A Dangerous Affair

Book 6 of the Branwell Chronicles

Judith Hale Everett

Evershire Publishing

A Dangerous Affair © 2024 Judith Hale Everett
Cover design © Rachel Allen Everett

Published by Evershire Publishing, Springville, Utah
ISBN 978-1-958720-04-2
Library of Congress Control Number: 2024909113

To Keely
My favorite oldest niece and a force to be reckoned with.

To my readers:
Make sure to read the Author's Note in the back for historical
information on concepts and events described in the story.

Books in this series:

A Near Run Thing
Two in the Bush
Romance of the Ruin
Forlorn Hope
A Knowing One
Piqued and Repiqued
A Dangerous Affair

To get *A Near Run Thing* for free and to find out more about the series, go to judithhaleeverett.com or scan the QR code below:

A Dangerous Affair

Chapter 1

A T FIRST GLANCE, the scene in the sitting room at Wesley Abbey could easily have been mistaken for one of unblemished domestic tranquility. A middle-aged gentleman sat at his ease in a wing chair near the fire, reading the newspaper, the possessor of both good looks and good humor. On a nearby sofa reclined a lovely young lady with golden curls and eyes of deep blue, which were now trained on a book that, if it could not be termed wholesome instruction, was at least very good entertainment, judging by the dimple often appearing beside her rosebud mouth.

Their surroundings, too, spoke of comfort, and were far from the austerity of former times, when monks and abbots frequented the Abbey's halls. Benches and trestle tables had long ago been replaced by an assortment of *bergères*, sofas, and dainty but useful tables, and an Aubusson carpet covered the stone floor. The massive fireplace of old had been bricked in and converted to an efficient Rumford, which filled the room not with smoke—as its predecessor had done with great regularity—but with warmth for a chilly autumn evening.

The third occupant of the room, however, in no way contributed to the illusion of tranquility. The lady of the house seemed utterly at odds with the peacefulness of her surroundings, and though possessed of at quite as much beauty as her daughter, was doing it little justice, continually screwing up her mouth and uttering various indications of disgust as she read the letter in her hand.

After a particularly violent gasp, her daughter—not looking up from the book she perused on the nearby sofa—remarked, "You might as well tell us what is distressing you so, Mother."

Mrs. Noyce ceased her mutterings and primmed up her lips. "Curiosity is vulgar, Clara."

"To be sure." Clara turned the page, glancing up with a smile. "But I am never vulgar."

"Then you ought not to ask what was in my letter."

Clara shrugged delicately and returned her eyes to her book. "I would never do that, Mother."

"But do not you wish to know?" inquired Mrs. Noyce with a huff.

"Not particularly. However, you are evidently eager to tell us, so you might as well do so and then we may all be comfortable again."

"Now, now," broke in Mr. Noyce, glancing over the top of the newspaper in his hands. "You must admit to *some* curiosity, Clara. After all that expostulation by your mother, I own *I* am dying to know what is in that mysterious letter."

Mrs. Noyce's affronted gaze flew to his, but as he was smiling in his cheerful way, with mischief in his beautiful, tawny eyes, her frown soon pursed into a repressed smile and she sat back in her chair. "I will tell *you*, William, though you do not deserve to hear it. You may listen if you wish, Clara, but I will not press you, as *you* do not at all care to know." She settled herself with an air of noble detachment, the letter before her. "Indeed, it is nothing very interesting, though it may surprise you, as it has me. It is from Drusilla, my dear friend Lady Gidgeborough. She writes that her daughter Athena has married."

The ensuing pause was pregnant enough to bring both pairs of eyes to her face once more, but she remained silent, her lips only slightly trembling, a look of injury in her countenance.

"Come now, my dear," said her husband, raising his brows. "Do not hold us in suspense. Is not this good news? Lady Athena has been out three or four years, I believe, and if I recall correctly, she is an excessively handsome girl. It is only a wonder that she was not snatched up in her first Season."

Something much like a snort emanated from Clara, causing her mother to lower her brows in her direction before replying to her husband.

"Lady Athena has been out three years, William, but has been on the town only two. Her fortune is magnificent and her birth impeccable. It was always expected that she make an excellent match. Thus, she has necessarily been shielded from innumerable—and I need not say ineligible—offers during those years, while dear Drusilla has cultivated the acquaintance of the most noble gentlemen for her. Drusilla is the daughter of a marquess, you know, and Athena is the daughter of an earl! As it turns out, however, she has married a mere gentleman, though his fortune, Drusilla assures me, is fabulous. She seems most gratified."

"Then it mystifies me that you are in a pucker, my love," said her spouse, raising his newspaper once more.

"Shame on you, Mr. Noyce," said Clara, smiling down at her book.

"You are not at all dull-witted, and it is beneath you to tease her. Surely you can tell what is the matter."

His quelling glance was wasted on Clara, who never raised her eyes but turned another page in the utmost unconcern.

"My dear Anamaria," he said, looking once more at his wife. "Your daughter does me an injustice. I cannot tell what is the matter, for I have not the experience of your habits as she does. Forgive me that in the two months of our marriage I have not yet learnt your likes and dislikes, and moods and whims, and do me the honor of taking me into your confidence."

Mrs. Noyce blushed as becomingly as the bride she was and blinked rapidly, her lips trembling on a tender smile. "Oh, William! You are so kind, and sweet, and conciliating! Not like—that is, I am not used to such treatment from—from a gentleman, or from anybody." She cast a look of ill-usage at her daughter but, as no response—repentant or otherwise—was forthcoming, she huffed and continued. "It is only that I am such a great friend of Drusilla, and though we have not been so close as we once were, it is not as though we are estranged! I have always visited her in Town when I have gone, and we have kept up a regular correspondence, and—and after all this, she did not say one word to invite me to the wedding."

"I see," said Mr. Noyce, rising and hobbling toward her, his legs stiff not from age but from a defect that had afflicted him from birth. He lowered himself onto the chair next to her and took her hand. "It is a disappointment when a friend is not as constant as one would wish. But there must have been extenuating circumstances, I am persuaded."

His wife looked away, absently stroking his hand with her thumb. "I suppose, for it was a small wedding, or so Drusilla informs me.

But I do not know that I believe it, for Lord Gidgeborough is as rich as Croesus!"

"Surely not Croesus, Mother," said her daughter, glancing up with a gleaming eye, "or you should have thrown Francis in Athena's way long ago."

"That I should not, Clara," said Mrs. Noyce, stiffening. "I may be Drusilla's bosom friend, but Lady Athena is far out of your brother's sphere—the daughter of an earl! Besides, Francis is an odious man, and though he is my flesh and blood, I should be ashamed to present him as a proper person for her to know—or any gently-bred young lady, for that matter."

"As Lady Athena has already found happiness in marriage," said Mr. Noyce firmly, bringing his wife back down from the boughs as only he could, "we need not bring Francis into it."

"Well, I hope she has," said Mrs. Noyce peevishly. "It was done is such a scrambling way—so quickly that there was not time, Drusilla claims, to send out even an invitation to an old friend! There were only themselves and such family and friends as were to be had in London. Imagine! At this season of the year, there could not have been more than a dozen persons in attendance, if it was as she says!"

"If she has said it, then it must have been so, my love," said Mr. Noyce, patting her hand. "There is nothing so remarkable about a speedy wedding, particularly when love is involved. You must recall how speedily we were married, my dear, once we had determined upon it."

"Yes, but we are fully mature, William, and knew our own minds!"

He gave her a significant look, saying gently, "Not at first, my dear, recollect."

She instantly averted her gaze, coloring and pressing his hand between her own. He smiled, bending forward to press a kiss to her forehead. "There now, love, that is all behind us."

"Yes," she said, meeting his gaze with tears standing out on her lashes. She raised his hand to her cheek, smiling sadly but gratefully, and kept it there for some minutes, until a movement from Clara broke her reverie, reminding her that they were not alone. With a little gasp, she released her husband's hand and bent to retrieve her handkerchief from her pocket. Patting her eyes, she cleared her throat and, standing resolutely, brushed out the skirts of her gown. "There is another matter that has distressed me, and it did not need talk of weddings to remind me of it, Clara."

Clara took a long-suffering breath, exhaling loudly before pointedly continuing to read.

"You have been out four years, Clara Mantell," her mother said sternly, raising her chin. "I could ask when you are to give up flirting like a common tramp and go with one of your poor, besotted beaux to church, but I will save my breath. You are too much like your father, I fear, and your brother."

"Thank you for the compliment, Mother," said Clara glibly, turning another page. "If I am anything like Geoffrey, I have done far better than even I had imagined."

Mrs. Noyce crossed to her and snatched the book from her hands. "Not Geoffrey, my girl, but Francis! Geoffrey never flirted more than was proper, and never raised unfounded hopes! And, I may remind you, he is married. I wish I could say the same for you and for Francis, but you know I cannot. It grieves me to the heart to see how you both go on, with the young men falling over themselves to be with you—"

"Do young men fall over themselves to be with Francis, too, Mother? You shock me."

"I am speaking of *you*, Clara! Though I do not know why I should bother. If you cannot behave with decorum to your own mother, you are a hopeless case, and I wash my hands of you."

"Thank you," said Clara, reaching for her book.

Mrs. Noyce held it out of reach. "You must marry some time, Clara, and it will only become more difficult the older you become. Though your fortune is excellent—thanks to Mr. Noyce's generosity— it may not be sufficient if you delay too long. Youth and beauty are generally required for captivation."

"Ah!" said Clara, withdrawing her hand. "I see I was precipitate in taking you at your word. As I never overstep the bounds of filial duty, I will not remind you that when one makes a pronouncement— especially one of such force as washing one's hands of someone—one is generally expected to abide by it. However," she added sweetly, as her mother's countenance threatened to turn purple, "perhaps you are right to give me another chance. Indeed, it may only want a change of society for my manners to improve. It has been some time since I have been in company with any young men who do more than fall over themselves, you know. Our Southam society is so unvarying and dull. Perhaps it may be prudent, as lecturing does no good, to try what London society can do."

"Now there is an idea," said Mr. Noyce, in a voice whose firmness belied the laugh in his eyes. Rising once more to his unsteady feet, he continued, "I have not been to the Metropolis in an age. We could go there at Michaelmas."

His wife looked horrified. "London at this time of the year? You must be mad!"

"But Lady Gidgeborough is in Town, is she not?"

"Only on account of the wedding, for Athena's courtship was

somewhat prolonged, and outlasted the Season. She and Lord Gidgeborough will have gone away by next week—indeed, they may already be at Kemmerton. No one of import will be left in Town by now, I assure you, William!"

Mr. Noyce glanced at Clara, a twinkle in his eye. "Not even enough young men to fall over themselves, I expect. Ah, well, I was never one for London, at any event."

"No, and if Clara does not know that, she is foolish beyond permission!" said his wife, in obvious relief. Pleased to have won that point, she returned to scolding the winner of the other. "Shame on you, Clara, to put your desires before your dear stepfather, who has been more than generous, and to whom you owe your present comfort!"

Clara exchanged a quick, humorous look with her excellent benefactor before bowing her head in deference. "You are right, Mother. It was shabby of me even to suggest London, at this season or at any other. Never mind that we have not been since Father's death, even though I begged for another Season. It was only from the shock of having lost your regard that this regrettable lapse could have taken place. I most humbly beg your pardon, ma'am. And yours, sir."

Mrs. Noyce was unamused, but her husband, shaking his head at Clara, took his wife's hand and kissed it, saying, "Never mind that little baggage, my love. You know she has not offered me an affront at all, for I would go to the end of the earth for either one of you, without a thought. No, no! Enough on that head. You are very tired, and we have pulled you sadly tonight. I beg pardon for the both of us. You deserve quiet and rest. Now, leave us to our consciences and go to bed." In a lower tone, he added, "I shall come up presently to see if you have forgiven me."

She colored, her gaze flitting from him to the floor and back again as she said breathlessly, "William, you are shameless—we are not alone! But—however—I own I am quite fatigued. I—I think I *shall* go to bed."

With that, she bade her daughter a stately good night and made her way from the room, leaving the gentleman and the young lady to regard each other with amusement.

"I fear the Mantell depravity is rubbing off on you, sir," said Clara archly.

He reached to take the book that Mrs. Noyce had discarded on the side table and handed it back to Clara. "Not depravity, my dear—not quite. Whatever it is, I find I quite enjoy it. I had only been living half a life until you and your mother came to Wesley Abbey. I shall ever bless that day, for it saved me from a lifetime of loneliness."

"Then you must bless the day my father finally succumbed to apoplexy, sir," Clara said, taking the book and flipping its pages to her place, "for without his death, you should never have had the opportunity to marry my mother."

He tutted. "Now you are trying to roast me, but you will not do it. I know you do not mean such an odious thing."

"Oh, I did not mean it to be odious, sir," said Clara, smiling disarmingly. "I am never odious. I simply do not speak untruths. I have never pretended to be sorry that he is dead."

His look softened and he dropped his gaze. After a pause, he said, "It is a small wonder that you are not eager to marry. But it need not be like that. I would that I could remove all your poor father's influence and give you a fresh look at men and marriage."

"You are too good, Mr. Noyce," she said, regarding him with wry affection, "too good to comprehend the real state of things. You would believe that men like yourself are the rule rather than the exception, just as you would not imagine that it is not my father's influence that motivates me, but my own evil tendency."

"It is hard to tell, my dear, for among you all there is quite a family resemblance. However, none of you is irredeemable. Just as Geoffrey has escaped the taint of your father's selfishness, I am persuaded you have not altogether absorbed it, and may yet escape it as well, if you try."

Clara pursed her lips. "Perhaps it is inherited from my mother, sir. I do not wish to disillusion you, but she is no angel."

"Ah, but she once was. Recollect, I knew her of old. Though she rejected my suit then, I did not forget her beauty of spirit, even while I watched it wither away under your father's callousness. She can be redeemed, Clara, and shall be, if I have anything to say in the matter. I will not give up hope, for any of you."

Clara smiled reflectively at the page of her book. "How vexing. Here I had determined upon employing my considerable genius in defying all attempts to manipulate my views, but you are so kind and reasonable that I find I do not at all wish to cross you." She looked askance at him, an impish smile curling her mouth. "I suppose it behooves me to try to make something better of myself."

Chuckling, he lowered himself onto the sofa beside her and placed an arm about her slim shoulders. "Do not put yourself out for my sake, my dear. I love you as you are, but I should like nothing better than to see you happy. If you will do anything for my sake, do not consign yourself to a solitary existence."

Clara laughed, tipping her head toward him. "I am never solitary, sir, depend upon it. While there are gentlemen to fall over themselves, I shall be very well amused. But marriage? I thank you, no! I am not yet so desperate. Indeed, my mother has the oddest notions of what would make me happy."

"She is not alone," he said, patting her hand. "Anyone who has found happiness in marriage naturally wishes that all may partake of their joy. However, if you do not wish to marry, you need not. But it would not hurt you to take the matter seriously, at least for a time—if only to make certain it is not for you."

She laughed again, sitting up to look at him. "With whom might I be serious, I ask you, sir? All the gentlemen with whom I am acquainted are the most foolish creatures imaginable. How my mother could expect me to marry any of them, I cannot conceive. I should be bored with the lot of them within a twelvemonth. Now that I am accustomed to *your* society, you see, I have become possessed of exceedingly nice notions."

"There is not a gentleman in the world so charming as myself, to be sure," he said gravely, pushing himself to his feet once more. "It is a quandary. We must put our minds to it—but not tonight! I am for bed. If you will take my advice, Clara, my dear, you will not stay up all night reading again. But much as I wish it, I do not really expect that you will take anything I say to heart."

Clara looked up at him, her mouth pursing against a smile. "You are in fine form tonight, sir! As though I could stand against you!" Putting her book aside, she stood beside him, taking his arm and supporting him to the chair where he had left his canes. "I would not dare discard your advice—what a sad pickle I would be in then! You are the only wise one among us, you know."

Kissing him soundly on the cheek, she left him at the door and returned to her seat on the sofa, taking up her book again. He watched her thoughtfully until she raised her eyes with an inquiring look. But he only smiled, winked, and was gone.

Chapter 2

CLARA WAS AS good as her word—she did not stay awake read-ing. Nor did she beguile the late hours gazing into the fire and considering her filial duty. This was something she had never been allowed to forget, and she was entirely familiar with its import, its urgency, and its utter futility. She was young—scarcely two-and-twenty—beautiful, tolerably skilled in every womanly art, and charming to a fault. However, she had a larger view than simply to waste these attractions on an early marriage. All the enjoyment of a woman's existence seemed limited to the period between her come-out and her marriage, where she could test, improve, and revel in her powers over the male sex. Marriage effectively ended such delights, for it not only consid-erably restricted her scope but removed the power of refusal, sentencing her to a lifetime of obedience and monotony—if not indignity.

That the man was not so restricted, either before or after marriage, was one of those inconsistencies with which the world was riddled, and which Clara observed with disdain. *She* would not suffer herself to be subjected to such inequality, and so marriage must wait. She meant to enjoy her salad days—just as a young man of her age was expected and even encouraged to do. But she would take care not to relinquish a jot of control into the hands of her admirers. There was much to enjoy in the company of young gentlemen without engaging in those forbidden acts which were only too likely to end her freedom.

Indeed, she could think of no inducement powerful enough to tempt her willingly to put an end to her independence—except perhaps the sort of attachment her brother Geoffrey had formed with his wife. But their situation must be extraordinary, she was persuaded, and quite unattainable for the generality of persons. They were lately married, and though they were bound together by law and in God's eyes, their happiness together seemed to know no bounds and had given them both an inconceivable freedom. Upon reflection, she was made to admit that Mr. Noyce's marriage to her mother was in a fair way to becoming such an attachment.

This really was most astonishing, for it flew in the face of everything she had understood of marriage all her life. Her mothers' first marriage had been entirely the opposite—a study in frustration and antagonism that had endured nearly thirty years. Nothing about that marriage had excited so much as a particle of longing in Clara for a husband, and she had grown to womanhood believing that true satisfaction belonged in remaining single. But Geoffrey and Mr. Noyce were of an entirely different stamp than Colonel Mantell had been, and it followed that the felicity of their marriages was due to their peculiar goodness.

It was precisely this aspect that gave Clara to believe she was incapable of achieving such a marriage herself. She was not so foolish as her mother, and would not make the mistakes she had, but neither had she ever been an angel. Clara took strongly after her father and her elder brother Francis in that she was entirely disposed to use her youth and beauty to tempt and to ensnare, to confuse and to vex members of the male sex. She did not strive to be worthy of the goodness that Mr. Noyce and Geoffrey extended to their wives. Indeed, though she respected and even envied their marriages, she considered them something akin to a faerie tale which one delighted in knowing but accepted the folly in aspiring to.

Though this conviction might have troubled some, Clara knew herself too well to allow it to affect her. Her mother may have found the faerie tale, but Clara most certainly would not end up like her mother. Thus, she did not waste much time in reflection after Mr. Noyce left her, but finished her chapter and went on her way to bed.

The following morning at breakfast, Mrs. Noyce looked cheerful and bright as she observed, "You are late to the table this morning, my dear. Almost as though we were in London, and keeping Town hours."

"As much as I could wish that were the case," replied Clara, matching her mother's bright tone, "I merely considered it my duty to come down when the family would be present, so that we might share our repast together. I had collected that you might rise late, for you were severely fatigued last night, and it would not do for me to have come and gone before even you had left your rooms."

Mrs. Noyce colored and sniffed, pouring herself a cup of coffee, but a sly glance from her husband transformed her pout to a dimpled smile, and she refilled his coffee as well, adding milk and sugar just as he liked it.

He turned a grave look upon his stepdaughter. "Your filial scruples did well to forbid your early rising, for we wished particularly to speak with you. In light of your expressed desire for a respite from Southam society, we have decided upon removing to Bath directly, for I generally spend some months there in the winter, and wish to carry you both away with me."

"To Bath?" inquired Clara, pausing in her surprise with her cup halfway to her lips. "Whatever for?"

"Bath is quite congenial in autumn—far more than London," said her mother. "And Mr. Noyce has need of the hot baths. But I ought not to have expected that you should be mindful of his needs, for you are ever selfish, Clara."

Mr. Noyce tutted. "None of that, my dear, for your opinion of our going was much the same last night. Ah, but I persuaded you otherwise, did I not? Let me try if I may persuade her as well. What say you, Clara? Shall you come with us to a watering place where there are plenty of fresh young men to fall over themselves, and parties and assemblies to divert one, or shall you keep yourself immured in the country with a paltry three or four unvarying admirers?"

Clara made a show of skepticism while ruminatively sipping at her coffee. After several moments, wherein her mother fidgeted in annoyance and Mr. Noyce looked amused, she set down her cup with a careless hitch of her shoulder. "Very well, sir. I shall accompany you to Bath. But I warn you, I haven't a stitch to wear."

Mr. Noyce's amusement gave way to a grin. "That's the spirit! I knew you would be sensible. You'll see, we shall have a wonderful time, and be prodigiously comfortable together, though it does cost me a pretty penny."

"How can you talk so, Mr. Noyce?" demanded his wife, putting down her coffee cup with a clink. "Clara is merely wheedling you, and you oughtn't to let her do it! She will do very well without anything new, for she has a whole room full of gowns that you bought for her at our wedding. A few of them may need furbishing up, but you need not pay more than a few guineas for that, I assure you."

"But my dear, that is just what I said of your wardrobe last night, and you very quickly undeceived me. I shall not be so sapheaded as to make that mistake again." He stood, offering her his hand to rise and go with him out of the room. "Clara's gowns must be in as sorry a state as yours after two months, and I will gladly lay out as much as either of you wishes, to fit yourselves out so that I shall not be put to the blush."

Their voices faded away as they strolled down the corridor and into the sitting room, and Clara smiled as she helped herself to more toast, lavishly spreading butter on it. Mr. Noyce was a dear, and even she, with her cold heart, adored him. She certainly did not repine that it was he and not Colonel Mantell who now presided over their meals and remonstrated with her mother.

When she had eaten her fill, she went upstairs to get her hat and gloves and, donning a pelisse against the cool of the morning, went out into the flower garden to tend to the roses. The former abbey cloister, having lost a wall to improvement, had become the garden, and had been tended by generations of Noyce ladies until it was the jewel of Southam. Clara, who enjoyed gardening more than any other womanly art, was pleased to do her small part in the succession.

It was at this noble task that Mr. Lawrence Simpford found her some thirty minutes later, snipping the shriveled heads off the late roses. He was a cheerful fellow of five-and-twenty, one of Geoffrey's good friends, and had known Clara since she was in leading strings. He was quite good-looking, with brown hair and brown eyes and a fine figure, which was displayed to advantage in a blue coat over a gold-and-blue embroidered waistcoat and buff pantaloons.

"Good morning, Clara!" he said, coming up to her on the gravel walk.

She put the shears into her basket and gave him her hand. "Hello, Lawrie. What brings you out on so fine a morning? It cannot be the glory of the sun that has seen fit to shine upon us at last."

Mr. Simpford grinned, bowing low over her hand. "Not the glory of the sun, ma'am, but the glory of your person, which cannot be compared."

"Fie, flatterer," returned Clara with a mischievous look. "But for that piece of flummery, you might have taken my basket and walked with me back to the house."

With an air of unconcern, he took the basket from her hands, offering her an arm. "As it is not my intention to return into the house, I am glad. I have a great desire to walk around the ruins instead."

"And if I have better things to do than to ramble about a lot of tumbled rock with you, sir?"

"Impossible," he said firmly, guiding her with exquisite cordiality toward the gate that led out of the rose garden and into the open area beyond.

Discarding the basket on an obliging bench, Mr. Simpford opened the gate for his companion to pass through, then followed her onto the flagstone path. Mr. Noyce had installed the path for the pleasure of his guests—his particular malady prohibiting his enjoyment of traversing uneven ground. The path led around the perimeter of the remains of the abbey church, now only crumbling walls and the occasional column laid out in the shape of a cross in the grass. It was a small ruin, but delightful to the imaginations of young and old alike and, Mr. Noyce being the kind-hearted and friendly man that he was, most of the neighborhood children had been allowed to run riot within its precincts at some period of their lives.

Mr. Simpford led Clara to the right of the nave, assisting her to scramble up onto a berm that had overgrown a fallen column. He laughed at her readiness to come with him, saying, "It is a happy occurrence that you were to be found in the garden on such a lovely morning, else I might never have persuaded you out of doors."

"I am not such a slug-a-bed, sir," she said, allowing him to lift her down the other side. "I imagined I should be spared the annoyance of visitors by absenting myself from the sitting room. However, I suppose your society is not so irksome as to entirely cloud my enjoyment of the day."

He grinned, sweeping off his hat and bowing at her compliment. Replacing his hat, he strolled with her along the path, which they had rejoined on the far side of the ruin. They paused beside a lonely portion of wall that stood apart from the rest and was oddly pock-marked, as though it had been used as a target for shooting.

"It is only right that you should bring me here, Lawrie," said Clara solemnly regarding the wall, "for it is a just penance to you for the impertinence of stealing the solace of my morning hours."

"I had forgot this place," he said, grimacing.

"Three times out of five I outshot you, sir! How could you forget?"

"It was only twice you beat me, Clara!" exclaimed Mr. Simpford, holding back a smile.

"Oh, no, sir! Three times. I never tell untruths."

"Perhaps. But I had beat you innumerable times before that."

She sighed happily. "Yes, but never after, recollect. I am become the better shot, and you must admit to it. There is the irrefutable proof."

"I am in no way obliged to admit to it," he said loftily, but his twinkling eyes belied him as he led her onward down the walk. "It should never have happened had Geoffrey not given in to practicing with you. How is he, by the by? Have you heard from him?"

"Yes. We had a letter from him only two days ago. They are safely embarked from Lisbon, and are looking forward to the long journey round the Cape. They will quite miss winter, for it is nearly always summer in much of Africa and India, you know."

"I see you are become an authority."

"And must, therefore, be accorded the respect I deserve, sir," she replied primly.

He chuckled, but after a pause said in a reflective tone, "I am glad Geoffrey has left the army behind and may be his own master. It is far less worry to have one's income dependent upon nothing more dangerous than the rents and the weather—or, in his case, his wife's inheritance. I own, I am glad never to be obliged to wonder at what cost my income will be given me."

Clara laughed. "No, unless your mama takes a sudden notion to become very expensive. Though, if she retains her aversion to London, I cannot conceive where she should spend her money. There are only the two shops in Southam, and even Warwick could not provide her with enough gowns or wares to exhaust all your funds, surely."

"I trust not," said Mr. Simpford, his brow creased in mock concern. "But perhaps she could find her way into one of the select gambling houses there, and ruin me after a few nights' hard play."

"As her character was ever vicious, one could easily imagine her capable of such a thing."

She caught his eye and they both burst into whoops at the vision of the comfortable and motherly Mrs. Simpford, who never left her couch if she could help it, and whose only vice was a partiality for rich foods. Their mirth was redoubled at Clara's suggestion that even were Mrs. Simpford to indulge in a fit of gaming, perhaps she would *not* lose, for having driven all the other players distracted with her voluble chatter.

"It will come as a welcome surprise to her," said her undutiful son, wiping his streaming eyes, "that her propensity for talk could be turned to such good purpose."

"Better not to suggest it, else she may imagine it her duty to try it, if only to improve your income."

"But then she should be obliged to leave the house, which she would not like," pointed out Mr. Simpford, nearly in command of himself. "I think my income is safe, for now."

"And a very good thing, too," said Clara, twinkling up at him. "Not many sons can boast such security."

"No," agreed Mr. Simpford, gazing down into her upturned face. His smile faded and he hesitated, the look in his eyes intensifying and his countenance becoming suddenly determined. All at once he stopped, turning to face her, and took both her hands in his own. "No, Clara, many cannot, which is why I must not take it for granted. I know I ought not—despite my fears that you—that is, I know it is not what you—but I simply must ask—"

Clara, recognizing to what this tangled speech tended, removed her hands from his grasp and said with embarrassed impatience, "Do not be a gudgeon, Lawrie."

He blinked at her as she studiously adjusted her shawl. "Clara, I—"

"You are trying to make love to me, Lawrie, and it will not do," she cut in, her tone all amiability as she took his arm again and compelled him at a meander along the path. "You know that I do not think of marriage. It astonishes me that you should allow yourself to be so carried away as to forget it," she added, with a significant glance.

His spirits palpably perturbed, he answered stiffly, "Pray, pardon me. I ought not to have overstepped."

"It is perfectly understandable," she said, pressing his arm in a comforting way. "Geoffrey is continually chiding me for that effect I have on gentlemen. It is very unjust, however, for I hardly ever intend to deceive them."

Her swain merely shook his head, and after casting him a sympathetic glance, she went on.

"I really have too much to consider at present. My mother lately married, the change in my home and circumstances—it is simply impossible that I should think of another change so soon."

"Certainly not," he said, his equilibrium returning.

"And we are very soon to remove to Bath. You see, I could not consider taking so significant a step before we are back."

His gaze flicked to her, his mouth puckering in irony. "If you are not intending to deceive me, Clara, you are doing a very poor job of it."

"Oh!" she said, making a face. "Forgive me. I sometimes forget just how well you know me. It is very bad of you to always be so very observant. But you must all the better comprehend my dislike of marriage!"

He sighed. "I do."

"I knew I could rely on you," she said, smiling up at him. "But you are always so obliging, and never take a pet. I should vastly prefer your company to any other gentleman—despite … everything."

"I may only hope that your sentiments prevent your forgetting me in Bath."

Clara pressed his arm. "How could I do so? We shall only be there until Christmas. That is not enough time to forget anything!"

"I hardly know what to say to such a compliment," he said, turning to take her hand. "But I suppose the best thing to say at this point is thank you for the walk."

He bid her good day, bowing over her hand with a perfunctory smile and walking away around the house. Clara, shrugging off whatever burden her conscience attempted to lay upon her, let herself into the vestibule, removing her pelisse and carrying it over her arm up the stairs. On the landing, she met Mr. Noyce.

"And what did young Lawrie have to say?" he inquired, winking. "He seemed mightily full of something."

"Only nonsense, sir, as usual," she said blithely, kissing his cheek as she passed.

"Clara."

She stopped at the unaccustomed gravity of his tone, turning to look an enquiry.

"Did he make you an offer?"

"He did, sir."

"And you refused him?"

"Of course."

He gazed ruminatively at her for a few moments. "If it had been Shelby Frean, I should applaud you, Clara, for he is nothing but a boor. But Lawrence Simpford is another breed altogether—a better breed. Indeed, I must tell you that he is an excellent man, Clara."

"To be sure, sir, and that is why he is not the man for me. I was not bred to excellence myself, and so I can find very little in it to tempt me."

Mr. Noyce tutted. "But what, then, could you look for in a husband?"

"Nothing, sir, for you know I do not think of marriage. There is very little scope for the imagination in marriage—at least for a woman. I wish for adventure and, indeed, a little danger, before I am tied by the heels to a man and a home."

"My dear," said Mr. Noyce, "marriage can be a grand adventure, and even a little dangerous at times. I recommend it highly."

Clara reached up to kiss his cheek again. "If I could find another such as you, sir, I should consider it, depend upon it. But I fear you are unique, and so I must make my own way through this world."

She went on her way to her apartments, and Mr. Noyce, after a protracted pause, shook his head and continued down the stairs.

Chapter 3

ON THE EVE of their removal to Bath, Mr. and Mrs. Noyce enjoyed the felicity of a visit from her eldest son, who had just come back into the country after a protracted visit in Northampton-shire. Mr. Francis Mantell's abode was not four miles from Wesley Abbey, but being a bachelor, he was often to be found from home. His mother deprecated this mode of life, which she scrupled not to stigmatize as a flagrant waste of a good manor. It did not occur to her that she had done much the same in her time at the Hall, having not wished to pass much of her time there while her first husband was alive. She had blamed this reticence on the vulgarity of their nearest neighbor, but the fact remained that the Colonel's libertine propensities in his own neighborhood had given her a disgust of home.

Francis was cut, she believed, from the same cloth as his father, having only been spared his fierce temper—Francis was rather easy-going by contrast. Still, Mrs. Noyce prophesied that though he could not expect an early demise from apoplexy, he would surely be killed by dissolution and debt.

"That," she said to Mr. Noyce as she completed her toilette before dinner, "or he shall be murdered in his bed by one of his doxies."

"Nonsense, my love!" replied Mr. Noyce soothingly. "To conclude anything of the sort, one should have to know something of their tempers, which, I fancy, you do not."

"But I do, William! Our maid, Jane, was one of his earliest conquests! And a more saucy piece I never did see. I should have turned her off instantly I knew of it, had Francis not been master at Gracely Hall by that time. But he would only have found another 'bit of muslin,' as he calls them, and he has. If the servants are to be believed, there is one in every town where he goes, and they are none of them decent or honest, by any means, my dear."

"Not every dishonest or indecent female is up to murder, however, Anamaria," he said, handing her the jewelry box with his customary thoughtfulness. "Now, my love, I do agree that his habits are most reprehensible. However, despite heartily deprecating the company he keeps, I must maintain the conviction that Francis need not fear for his life just yet."

Mrs. Noyce might, in a former time and with a former adversary, have battled the point to the death, but as Mr. Noyce was never contentious, she had become less and less disposed to it, and gave it up now with hardly a murmur. Her reward was a kiss and a warm look full of promise, and with a happy pattering of her heart, she took his proffered arm, and went down with him to join Clara in the sitting room to welcome their guest. So well-timed was their entrance that they had scarcely greeted Francis when dinner was announced, thus precluding the possibility of any argument arising before they were safely ensconced at the table.

"So you are for Bath, then?" inquired Francis, taking some boiled spinach and potatoes onto his plate. "I am glad I do not go with you. I detest Bath!"

"I cannot perceive why, Francis," said Clara, smiling with deceptive innocence. "Mr. Noyce assures me there are gentlemen aplenty in Bath, and Mother is of the opinion that this is a circumstance to please you."

"Clara!" cried Mrs. Noyce, coloring deeply. "I think nothing of the sort. Do not put words into my mouth."

"I never presume to put words into people's mouths, Mother. You certainly said—"

"It does not signify what I said—provoking child!" Mrs. Noyce looked pointedly at Francis. "Bath is an eminently respectable place, with delightful society. You need not worry for our sakes."

"Oh, never fear, Mother," said Francis, flicking a knowing glance at Clara. "I do not fear for you. Indeed, I am glad for you all, for I do not doubt Clara is pining to rake about town somewhere. Better in Bath, where she can do the least harm."

Clara was all astonishment. "But this is a new come out for you, to be sure. You have never cared a rap for any gentleman beside yourself before."

"You mistake me, dear sister." He smiled, refilling his wine glass before saying, "Even were the majority of male inhabitants of Bath not invalids and elderly persons—yourself excepted, of course, sir—" he said, nodding to Mr. Noyce, who acknowledged this civility with perfect gravity, "the remainder are such as could never be brought under so unsophisticated a spell as you might cast."

"Oh, no?" inquired Clara in a challenging tone. "Though I do not pretend to any higher degree of beauty than the next nonpareil, and I certainly do not admit to raking about the town, I do recall having had some small success with gentlemen in the past."

Francis regarded her in amusement. "Bath is not Southam, nor is it London. You may depend upon it that men—such as would attract you, that is—who find themselves obliged to be in Bath are there only for the purpose of rustification, which assumes they are men of experience and action, and not to be tempted or flattered by a chit of a girl from the country. You may practice your wiles upon them with a free conscience, knowing they will none of them be affected in the least."

Clara pursed her lips and directed her attention to the cutting of the green goose on her plate. "Your observations, as ever, my dear brother, are edifying. However, I must inform you that you have misjudged my purpose in going to Bath. Far from imagining myself to be descending upon a Mecca of unsuspecting suitors whose hearts I mean to enslave, I go only to be a companion to my mother—and to our dear Mr. Noyce, of course."

"I am her model of manly charms, after all," said Mr. Noyce, the ghost of a smile betraying his rich enjoyment of this interaction. "Clara has declared that all other gentlemen are eclipsed by me, thus any amorous purpose for coming with us to Bath would be vain."

"You see, Francis?" said Clara virtuously. "My motives are of the purest, and your obliging warning is utterly wasted."

Francis merely smirked. "You had better watch out, Mother, lest you find yourself ousted in Mr. Noyce's esteem by this snake in the bosom."

"How can you talk so?" cried Mrs. Noyce, staring at each of her offspring in turn. "It is all nonsense, of course, and I will have no more of it. We go to Bath for Mr. Noyce's benefit, and Clara comes to enjoy a change of scene. She will, of course, behave with propriety while she is with us."

"I can certainly believe that, at least," replied Francis, returning to his potatoes. "It is what she will do when she is not with you that you may wonder at."

"I will not have such indelicate conversation at table!" his mother retorted, and signaled for the next course to be brought in.

She had her wish, for Mr. Noyce exerted himself to keep his two unruly stepchildren within bounds more felicitous to the peace. His efforts were crowned with such success that, at the end of the second course, Mrs. Noyce rose almost regretfully to repair with Clara to the sitting room, where they would await the gentlemen. Clara, quite willing to be spared her brother's company for a quarter of an hour, went with her mother unprotesting, but when they had settled themselves, had cause to regret her meekness.

Mrs. Noyce immediately began with, "It is useless to pretend that you go with us only to be a companion to me, Clara, for I am no simpleton. Francis had the right of it, I daresay, though I cannot conceive what the enslavement of hearts has to do with anything, when you do not pursue marriage. You may as well remain here, as go to Bath, for all the good it will do you."

"But Mother," replied Clara imperturbably, "I must practice how to inspire an offer, if ever I am to accept one."

"Do not be provoking," said her mother, picking up her workbasket and fishing out some linens to mend. "You have quite enough practice in that, from what I have heard. What possessed you to refuse Mr. Simpford, I cannot comprehend."

"Lawrie? Oh, Mother, you could not wish me on poor Lawrie for all the rest of his life."

Mrs. Noyce humphed. "I begin to wonder if there will be any gentleman I could wish you upon. Perhaps you shall find yourself a spinster before you are too much older, and shall live to take my place at Mr. Noyce's side when I am gone."

Chuckling appreciatively, Clara picked up her book and became as absorbed in it as her mother was in her needlework, until the gentlemen came in. Then, considerate of her husband's comfort as she had yet to learn to be with that of her children, Mrs. Noyce put away her needlework to ensure he was settled in his favorite chair, near enough to the fire but not too near it. She then brought her own chair closer to his so that they could converse in low tones, heedless of the others in the room.

Shaking his head, Francis took a seat beside Clara on the sofa. "She is overdoing it a trifle, don't you think? I suppose I frightened her into this little display of wifely virtue."

"On, no, Francis," responded Clara, glancing up from her book to take in the domestic scene before her. "This is quite ordinary behavior, but I am not surprised at your incredulity. You have made it your business to be away, so you can have no idea of their devotion."

"I am glad of it. It turns my stomach."

She favored him with a shrewd look. "Only because you have not the power to inspire such devotion yourself. I am persuaded none of your inamorata would—or could—dote upon you in this way."

"Not a chance of it, and devilish glad I am, too! How he stands it, I don't know."

"It is because he loves her," said Clara simply, returning her gaze to her book.

Francis huffed a laugh. "As though you know anything of the matter." When she only raised a brow without lifting her eyes, he pursued, "What do you know of love, you Jezebel? When have you felt anything akin to love in that cold heart of yours?"

"I have not," she said, still disdaining to look at him. "Indeed, I do not know if I am capable, just as I am almost certain that you are not. We have too much of our father in us, I believe. But I have seen quite enough of love to begin to comprehend what makes it so desirable to the generality of humankind."

"Storybook love! Nauseating drivel," he said, indicating their mother and stepfather with a wave of his hand.

"Well," said Clara, shrugging a shoulder, "I cannot say if I would like it myself, for though I have had any number of gentlemen dote upon me, it has never been quite so—how do I say it—endearing. But I do not pretend to love them. Yes, one imagines such attentions would be quite endearing, if one had any sort of feeling for the man. But whether that is ever possible, I do not know. Ah, well. One does what one must to make do, does not one? You certainly do."

Francis pressed his lips together, settling back into the sofa with his arms along its back and gazing at Mr. Noyce, who looked with real fondness upon his wife while resisting her importunities to put his feet up on a stool.

"I would never have imagined her capable of *tenderness*," he mused after several moments. Then, shaking himself, he said, "I declare I should find such attentions stifling. I prefer my freedom."

"As long as there is a winsome little thing awaiting you at the end of the day?" inquired Clara sweetly. "I wonder, just how satisfactory was your freedom when you cast off poor Janet? And how quickly did you move on to another fancy piece?"

"That is a term you should know nothing about, young lady," he said, with a disapproving grimace. "Though it should not surprise me that you do, for it is only of a piece with your own thinking, you know. How satisfied were you upon refusing Mr. Frant last year? Or Mr. Spelling?"

Clara waved the mention of these gentlemen away like gnats. "They were nothing—mere flirtations. Their hearts were no more engaged than mine."

"And what of Lawrie Simpford?"

She looked sharply at him. "How come you to know of that?"

He chuckled. "Rankles, does it, that your refusal is common knowledge? Perhaps you are more keen there than you would have yourself believe. Have no fear that gossip has discovered you, however. Mr. Noyce informed me of it over port. Very wise of you to refuse. Lawrie Simpford is not for you. You would eat him up within six months."

"Of course he is not for me. Pray, why else would I refuse him?" She tossed her head. "At least I have conscience enough not to pretend at love when I mean only to take him for all he is worth before discarding him."

He was ruminative for a time, then eyed her askance. "I didn't, you know."

"Didn't what?"

"Cast Jane off." He adjusted his seat on the couch, not looking at her. "It came to my notice that the butcher's son was head over ears in love with her. It seemed a good match, considering her ... shall we say, previous attachments. So I gave them the means to marry—that is, I encouraged the match. She seemed pleased, at the end."

Clara gazed at him with unrestrained wonder. "I have wronged you, Francis. Such nobility—I am without words. Now you must only say you miss her to bowl me out entirely."

"I shan't." He shrugged. "I was beginning to tire of her, actually. And as Pritchard has the estate well in hand—I finally pensioned off old Brompton—the rents are flowing in, and I am at liberty to go where I please. I could not very well take a housemaid with me."

"I suppose not," mused Clara. "She would be somewhat out of place amongst your belongings. I don't suppose it would have been looked kindly on for you to strap her to the back of your curricle with the rest of your baggage, at any rate. Nor would she have liked to perch up behind you and your groom, to be sure."

"No," he said quellingly. "Hatten would not have suffered it, and nor would I. I never drive females."

Clara laughed, settling more comfortably into her corner of the sofa. "As you claimed last year when you taught me to drive."

"I did not teach you!" he disclaimed. "You took advantage of me in a moment of weakness."

"A moment which lasted all the way from the turnpike road to Gracely Hall."

"You refused to relinquish the ribbons and we should have run into the ditch! It was only my very great concern for my horses that decided me to humor you at all."

"I know it," she said, smiling reminiscently. "I shall never forget my triumph that day."

"And you shall never repeat it, my girl," he said firmly.

She looked down her nose at him. "I want no more instruction, I will have you know. Between Geoffrey—who is a far better and kinder brother than you will ever be—and Lawrie and Billy Thornton, I am become quite a fine whip."

"And yet you shall never again drive my horses. Not though you tease me half to death."

"I never tease."

"Regardless, I mean what I say this time."

"And I never beg, Francis."

At this point, Mr. Noyce, having convinced his doting spouse that he had been cosseted long enough and seen her settled again at her needlework, spoke across the room to them.

"What are your plans, Francis? Do you stay for any length of time at Gracely Hall?"

"I shall go into Leicestershire for the shooting, sir," Francis said. "My hunting box is quite snug, and Charles Wraglain goes with me. Depending on our luck, we may go on to Penhurst Lodge. Nathan Willoughby has invited a few old schoolmates, and we shall make a lively party."

"Too lively to return before Christmas, I'll wager. Well, neither shall we return until then, but we depend upon your coming here for the festivities. I still have a yule log dragged in, you know, for the Great Hall. And mistletoe."

Mrs. Noyce broke in peevishly, "Do not encourage him so, William! He will only use that charming tradition to ruin your maidservants, and cause an uproar. I shall not have it! There was enough of that at Gracely Hall, without it following me here."

"We must only keep our eye on him," Mr. Noyce said gravely, though his eyes danced. "I leave it to you to warn the housemaids so that they will not be deceived, even if he is as mild as a lamb. And Clara, too, will behave herself, won't you, my dear?" He lowered his voice and added to Mrs. Noyce, "I cannot go entirely without mistletoe, my love."

She blushed and lowered her eyes demurely, murmuring something incoherent, and Mr. Noyce turned again to Francis.

"What say you, my boy? Will you come for Christmas?"

"If you are revived by the hot baths, sir, then I must hold myself obliged to come to you then, if only to celebrate your safe return from the drudgery of Bath."

Satisfied, Mr. Noyce challenged him to a game of piquet, and the family whiled away the evening hours in comparative camaraderie until the ladies declared their intention to retire.

Francis, rising to take leave, said to Clara, "My best wishes for your survival of the coming months, dear sister."

"Thank you, but I believe I shall do very well. You have given me a challenge, after all."

He huffed. "Recollect, your motives for going to Bath are of the purest, and do not include the enslavement of hearts."

"However, you and Mother between you have convinced me of the need to replace Mr. Noyce in my estimation. I shall therefore endeavor to be amiable to the gentlemen I meet. Enslavement of hearts, should it occur at all, shall be merely coincidental."

Francis raised his brow at this, saying, "I shall watch for news in the *Courier* that you have made a great noise, then."

Clara smiled, pleased at this prospect. "Do."

Chapter 4

THE JOURNEY TO Bath comprised three days, for though Mr. Noyce advocated to take advantage of the waning daylight, Mrs. Noyce declared she could not bear to be on the road longer than eight hours at a stretch. After their dinner at Oxford, Clara and Mr. Noyce ventured out with into the town but, due to the anxiety of travel and her fear of the tenor of university boys' amusements, Mrs. Noyce forbade them to stay out past ten o'clock.

"I will not have our departure tomorrow postponed by an accident, which I do not doubt will result from one of those horrid pranks!" she cried, shuddering. "Francis was forever getting up to them while he was at school, and they more often than not ended in some sort of injury, either to some poor, unsuspecting person or to their property. The number of times he was sent down—I do not wish to recollect. I am persuaded we shall do very well making an early night of it so that we may arise betimes."

No heedless prank upset their plans and they resumed their journey after a hearty breakfast served in their private parlor. A downpour made the going at one stretch rough, for McAdam's experiments in road improvement had not extended past Bath, and the horses' hooves squelched in the mud. They were forced, therefore, to break their journey early, in Wootton Basset, which Clara thought had only its preponderance of double letters to recommend it. Indeed, she could not know that the town was generally held to be quaint and charming, for she was prevented a proper view of it by the rain and dirt.

Mrs. Noyce's temper was shrill and Clara's glowering as they regarded the prospect of a night cooped up in the small inn. But Mr. Noyce opined that it was all for the best, "for it is my opinion that a jaunt in this rain would surely deprive you of both daughter and husband, for we would certainly sink into the mire and never be seen or heard of again."

So saying, Mr. Noyce settled down to entertain his lady with a game of backgammon, and Clara reflected that he was far more cheerful in his lot than she could ever be. She followed his example as far as she could, however, and whiled away the evening hours with multiple games of Patience, until Mrs. Noyce announced that it was time to seek their beds.

They set out in the early morning, arriving in Bath at midday under a leaden sky. Mr. Noyce had taken a house in Laura Place with a pleasing view of the river and easy access to the baths across the Pulteney Bridge. Though the place was far smaller than Wesley Abbey, Clara could find no fault in it. Her apartments were both adequate and elegant, and the town certainly was larger than Southam—and more promising, too. Already, as they had bustled about getting themselves and all their bags, parcels, and portmanteaux from the carriage to the front door, she had seen two very handsome young men, and to judge by their appreciative glances, they had taken notice of her as well.

Undoing the strings of her bonnet, Clara set it on the bed and wandered to the window to look out. A mist was forming over the undulating fields as the rain began to fall, and though it was quite lovely, she could not greet the circumstance with satisfaction. Her mother was bound to insist upon their staying at home again, both to avoid the rain and to recruit their strength after the journey. After three days without a reprieve from her parent, Clara did not view the prospect of another evening *en famille* with any degree of pleasure.

The evening proved less tiresome than she imagined, however, for Mr. Noyce insisted on taking her on a short walk across the bridge, which both eased her fidgets and stretched her legs, and the night brought an improvement in the weather. By morning, Mrs. Noyce had fully recovered from the journey and was bent on venturing out to find out what society Bath had to offer. Mr. Noyce graciously engaged himself to ensure they were settled before confirming his appointment at the baths on the morrow.

"We will appear at the Pump Room, Clara," said Mrs. Noyce over breakfast. "I declare if a taste of the waters will not set me up again after our long journey, and I advise you to try them."

Mr. Noyce, who had more experience of the Bath waters than his wife, intervened, saying, "I expect a promenade about the Pump Room will set you up much more readily, my dear, and it would greatly surprise me if Clara wished ever to taste those horrid waters. However, she will wish to see and be seen as soon as may be. Will you join us, Clara? Your mother looks to such advantage with you by her side."

"Pooh, William!" cried Mrs. Noyce, coloring prettily, "I look to best advantage with you by my side. Clara may take your other arm, and carry your canes for you."

To this Clara gladly agreed, and the three sallied forth, walking over the bridge and into the High Street. Mrs. Noyce remarked upon Bath Abbey as they passed, declaring that they all should attend services there on Sunday, and Clara observed that it was a pity their own abbey did not still have a church attached.

"For Mr. Noyce would, of course, have made an excellent vicar—besides being the owner and benefactor—giving you, Mother, a whole congregation upon whom to exercise your influence, rather than only myself and your husband."

Mrs. Noyce's sputtering was calmed by her husband commenting ruminatively, "I have often imagined I had missed my calling there. I can easily imagine the satisfaction it would bring to a vicar to have so thoughtful and careful a wife as you, my dear Anamaria, at his side."

With this adroit handling, the two ladies arrived at the Pump Room in tolerably good spirits. After signing the visitor's book, Mrs. Noyce checked the list of names, pleased to find one or two acquaintances among the many strangers listed. Glancing about, she found one of them still in the room, and crossing to her immediately, lost no time in renewing the acquaintance and making the introduction of her new husband. Mr. Noyce made his usual charming impression before excusing himself to make his inquiries of the bath attendant.

"He has a fine figure," said Mrs. Wellstone, gazing after Mr. Noyce as he made his awkward way across the room, his canes tapping on the floor. "Such laughing eyes. I do not know when I have met a pleasanter man. You are to be congratulated, Anamaria."

Mrs. Noyce simpered. "I declare I could not have chosen better. I have always thought him to be the most charming man of my acquaintance—that is, the Colonel could be quite charming—however, it was not long before I came again to realize—what I mean to say is that Mr. Noyce really is beyond compare."

As this tangled speech wound to a halt, Mrs. Wellstone nodded, her comprehension of how it was writ on her face. A lesser female might have been tempted to make a sly comment on Mrs. Noyce's principles, but the vicissitudes of life had taught her much, and she, for one, had long outgrown such posturing. Besides, Mrs. Wellstone had known something of the late Colonel, and herself blessed with a faithful and good, though also deceased, husband, had often felt much compassion for her friend, who had been made to regret her poor choice for nearly thirty years. Indeed, rather than feel the smallest triumph over poor Anamaria, her only hope was that this second marriage would be the making of her friend.

Thus, Mrs. Wellstone smiled kindly and turned to Clara, inquiring, "This is your daughter? I do not believe we have met."

"Oh, perhaps not," replied Mrs. Noyce, grateful to shift so painlessly to another subject. "This is Clara, my youngest. My eldest, Francis, you know, is busy with his estate, while Geoffrey is lately married."

"Ah!" Mrs. Wellstone regarded Clara, her gaze taking in the lovely face and golden locks. "You are the image of your mama. With so much in common, I am persuaded you are her dearest friend."

"Yes, ma'am," said Clara, assuming an angelic look and extending her hand. "We are such good friends that my only ambition is to be a prop for Mother. Indeed, that is why I am come to Bath, to be her companion when Mr. Noyce is otherwise disposed. To me, there is not a more enchanting prospect than to sit side-by-side with Mother, day after day, and absorb the words of wisdom that bubble so freely from her lips."

Mrs. Wellstone raised her brows, again seeing more than was perhaps intended, but her smile never wavered. "I must beg your patience, then, my dear, for I fear my presence must necessarily interrupt your idyll. Now that we have become reacquainted, you understand, I intend to place myself often at your mother's disposal."

"I shall endeavor to overcome my disappointment, ma'am," said Clara pleasantly. "To be sure, it will be the greatest comfort in the world to me to know Mother has another friend in Bath to whom she can turn in times of need."

Admirably preserving her countenance, Mrs. Wellstone looked to Mrs. Noyce with such twinkling sympathy that her old friend lost her frozen look and instantly expressed her great desire to know all that had taken place during the several years since they had last been in company. This was agreed to, and the three ladies linked arms as they took a turn about the room.

As the elder ladies talked, Clara allowed her gaze to travel over the groupings scattered about, taking note of the younger gentlemen in attendance. Though Francis had thought to discourage her with his descriptions of Bath gentlemen, the effect had been contrariwise. She fully intended upon captivating one or two of these so-called worldly-wise gentlemen, for it would prove her superior powers without the need for a twinge to her conscience.

Her gaze took in several young gentlemen who looked promising, but she would require more than one outing at the Pump Room to determine those most suited to her purposes. One gentleman, however, did catch her notice. His cynical air and roving eye bespoke the rake as he flirted effortlessly with two ladies, one older and one younger than Clara. Without losing sway over his companions, he bowed to Clara as she passed and she, making an unequivocally inviting response, did not doubt his ability to discover the size of her fortune within twenty minutes.

They continued on their round, being introduced to a few of Mrs. Wellstone's acquaintances before taking seats on one side of the room. Presently, Mr. Noyce returned with two gentlemen and a lady in tow, whom he introduced as Mr. and Mrs. Finholden, and their nephew, Mr. Picton. Clara instantly recognized this last as the gentleman who had bowed to her earlier, and she smiled in satisfaction—he had been even more prompt than she had anticipated.

"Mr. Finholden, I find, is come also to enjoy the baths," said Mr. Noyce.

Mr. Finholden coughed deprecatingly. "The rheumatism, you know. Nothing for it but to try the hot baths. Didn't like to go to Harrogate at this season. My good lady doesn't much like the cold. Besides, depressing place. Not a decent face to be seen."

Tittering at this speech, Mrs. Finholden extended a languid hand to Mrs. Noyce. "Pray, excuse poor Finholden. He is candid to a fault. To be sure, one would never contemplate going north so late in the year. Unless, of course, one is a native! Such hardy people, northerners. They have my deepest respect. But Bath society is vastly superior to anything, I am persuaded, excepting London, to be sure. We could not go anywhere but Bath in the winter."

"As we could not," said Mrs. Noyce. "When Mr. Noyce made up his mind to a course of hot baths, I would not hear of his going anywhere so vulgar as Harrogate."

Mrs. Finholden, recognizing in Mrs. Noyce a kindred spirit, proceeded upon a panegyric of all other hot springs, while their husbands embarked on a discussion of the treatment they were to expect. Mrs. Wellstone quietly excused herself. This left Clara and Mr. Picton to regard one another with interest. Clara looked with appreciation on the tall, well-built man of about thirty with dark pomaded locks and steel grey eyes, whose coat and breeches fitted exactly to his powerful frame, proclaiming the Corinthian. Mr. Picton seemed rather pleased by the prospect of a lovely girl with deep blue eyes and golden locks, whose cherry lips seemed ripe for a flirtation.

He cocked an eyebrow. "Have you tasted the waters yet, Miss Mantell?"

"Indeed, I have not, sir, nor do I intend to do so," she said coolly.

He pressed a finger to his lips, glancing significantly over his shoulder at her mother. "Do not say so aloud." Keeping his satirical gaze upon Clara, he said to his aunt, "Miss Mantell has an overpowering desire to taste the waters, and I find myself disposed to escort her. With your permission, ma'am, we shall return presently."

Mrs. Finholden and Mrs. Noyce paused long enough to smile their acquiescence and, offering his arm to Clara, he led her away.

"Now you may say what you like of the waters," he said dryly, "or, indeed, of anything else. I have extricated you from that abominably dull conversation and have you to myself for—" He consulted his pocket watch— "a quarter of an hour at least."

"You are incorrigible," said Clara, quite delighted. "Nonetheless, as you have gauged the situation exactly, I believe I shall find it in my heart to forgive you. If you expect me to taste the waters, however, merely to complete the farce, you will be vastly disappointed, sir."

"Oh, no. I could not, as a gentleman, force that upon you. They are ghastly." Nodding toward the bar where the waters were being dispensed in pewter tumblers, he grimaced. "A pack of fools, if you ask me, lapping it up like dutiful children their medicine."

Clara looked mischievous in her disastrously charming way. "But they have come here to be cured, and so they must be seen to submit to physick. Poor dears. If everyone simply acknowledged how awful the waters are, I am certain no one would take them, and then where should we be? No one would come to Bath, and gentlemen like yourself would have nowhere to rusticate."

"There are still the hot baths." She cast him a scandalized look, but he merely went on, "As long as they are hailed as a cure for any ailment, people will converge upon Bath forever. But I am certain it is not so with you, Miss Mantell." He favored her with a roguish smile as his eyes took in her rosy good health, from head to feet. "You are not here for the cure."

"How would you know, I wonder?" she replied archly. "One's gaze cannot penetrate all, sir."

"And what a pity."

She opened her eyes at him, but laughed. "How odious you are! To say such naughty things, and in so respectable a place! I fear I know your sort."

"But how so, Miss Mantell? As you said, one's gaze cannot penetrate all. I am only forthright, and say just what I think."

"Then you must often be in trouble with the ladies. Do not you know that we must be flattered and adored, and our charms made into poetry?"

He gave her an appraising look. "I am certain it is not so with you, and just as well, for I should as likely choke as write a sonnet. But that does not mean your charms are not such as might inspire me to some other great endeavor."

"Oh, my," said Clara, pressing a hand to her bosom. "This passion overwhelms me! I might say it becomes you, sir, but that, I am persuaded, would be to court disaster. A man so conceited as yourself ought never to be encouraged."

His lips curled appreciatively. "Minx. I was right about you."

She smiled impishly. "Come now, enough nonsense. Tell me why you are in Bath. *You* certainly cannot have come here for your health."

"No, but it seems I was unwise not to, for you have driven my spirits unaccountably low! You think me conceited? I, who am used to be styled arrogant—how am I to recover? There may be nothing for it but to take the waters."

"Oh dear! I could never forgive myself if you did. Only imagine what a flaming reputation they would get from such a specimen as you taking them! Very well, sir. If you will undertake to be serious, then I shall undertake to withhold my opinion of you."

He looked at her, something stirring in his steely eyes. "I cannot accept. For though you think very little of me at present, ma'am, I apprehend that someday your opinion will be excessively interesting to me."

Clara blushed becomingly, quite satisfied that this Mr. Picton was prodigiously fitted to her purposes while in Bath. He was as ready to toy with her as she was with him, which suited her very well, for she loved nothing better than a game of wits. And if it all ended with one heart broken, that would be a shame, yet well worth the cost—especially as the heart would not be hers.

They returned again to their chaperons and the group soon broke up. Mrs. Noyce was infinitely pleased with her new acquaintance and was profuse in her approbation of Mr. Noyce's friend.

"But he was not my friend, my love," he said as they made their way back up the High Street and onto Pulteney Bridge. "Mr. Finholden approached me to make the acquaintance. A personable fellow, to be sure."

"Oh, and Mrs. Finholden is the most delightful woman! It is as though we were friends from girlhood! We are very alike, she and I."

"Precisely, Mother," said Clara, looking askance. "I could see that at once. The other one, however—Mrs. Wellstone. I do like her."

"Yes, my love," said Mr. Noyce, picking up this more felicitous thread. "Where did you know her, Anamaria?"

"We met in London, my dear. It has been, oh, an age since first we met. But we have corresponded here and there. She is altered, to be sure, but not prodigiously. I do not know if I like it. She is quieter, and more—more—"

Mr. Noyce offered, "I thought her very kind, and exceedingly elegant. I hope she will grow again upon you in time. It is just as I had wished for you, my loves, to have acquaintance immediately upon coming to town."

"And Mr. Picton is excessively handsome!" cried Mrs. Noyce, easily finding words to describe a fine gentleman who obviously admired her daughter. "And rich, too, I should imagine, from the fine clothes he wears. His coat was perfectly fitted to him! Made by Weston, I've no doubt."

"Yes," said Clara. "He has the look of a town beau about him."

Mr. Noyce regarded her, a smile playing about his lips. "Did not you like him? You seemed to go along famously."

"We did! I did not mean to abuse him, sir, not in the least. He is exactly the man for me."

His smile vanished at this, but while he continued to regard her for some minutes, he did not reply.

Chapter 5

AFTER TWO WEEKS in Bath, Clara considered she had enough news to warrant a letter to her brother Geoffrey in India, and sat down at her writing desk to compose it.

> *10 October, 1818*
> *8 Laura Place, Bath*
>
> *My dearest Geoffrey, and of course, Emily,*
> *Your last from Lisbon we received most probably as you passed the uppermost part of Africa, and if you had had the decency to take me along with you, I should have enjoyed waving to the natives along the shores. I am certain they must cast off all their duties simply for the delight of hailing passing ships, for I certainly would. If you can tell from your vantage at the ship's railing what*

it is they do all day in those strange countries, you must enlighten me. It surely is of more interest than what I do all day.

We, as you have perceived from my direction, are in Bath, which is a lovely change of scene, but hardly so interesting as the scenes which must continually pass before your view. Perhaps I will seek out a handsome captain bound to serve in the East India Company and marry him, simply so that I might see something new and different. But then again, I should have to be married, which is something I do not at all wish for.

I can hear your exclamation at this all the way from India, dearest Emily, but I assure you that the marriage state would not suit me nearly so well as it suits you. Recollect that I am a selfish, heartless creature with no opinion of men, while you are quite the opposite. I am persuaded your first experience of marriage—to the never-to-be-mourned Mr. Crowther—is more usual than your present, and as such, could not be envied. It will comfort you to know that I do envy—at least a little— your present marriage, for there is something wonderful about your meeting of both minds and hearts that I would give much to experience myself.

But my brother Geoffrey is such an excellent fellow that one does not believe there are any more like him in the world. Let us not go down that road, therefore, for it is a rutted and many pot-holed one, and I had much rather write of my new adventure here in Bath. (It is strange to think that I write you from Bath but you may not read it until I am returned to Southam, for the post takes so long by ship to India. However, it only lends mystique to what I write, and gives me the illusion of a captive audience.)

In the week since our arrival, we have met many acquaintances, old and new, and have nearly settled into a routine. Lady Drayford is here with dear Angeline—do you recollect our stay with them in Northamptonshire? How glad I am that she and I are not obliged to entertain one another day in and day out here in Bath! One can only take so much talk of millinery and embroidery and marriage prospects—you will collect that she has not changed a whit in three years. I will be forever grateful that you did not fall in love with her, Geoffrey, for Emily is so very much more sensible.

Our circle is much larger here than in Southam, as you might imagine, Bath being quite four times larger than our little town, and a hundred times more fashionable. Every sort of person is to be found here, from rich to poor, handsome to plain, hale to invalid. That last makes up the majority of the population, and all the rest is tied to it in some way, for no one comes here but in the train of an invalid, except perhaps those who hope to be benefited in some way by the society that has grown up around the baths.

These persons are many and varied, and include some of our new acquaintance. Mother has become a great friend to a Mrs. Finholden, who is every bit as supercilious and meddlesome as herself. At least, as she once was, for you would be shocked at the change Mr. Noyce has brought about in Mother, all in a matter of a few weeks. It is slow going, but he is as patient as he is persistent, and I am much mistaken if he will not win out at last, and recover the sweet, lovely girl she once was—for he asserts that she once was a jewel among women. I am yet unconvinced of her past perfection, but I am a skeptic.

I am also her daughter, and have lived with her too long, and learned too many of her habits to give in easily to credulity. But as Mr. Noyce (like myself) never tells untruths, I must allow at least for his memory of her innocence. And it may only be that I, myself, cannot change—for I assure you, it is impossible, as I do not really wish to do so—thus I cannot imagine someone like our mother to be capable of it. It would certainly take a miracle for her to do so—but Mr. Noyce is something of a magician with her—you witnessed some of his magic before your departure to exotic lands, where fantastical powers are not so rare—and so you may join me in believing that he might, eventually, manage the impossible after all.

But I digress. Mrs. Finholden I will assert is a treasure, for she affords me much amusement—indeed, nearly more than she affords me grief. She was made known to Mother only by her interest in my fortune—but more on that later—and she is a silver-tongued, flint-eyed, fashionably-dressed harpy, with whom our dear mother gossips half the day. Mr. Noyce and I are agreed that we do not like Mrs. F nearly as much as our mother's other *bosom bow, Mrs. Wellstone, who is quite another creature altogether, and infinitely more tolerable.*

Indeed, tolerable is not nearly the proper term for Mrs. W, for she is a motherly, gentle and kind sort of woman, full of great good sense, and it is a wonder that she ever thought of our mother as a friend. They met in London some years ago—when I was a little girl, I am told—and perhaps Mother had not yet sufficient time to become horrid. In any case, I am glad Mrs. W did not take Mother in dislike on her reunion with her in Bath, for she is a balm to the soul after we have had Mrs. F with us. Mr. Noyce promotes the former's visits, and does his best to absent himself during the latter's. I, unfortunately, am not so lucky as to have the excuse of the baths to take me away.

Mr. Noyce, dear soul, has received much benefit from the hot baths—indeed, it has been his custom to spend some part of every year in Bath as it is so healthful to him. I could not wish him to do anything but what gives him comfort, for he is the best of men, except that his frequent absences leave our mother too often to choose her own companions. She does have me, of course, to support her in her lonely hours, but I have proved to be poor company, for I do not simper and smirk and make sly comments on peoples' looks—but I am unjust, for Mother does not indulge in this behavior more than half the time anymore. When she is in Mrs. Wellstone's company, she is perfectly tolerable (a better use of the word here)—I only wish I could say the same of her in Mrs. Finholden's company.

But what, you ask, can I have found to make all these disagreeable moments worthwhile? For you know me too well to imagine that I would not have taken the first stage out of Bath if this was all to which I could look forward each day. And you are perfectly right—I should have taken the mail coach at once, and perhaps even tooled it, had I not found much to excite me here in Bath—that is, to excite my philanthropy.

Before you take exception to my claim to such an attribute, allow me to explain. The unique formulation of Society in Bath has brought, as I previously alluded, many who wish to take advantage. These include Mrs. Finholden and her ilk, who are hangers-on and peekers-in; young ladies and gentlemen who missed, for one reason or another, the Season in London, and who wish to make up for it here; and those who have, for various reasons, a wish to live cheaply but with good Society. This last are what chiefly interest me, for among them are men of whom Francis, in his goodness, warned me—but you can guess how I intend to heed him.

There is a preponderance of gentlemen much like himself, but whose style of living has proved too hot for London, and so they come to see what Bath can offer them—and it offers them plums ripe for the picking. You can imagine how this has interested me, for you know well how I view the activities of such men as our brother. Indeed, there are ever so many witless young ladies in residence that all the rakes would be having a heyday but for me. You will see what a generous, unselfish creature I am become when I tell you that I have made it my business to use my considerable powers of persuasion to claim the attention of these gentlemen, which saves the innocents much trial and hardship—not to mention probable flights to the border.

My first conquest of this sort is a fine specimen of nobility, chicanery, and deceit. His name is Lord Boltwood, and I made his acquaintance upon my third day in Bath, at the Pump Room—for that is where everyone meets, whether or not they imbibe the waters. I had observed him there once before, and recognized the signs immediately as he imparted sweet nothings to one of the aforementioned innocents—but she can hardly be blamed for swooning over him, for even her mother was dewy-eyed! I shake my head even now, as I write, Geoffrey, for I wonder how it is that females can be such gudgeons! Give them a handsome face and a brooding air and they straightway lose possession of their senses. Make the gentleman a rake, and their hearts flutter almost as wildly as their imaginations.

What is it, I ask you, that gives a girl to believe that a man who flits from flower to flower, greedily gorging himself on whatever he can take, has any sort of a heart? How can they wish to throw themselves into the power of such men, to resign to them their faith, their virtue, their fortune—indeed, all they have and are—and hope to receive anything but degradation and disdain for their pains? You and I, Geoffrey, know too well how men of this kind regard their conquests, for our father was just such a one.

I almost said our brother as well, for you know how Frances comports himself. You will be as shocked as I to find that he has not only given up his little Janet from the Hall, but rather than simply discarding her as our father was wont to do with his light 'o loves, he has actually forwarded a match for her with the butcher's son! There's for you! Perhaps there is hope for him after all, just as there may be hope for our mother. Only do not hold your breath, for we might find, to our grief, that you have expired from the strain of it, and with nothing to show for your sacrifice.

I was holding forth on the cod's headedness of females over a handsome and rakish gentleman. Males are almost as ridiculous as females in this regard, to be sure. Lord Boltwood, who looks like a golden Corsair and whose passions storm quite as easily as that fictitious personage, had one glimpse of me and was smitten. It was almost comical how he turned from Miss Pitchling and swooped after me, hardly recollecting himself long enough to take leave of her. In all honesty—for I never boast of my personal charms—I expect he had heard of my fortune.

There is something inherent in a fortune, I have found, which makes it impossible to hide no matter how assiduously one guards the secret. The larger the fortune, the quicker it is found out, and the more obsequious and false the persons who flock to the possessor. But however tedious such persons may be, and however great the inconvenience of having them among one's acquaintance as a consequence, I must say the size of my fortune is a great comfort to me in other respects. Not only shall it support me no matter how I choose to dispose myself in future, I can also depend upon its forwarding my designs now, in ensnaring precisely his lordship's sort.

It was not difficult to keep Lord Boltwood's interest, once engaged, for he is as predictable as he is false. I find it most effective to blow hot and cold on him, and his passions do the rest. Indeed, his lordship is now sworn off Miss Pitchling, and is devoted to me. And though that young lady mourns his loss, she will not for long, I am persuaded. She is quite pretty, and though I find her insipid, I have heard her described as very taking, which gives me to believe she will soon attract another—and we may all hope a more worthy—suitor. Contrary to Francis's claim, there are several upstanding gentlemen about who would do for her very well.

No, Emily, I do not consider these gentlemen for myself. They are better left to the insipid and pretty young ladies, for I cannot be trusted with their hearts. You may not comprehend me, for you are very good with hearts, and are wondering what it is that gives me trouble—Geoffrey may be of assistance in explaining in my absence, but for your sake I will try. It is simply that, having no heart of my own, I care too little for those that could be broken. The men I have to do with are those with hearts of stone, that cannot be broken but by a tremendous force. This alone may save them—though, to be sure, I am a force to be reckoned with.

Another gentleman I have met with frequently is Mr. Picton, and though he is also a fortune-hunter, he is a different breed altogether. He is far more subtle and experienced than Lord Boltwood—who in contrast is a mere puppy—and thus he is a terribly exciting challenge. I have reason to believe that Mr. Picton's financial state is quite precarious, for he does not take up with just any young lady. Mrs. Finholden likes to tout his position as heir to a baronetcy, but it must be either a small holding or a poorly-managed one, for though his dress is the height of fashion, he lives in Bath with his relations. If he does not have the funds to live in bachelor rooms in London, the expectancy must not be worth much.

This does not make him desperate in the least, however. He has not, like Boltwood, professed his devotion to me yet, but continues to pay court to several young—and wealthy—females. It is an attempt to make me jealous, I think, for there is nothing in his manner to suggest he is particular with any of them. They are, of course, entirely taken in by him—he is a rake after all—but he holds himself aloof, and he takes no pains to hide his cynicism and satirical air. This makes him too intimidating for most of the young ladies in residence, which suits me very well. I do not fear for competition, I merely do not wish to be forever hinting away females who are too silly to look after themselves.

Mr. Picton is very much like our father, I believe, for he makes much of beauty and little of respect. I am certain he has a string of mistresses strewn across the country—what fun if I were able to find even one of them and convince her to leave him! It would certainly be a leveler, for he is *unlike Father in that he is excessively sophisticated, and dances continually out of reach. The young ladies in his sway find him tantalizing—it is my great ambition to make him dance to my tune. You may warn me against it, Geoffrey, but I am determined. There is something exceedingly satisfactory in attracting a man who believes himself dangerous—much like walking about with a tiger on a leash, I should imagine. You must find one of these tame tigers I have heard of, that lounge about in rich men's houses in India, and tell me if I am wrong.*

I do have a few other beaux—mere dabblers, to be sure, and nothing to speak of—pretty fellows who ease my boredom when no better game can be had. One you will remember from my London career—Mr. Frant, whose offer I refused last year. He has re-attached himself to my train, and will not be shaken off—I did, in good conscience (or at least in good principle) try, Geoffrey, I assure you. I have decided, therefore, to humor him, for he has been given his chance and now must abide by the consequences. Do not worry for him, Emily, for he is in no more danger than from the pain of a fresh disappointment, the first of which he survived, I can attest, very well.

Thus, you can imagine what a time I will have, with so much to entertain and to challenge me. I am very well satisfied. We plan to stay until Christmas, and thus I have more than ten weeks to exhibit my talents and to count the spoils. Wish me luck, as I wish you the best,

Yours affectionately,

Clara

Chapter 6

THE FOLLOWING DAYS settled Clara and the Noyces more firmly in Bath society, and any fear of boredom fled before the continuous round of card parties, balls, dinners, plays, concerts, and outings that beset them. Mrs. Noyce graced the Pump Room every morning and afternoon, and Clara and Mr. Noyce—when he was not in the hot baths—attended her. Mr. Noyce delighted in pointing out to Clara certain women who were part of a set referred to satirically as the Bath Quizzes, for they were prodigiously busy about everyone's business.

"Watch that you do not come under their scrutiny, my dear," he said, more serious than not. "They have the power, much like the Patronesses at Almack's, to wreck a person's fortunes here in Bath, if they observe something they do not like."

Clara watched that particular trio of ladies make their round of the Pump Room and smiled. "You know I never mortify my relations, sir, and so you may rest easy."

"I doubt I shall rest easy until you are on some other man's hands, my dear," he said blandly.

"Goodness me! You are in for a long period of restlessness. But you have only yourself to blame, for I have never yet crossed the line."

"Ah, but those who dance too close to the line are prone to lose sight of it ere long."

She patted his arm where it looped through her own. "Never fear, sir. I am too accomplished a dancer."

And to prove her point, she moved off to make the rounds of the gentlemen in her train, beginning with Mr. Frant, whom she saw as a sort of hors d'oeuvre before the first course of her more stimulating admirers. She handled him with the same laughing coquetry she had used with Mr. Simpford, but with less regret, for though she had refused them both, Lawrie was her oldest friend and she held him in high esteem.

After a correct fifteen minutes, she moved on to a Mr. Dysart, who had been showing an alarming tendency to fall in love with her, which Clara could not allow. He was just the earnest, good sort of fellow she did not want, and who would drive her mad within a week. Thus, she took steps to end his attentions very efficiently by introducing him to Miss Pitchley, who had been regarding her sourly whenever they met. The meeting was felicitous, and Clara left them to take Lord Boltwood's arm, what there was of her conscience satisfied.

Clara's flirtations were not confined to the Pump Room. She often went driving with her beaux, and nearly as often convinced them to allow her to take the ribbons. Mr. Frant could not refuse her anything and Lord Boltwood, though he thought it somewhat beneath his dignity to be driven by a female, did not wish to displease her, and made the sacrifice. But Mr. Picton would not give in, and if she tried a pout, he only laughed at her. Once, she gave him the cut direct after one of these unsuccessful sessions, but he merely took up a flirtation with another young lady until Clara decided that she must take another tack or risk losing the game to him altogether.

She had certainly taken up the gauntlet, and she would by no means cast it from her before her victory was complete. Managing two worldly-wise suitors at once was a greater challenge than she had heretofore known, and she found her interactions with them both taxing and exhilarating. It would be quite a feather in her cap to have bested two rogues in one season, and she was determined to do it.

As Clara schemed for victory, Mrs. Noyce planned for superiority amongst her set, and she set about it in her usual way. In an attempt to outshine other hostesses, she planned a card party with supper, a rout that ended in an impromptu hop, and an evening at the theater, all within a week. But unlike her former successes, these victories and the increased pressure to perform did not energize her. On the contrary, she began to feel unaccountably fatigued and increasingly dissatisfied.

"It must be that I have not been used to entertaining of late," she complained to her husband one night, as she brushed out her platinum locks at her dressing table. "How easily I am tired now, and we have only had one party this week! There was the evening at the theater, to be sure, and dinner at the Finholdens, and the ball at the Assembly Rooms, but they were not of my contriving. In London it was not uncommon for me to attend three parties in one night, and sometimes that three times in a week!"

Mr. Noyce came to take the brush from her hands and stroke it through her hair himself. "I sometimes wonder if it is not the number of entertainments that weighs upon you, my love. It is true that you are perhaps not so energetic as you once were, but that would be nothing if you were surrounded by persons who were more ... satisfactory to your feelings."

She looked quickly up at him in the mirror. "What do you mean, William? All our acquaintance are excellent *ton*. The Finholdens, the Drayfords, the Ashwickes, the Gravesthwaites—all are the cream of Bath Society!"

"What of Mrs. Wellstone? I could wish that you were more in her company, Anamaria."

"Oh! Olivia is the sweetest creature, and so very restful. You were right about her, William. I no longer think the change in her odd." She averted her eyes, fiddling with the hand mirror on the table in front of her. "Perhaps I ought to cancel my appointments tomorrow, so that I can be recovered for the dress ball on Thursday."

"An excellent scheme, my love," said Mr. Noyce, putting down the brush and bending to kiss her forehead. "And as Clara is not likely to stand by her intention of being a companion to you, perhaps you ought to send round a note to Mrs. Wellstone to keep you company."

"Oh, dear," his wife said, turning to regard him with a frown. "I could not let Clara go out alone—her maid cannot go with her to the Pump Room. William, you know very well that she must be properly chaperoned or heaven only knows what people will say."

He smiled, taking her hand and raising it to his lips. "That is why I shall escort her to the Pump Room, or wherever she should like to go, my love. Never fear, Clara shall not lose her reputation while I am standing by, for I shall require her to take my arm so that I may lean upon her."

Her frown was replaced by a dimpled smile, held back without much success. "You are a complete hand, William! Very well. I shall take the day, and I shall send a note tonight to Olivia. I think I shall order some cakes from LeBlanc's bakery, and we may have chocolate in the afternoon. How lovely it will be!"

Clara's feelings upon the morrow when apprised of her mother's plans were mixed. She adored her stepfather, and should at any other time have been delighted at the prospect of spending a day with him as her chaperon, but today she had planned to slip her mother's escort to make a visit to someone her mother would not approve—one of Picton's inamoratas whom Clara had discovered at the theater. Mr. Noyce, however, was far more percipient than her mother, and Clara was not foolish enough to imagine that he would believe her proposed outing with her maid to be entirely innocent.

An attempt to convince her mother to go with her early to the Pump Room failed utterly.

"Indeed, I cannot, Clara," said Mrs. Noyce, who had taken her rest day so completely to heart that she had ordered her breakfast to be brought up to her in bed. "Mrs. Wellstone is to come to me at eleven o'clock, and I couldn't possibly be up and dressed and to and from the Pump Room by that time. But I do not know what can be the matter with Mr. Noyce taking you. His company has never been odious to you before."

With an effort, Clara forbore to roll her eyes. "His company is not odious to me, Mother. I simply do not believe he would wish to be saddled with a gadabout like me all the morning. I might have Mary accompany me, or perhaps—perhaps you might send a note to Lady Drayford inviting Angeline to spend the day with me."

Mrs. Noyce looked sharply up from her coffee. "You cannot abide Angeline Drayford, Clara, not since your London Season together."

"Perhaps not, but since she stopped in Bath I have discovered that she is quite tolerable ... in small doses."

"That is all very good of you," said Mrs. Noyce with some asperity. "But this sudden generosity of spirit is nothing to the purpose, for Mr. Noyce has undertaken to be your chaperon for the day."

Clara recognized defeat. "Very well. I shall go with Mr. Noyce to the Pump Room, though I shall maintain to the last that it is a great imposition. He will insist that we walk, you know, and he cannot like it."

"Nonsense. He enjoys the walk, for he likes the exercise and assures me it is good for his legs."

Without recourse to another excuse, Clara went down to the breakfast room, where she met Mr. Noyce and tried on principle to convince him that his going out with her was unnecessary. But with his ironical gaze never leaving her face, he assured her with all gravity that it was not the smallest imposition for him to take her to the Pump Room. Indeed, he had cleared his calendar for the day and should otherwise have nothing else to do.

"I declare, I had looked forward to it, for your beauty on my arm gives me immense consequence. You would not deny me this treat, would you, my dear?"

Thus cajoled, Clara could do no less than chuckle and say that she would be the greatest beast in nature to do so, and they soon collected their coats and hats and went away together. The Pump Room offered them each some enjoyment, for Mr. Finholden was there with Mr. Picton, who handsomely took Clara on his arm to allow Mr. Noyce to sit and chat with his uncle. His self-assured flirtation only strengthened her determination to bring him down a notch, and she resolved to meet with his actress as soon as may be.

But as this would require strategic planning, she resigned herself to putting off the attempt to another day, and she was quite ready to rejoin Mr. Noyce after three quarters of an hour and make their slow and ungainly way home.

But part way across Pulteney Bridge, they stopped in amazement.

"Lawrie!" cried Clara and Mr. Noyce together.

Mr. Lawrence Simpford, coloring, removed his hat and bowed.

"Lawrie, my boy! How come you to be in Bath?" Mr. Noyce inquired, extending his hand.

Mr. Simpford smiled somewhat sheepishly. "I—I came in search of amusement, sir. It is quite dull at home."

"I see," said Mr. Noyce, glancing sideways at his stepdaughter.

Clara, who had recovered herself and lost the look of consternation that had overcome her countenance at sight of him, smiled affably and gave him her hand. "Dearest Lawrie! What a delightful surprise. I had not thought to see you again until Christmas! What a start you gave me. I am quite tempted never to speak to you again, but I suppose I must. After all, it is only natural that you should flee to Bath, of all places, in search of entertainment."

"I beg your pardon for coming upon you unawares in the middle of town," he said, bowing over her hand. "It had been my intention to startle you in your sitting room, where a scene could be contained. But knowing you to be a hardy young lady, and not prone to the vapors, I took my chances and came to meet you where Mrs. Noyce conjectured you would be."

"A very good notion, my boy," said Mr. Noyce with a wink. "Now, how did you travel here—with your curricle? Are you just come?"

"Yes, sir—and no, sir. I am arrived this half hour, but I took the mail coach to save the expense of boarding my horses."

"Dear me, Lawrie," said Clara, raising a brow, "you must be in straightened circumstances! Do not tell me your mama has taken to gaming after all!"

"No, no, none of that," laughed Mr. Simpford, rubbing his nose and looking surreptitiously at Mr. Noyce.

But Mr. Noyce merely chuckled. "I would rather think Diedre Simpford more likely to fritter away her son's fortune on sofas upon which she may recline. Is there not one in every room, Lawrie?"

"Not in the dining room, as yet, sir. And there is no occasion for concern over my circumstances. They are not straightened in the least! I simply have a turn for economy."

Clara looked dubious, but Mr. Noyce only nodded approvingly, his eye twinkling. "A fine thing in a young man. Can't always be throwing good money out the door, not if you plan to settle down some day."

"No, sir," said Mr. Simpford, looking a trifle discomposed.

Mr. Noyce glanced between him and Clara again and said, "If you are not too eager to go exploring about the town, will you walk back with us? I think I am about done for this morning, and I am tolerably certain Clara has thought me a dead bore these twenty minutes and more. I would count it a great favor if you would come in again, for Clara has need of a new face about the house."

"Nonsense, Mr. Noyce," chided Clara. "I am very well content with both your company and your face, and should not like to give my arm to anyone else."

"That I know to be false, my dear," retorted her stepfather, accepting Mr. Simpford's arm and relinquishing Clara's. "You are far happier on Lord Boltwood's arm than my own."

Mr. Simpford glanced quickly at him. "So Lord Boltwood *is* here. I had heard as much. Is Ferdinand Picton also?"

"Now, how had you such minute intelligence?" inquired Clara, piqued. "Do you know the gentlemen? Otherwise, I must suppose a little bird told you. It is a strange migration, however, from south to north at this time of year."

"In fact, I do know the gentlemen. But it was not from them I heard of it," he said, not meeting her eyes. "Arabella Thornton informed me. She had it from Miss Drayford—you know Angeline Drayford is in Bath."

Clara pursed her lips. "Certainly I do. How kind in her to report all the Bath gossip to dear Arabella. And for Arabella to so obligingly repeat it to all my acquaintance."

They had reached their door, and Mr. Noyce welcomed Mr. Simpford in, taking him straight up to the drawing room, where Mrs. Noyce sat with Mrs. Wellstone.

"My dear!" she cried when she saw her husband being supported by her guest. "You have gone and fatigued yourself again. Come, come, sit! For shame, Clara, to have disregarded his comfort. But it was ever so with you! Heedless child."

"My dear Mother," said Clara, with an air of saintly resignation, "as you practically forced us out of doors together this morning, it is too provoking of you to lay me the blame, for you know what Mr. Noyce is once he is out in the fresh air. I have never known a man for so much walking!"

Mrs. Noyce had settled her husband into a large wing chair by the fire and was fussing about him, leaving Clara to see to the disposition of their guest.

"But indeed, my dear," said Mr. Noyce reasonably, "we went only to the Pump Room and back, and I was seated there with Mr. Finholden quite half an hour."

As Mrs. Wellstone added her calming voice to the matter, Mrs. Noyce was induced to let it pass, and recollected her civility enough to greet Mr. Simpford for a second time, and to invite him to take a nuncheon with them. She then resumed her ministrations to her husband, who protested in vain against them, for she was determined to be a good wife, and he was too much in love to resent it.

Mr. Simpford took off his hat and gloves and, seeming reluctant to speak *tête-à-tête* with Clara, engaged to make himself agreeable to Mrs. Wellstone. This amiable lady had taken quite a fancy to him during his first visit half an hour before, and by the time the nuncheon was served, had made him a friend.

"There are several walks to which I should be glad to direct you," she offered. "There is nothing so lovely as the woods and hills hereabouts—though I suppose you have plenty of that in Warwickshire. But when one is in a town like this, surrounded by stone and people, one does yearn for a taste of the country."

"It is precisely why I have come to Bath, ma'am," Mr. Simpford assured her, to which Clara made a noise very like a snort.

Mrs. Wellstone regarded her with surprised inquiry, but Mr. Simpford quickly begged for her recommendations, ignoring Clara with as much civility as possible until Mrs. Wellstone took her leave. Then Mr. and Mrs. Noyce dozed off by the fire, forcing him to face his old friend at last. Her bland gaze seemed utterly to discompose him, and when she opened her mouth to speak, he blurted, "I suppose I must make an appearance at the Pump Room."

But her gaze only became more ironical. "Dear Lawrie, what a cawker you are. As though I should believe your turn for economy brought you away from your comfortable home in the middle of the shooting, to make an appearance at the Pump Room."

He glanced guiltily at her. "There is nothing in that. I may shoot at any season, if I wish."

"And I suppose at present your only wish is to spoil both your own sport and other people's."

"I may tell you that I bagged so many birds last week that I doubt there is another on my manor," he returned with spirit.

"You may tell me that, and I may not believe you," said Clara, but a dimple quivered in her cheek.

He huffed, smiling as well, and said, "Very well, Clara. I came to see how it was you had managed, in only a few weeks, to make the acquaintance of two of the rarest rakes in England."

She sat up, infinitely pleased. "Are they? I might have guessed. In all my worldly experience, I have never met their like. But they are perfect gentlemen in company, you know."

"Not in my experience," he said, but he looked away. "I must own it has been some time since I have been in company with either of them, however."

Clara frowned. "But they cannot have changed so very much since then—not more than a few years, I conjecture. I must own, I hope you are not mistaken, and find they have reformed. I shall be excessively disappointed."

Mr. Simpford pursed his lips and said, "At any rate, I am here for a week or a fortnight, and shall find out one way or another."

Clara rolled her eyes. "And here I was under the illusion I had outgrown a governess."

"Clara—"

She laughed, reaching to pat his hand. "But at least you are a handsome one, and can make me laugh."

He managed a smile at this, only looking a trifle put out.

Chapter 7

MR. SIMPFORD CHIDED himself all the way back to his hotel. It was only what he had done the whole of the uncomfortable journey to Bath on the mail coach—a choice of transport he had ample cause to repent. His initial fever of anxiety had lasted only a few coach stops, when the inconvenience of being without his own horses and curricle, for an unspecified length of time and in a strange town, had been borne in upon him. He also began to reconsider the wisdom of his haste, for not only was his right to meddle in Clara's affairs questionable, it was imprudent in light of her feelings for him—or more precisely, her indifference to him.

He was in something of a bind, and he was uncertain whether he would be able to extricate himself. He had known Clara Mantell all his life, was fully aware of her outrageous tendency to flirt, and deprecated her insistence upon taking up with the worst sort of men—and yet he had been in love with her for years. He could not say exactly how it had come to pass, for he knew very well that she regarded him only in the light of a friend.

But they were exceedingly good friends. He delighted in her satirical humor and enjoyed their camaraderie, and he often saw a goodness and generosity in her that was hidden from others less intimate with her. Indeed, she had been instrumental in saving her sister-in-law's life, and in forwarding the match between that lady and her brother Geoffrey. She insisted that she had no heart and that she was incapable of caring, but Lawrie knew her better. Perhaps that was his problem—he had been captivated by the kind and generous soul that occasionally enlivened the jaded coquette.

Clara certainly had the power to wind him round her finger— indeed, getting her way was one of her finest skills, and Lawrie was not her only victim. It was Lawrie who had first taught her to handle the ribbons, and it was Geoffrey who had been made to teach her to drive to an inch. Francis had given in to purchasing her a fine pistol in London, but Lawrie had been cozened into teaching her to shoot. What unorthodox pastime she would decide to take up next, Lawrie could not say, but he felt sure she would find some gentleman to aid and abet her in accomplishing it.

It was not as though he begrudged her the satisfaction of mastering a new skill—no matter how improper it might be considered—for she seemed unable to fail at anything to which she set her mind. He naturally felt some pride that he had had a hand in uncovering these talents, but he could not help worrying over how they would encourage her ongoing fascination with danger. She was too headstrong to beware, and he felt as though, like a moonling, he had assisted her in opening Pandora's box.

Thus, upon learning from the obliging Miss Thornton the state of things in Bath, Lawrie had not wasted many moments in deliberation. He knew Mrs. Noyce to be unfit for the care of Clara—indeed, it was his belief that Mrs. Noyce saw nothing untoward in Clara's easy charm. And though he held Mr. Noyce in the highest esteem, that gentleman had been a bachelor many years before marrying Clara's mother, and was too inexperienced in the ways of coquettes, and too kind in general, to be trusted to recognize the danger. So, within two hours of having received Miss Thornton's report, he was on the overnight mail headed to Bath.

If his interview with Clara had done little to ease his forebodings, the scene upon his arrival at the Pump Room the next morning offered no more comfort. Clara stood on the far side of the room, coyly denying a gentleman he recognized instantly as Mr. Picton a view of her brilliantly shining eyes, while her admirer employed all the techniques of an experienced man to tease and to tantalize her. Sweeping his gaze about the room, Lawrie discovered Mrs. Noyce to be sitting several paces from them, heedlessly gossiping with another lady. Of Mr. Noyce there was no sign.

After a brief inward struggle, Lawrie marched up to Clara and her companion and smiled with all his teeth. "Picton! How do you do? I heard you had come to Bath."

Mr. Picton blinked at him once or twice before recognition dawned in his steely blue eyes. "Ah, Simpford, isn't it? I declare, it's been an age. How do you do? May I introduce you, Miss Mantell? An acquaintance from the club in London—you know one another? All the better. Then we need not stand on ceremony. And how have you been keeping yourself, Simpford, up in the wilds of—was it Warwickshire? Oh! I see. That is how you know Miss Mantell."

"Yes, we are old friends, Lawrie and I," said Clara, sparing an amused look for her old friend.

Mr. Picton did not need this warning, it seemed, to pass his new rival under review. His cold gaze took Lawrie in, from the tips of his Hessian boots to the top of his carefully tousled hair. He smirked gently, his eyes narrowing only slightly before returning their gaze to Clara.

"How fortunate for you, ma'am, to have an old friend here, so far from home. It must remind you of the country, with all its simplicity and freshness."

Lawrie's nostrils flared at this jab, but his smile did not dim a whit. "Anyone who knows Miss Mantell will understand how little she regards anything connected with home as simple, sir. I expect she is glad to be so far away, and does not allow recollections—no matter how fresh—to cloud her enjoyment of what is new and delightful."

"Can it be that you dislike Warwickshire?" inquired Mr. Picton of Clara, in approving accents. "I must say I am relieved. With Simpford's appearance, I expected to be inundated with remembrances between you, and there is nothing more tiresome than to hear one prose on about one's country acquaintance."

"Lawrie knows me better than to attempt such a thing," said Clara, removing her hand from her swain's arm and taking Lawrie's. Her smile held a challenge. "I am never tiresome."

"That you are not, ma'am," returned Mr. Picton, seemingly unaffected. "Nor am I, and as you have given me my *congé*, I believe it is my duty to retire. Good day, Miss Mantell. Good day, Simpford."

He strode away to another part of the room, where a very pretty young lady seemed infinitely gratified to receive him. Lawrie did not watch him go, but he watched Clara, who seemed piqued at this desertion.

"You are not so silly as to fall for that old trick, are you, Clara?"

She looked up at him askance. "Certainly not, Lawrie. Do not you know me better than anyone here?" She stepped forward, signaling, Lawrie hoped, that Picton was forgot and they could move on. "I wish you will not make it your business to explain all my dearest concerns to everybody while you are in Bath. It will give all my acquaintance a disgust of you."

"Your dearest concerns?" he echoed. "Even did I know them, I could not explain them. For if you will have me believe your family and home to be your dearest concern, you have misjudged your mark."

She huffed a laugh. "You do know me too well, old friend. I had much rather not think of Gracely Hall, or of Southam in general. Surprisingly, I will own that Wesley Abbey is become almost a refuge to me—if my Mother were not also in residence. However, as we are to inhabit it together for some time, it is well that she provides me endless amusement. She is so easily vexed! Mr. Noyce, however, is a dear, and I should very much dislike to be without him. So I will not repine."

"Is that what you have told all your beaux in Bath?" inquired Lawrie conversationally.

"You may depend upon it that I have not, sir. Did not you hear Mr. Picton? It is tiresome to be told of one's life and interests. One must only flatter and fawn and say pretty nothings."

Their circuit was soon complete and another gentleman came up to them, and Lawrie found, after a brief period of unrecognition, that he was to be privileged to renew his acquaintance with her other rake as well. Byron Groves, Lord Boltwood, was blond and classically handsome, with stormy green eyes and a slender but manly figure. But unlike his Oxford days, he had adopted a style of dress that was artistically careless, his cravat tied in an unsophisticated knot, his coat open to reveal a red and gold embroidered waistcoat that brought the garb of a pirate to mind. Rings glinted on the fingers that gripped not a sabre, as one might think of this blond Corsair, but the head of an intricately carved cane. His manner, also, had lost its swaggering *ennui* and become brooding, his air tragic and calculated, Lawrie assumed, to be hopelessly romantic.

"Miss Mantell, I trust I don't intrude," his lordship said in a faintly melancholy voice. He kissed her fingers before turning to Lawrie. His countenance was impassive as he blinked slowly. "I feel I should know you, sir, but it may be my poor memory. It has often played tricks on me—the tragic effect of a youthful accident. But your face *is* terribly familiar."

With an effort, Lawrie did not grind his teeth. Lord Boltwood had been one of Lawrie's circle at Oxford for more than a twelve-month, before finding his feet—and his favorite vices—within the gamesters' set.

"It is your poor memory, sir," he said kindly. "I know it of old. Lawrence Simpford. We met at Oxford—a trifling acquaintance, to be sure."

Lord Boltwood's stormy eyes flashed, but he said only, "A pleasure to meet you again, Mr. Simpford. By your leave, I should like to take Miss Mantell on my arm. We were interrupted some days ago in a discussion of Byron, which I yearn to continue."

"Lawrie will certainly give me up, I am persuaded," said Clara, transferring her hold to Lord Boltwood. "Firstly, he takes not the least interest in Gothic poetry, and secondly, he has been with me this half hour. It would look very particular indeed if I were to walk with him longer, which I should be loath to do. I never mortify my family, and they would be if I were to appear fast in Bath Society."

"I could not forgive myself if that were to happen on my account, naturally," Lawrie said, knowing full well Clara took even less interest than himself in Gothic poetry. But he merely bowed gallantly and said, "I trust you will enjoy a fascinating discussion. Servant, Boltwood."

Lawrie did not intend to gaze after them like some lovesick fool, but he was curious whether Boltwood's methods had altered much since last he had known him. As soon as he was out of earshot, Boltwood bent down to whisper something in Clara's ear, their heads so close that their golden curls intermingled, and Clara's answering appreciative laugh made Lawrie's teeth grind together. The arts of this Golden Corsair persona seemed quite effective.

He turned stiffly to find Mr. Noyce making his awkward way toward him. "You must not look so thunderous, Lawrie," he said, urging him to a seat beside Mrs. Noyce, "or you will give away more than you care to."

"If you mean that those scoundrels will know how I feel about Clara, I am glad of it, for they shall be given to understand that she is not, as they are made to believe, unprotected."

"Now, now, my boy, you are uncivil. I and Mrs. Noyce are her rightful protectors, and as you see, we are here in the room. Unless Lord Boltwood means to carry her off under the watchful stares of the half of Bath Society, I believe there is not much more for us to do."

Forced to accede to this reasonable response, Lawrie blew out a sigh and made an effort to command himself. "Forgive me, sir. She is far too confident for my liking. There are many places where she may be got alone, and I cannot help but worry that she will come to harm."

"As do I," said Mr. Noyce, his eyes following Clara and Lord Boltwood on the far side of the room as they promenaded along the perimeter. "But we are not as helpless as we might imagine, my boy.

We have the Bath Quizzes on our side—a formidable lot to be sure! Their eyes are everywhere, and their tongues excessively sharp. No gentleman—or lady for that matter—would last a day in Bath once the Quizzes went against them."

"But then all that need be done is to carry her off, as you said."

Mr. Noyce looked at him with a humorous twinkle in his eye. "Were that to happen, you cannot imagine Clara would go quietly, can you?"

Lawrie hesitated for a moment, caught by the vision of Lord Boltwood trying to coax Clara into a post chaise and four, her eyes flashing and fists flying, and his elegant cane being used against him. He relaxed somewhat and gave a reluctant smile. "No, sir, I cannot."

"Then we must not waste our energies in worrying," said Mr. Noyce, surveying the room once more with utmost unconcern. "She is testing her limits, and I am persuaded we would be wise to let her do it. The more adventurous she is able to be here, away from the staid sameness of home, the more content she will be when at last we must return." He turned his cheery gaze upon Lawrie once more. "And perhaps she may learn to be more careful, or to wish more for those things that will bring her lasting happiness."

After a moment of reflection, Lawrie said, "I fear I have wronged you, Mr. Noyce. I imagined you not up to Clara's weight. But you seem fully capable of managing her, though she is the most provoking little chit I have ever had the ill-luck to know."

Mr. Noyce chuckled. "She is certainly out of the common way, my boy. But I would not have her any other way. It is good for a man to be challenged, I think," he added, with a sly look at Lawrie.

"Only if the challenge brings an equal reward," said Lawrie grimly, again regarding Clara and her beau.

But rather than remaining an unseemly length of time in one gentleman's company, Clara passed from Boltwood to another gentleman, whose waistcoat set the eyes to watering and whose person was beset by fobs and rings. After blinking away his amazement, Lawrie recognized him as the same Mr. Frant she had refused last year. She soon abandoned Mr. Frant for yet another gentleman, and Lawrie, perceiving that she flirted quite differently with each of her beaux, was reluctantly appreciative of her methods, for she did read her companions excessively well. After watching her, he was willing to hope that she was in little danger from the last two, if not from Boltwood and Picton. Whether his hope would be realized remained to be seen.

Though he was somewhat relieved by his observations, it was hard work watching the flirtations of the handsomest gentlemen in the room with the girl he loved, and Lawrie rose to take his leave of Mr. and Mrs. Noyce. But as he was threading his way through the throng to the door, he heard his name called, and he turned to see an old acquaintance from London, a Mr. Hiddeston, making his way smilingly toward him.

"Hallo, old boy!" cried Mr. Hiddeston, slapping Lawrie on the shoulder. "Haven't seen you in an age! What brings you to Bath?"

Lawrie, unwilling to divulge his real motive for being there, fobbed him off with the same excuse of boredom he had given Mr. Noyce, which his friend was more than happy to accept. At Hiddeston's inquiry as to his plans, Lawrie darted a look again to where Clara now talked with Mr. Noyce.

"I believe I shall stay until Christmas," he said.

"Capital! I'm here for the winter—can't quite afford London at the moment, if you take my meaning. Dashed bad run of luck, but I've learnt m'lesson. Keep away from the gaming tables, don't you know!"

"I'll join you, and gladly," said Lawrie. "Never been much of a dab at cards anyway."

Hiddeston clapped him on the shoulder again and they moved to the door. "What of your lodgings? None yet? Mustn't hole up just anywhere, you know! Don't want to come off as bad *ton*. A hotel is a start, but you'll be well-advised to take more permanent lodgings."

Hiddeston rattled on about fashionable streets and tolerable quarters as they went up Union Street, but Lawrie's attention was arrested by Mr. Noyce's name on a stranger's lips somewhere behind them.

A woman's voice was remarking, "I wish Mr. Noyce would not walk about town so. There are chairs aplenty to be had, and yet he never avails himself of one. It is almost painful to see him walk in his unsightly way. I am most discomfited whenever I see him."

"I could wish he would not lean upon Miss Mantell's arm," put in a man, whose voice Lawrie could swear belonged to Mr. Picton. "It is a jarring picture—that lovely creature with a ghoul to support her."

Lawrie risked a peek over his shoulder and saw that it was Mr. Picton, and the woman with whom Mrs. Noyce had been gossiping at the Pump Room with another gentleman who he took to be her husband.

"One may almost forget he is crippled while he is sitting," the lady continued, "for he is quite gentlemanly, and knows just how to address a lady."

"He has taught himself many tricks, I expect, to make himself agreeable."

The other man coughed and said, "And he is—very agreeable."

The lady tittered. "I cannot conceive how he came to address himself to dear Anamaria—and successfully! It is quite shocking!

That so lovely a woman, and so accomplished and fashionable, should even look at such a man."

"They say he is rich as a Nabob," offered Picton.

Lawrie tensed, but could do nothing—he ought not to eavesdrop, after all.

"To be sure, that would account for it," the lady went on. "Though Anamaria's late husband did not leave her penniless, from what I have heard. And her eldest son not married—she could have lived comfortably at Gracely Hall for several years to come. There is even a dower house, I believe. But money *is* a consideration, even when one is quite comfortable. Independence is fine and good, but wealth—that is infinitely preferable."

The husband grunted. "You were very well-satisfied when I inherited my uncle's fortune."

"Oh!" cried his wife, hesitating. "But that is nothing to the point, my dear, for we were already married, to be sure. I thought nothing of the expectation, I assure you. Ferdy, do we attend the assembly tonight? Or should you rather play at cards?"

Luckily for Lawrie's sense of decorum, they turned up another street, and he was able to return his attention to Hiddeston, whose ramblings had run on to Bath and its environs, and the enjoyment to be got in town. But Lawrie's mind would not be kept from Picton and his horrid companions, and he wondered if either Clara or Mrs. Noyce was aware of their sentiments. They couldn't be, for that was one area where Clara's goodness came to the fore—she would never tolerate insult to Mr. Noyce in any form, or for any reason, and nor would Mrs. Noyce. If they suspected anything resembling distaste of their dear Mr. Noyce in their companions, they would reject them instantly.

The thought relieved him somewhat, for there was one way Picton, at least, could not impose upon Clara, and he was able to join more properly with Hiddeston in conversation as they entered the gentleman's club.

Chapter 8

ONCE CLARA HAD adjusted her ideas to Lawrie's presence in Bath, she was able to forgive him his impertinence in imagining that she should not be well up to the task of beating two odious rakes at their game. He ought not to have doubted her, for he had witnessed years ago how handily she had put their odious neighbor Shelby Frean in his place—and had kept him there—and knew from various incidents how well she dealt with Francis. But, upon reflection, she allowed that Shelby Frean was not a rake, precisely, but a bully, and Francis was only her brother. Thus neither of them rated very highly in her successes, and Lawrie could be forgiven his lack of faith. Now that he was here, he could be made to be useful, for he was just the companion she required when her beaux grew tiresome, or when her mother succumbed to an attack of blue devils.

Mrs. Noyce endured another the very day after Lawrie had come to the Pump Room, and she could not, again, account for it. The day before had been delightful, she maintained to Mr. Noyce, for she had been conversing with Mrs. Finholden on the best millinery shops and modistes to be had in Bath, a subject that had always held satisfaction for her.

But what she could not explain was that, during this particular conversation, she had become conscious of a headache growing, and of a creeping dissatisfaction with her companion. That this should be so was baffling to her, for she had always loved fashionable people and fashionable things, and to sit happily chatting with a friend on so delightful a topic had never before been productive of so contrary a feeling. Indeed, she had sat for two hours together only the previous day with Mrs. Wellstone, conversing on much the same topic, without even a hint of dissatisfaction, and had arisen from the *tête-à-tête* refreshed. But it was with a feeling of relief that she saw Mr. Finholden come to claim his wife, and to take leave of her and Mr. Noyce.

"I really am almost convinced, my dear," she said to Mr. Noyce as they prepared for bed, "that I am coming down with an infection. Perhaps I ought to shut myself away for a few days, if only to ensure it is not catching."

Mr. Noyce gravely agreed with her while inwardly rejoicing at the circumstance, for he did not like Mrs. Finholden half so well as he did her husband, but it was difficult to tell his wife so without provoking awkward questions. When she awoke the next morning languid and cross, he kissed her soundly, tucked her up again in bed, and requested a tisane and toast to be delivered to her later that morning, with orders that no visitors—excepting Mrs. Wellstone—be admitted during the day.

Clara, finding great satisfaction in the circumstance of her mother's being indisposed, and knowing Mr. Noyce to be going down into the baths that morning, easily obtained her stepfather's consent to seek Lawrie's escort for the day. She sent a footman with a note to Lawrie's hotel, requesting that he attend her on errands, and received the good tidings that he was available and agreeable. He called for her at the house betimes, and they set forth over the bridge.

"It is kind in you to notice me so particularly, Clara," said Lawrie, "when you have so many beaux."

She laughed. "Perhaps none of my numerous beaux were available this morning to gallant me about town."

"Or perhaps they all were still abed."

"Very likely," she said with a saucy glance. "Or perhaps I simply wished for an old friend this morning."

Lawrie paused, narrowing his eyes. "What are you up to, my girl?"

"Oh, nothing outrageous, I assure you, Governess Simpford. Indeed, I may faithfully promise that I am on an errand of mercy— no more, no less."

"Very well, ma'am," he said, continuing up the street with her on his arm. "And am I to know to whom this errand is directed, or to what purpose?"

Clara smiled impishly, her dimples peeping. "I am reclaiming a soul, my dear sir—bringing enlightenment to the sinner."

"This is a subject you know intimately," he said, eying her askance, "at least from one angle."

"Precisely," she said, unperturbed. "When one has been raised in a household with not one, but two debauched persons, one learns quickly."

Lawrie exhaled, and allowed himself to be talked to of other things—the number of chairs transporting infirm individuals to the baths, the coal heavers' noise as they made their deliveries, and as they came up to the Theater Royal, the relative newness of the building.

"Yes, it has been a great asset to Bath, I am told," said Clara, leading him blithely up the steps.

Lawrie hesitated a moment on the flagway, watching her warily. "Clara, you were serious? There is a soul here you intend to reclaim?"

"Do you doubt it? Recollect, I never tell untruths. Else, why would I bring you here? There is no performance so early in the day. They can only be practicing."

Clara swept into the building, and after a moment Lawrie followed her, stepping somewhat consciously through the foyer and into the pit of the theater. There was a small group of actors reading lines on the stage and Clara marched up to them, inquiring after one Miss Pratt, whom she was informed, by a finger jabbed in that direction, was behind the curtain offstage. Thanking her informant, Clara tripped up the steps beside the stage and ducked behind the curtain, leaving Lawrie to decide whether to follow. When he did not do so, Clara owned to some relief, for the conversation she meant to have was to be fiddly enough without his delicate sensibilities getting in the way.

Behind the curtain, she found herself in the wings, where a lovely young woman of about twenty, with long, black hair tied in a tail, was practicing with a smallsword. Pausing to watch her, Clara could not but admire the precision of her movements, and the surety with which she handled the weapon. After several minutes, the woman noticed her and stopped.

"What do you want?" she asked, looking Clara up and down.

"You are prodigiously talented," said Clara, gesturing to the sword. "Where did you learn?"

The woman stepped closer to her, swishing the sword as she went.

"Master Lorenzo, in Corn Street. But he ain't in the habit of training just any female. Is that what you want? To learn swordplay?"

Clara tipped her head. "I believe I might. However, that is not what brought me here today. You are Miss Pratt? I am Miss Mantell. We have an acquaintance in common."

"Oh?" said Miss Pratt, shaking the gloved hand warily. "And who might that be? I know a lot of the nibs and nobs."

"Mr. Picton."

Miss Pratt stilled, her eyes narrowing. "You're the girl what was with him last week. Are you his latest flirt?"

Clara shrugged a careless shoulder. "I suppose so, though it is of no consequence. You and I both know he is rather indiscriminate in his attentions."

The actress was silent, appraising Clara with an unabashed gaze. At last, she said, "Ferdy is as Ferdy does, is what I say. What's it to me if he likes 'em all ways? They none of them lasts long." She averted her gaze for a moment, then looked again at Clara, gesturing with her chin. "What do you want with me? Trying to warn me off?"

"Oh, no," said Clara, removing her hat and gloves. "I never intrude in personal affairs. Might I try your sword?"

Looking warily, Miss Pratt nevertheless handed Clara the smalls-word, and Clara made a few passes with it in the air. "It is even lighter than I expected. Have I got it right?"

Miss Pratt unbent a trifle as she helped Clara to adjust her grip and showed her how to draw the blade back and forth so it almost sang. They traded the sword between them for a few minutes, Miss Pratt demonstrating simple postures that Clara then imitated. She led her pupil through the positions of guard, lunge, and retreat, with some instruction as to angles of the wrist. At last, Clara returned the sword, smiling widely.

"Exhilarating," she said, regarding the actress thoughtfully. "You have a prodigious talent, as I said before. I wonder that someone so accomplished should waste her time with such a man as Picton."

Miss Pratt's eyes narrowed once more. "You *are* trying to warn me off."

"You mistake me," said Clara with a compassionate smile. "I came here to see if I might discover how far he has imposed upon you. Has he, for example, told you he loves you?"

The actress snorted. "Not he. But what would I want with pretty words?"

"They are worth nothing, to be sure," said Clara, pleased with this much of Miss Pratt's understanding. "But perhaps he has promised you security and comfort if you allow him to take you into his protection."

Miss Pratt's beautiful mouth hardened into a thin line. "What would you know about it, eh? Has he promised you the same thing? And here I thought you was respectable."

"Dear me, I have given you a wrong idea. He has done no such thing, nor would I wish him to. For I must tell you, Miss Pratt, that I would never in a million years believe him if he did."

"You don't think he's as good as his word?"

"I imagine he should be good for it as far as setting you up as his mistress, but how long would that last? And just how secure and comfortable would you be? Do you believe that, once he has got what he wants from you, he should be eager to support and care for you the rest of your life?"

"Rumor has it he treats his mistresses well."

Clara gazed significantly at her. "Mistresses—plural!"

"They ain't all at once!"

"All at once, or one after another, it comes to the same thing," replied Clara firmly. "He views you as lovingly as he does his horses. He will train you to his satisfaction, house you to keep you at his beck and call, and ride you as hard and as long as he can. That is, until you throw a shoe, or strain a hock, or—I'm afraid that is as far as I wish to take that metaphor. But you may depend upon it that his approbation will be harder and harder won, and his eye will be constantly roving in search of the next beautiful woman—who is younger or more shapely or more willing. When he finds her, it will be that—" she snapped her fingers— "for your security and comfort."

Miss Pratt frowned, dismayed but thoughtful. "You've a way with words, Miss Mantell. How would a fine lady like yourself come to know of such things, I wonder."

Clara smiled grimly. "If you knew my father, you would not ask. He certainly did not take much trouble with his mistresses once they were in his power."

The actress exhaled, gazing off into the rigging of the stage curtains. "Ferdy's take on it was far prettier said than yours, to be sure. I'll think on it. But hey, why do you take on with him, if he's so bad?"

"A lifetime under my father's influence has engendered in me an overwhelming desire to cut his kind down to size," replied Clara, patting her hair back into order and replacing her bonnet. "And I do like a challenge. I am only in Bath until Christmas, and wondered if I could capture and break a heart or two in that short time. It is something of a hobby with me, I suppose—as is putting a useful word into needful ears. Thank you for the fencing lesson—it was exceedingly eye-opening."

She turned and walked back out onto the stage, almost bumping into Lawrie, who awaited her just beyond the curtain.

"Why are you skulking here, Lawrie?" she inquired lightly, descending the steps from the stage and nodding her thanks and goodbye to the other actors.

"I was not skulking," said Lawrie, hastening to keep up. "I had only just come up to see what took you. What can you have meant by speaking with that woman, Clara? She is clearly Picton's mistress—and you should not know of such things!"

Clara laughed. "Poor Lawrie. Have I injured your sensibilities? I had not believed you to be one of those men who are so obtuse as to believe every member of the female sex to be as unobservant as they are themselves. How one can imagine a woman could mistake the ogling of a gentleman for a single actress on stage, and her returned ardent gazes, for anything but an *affaire*, boggles the mind."

"Picton had the audacity to invite you to the theater—" gasped Lawrie, incensed, "so that you could witness him flirting with his mistress?"

"Mr. Noyce brought me there," said Clara soothingly, taking his arm again and pressing it, "and Mr. Picton just happened to be one of the party. But the coincidence is no excuse for idleness on my part. If I am to win his game, I must be awake on all suits."

He pursed his lips, a scowl on his brow. "You came to frighten her away, then. Clara, it is a fool's errand, I am persuaded. I woman like that—"

"Men are continually underestimating women," Clara broke in crisply. "That woman happens to be a fairly intelligent one—and an excessively talented one with a sword. Do you know, Lawrie, I believe I should like to learn to fence."

Lawrie shook his head impatiently. "She cannot have agreed to give up Picton. A prize like him—he must give her dozens of gifts, and expensive ones—Oh lord, I oughtn't to be speaking to you of this." He ran a hand over his face. "Clara, to what does this tend? Do you—do you hope to have him to yourself?"

"Certainly," she said archly. "But only so that I might serve him with his own sauce. He has offered her a *carte blanch*, but she has yet to close with him and I think—after our discussion—she never will. I have enlightened her as to his true intentions, you see."

He closed pained eyes. "I ought not to be surprised. Never mind that it is utterly indelicate to consider such things."

"But you must own that it ought to be considered!" She sighed. "Truly, Lawrie, it was an errand of mercy. If women do not take each other's part, who will?"

"Perhaps more than you think," he murmured, exhaling heavily. Then he said, "But as we are being indelicate, I can only agree that you have done right. I suppose there was no one else to advise her."

"Precisely!" said Clara, eying him with approbation. "And now we have relieved our minds, will you take me to Corn Street?"

Lawrie blinked at her. "Corn Street?"

"Yes, to the establishment of a Master Lorenzo."

"Clara, I will not take you to flirt with one of your beaux—"

"He is merely a fencing master, and an excellent one, by the looks of things. I wish to persuade him to teach me."

"Good heaven—Clara, no!" He stopped still to stare at her in vexation.

Clara turned her blue-eyed gaze upon him. "I do not understand why not."

"Clara! You cannot justify it to me, for there is no purpose for you to learn swordplay! Driving and shooting I can comprehend, for they are reasonably useful to a lady, but fencing?" He was not unmoved by her clear gaze, but he made a decisive cutting motion with his hand. "It is the outside of enough!"

"You have only to walk with me there and back."

"No, for I am responsible for you when I am your escort, and this will come back to haunt me, I am certain of it!"

"It will not, I promise you," she said, leaning into him a little.

He paused, transfixed by her melting gaze. She averted her eyes, so that her lashes fluttered against her cheek, and when she peeped up at him again, he swallowed. With a tremendous effort he shook his head, striding away over Pulteney Bridge.

"No, you will not do it again," he said. "I will not be used to your ends—and for what? So that you can murder someone?"

"I do not shoot people simply because I have learnt to use a gun!" she cried, catching him up and taking his arm again in a tight clasp. "Only think what talent may be latent in me, and I will have you to thank for assisting me in developing it."

"Your mother will not thank me, nor will Mr. Noyce, I daresay."

"But they shall not find it out, for you may depend upon my keeping it a great secret. I know just how it is to be done, too."

"That I don't doubt," muttered her companion, walking on with jaw set.

"But it is just the sort of occupation for me, Lawrie. I am a capital whip, and a finer shot even than you, now," she pressed, hastening to catch him up. "I am persuaded I shall be equally talented at fencing."

"It is madness," he said, and his jaw clenched as she clung more tightly to his arm.

"Not madness, but an idea before its time. Women already are showing great skill in manly pursuits—boxing, riding, shooting—it is only reasonable that swordplay will come next." She tugged at his arm to stop him, looking pleadingly into his eyes once more. "If an actress may fence, why not any class of lady?"

Lawrie hesitated, nearly overpowered by this argument—not to mention the beguiling depths of her blue eyes—but said manfully, "Because a lady has no use for fencing. Clara, I would do anything in the world for you, but this—I am persuaded it is imprudent in the extreme! Fencing is a competitive sport, meant for fighting. It is not uncommon for accidents to happen, even in practice. You could too easily come to grief!"

Clara's lips turned down in a pout. "I wonder at your claim that you would do anything for me, and yet you refuse this one, trifling thing I would ask of you. I begin to believe that you do not wish to please me at all."

"Now, Clara, that's too much!" cried the ill-used Lawrie, stopping before her door. "Assuredly, I wish to please you—only not in so—so reckless a way!"

She eyed him sidelong. "You mistake, Lawrie, if you believe I have taken up shooting and driving and all that for some radical cause. I have not! Does not it occur to you that I might fall into some danger, and wish for a means of escape?"

"It did, Clara," he said, bending to look her in the eye, "when I learned that you were entertaining the likes of Picton and Boltwood here in Bath. I have not ceased to worry over you, nor to discourage you from your course, and yet you will plunge on like an untried colt at a gate. And now you wish me to put a sword in your hands! No. I will not allow you to enlist me in this madness. I will do anything for you that is right and good, but I will not be drawn into this."

She pursed her lips, glaring in sullen irritation. "Well, then, I shall be obliged to recruit the aid of a better friend."

He swallowed down a sudden constriction in his throat, reaching to take her hand and holding it tightly between his own. His voice a trifle thick, he said simply, "You may depend upon my being a better and truer friend than any other you have made, here or at home, or anywhere else. That is why I tell you no."

Releasing her hand, he stood away, bowing punctiliously before turning to stride across the street toward his lodgings.

Chapter 9

CLARA HAD OCCASION to witness the fruits of her dialog with Miss Pratt the following Thursday, for Mr. Picton invited her with Mr. and Mrs. Noyce to the theater, along with his uncle and aunt Finholden, to view the first performance of *The Inscription*, a play promised to deliver high drama taking place on a sailing ship. He reserved one of the best boxes, and though he acted the part of attentive suitor throughout, she did perceive his slight annoyance that a certain lady sailor—whose prowess with the smallsword was unparalleled on the stage—scarcely glanced his way.

At the interval, he made no show of approbation for the performance, but rather languidly moved to seat himself beside Clara. The Finholdens—at their nephew's behest, Clara was persuaded—drew Mr. and Mrs. Noyce into conversation at one end of the box, leaving Mr. Picton and Clara quite to themselves.

Clara turned shrewdly laughing eyes to him and observed, "You did not seem to enjoy the performance, sir. Not even a 'bravo' for the beautiful Matilda! I own myself astonished, for she received adoration aplenty from the pit."

"I suppose my experience of the theater runs rather more broadly than yours, Miss Mantell," he drawled. "I have seen better performances at Southampton docks."

"You are severe! But it must be that this play did not suit the troupe, for two weeks ago you were in raptures over *Bachelor's Miseries*."

He gave his usual satirical smile. "It was more to my taste, I own."

"Or perhaps it appealed more particularly to your sympathies," said Clara archly.

"Very likely," he said, pausing to herald the arrival of the porter, and to hand her a glass of champagne. "It is a miserable business to be a bachelor, to be sure."

Clara tutted. "You do not seem at all miserable, sir. Else why should you remain a bachelor so long?"

"Alas, I must await the pleasure of the lady I desire," he said, casting her a droll look.

Clara sipped at her champagne, regarding him in coy admiration. He truly was magnificently impudent, to profess himself devoted to one lady while handing out *cartes blanches* with his left hand. Well, if he wished to play a double game, he was worthy of a double disappointment, and she wished him joy of a miserable bachelorhood.

A noisy eruption in the pit drew their attention. "Dear me, the pit is in an uproar tonight," she remarked, leaning forward to peer over the balustrade. "I declare, those two gentlemen look about to engage in fisticuffs. I wonder what has inspired such passion?"

"Matilda," Picton replied promptly, looking smug at her quick look. "Oh, decidedly. You observed yourself that she drew the admiration of the audience."

Clara pursed her lips and looked away. "She is prodigiously talented, to be sure. Her swordplay is excellent, but so too is her acting. One marvels at the ease with which she assumes such dissimilar roles. Why, only last week she was the demure Miss Laura—a role I believe you prefer, for you did give her a standing ovation. I, on the other hand, admire her better as the cold-blooded adventuress."

"I did not own a preference for a role, Miss Mantell, if you recall," he said, regarding her in wry amusement. "Though I cannot admire this particular play, I do like a cold-blooded female."

"Pray, how am I to take that, sir?" inquired Clara. "Do you admit to admiring Miss Pratt?"

He let his eyes wander over her face. "At present, I only admire the beautiful lady in my box."

"Next you shall tell me I am cold-blooded," she said archly, turning her cheek. "I cannot conceive what you can hope to achieve by that."

"Can you not?" he inquired, reaching across to refill her champagne glass and helping himself to a judicious view of her decolletage. She turned her face toward him, and with mesmerizing deliberation, he allowed his gaze to rove up her white neck and to her cheek, meeting her eyes. "I trust your powers of observation are more keen than you claim."

Their lips only inches apart, Clara reveled in the danger of his nearness—but was not spellbound by it. She took greater satisfaction in the power she held over him, which relied upon her remaining in control.

She inhaled his scent of lavender and citrus and sighed, "Indeed, I do not miss much, sir."

"Nor do I." His eyes traced her features, from her brows to her hair, down her nose to linger on her lips.

She opened them again to say breathlessly, "I believe what attracts you to Miss Pratt is her range of skills."

He blinked slowly. "Pardon?"

"It only remains to be seen," she continued in the same intimate tone, "whether her demure lady can stand against the cold-blooded adventuress."

He sat back, resting his chin in his hand as his heavily lidded eyes regarded her.

Clara took a ruminative sip of her champagne. "It is my opinion that a woman is ten times as alluring with a sword in her hand. I believe I should learn to fence. One imagines it would greatly broaden one's horizons, as with Miss Pratt. Indeed, I am determined."

"Miss Mantell, you are already a proficient fencer."

She cast him a derisive look. "Words are not always the weapons one should like them to be. One may only wound with words, but that is not sufficient in some situations. One requires more in one's arsenal—females especially."

"I, for one, Miss Mantell," said Picton, his lips turning up in an ironic smile, "have great respect for your arsenal, as it presently is."

"That is as it should be," she replied lightly. "One cannot be too careful. Indeed, one must prepare for every eventuality, if one can. I have already learnt to handle a gun, for example, and in Southam I am accounted a very fine shot. You may ask Mr. Simpford."

"I suppose he would know. He has been wounded by you, to be sure."

She gave a short laugh. "A graze only. And quite accidental, at least on my part. When I shoot, I aim to kill—" Her mirth vanished and she looked away, taking a sip of champagne— "And he got in the way."

A cynical smile curled his lips at her careless air. "I am not so foolish."

Her eyes flicked to his face and she said pleasantly, "I should hope you are not, for I do not intend to give up shooting."

"I find a woman who handles a gun vastly attractive," he said, taking her hand and kissing it. "Only do not try to shoot me."

He held her hand for an instant too long, but she soon regained it, saying archly, "I will only engage not to shoot you if you do not give me cause to wish to."

"Then I must beg you not to kill me."

"But I never do anything by halves, sir," she said, one dimple peeping impishly. "Perhaps you had better resolve never to give me cause to wish to kill you."

He chuckled. "You truly are a cold-heart."

Clara reflected that he might be looking in a mirror, but said merely, "Only think how you should like me with a sword in my hand."

"Do you think to outshine Miss Pratt?" he inquired, a roguish twist to his lips as he leaned closer to her. "You need not fear her influence, Miss Mantell. I can assure you, she is quite outside my thoughts."

Clara averted her eyes from his smoldering gaze. He was very good at his game. Perhaps Francis was right, and Clara had got in over her head with this particular rake. But she scorned this craven thought, putting it from her mind. She was still very much in control—she knew precisely with what kind of man she had to deal, and he was not of a sort to deal handsomely with any woman, once he had got what he wanted. With an silent exhale, she said, "You mistake me, sir. I have only taken a fancy to add to my very respectable arsenal."

"But what must I understand by that?" he inquired with a wry look. "Perhaps I ought to brush up on my fencing skills, so that I might recall how to deflect a well-executed *flanconade*. Though I am persuaded my superior size will be sufficient to defend me."

She shrugged a white shoulder. "Or you might teach me. It would be one and the same to you, for you would get your practice and I would get my wish. A winning compromise."

He laughed. "I wouldn't dare. It would be to bear the responsibility of having given you the power to wield yet another deadly weapon—such a circumstance would cause me grave disquiet. Recollect your dire warnings to me."

Clara's brow rose as she tamped down a sudden rush of pique at his mockery. "You are wise to heed my warnings, sir. One never knows when one will be called to book."

His smile became devilish. "If you are to call me to book, Miss Mantell, I welcome it."

"Then you are a fool, sir."

The gas lights dimmed, signaling the beginning of the next act, and she turned her face away, regarding the rising curtain with outward calm. Her mind, however, was abuzz with annoyance. He certainly was arrogant. To think that she was so easily to be captivated by masterful ways, like some dewy-eyed young lady fresh from the romantic novels hidden in her couch cushions. He knew nothing of her. She had seen what happened to young girls who gave themselves to greedy and controlling men. Even were he to marry her, he would never love or respect her enough to see her as more than a possession. He would take what he wanted, for as long as he wished, and then move on to his next fascination.

But she was no innocent miss ready to sacrifice herself to some misbegotten notion of Gothic romance. On the contrary, she knew just what she was about—and more importantly, she knew just what he was about. She was quite as cold-hearted as he had accused her of being, and it was time he felt it.

At the end of the play, she allowed him to take her on his arm to the foyer and to speak commonplaces to her while they awaited Mr. Noyce's carriage, but she treated him with only cool civility. When he kissed her fingers after handing her into the coach, she merely smiled and nodded, as though he had been a footman, and did not let her eyes linger on him as they pulled away. If she had, she might have seen them narrow as they watched her out of sight.

The proceeding two days, she continued to handle Picton with tepid interest, displaying more than an ordinary delight in the presence of her other beaux and betraying no hint of preference for him. She had meant to chasten him, but in this she was disappointed—he did not dance to her tune as she had intended. His attentions to her waned, and he began to make up to a Miss Omber, who was plump and pretty and who was rumored to have twenty thousand pounds.

Understandably annoyed at this turn of events, Clara was again reminded of Francis's warning, and wavered for half a day between attempting to re-engage Picton or acknowledging defeat. But she was no faint-heart, and she certainly was not in the habit of giving up even the smallest point. She had set a course and she meant to see it through. He was merely giving her her own again, in an attempt to humble her, but he would be the one to fall to his knees.

She turned her energies, therefore, full on Lord Boltwood. He also had been throwing out lures to Miss Omber, but only half-heartedly, for Clara suspected his debts were such that a paltry twenty thousand would not cure them. He responded to her advances with alacrity, therefore, and gladly took the place of her favorite.

One day, as Lord Boltwood walked arm in arm with her along the Gravel Walk, he began to recount a tale of his having bested Sir Wallace Heatherby at Angelo's Fencing Academy. Clara's attention, which had been wandering, was instantly caught, and she listened with great interest. She had by no means lost her fancy to take up fencing and now perceived a means whereby she could achieve her desire.

When his recital was finished, she said admiringly, "I should dearly love to see you fence, sir."

He looked gratified, but did not meet her eyes, saying, "But Miss Mantell, it would be too distressing for you, I am persuaded."

"Not in the least!" she replied. "I should find it terribly exciting, I assure you."

He at last turned his green gaze upon her, stormy with concern, and said, "But it is so dangerous, and a lady such as yourself could not bear it without swooning."

"Pooh! A match with buttoned foils? I think not."

"You do not know how it is," he said, taking her hands and speaking intently, "to watch as two mortal men—perhaps one for whom you care deeply—fight as though to the death—"

She pulled her hands from his grip, pointedly walking onward. "I see. I might have known you are not quite so skilled as your assertions may suggest."

"It is not that, Miss Mantell!" he cried, coming up with her again. He hesitated a moment, then continued, "A fencing match is too close to true swordplay to be suited to a lady's taste. The foils, though capped with a button, are still sharp-edged, and blood is often spilt."

"I suppose you think me a poor, squeamish girl."

"Indeed not, ma'am! But the clashing of the foils is most shocking to the nerves," he persevered.

She turned to him, her deep blue eyes raised in sudden admiration. "But not to *your* nerves, I am persuaded."

"Certainly not, ma'am," he said, suitably caught. He puffed out his chest a trifle. "But I have steeled myself to it."

Clara put up a hand to straighten the folds of his cravat in a wistful manner. "Will not you show me? Indeed, you need not have an adversary, only yourself."

But he disdained the notion. "It would be nothing without an adversary—mere posturing. Even at Angelo's we never practice alone."

"It is my dearest aspiration, my lord," Clara said, raising her luminous eyes to his once more.

He returned her look, but with something she took for panic lurking in his own. Suddenly, he clasped her hands against his chest so that her forearms pressed against him. Ardor replaced the fear in his eyes and Clara was thrown completely out of her stride.

They had reached the path across Crescent Fields and were quite alone—if he chose to kiss her, there would be very little that she could do about it. Mary, her maid, was dawdling quite far behind, and for the sake of her purposes, Clara had encouraged her to be deaf and blind to these sorts of assignations. But Clara also had seen that hint of panic, and suspected that his lordship was hiding something. She therefore maintained her calm and awaited events.

"You must know how I long to fulfill your wildest dreams," he said, his voice reverberating with suppressed passion.

"But sir, you have only just refused my one wish."

"I could never refuse you, my darling."

She lowered her eyes demurely. "You will not show me how to fence."

"I will do more than show you," he said in an intimate whisper, releasing one of her hands to steal an arm about her waist.

Twisting quickly from his grasp, she clapped her hands. "Then you *will* teach me to fence? I am so glad. I should dearly love to wield a foil, and to learn more of the positions."

"What? No! Miss Mantell—"

He reached to take her hand again, but a shout and a rush of footsteps nearby brought both their eyes around toward the end of the path. Lawrie was hastening toward them, his face set, and his eyes murderous. Lord Boltwood stepped back a pace, and Clara watched her friend's approach with both interest and annoyance.

"Are you injured, Clara? Did he harm you?"

"Certainly not, Lawrie. We were discussing fencing."

Lawrie grimaced, taking her hand and putting it on his arm. "I very much doubt that," he said under his breath to her. Then, louder, he added, "But if that is all, then his lordship can have no objection to my joining you, for your maid, I perceive, is doing no good to anybody so far away."

"On the contrary, sir, you will be very much in the way," said Lord Boltwood, attempting to retrieve his place at Clara's side.

But Lawrie stepped quickly forward, carrying Clara with him and out of his lordship's reach. "If your lordship does not mean to take care for Miss Mantell's reputation, I will. And as Mrs. Noyce desired me to find her, I would think myself remiss if I did not deliver Clara safely back to her."

"I thought it was a very lucky thing that you had come upon us," said Clara dryly.

Lord Boltwood, coming up alongside to take Clara's other arm, murmured, "Do not you mean unlucky, ma'am?"

"No, I do not, sir," she said, in a voice not low enough for privacy, "for I am much mistaken if you were not about to go back on your word, and say you will not teach me to fence after you had said you would."

"But I did not! Miss Mantell," he lowered his tone again, "I am persuaded you understood me."

"Certainly, I did, my lord. You agreed to my request, and I am exceedingly grateful to you. It is most exciting, and I cannot wait to begin."

Lawrie was plainly consternated. "Clara, you cannot be serious. Lord Boltwood could not agree to so improper a thing—indeed, he said he did not."

"That was only quizzing me," said Clara, subjecting his lordship to her most melting look, "for he promised he could never refuse me anything."

Lawrie's jaw tensed. "Then he is not the gentleman I thought him."

"Recollect, Lawrie," Clara said, *sotto voce*, "you never *did* think him a gentleman."

Lord Boltwood, his romantic instincts having sustained by this time too many blows to bear, said stiffly, "I would call you out, Simpford, if there was not a lady present."

"Good gracious!" said Clara. "You see, Lawrie, where your interference has got you? You had better hold your tongue, I am persuaded."

Lawrie scowled. "I am not afraid to meet him, if he wishes to make a fool of himself."

"Come now, you are not so good a shot as that," said Clara repressively, then she had a striking thought. "Dear me, what if he chooses swords? Take care, Lawrie, what you say, for I have it on the very best authority that he is a proficient in the swordsman's art."

They had rounded the Royal Crescent and had entered the Circus, and Lawrie hastened their pace, saying, "Perhaps you had better take care what you say, Clara. Lord Boltwood does not know you as I do, and might mistake your meaning. You would not wish him to believe you to be pitting us against each other."

"Lawrie," said Clara, giving him an amused glance, "you are chattering, and will give Lord Boltwood a headache, not to mention a wrong idea of your manners."

"I am in no uncertainty as to his manners," muttered his lordship.

Lawrie ignored this, saying briskly, "I believe your lodgings are in this street, Boltwood. We will leave you now. Good day. I will relay your compliments to Mrs. Noyce."

Perceiving Lord Boltwood's furious countenance, Clara gave a sympathetic chuckle, letting go Lawrie's arm and walking his lordship another few paces away. "Do go along, my lord. I really must speak to my dear old friend, and you would only be underfoot. No, no, I insist you go away, for I mean to give his head a washing, and it would be quite flat if you were to witness it. I shall depend upon meeting you tomorrow at the Pump Room."

With a parting look of surpassing sweetness, she waved him goodbye, turning back to Lawrie with glittering eyes.

Chapter 10

LAWRIE WAS SOMEWHAT taken aback by the look in Clara's eye, for it suggested she had really meant what she had said about putting him in his place. A sudden conviction that she intended to cast off his friendship washed over him, and he experienced a moment of despair at the thought of an estrangement from her. But on closer observation, he recognized her manner not as angry but annoyed, and took hope. Gazing uncertainly at her, he waited to receive her remonstrations, but she merely took his arm and led him over to George Street.

She was silent until about halfway down the street, when she said, "You are making a very great noise about nothing, you know."

Lawrie's brow furrowed and he looked askance at her. "Nothing, that you are entertaining the advances of a *roué*?"

Clara laughed her delightfully musical laugh. "He is scarce six-and-twenty! And he is hardly dangerous."

"Clara, you must not underestimate him," Lawrie said firmly. "I have known him longer and more intimately. I assure you, he is no brooding poet! You know not what you are playing at."

"There you are wrong. I know precisely what I am playing at, and Lord Boltwood cannot harm me. Truly, how could anyone take such a play-actor to be anything but amusing?"

"It was not amusing that he had you locked in his arms!"

She tutted. "I was not in his arms. He held my hands only. He did not even get one arm about me before I was away. You have mistaken the matter, Lawrie."

She walked on as Lawrie considered what he had mistaken. But several moments were not enough to enlighten him and he exclaimed, "I cannot comprehend why, if you know how dangerous he is, you insist upon pursuing this flirtation!"

"Do not put yourself about." She patted his arm reassuringly. "Recollect, I count one of the most odious rakes among my near relations. There is nothing I respect more than a man who walks through Society exploiting vanity and stealing hearts, for he is what I abhor. As I am good for very little else as a female, I intend to do my part in schooling men of that ilk. Picton and Boltwood are my finest challenges to date, and I am determined they shall number among my greatest achievements. Indeed, I am doing Society a great service by taking their notice, you know. Only fancy, Lawrie, what it would do for the females of our great kingdom if these stone-hearted men could be broken, before ever they wormed their way into matrimony. It would make them think twice before putting their tricks over on an innocent woman, and perhaps allow her to keep her self-respect and dignity—and possibly even her heart—after she is married."

Lawrie did not reply, utterly dumbfounded. She led him resistless across Milsom Street as he pondered the revelation she had just made, and how it had affected his sentiments. It cleared some of his uneasiness at loving her, to be sure, for she did seem to possess more conscience than she had ever admitted to. But no matter how he tried to justify her, he could not dismiss the fact that the means she had chosen of achieving her ends were flawed and, he was certain, doomed to failure.

As they came into the High Street, he at last found words to express his feelings, saying, "I will commend your purpose, Clara, but must condemn your means as folly. It seems I can do nothing to stop you, however. My only hope is that your reputation may survive this foolhardy course."

She clucked her tongue. "Oh ye of little faith!"

He sighed, passing a hand over his face. "Will you at least promise to be careful? For my sake?"

"For your sake? No, dearest, for that would only make you conceited," she said, smiling. "But for my own sake, yes, you may depend upon my being excessively careful."

And so saying, she pulled something out of her reticule, lifting it to show him. It was a small but serviceable pistol, just big enough to fit in her hand, and fitted with silver and mother-of-pearl.

"Where had you that?" exclaimed Lawrie, reaching for it.

She whisked it back into her reticule. "Francis bought it for me in London last year."

"The devil he did!"

"Certainly he did. He may be an odious rake, but he has his uses."

"This is the second gun he has got for you! He would do better to concern himself with his sister's safety."

Clara gave him a derisive look. "You are beginning to sound like Morley, our gamekeeper. Come, Lawrie, it is some years since I first took up shooting. I believe I have proved myself capable of handling a gun."

Lawrie gritted his teeth, but sighed. "It is not that, Clara. I know full well you can handle a gun. It is only that it strikes me as exceedingly unwise. I had no notion you carried such a thing about on your person!"

"It is only for special occasions—none of which occurred at Southam. Perhaps you have not observed, Lawrie, that we live in the most unexciting little backwater of a town. No rakes—besides my dear brother, and I could scarcely shoot him—no highwaymen, not even a cutthroat! But here, the possibilities are vastly multiplied! One might reasonably be approached by a desperate character. Indeed, it will comfort you to know that I consider both Picton and Boltwood exceedingly desperate. I make it a practice to carry my little pistol with me when I am with them—I shall not be caught napping."

Lawrie swore, gripping his hair with one hand and turning away from her. How could she be so cool and yet so unreasonable? A lady could certainly wield a gun, but whether or not she could protect herself with it was another matter. A gentleman of any decent strength could easily wrest the gun from her, and then—but he could not think of such things. It was not his place to advise her—even should she be amenable to advice. Only Geoffrey had ever seen success in curbing Clara's ridiculous starts, and he was halfway across the world.

With a heavy exhalation, Lawrie turned pleading brown eyes to Clara. "Do not—I beg of you, do *not* rely upon your own strength with these men. It will not answer, and I—that is, your mother and

Mr. Noyce, and Geoffrey, and possibly even Francis, would mourn for you. If you do not care for yourself, at least care for their feelings, for if it was not your death, Clara, it would be your ruin!"

She regarded him intently for a moment, then lifted onto her toes to kiss his cheek. "You are a good friend, Lawrie. Would that I deserved you! But I am a worthless baggage, and of no use to anyone so good as you. I promise that I will take great care—indeed, I always do. Do not fear for me."

She went swiftly up the street to Number 8 and disappeared inside, and Lawrie gazed after her, resisting the urge to touch his cheek where she had kissed it.

After a rather disturbing night filled with dreams of Boltwood and Lawrie fencing to the death, Clara took her breakfast in bed. Though Lawrie's concern had moved her more than she would like to admit, she was not about to abort her plans simply to pander to his scruples or Society's absurd prejudice. She had learnt to drive and to shoot, and she would learn to fence. The notion had taken strong possession of her imagination, and she had set her heart upon it. The thrill of the blade whistling through the air or of Miss Pratt's graceful movements—she did not think she would ever forget it. She must learn or she was persuaded she should regret it the rest of her life. It was only a pity that she could not contrive it herself.

When she arrived at the Pump Room that morning with her mother, she made directly for the little knot of persons surrounding Lord Boltwood. Stretching out her hand, she smiled warmly at him, and he instantly excused himself to his other admirers and came to her.

"How do you do, my lord? It is a very fine day, to be sure," she said sweetly.

"Until you graced the room, ma'am, it was a very dreary day," he replied, kissing her hand with deep reverence. "But now the sun shines almost too brightly."

She simpered. "I am pleased that you did not take a pet over yesterday's folly. It was too bad of Lawrie, but you must forgive him, poor boy. The truth of the matter is that he has been in love with me for an age, and I have not yet been able to get him over the idea."

"It will be my honor to help him see reason, ma'am," said Lord Boltwood, his eyes glinting. "But say the word."

She retrieved her hand. "Oh, no, my lord, I could not. And you will not do anything rash, for I should not like it, you see, for it would rob me of two friends at once."

"Two friends?"

"Indeed, for if you were to interfere, I should never forgive you, for Lawrie would never forgive me. I would not give up Lawrie's acquaintance for anything, you see, even if he is quite provokingly misguided in his notions."

His brows raised and he regarded her with his intense green gaze for some moments before bowing gracefully. "I am your servant, Miss Mantell."

"You are very good," she said with returning warmth, taking his arm and compelling him to take a turn with her about the room. "I have occasion to be glad of it, for I have been meaning to find out when we shall begin my fencing lessons."

He lowered his gaze to hers and murmured, "Ah, but we already have."

She paused, the smile vanishing from her lips. "Dear me, you are not on about that again, are you? I thought I had made the matter plain to you—or do you intend to take me into your arms here in the Pump Room?"

"Only if you wish it, ma'am," he said, his eyes smoldering.

"Wretch," she said, favoring him with an amused dimple before moving forward again. "I do not wish it. Need I remind you that our reputations hang upon a thread in this town, my lord?"

He bent his head nearer her ear and said, "And what if I said I do not care a button for my reputation when you are near?"

"I would say you are exceedingly foolish, sir. For while a gentleman may do any amount of harm to his own reputation and recover, it is not so with a lady. You do not imagine I should be so unwise as to allow improper attentions in the full view of the public?"

"Am I to hope that you would in private, ma'am?"

She glanced mischievously at him. "You may hope, sir. But you must admit that I have very little cause to allow you any extraordinary favor."

"What more must I do, Miss Mantell? I have already proclaimed myself your servant," he said, fervently pressing her hand where it lay upon his arm. "Ask, and it shall be done."

"Teach me to fence," she said simply.

He opened his mouth and shut it again, pressing it into a line. "I could not do it."

"Not you, too!" Clara raised her eyes heavenward. "If now you will say that it would be improper, I do not know how to believe you are serious. To preach propriety after such a dialog—"

"No, ma'am. You mistake me. I simply could not do it."

She looked at him, brow furrowed. His usual swagger was gone, his expression impassive, his posture stiff. She suddenly comprehended the matter.

"You do not fence."

His only answer was a slight tightening of the lips. She looked away, amazed at her own lack of foresight. He had boasted so convinc-ingly of his fencing conquests that she had not considered the possi-bility of deceit. But she ought to have foreseen that he would be false, in this as in everything else.

She put a little distance between them, lifting her chin. "Well. There does not seem to be anything else to say in the matter."

"Miss Mantell—"

"No, no, do not attempt an explanation. The matter is plain, and further discussion would be useless. I see now that you are not to be trusted. Goodbye, Lord Boltwood."

But when she would have disengaged from him, he held her back by pressing his hand again over hers on his arm. "Ma'am, pray hear me out." He paused for several moments, as though overcoming his feelings with an act of will, before his green eyes lifted to hers. "It was cowardly to boast of accomplishments not my own. All my life, I have been too keenly aware of my shortcomings, which were the fault of a negligent upbringing, and I could not bear to be compared with other gentlemen. Thus have I allowed myself to fall into this deplorable habit, and I do not excuse myself. I ask only your pardon, and give you my word, as a gentleman, never to deceive you again, if only you will find it in your heart to forgive me."

"Your application is moving, sir," said Clara, utterly unmoved, "and I forgive you as a Christian, but I cannot pretend that I am not vastly disappointed."

"Would that I knew someone who possessed the skills necessary to teach you what you wish, Miss Mantell," he said, eyes averted to his fingers that now stroked her hand gently, "for I should engage him without hesitation."

She beamed. "Then all is right, sir. It happens that I have heard of a Master Lorenzo who is a fencing instructor here in Bath. Will you take me to him?"

He hesitated, his glance flicking away and back again, but after a few moments he exhaled and said, "To be sure—but first I must negotiate with him, Miss Mantell. He may refuse to teach you."

Suppressing a feeling of triumph, Clara said, "I do not think so, sir, for he teaches the actresses at the Theater Royal. I am certain he will be willing to teach me. Particularly as you are so very persuasive," she added, fluttering her lashes.

Lord Boltwood seemed to discard his reticence, and setting a meeting with her for the morrow, he bowed and quitted the Pump Room. The following day being Mr. Noyce's day in the baths, Clara was able to slip out of the house with her maid while her mother entertained Mrs. Finholden and another particularly chatty lady. She met Lord Boltwood in Abbey Lane and they proceeded thence into a less fashionable area of town, stopping at Lorenzo's Fencing Academy in Corn Street. Upon entry, they were ushered up a cramped stairway that led to a room extending the length of the house, with large windows in the front and back walls, sawdust strewn on the floor, and racks of foils and shortswords against the side walls.

Clara's gaze was caught by these, but quickly found an object of even greater interest in her instructor, who came forward from a desk in the far corner. He was of no more than middling height and build but walked with the grace of both a dancer and an athlete, his wiry frame lithe and powerful beneath his linen shirt and frieze breeches. His throat was bare, the collar of his shirt open, and he wore no coat over his plain stuff waistcoat. His coloring was dark—dark eyes, dark curly hair, and the deeply tanned skin common to the Mediterranean. Those eyes took in his student with unmasked appreciation.

Clara felt her heart patter and a blush of heat come into her cheeks. She was thoroughly impressed with Master Lorenzo, and no part of her plan demanded that she save her admiration for eligible gentlemen. Indeed, she could see no occasion to make the attempt, and returned his appreciative gaze with her most entrancing smile.

"Signorina Mantell," he said, coming forward and bowing with a flourish. Turning to Lord Boltwood, he said, "When we talk, you do not say she is *così bella*, Signore, and *unna donna*. I expect a *mascolino*—a girl with the body and the mind of a man."

"It was unkind in you, signore," said Clara, offering her hand.

He took it, a roguish smile in his eyes. "A thousand apologies, signorina," he said, bringing it to his lips. "I most humbly beg your forgiveness."

Lord Boltwood coughed. "Yes, well, we haven't much time, Master Lorenzo. Miss Mantell wishes to learn the basics of fencing, which ought not to take long, I fancy."

"*Ma dai*, Signore," said Lorenzo, tearing his gaze from Clara's fascinating features to roll his eyes at his lordship, his hands pressing together as though in prayer, "I tell you yesterday, I promise nothing. But now I see Miss Mantell—her grace and form—" He gestured eloquently to her feminine shape— "I am satisfied. She will learn all."

"We are not here to satisfy you, sir," retorted his lordship stiffly. "Miss Mantell does not require more than the rudiments—"

"I beg your pardon, my lord," interrupted Clara, regaining her hand from the fencing master and turning with an arch look to Lord Boltwood, "but you are quite mistaken. I wish to learn to fence not simply so that I might be satisfied, but so that I might become proficient. That, I believe, will require much more than a rudimentary knowledge."

Lord Boltwood's rigid and unsmiling countenance suggested he regretted his rash decision to bring his fair one to what had amounted to no less than the camp of the enemy. "I can hardly guess how you imagine you should require such skill, ma'am."

"Cannot you?" she inquired, in a tone of surpassing innocence. She turned again to Lorenzo. "I do hope you might accommodate me, signore."

"*Di sicuro*, signorina. With me, you have no fear."

She bestowed yet another charming smile upon her new preceptor. "Then I place myself wholly in your hands."

Apparently finding nothing in this against which to protest, Lorenzo led her over to the desk, where he helped her to remove her pelisse and hat. He expressed approbation of her serviceable gown of plain cotton, cut high to the throat—a circumstance which he seemed privately to deplore, but could not, as a professional, criticize—and boots of pliable but sturdy leather.

Shepherding an even more than usually brooding Lord Boltwood to the side of the room, Lorenzo proceeded to demonstrate, with rather more flair than was perhaps necessary, the first position to draw a sword. But Clara quickly showed she had already mastered that and the guard in carte and in tierce with Miss Pratt's assistance, and he gladly moved to advancing and retreats.

The lesson proceeded quickly, for Clara was an apt pupil, but at the end of an hour, Clara conceded to Lord Boltwood's insistence that he return her to her home. He was paying for the lessons, after all, and she well knew Mrs. Noyce would not view a longer absence with complacence, and might ask awkward questions. She therefore shook hands with Master Lorenzo—who showed his disdain for such an affable exchange by turning her hand so that he could salute it with his lips—and took leave.

She was at some pains to soothe Lord Boltwood's feelings, which had been ruffled at Master Lorenzo's too passionate manner, but managed by the time they had come again to Abbey Lane to pacify him into a promise of repeating the exercise the following day but one, when Mr. Noyce would again be in the baths. They then parted, with Clara conscientiously stopping at a few shops to provide herself with incontrovertible proof that she had, indeed, been innocently doing errands with her maid, though her mood was unusually jubilant for so routine an activity.

Chapter 11

OVER THE NEXT four weeks, Clara met often with Master Lorenzo, and he was so voluble at her increasing skill that she became quite overflowing with excitement. She had been right to press her point, and to insist upon learning to fence—she only wished that she could share her progress with someone other than Lord Boltwood. Though she often enjoyed convivial conversations with Lawrie during this time, she knew he continued to look askance at her usage of Boltwood in particular—and her flirtations in general—and did not feel it likely he would appreciate her confidences regarding fencing.

Lord Boltwood, however, had begun to display a distressingly proprietary air in their interactions. She supposed she did not fault him, for he had done her a great service in providing the lessons, but as she did not allow it to weigh with her, she considered that it was rather ill-bred of him to do so. Still, she could not give him a set-down as yet, for she required his assistance to continue her lessons. She therefore was obliged to tread a fine line with him, gradually increasing her attentions toward Mr. Frant and her other beaux, while making sure to impress upon Boltwood her preference.

The circumstance seemed to effect Mr. Picton's unapologetic return to her court. He simply resumed his attentions to her, in all the arrogance with which he had begun, but Clara recognized the great victory in this concession. Thus, she welcomed him back after only a few days of coolness.

One morning in mid-November, Mr. Noyce met Clara and her mother in the breakfast room, and Clara instantly mistrusted the look in his eye.

"Ah, my dears," he said pleasantly, "and how do you intend to employ yourselves today? I must go down into the baths again, but that need not keep you from your pleasures." He shot a knowing look at Clara. "Indeed, I know it never does."

Clara's eyes widened a fraction, but she quickly took refuge in studiously cutting her bread into slices. Her mother, however, sighed mournfully.

"I do not think I shall go out today, William. Mrs. Wellstone is with her sister at Bristol, and I do not find myself equal to the Pump Room without her."

"But I shall be with you, Mother," said Clara, eager to keep the attention off herself, "and Mrs. Finholden is always in attendance in the morning. You may sit with her."

"Yes, but it is so tiresome always to be talking of fashion and gossip and—that is, Penelope's ideas are so narrow, and even vulgar, it seems. I wonder that it did not strike me before. But I cannot wish to be at her mercy this morning. I am sorry, Clara, that I will be unable to take you."

Clara patted her hand. "It is of no consequence, Mother. Society is nothing to me. Air and exercise are the thing! Perhaps I will take Mary with me to do some shopping. I must get new gloves, for these are shockingly stained, and the palm has worn quite through."

Mr. Noyce settled in a chair beside his wife, glancing dryly at his stepdaughter. "An excellent notion, and a very good use of your time. Besides being capital exercise—I believe you have been patronizing a shop as far away as Corn Street, have not you, my dear?"

Clara's knife stilled as she stared at him a full three seconds before recollecting herself and assuming a look of amused inquiry. "I had not imagined you would concern yourself so minutely with my habits, sir. Yet, I wonder how you can have learned of that? *I* would not bore you with such a paltry detail."

"Mary mentioned it to me last night." He paused a moment to stir sugar into his coffee, tasting it and adding more before continuing, "I inquired of her how she likes Bath and urged her to acquaint me with all the most interesting places you have taken her. She was very obliging— seems quite taken with the place, and has found ever so many trifles to send home to her family. It was kind of you to make her so many little gifts of money as you have, Clara. A young girl far from home might become homesick, but you have given her every reason to feel herself useful. And in return, I find she has taken prodigious good care of you! A very good girl—an excellent maid. I gave her a little gift myself, to thank her."

As Mrs. Noyce added her approbation to this, Clara could not raise her eyes from the excessively interesting arrangement of bread and ham on her plate. After a few moments, however, she risked a peek at Mr. Noyce, who gazed back with a wry twinkle.

Reassured, she said, "Mary *is* an excellent maid, sir. I do not know what I should have done without her, with Mother's health so indifferent of late. It would be unseemly for me to go about Bath alone, you know, and it is a great comfort to me that I need not be cooped up."

"Exercise is excellent for the complexion," said Mrs. Noyce, moodily stirring her tea. "The proper circulation of blood to the face is essential for an even tone to the skin."

"Why do you not go out with Clara on her errands, my love?" suggested Mr. Noyce, as though he had come upon a wonderful idea.

Clara's gaze went quickly to him, but she need not have been anxious. Her mother declined, pronouncing herself to be far too fatigued.

Mr. Noyce patted her hand. "Well, my dear, perhaps you might write to Mrs. Wellstone to hurry her return."

"I could not do that, William, for she is to come back tomorrow."

"Well then, you must only push through today," he said, kissing the top of her head as he stood. Turning again to Clara, he said, "Mary will be a great help to you today, Clara, I have no doubt."

Clara watched him reflectively as he quitted the room, then said lightly to her mother, "I am glad Mrs. Wellstone comes tomorrow, Mother, for I should not wish to miss the assembly."

"Certainly not, Clara. However, I could wish that you did not show particular attentions to Mr. Picton."

"Mr. Picton? But he has been your favorite of all my suitors, Mother."

Mrs. Noyce shrugged a petulant shoulder. "He is as vulgar, I fear, as his aunt. I would not say so in Mr. Noyce's hearing, but Mrs. Finholden has been rather impertinent of late—teasing me to know the extent of your fortune, and wondering what induced me to marry Mr. Noyce. As though that was any business of hers!"

"To be sure," said Clara, stiffening. "I never liked Mrs. Finholden. However, it does not follow that her nephew is of a mind with her,

Mother. Besides, I fear I shall be obliged to dance with Mr. Picton at the Assembly Rooms. He is an exquisite dancer, and such an amusing companion. And his company gives me consequence—but do not allow it to fidget you. Rest assured, I do not mean, nor do I wish, to attach him. It would not do."

Her mother glanced up quickly, appraising her. "I see. I suppose it is wise to take advantage of his consequence—though he is only heir to a barony. And I am certain that if he does not keep the line, you are qualified to give him a set down."

Pleased to have got through that unscathed, Clara left her mother to dawdle in a brown study over her breakfast, going upstairs to confront her maid. She was not angry. The girl had only done as she was bid, by both her young mistress and her master, and Mr. Noyce's authority was higher than Clara's. She merely asked Mary what Mr. Noyce had said, and was given the intelligence that the maid had promised not to go with her again to Corn Street.

"Or with any gentleman what don't call for you first at the house, miss," Mary added guiltily.

Clara sighed. Her stepfather had certainly put a spoke in her wheel. Without Mary to lend propriety to her outings, Clara could not enjoy more clandestine meetings with handsome fencing instructors or unenlightened mistresses.

"Very well, Mary," she said, pulling on her pelisse and hat. "You shall keep your word, and we shall go to buy gloves."

This was accomplished within half an hour, and Clara, disliking to return so early to the house, had determined upon walking up to the Circus when she was hailed by Lawrie, who appeared out of Cheap Street.

"Good morning, Clara! What brings you out on this dreary day?"

"Merely necessity, Lawrie. Mr. Noyce is in the baths and Mother is too fatigued to gossip with her friends, so I am left to my own devices."

"No assignations today?" he inquired, quizzing her.

She lifted her chin. "No, sir. I have turned a new leaf—or rather, a new leaf has been turned on my behalf."

"Ah! You have been bubbled. I thought it was not far off. The Bath Quizzes have eyes everywhere, I am told."

She huffed. "That is how little you know. Mr. Noyce merely questioned my maid."

"A simple and elegant solution. How very like him."

"Yes, and excessively unlucky, for I am obliged by the circumstance to be good. It is a great bore."

He chuckled, taking her parcels and drawing her arm within his own. "Then I must, as a gentleman, place myself at your service. Where shall we go? What shall we do? I am yours to command."

"You are a very good friend," she said, succeeding only partially at hiding her smile. "Unfortunately, you do not pass muster. Mary, as Mr. Simpford did not call for me first at the house, I do not conceive how I may go about with him. Do you?"

The maid said quickly, "Mr. Noyce says Mr. Simpford is approved, miss," as though eager to give good news to her mistress.

Clara opened her eyes at that. "Well! How extraordinary. You are a lucky man, it seems, Lawrie! How does it feel to be approved, I wonder?"

"You are not likely ever to find out, Clara," said her friend, turning toward the Abbey. "But I shall do my best to be worthy of the honor. Perhaps we may go to the Orange Grove, or to Sydney Gardens."

"Capital! I am fond of insipidity and sameness. It will do very well, for according to Mr. Noyce, I am now devoted to fresh air and exercise."

"I see. He is as percipient as he is resourceful. If you do not wish to go to the Gardens, where do you wish to go?"

She turned speculative blue eyes upon him. "There is a very nice walk along Beechen Cliff. Will you take me there?"

"Certainly, ma'am," he said, a challenge in his own eye. "I will only warn you that I do not intend to give you up to any other gentleman we might meet."

"You cannot suspect me of that," she said, looking disdainfully. "I am merely sick of the town and wish to be away from it for a while."

Taking her at her word, Lawrie led her down Stall Street, the maid trailing behind, and over Bath Bridge onto the path up Beechen Cliff. The day being overcast, they met no others on the path, and when at last they reached the top, they found themselves alone.

As they gazed out over the city below, she said archly, "Now you may see how you have wronged me, Lawrie. Witness, no gentlemen await to snatch me from your side."

"I most truly beg your pardon, Clara."

She allowed it, adding handsomely, "Do you wish to know what I had planned to do today, Lawrie?"

"Before you were bubbled, you mean? Tell me."

"I was to have gone to my fencing lesson."

He turned to her, the laugh going out of his eyes. "Who has been teaching you?"

"He is an Italian master named Lorenzo—the same who taught Miss Pratt. He is highly skilled, and excessively handsome. Is he not, Mary?"

The little maid quickly corroborated it, and Lawrie's dismay was somewhat checked.

"You had your maid with you? All the time?"

"Certainly, sir. You do not think me so careless as to be alone with *two* handsome and dangerous men."

He did not deign to answer this but inquired brusquely, "Did Boltwood arrange it?"

"He did. He also accompanied me. However, I think he has since repented the celerity with which he accommodated my request. Even the frequent glimpses of my ankles seem not to be worth the cost of watching me with Lorenzo."

Lawrie's eyes closed tight as he pinched the bridge of his nose. "Will you never learn, Clara? You are playing with fire."

"Not fire, Lawrie. Hearts—and hearts of stone. They are as hard as mine, you know." She paused, regarding his consternation with sympathy. "But it is all at an end, Lawrie. Mr. Noyce made that clear to me this morning. Mary may no longer abet me in clandestine behavior, and so I may no longer go to my fencing lessons."

His eyes opened and he looked keenly at her.

She assumed a martyred air. "It is really too tragic. I was coming along so well. I have a talent for it, or so Lorenzo says. I am better even than the actresses he has trained. He is persuaded I could easily be a master myself one day, and perhaps even open my own fencing academy, for females. Just think of the triumph! But it is not to be. I have not even the latitude of an actress. The life of a gently-bred female is so very dull."

"Come, come, Clara," said Lawrie, softened. "You have got your way—yet again—and may be as proud of your accomplishment as you wish, for no one is the wiser."

"Except Mr. Noyce," she said, looking at him askance. "But I do wish I could continue."

Hesitating a moment, he frowned. "Now you are endeavoring to wheedle me into continuing your lessons, but it will not do! I care more for your reputation and safety than Boltwood! Italian master, indeed."

"I am entirely of your mind," she said, taking him out of his stride. "I am firmly of the opinion that I have learnt enough to make a teacher unnecessary. What I need now is practice."

After a brief, astonished pause, he turned away from her, crossing his arms over his chest and shaking his head.

She bit her lip, her dimples peeping. "Only let me show you. Pray, Lawrie, humor me for a little while. It is so very exciting to have learnt what so many said I could not. I only wish to show my small accomplishment to someone."

He glanced her way, the merest hint of curiosity in his gaze, and Clara knew he was caught. He squeezed his eyes shut for a moment, then looked heavenward with a gusty sigh. "Very well! Very well. Show me."

She clapped her hands and blew him a kiss, then ran into the wood, searching about for a small sapling to use as a foil. She came back presently with two, switching them through the air in satisfaction.

"These shall do exceedingly well, I think," she said, handing him one.

"What am I to do with this? I am not fencing with you!"

"Now do not be a cod's head, Lawrie," she said as she removed her pelisse and hat, handing them to the maid. "I cannot display my skill without an opponent, and as poor Mary knows nothing of the art, it must be you. Stand where you are. *En garde!*"

He blinked at her as she performed the steps of the salute, ending with her sapling pointed straight toward his heart, her left arm held exactly two feet from her left thigh.

"Clara, you are not serious. I might injure you!"

"With a twig? I think not. Come, Lawrie, don't spoil sport. If you harm me at all, I shall let you know of it, and the match will end instantly."

"I foresee that I shall lose my approved status with Mr. Noyce directly," grumbled her adversary, as he nevertheless took up a pose mirroring hers.

She advanced with two quick steps, testing his blade with a quick parry and lunging forward in carte to pin him near the shoulder. "Ha! You do not take me seriously. That will show you. Again!"

He made a face but set himself *en garde* again, retreating as she advanced again in tierce, this time returning her parry. She laughed in delight and retreated, coming at him again with a lunge in carte. He parried but she reversed her wrist in a masterly movement, flashing her sapling up and over his to again pin him in the chest. Her triumphant chuckle was met by a determined huff as he removed his coat and cravat and set himself again *en garde*.

This third volley was longer, going back and forth, with each lunge parried again and again, as Lawrie exerted himself to meet her skill without either exceeding it or insulting her pride. He had not been in the habit of fencing since his school days, and therefore made but a poor showing at first. However, his limbs quickly remembered the motions drummed into them years ago, and he presently found himself able to assume, in good measure, the control he once had. He was glad of it, for he was well aware that a careless movement, even with so harmless a weapon as a sapling, could draw blood, and it was no part of his intention to inflict such a mark upon the woman he loved—even though she did not love him back.

Clara did have a talent for fencing, her native grace lending a smoothness to her movements that Lawrie had always admired. However, one was forced to suspend one's admiration or one was caught off guard, and pierced by that dratted sapling again and again. Their engagement became quite intense, therefore, each laughing in triumph or crying out in dismay as they tread back and forth across the hangar. At last, they both lunged at the same moment, twining their saplings in a parry as their arms were forced above their heads.

Lawrie caught her left wrist as she brought it up to push him away, and they paused, each breathing heavily. They were almost chest to chest, their flushed faces close together, their eyes, bright with fierce delight, searching each other's. After a moment, his gaze dropped to her parted lips and she blinked, the martial light in her eye softening with surprise. She did not draw away, however, until he exhaled, letting go her wrist and stepping back.

He drew out his handkerchief and passed it over his brow, tossing away his switch and averting his eyes in awkward silence.

"Own I have some skill," she demanded lightly, patting her own perspiring face with a lace-edged handkerchief.

He huffed, but could not suppress his grin as he owned it. "I had not thought it possible in so short a time."

"I did, however," she said smugly. "I am persuaded that I am eminently suited to such activities. Only think what I could do in two months, or a year!"

"You cannot continue, Clara," Lawrie reminded her gently but firmly. "It is too much of a risk."

She pursed her lips, patting her hair back into place and retying her ribbon. "I suppose you are right. But even you will allow it is the greatest shame that I must."

This forced a chuckle from him, but he shook his head. "Clara, it is a shame, but there is no need. For what would a lady use such a skill?"

"I cannot say," she said, lifting a shoulder. "Men use it to defend their so-called honor. If Society were not so odiously unjust, perhaps ladies would be able to defend their own."

His look gave her to understand precisely what he thought of that, and she laughed her melodious and delightful laugh that never failed to touch something deep within his chest. Smiling despite himself, he shrugged again into his coat, tied his cravat in a hasty knot *a la Colin*, and offered his arm to her. With an arch look, she took it, practically dancing her way back down the path and into town.

Chapter 12

CLARA ARRIVED HOME in Laura Place in time to greet Lord Bolt-wood, who had come to inquire after her health but surreptitiously whispered that he had been amazed at her missing their appointment that morning. Her succinct explanation seemed at first to annoy him, but then his countenance brightened considerably and he said it was all for the best, to be sure, and went on his way. Taking this to mean he was glad to be rid of another rival, Clara went upstairs to change her walking dress of plain cotton for a morning dress of twilled muslin.

As Mary dressed her hair with a blue ribbon, she said, "Mr. Simpford seems right taken with you, miss."

Clara wrinkled her nose. "He has been taken with me these three years, I expect. There is nothing in that."

"Yes, miss." She hesitated. "Begging your pardon, miss, but I thought you was taken with him, too."

"I'm taken with every handsome man in my vicinity, Mary," said Clara lightly, "or have you not noticed? I advise you to ignore the little nothings if you cannot see everything."

"Yes, miss."

But after Mary left her, Clara's vaunted unconcern faded quickly away and she sat gazing past herself in the mirror. She could not help recalling Lawrie's liquid brown eyes as he had stared at her, and the swirling sensation in her chest while they had stood so close, and the sudden realization when he looked at her lips that she wished for him to kiss them. It had struck her very forcibly, and for a moment she was tempted to encourage these feelings, but she quickly concluded this would be folly. Her heart was too cold for the likes of Lawrence Simpford, and she liked him too well to serve him such a trick, which could end only in the ruin of their friendship, and endless regret.

But her resolution could not erase the moment on Beechen Cliff, nor could it prevent her longing for another such moment to occur between them. She spent a distracted evening, during which she inadvertently allowed Lord Boltwood to draw her away into a secluded alcove, where he almost succeeded in stealing a kiss before she was able to extricate herself. Telling herself firmly that she was losing her grip, she forced herself to recall all the horrid pranks Lawrie had played on her as a boy, but this only sent her into fond reminiscences punctuated by unladylike giggles.

On the next evening, she was sorely tested upon meeting Lawrie at the Assembly Rooms. He asked her to stand up with him and she considered refusing, but somehow the words would not come and she found herself holding his hands and laughing delightedly up into his smiling face. It was so comfortable that she felt bereft when he relinquished her to Mr. Picton for the next dance, who earned an impatient toss of the head when he suggested they steal away into the corridor for some peace and quiet.

She had almost succeeded in putting Beechen Hill from her mind by Sunday, when Lord Boltwood enticed her out for a ride to Lansdown. When they had alighted at the monument, his lordship was obliged to repeat himself only once before he succeeded in claiming her attention, though he was very eloquently expressing his dismay at Mr. Noyce's feeling it necessary to send a groom with them.

"For I know how you value your independence, ma'am, and cannot but deprecate the mistrust and austerity of a guardian who calls himself so easily your father."

Clara's brow rose. "Mr. Noyce is a darling, my lord, and I will not have him slighted, even by you."

"I would not injure your exquisite sensibilities for the world, Miss Mantell," he said, turning to clasp her hands and lowering his voice to an urgent whisper, "but I yearn to remove you from so unfeeling a household. Would that I could claim the right to take you in my arms, and to kiss those lovely lips that even now inflame me with their perfection!"

Clara removed her hands from his grasp, casting a significant look toward the groom, who stood not ten paces away. "Perhaps that is why Mr. Noyce insists upon a groom, my lord."

He was visibly annoyed, but Clara only treated him coolly until he seemed suitably chastened, and returned her to her horse with only a gusty sigh. Their return ride was uneventful, he being taken by what Clara could only term a fit of the sullens, and he gave her back into the hands of her unfeeling household in time to dress for dinner.

Monday, Mrs. Finholden called unexpectedly on Mrs. Noyce, who was unable civilly to repel her. Clara and Mr. Noyce were so lucky as to be in the library at the time, and when apprised of the caller's identity, callously abandoned Mrs. Noyce and fled the house to do some shopping.

As they sorted through reticules at a stall in the Guildhall market, he observed, "These are not near large enough for that pretty pistol you carry, my dear."

Clara gazed at Mr. Noyce in astonishment. "How did you— no, I shall not ask. I must learn never to be surprised at your perspicacity, sir. I shall only agree with you, for you are right, after all. They are too small."

They directed their attention to another assortment of reticules, among which Clara found a lovely green one that would just match her new silk. "I shall take it to the Assembly Rooms tomorrow night."

"The pistol? Not a bad notion, with the company you keep," said Mr. Noyce wryly. "I must advise against it—purely on principle, you understand. However, the reticule would go well with Lord Boltwood's eyes. It is my belief that they have become even greener while he has been in Bath. Could it be the waters? Or is it the Italian influence? Perhaps you ought not to dance with him twice again, or you might have occasion to use that pistol."

"You ought to be ashamed, sir," said Clara, failing utterly to hold back a smile. "Poor Lord Boltwood cannot help that his is a sleeveless pursuit. But it is all of a piece with men of his stamp. They *will* lay claim to the prettiest ladies, and so inevitably find themselves at odds."

"Perhaps if the prettiest of the ladies was less free with her smiles and encouragement, they should have less trouble."

Clara cast him a quick look before turning back to sort through the reticules. "But how flat! You are too kind-hearted, Mr. Noyce, and misjudge my suitors. They like the trouble, depend upon it."

"I cannot but feel, however, that we ought to take pity on them and whisk you away home to Warwickshire."

"Our pity would be wasted on them, I assure you," she said with a laugh. "They should only find another pretty young lady of fortune to squabble over, and she might not be so wise, nor so capable, as I. When I am done with them they will think twice before trying their tricks again. Besides, I wouldn't dream of taking you away from your treatments. They seem to be doing a vast deal of good to your legs."

"They certainly promote relaxation. Unlike your activities, my dear. I own I should like to see less of flirtation and more of real attachment."

Clara showed him an injured look. "You are so eager to be rid of me, sir? But I ought not to be surprised. My mother is so very charming, especially now she has given over her predilection for horridly fashionable gossips. You both have found something of a cure here in Bath."

He smiled, patting her hand where it rested on his arm. "Would that you could also, my dear."

Clara merely smiled sympathetically, but his words niggled in her brain. She had never considered herself curable. Once a cynic, always a cynic, was not the saying? She supposed it possible that sayings could not always be true, but they became sayings for a reason. And after all, she did not wish to be cured, precisely. She thrilled at the hunt, the game, the conquest—the triumph of keeping a whole heart while another hardened heart was left bruised and sore, if not in pieces—and she could not do that without at least a portion of cynicism.

They arrived home to find Mrs. Noyce alone and in a sour mood. Mr. Noyce did his best to discover what the matter was, but she would only say Mrs. Finholden had overstayed her welcome. Later, however, she confided in Clara that she thought the Finholdens horridly underbred.

"She had the impudence to inquire what sort of fortune Mr. Noyce has, as though she would question my attachment to him! It was coming and rude, and I'm afraid I sent her away. I did not wish for her visit, nor do I like her, and I certainly will not entertain her again."

"Bravo, Mother," cried Clara, marveling at the startling power of love to transform characters. "I know I never liked her at all, and I think you are exceedingly wise to end your acquaintance."

Mrs. Noyce sniffed. "If only you would not allow that nephew of hers to dance so much attendance on you. I am persuaded he is as impudent as his aunt."

"To be sure, Mother. However, I only allow him as it amuses me. Be assured, I do not intend to give him even an inch."

This mollified Mrs. Noyce somewhat, and Clara was struck with the disquieting realization that her mother saw her as almost a copy of herself. It was lowering, to be sure, for she abhorred her mother's weakness, and it renewed her determination to prove their dissimilarity by triumphing over—rather than submitting to—her rakes.

The following evening at the Assembly Rooms, Clara went against Mr. Noyce's advice and brought along her little pistol. She did not, however, dance twice with Lord Boltwood, though he pressed her to do so, instead accepting Lawrie, who complimented her on her Pomona green silk gown.

"Did you have the gown made to go with that reticule?" he inquired politely. "From the size of it, I imagine it holds that horrid little pistol."

"Certainly it could," she replied, unconcerned. "But I have determined that dancing with a pistol dangling from my wrist is simply too awkward. I have it in my pocket."

"I rejoice in your prudence," was Lawrie's wry reply.

"I said I meant to be careful."

"Surely there can be no occasion for keeping a pistol on your person at the Assembly Rooms."

She cast him a sly look. "As long as you are my partner, there will not be the smallest occasion for it, I assure you."

His lips twitched and he said, "I suppose I am flattered. It occurs to me that I ought to acquaint your other partners of the danger they are in."

"Not for the world, sir. It shall be a test of their worthiness, which they could not pass if they knew the consequences beforehand."

"Very true."

Their dance ended, and Clara did not watch him go away into the crowd, though she was sorely tempted—his coat fitted so well to his broad shoulders, and his hair was quite artfully done. She reminded herself that she was no moonling, and to gaze after him would give the Bath Quizzes—not to mention Boltwood or Picton—the notion that she felt more for him than an old friend ought.

It was perhaps lucky that Mr. Picton came up to her then and saved her from further temptation to seek out Lawrie's tall form in the crowded room. He claimed her for the next set, but at the end of the first country dance, professed himself fatigued and suggested they sit out the second dance. Clara, a little flushed herself, agreed, and they retired to the side of the room.

Mr. Picton went away to procure her some lemonade and on his return he said with his characteristic languor, "I am bid to tell you your mother requires your presence instantly. She has apparently been overcome by a sort of fit and has been taken to recover in one of the dressing rooms by the cold bath."

Clara, taken aback by this extraordinary information, blinked.

"Downstairs? How odd."

Mr. Picton shrugged. "They are cool and quiet, I daresay, which would be soothing to the nerves."

"I suppose you are right." She stood, looking about. "I must find Mr. Noyce."

"No need. There is such a press that it would take an age for you to reach him, and by then your mother might be in a worse state. I had better take you to her myself, and then I will find Mr. Noyce and bring him to you. Come."

He led her out of the ballroom and through a short corridor, at the end of which was a flight of stairs leading down to the cold bath. They descended together, Clara frowning over what could have happened to overset her mother and suspecting that Mrs. Finholden was at the root of it. The corridor at the bottom of the stair, however, was lit by only a single candle, casting the way to the bath in deep shadow. Clara peered down it, surprised that more light had not been provided. Suddenly, Picton pulled her into a dark room and pressed her by the shoulders against the wall.

"Now, my sweet, we are alone," said Mr. Picton, looming over her in the shadows. "Do you know how difficult it has been to accomplish this feat? Certainly you do, for you are guarded most jealously, if not by your dear stepfather's prudishness, by your own nonsensical designs. What other end could you have in mind than this? Better to have done, my darling."

He would then have seized her in an inescapable embrace, but for the unmistakable sound of a pistol being cocked. He stilled, and Clara chuckled, pushing the pistol into his stomach.

"Yes, sir, it is a pistol, and a very serviceable one, too. I would let go now, if I were you."

He huffed. "You cannot expect me to believe you will shoot me. Here, in the Assembly Rooms?"

"But I would, sir, without a thought, just as you would have ruined me without a thought. You see, I am quite as cold as you, and also just as clever. I do not like my hand to be forced, literally or figuratively, and have taken steps to ensure it. Let me go."

He did so, and she took a step away from him, toward the door, the pistol aimed unerringly at his heart. "Thank you, sir. It was very wise of you. If you will take more advice from me, you will leave Bath, and not attempt to see me again. I have grown rather tired of you."

"Come now, Miss Mantell, you cannot convince me that you did not understood me long ago."

"Oh, I did, and have quite enjoyed watching you dance to my tune. However, that must be at an end. I will leave you now to your conscience, but I fear you will have a lonely time of it."

She backed to the doorway, reaching to the side for the door.

"It is my belief that you do not even know how to use that thing."

She chuckled again. "Men like you are forever underestimating the female sex. I believe I mentioned once that I like to shoot, and that I shoot to kill. Should you like to try me?" The silence confirmed her answer. "I thought not. It was not an idle tale. Good night."

She backed into the corridor, shutting the door and hastening back up the steps, holding the pistol in the folds of her dress in case Picton came upon her again. She was thrilling with conflicting emotions—triumph at having bested Picton, horror that he had so easily deceived her, and grim satisfaction that her insistence upon carrying her pistol to the Rooms had been justified.

She paused at the top of the stair to breathe deeply and to attempt to set her emotions in order. It was a shame, really, that the game was up so soon. Picton was an able adversary, and she had enjoyed matching wits with him—Boltwood was nothing to him. But she had allowed herself to be distracted—by Lawrie of all persons!—and so had been forced to end it. Drat Lawrie! He had become a thorn in her side.

She was startled by a scuffle and a low cry behind her in the empty corridor. She whirled, bringing up her pistol, and saw Mr. Simpford bearing down upon her, his eyes flicking angrily about.

"Where is he? Good gad, Clara! What in heaven's name do you think you are about?"

Exhaling sharply, she returned the pistol to her pocket. "Need you ask? My partner overstepped the line." She pushed past him down the corridor.

"But I saw you go with him, as willing as a lamb!" he hissed, hastening to intercept her. "Did you not know what he meant to do? I cannot believe you to be so stupid."

"Thank you, Lawrie," she said in clipped accents, her brows raised. "And you are right, I am not so stupid. It is true that he tricked me into following him to the basement, but as soon as he made plain his intent, I had my gun out and trained at his heart. He scarcely touched me."

"Then you are lucky, my girl!" he replied, taking her wrist in an ungentle hold. "What if he had knocked the gun from your hand, or worse, taken it from you?"

She huffed a derisive laugh. "I never would be so foolish as to give him the chance."

"Clara!" he said, controlling himself with an effort, his gaze wild with real concern. "Why must you take such risks? Why this fascination with danger? It is alarming—and foolish!—how quick you are to leap into situations that only a woman in a hundred could hope to survive unscathed."

"But I *am* a woman in a hundred, Lawrie," she said, extricating her wrist with deadly calm. "You are as bad as Picton and Boltwood—they also underestimate me. When will you learn that I am no innocent lamb? I was perfectly in command of the situation and will thank you to cease your needless interference in my concerns."

His jaw clenched. "Only when you show an ounce of prudence, or even restraint! I know I am not welcome in your concerns—oh, how well I know it—yet I cannot simply stand idly by as you walk into danger again and again."

"Your solicitude is moving, Lawrie, really it is," she said, baring her teeth in an angry smile. "However, it has me in a puzzle why you continue to believe me to be without counsel. I am not motherless, nor am I without a proper protector. My brothers may be unavailable at present, but my dear Mr. Noyce is fully capable of advising me. It pains me to be obliged to remind you that you have no right to chastise me."

"But you do not heed Mr. Noyce, nor your brothers! You rush headlong into whatever outrageous scheme comes into your head, thinking only of another conquest, whether it be in besting a man or in besting Society." His voice became gruff with emotion. "You persist in the belief that your actions harm only those who deserve to feel pain and disappointment, Clara, but you cannot remain heedless to the pain you inflict on those who love you."

The pain he spoke of showed plainly in his countenance but Clara was too angry to feel compassion. "I never asked to be loved, Lawrie. I was not reared to expect it, and I certainly do not crave it now. I know I am selfish and cold and spiteful and thoughtless and too unlovable to reclaim, and thus I do not waste energies in the attempt. Only a fool would try to love me."

A flash of something terrible crossed his countenance and then was gone. The fire of his eyes dimmed and his expression became inscrutable. He stepped back. "Very well, Miss Mantell. You have made yourself exceedingly plain. I have only to beg pardon for my blindness and to promise that I will no longer annoy you with my irksome society. My best wishes for your health and happiness. Good night."

He moved past her with scrupulous civility, and was gone.

Chapter 13

CLARA HAD AMPLE time in which to regret her hasty words. The next day, her mother, accepting on her behalf an invitation by Mrs. Wellstone to make a visit to her sister in Bristol, carried Clara thither for a week, the whole of which was spent in visiting, shopping, and attending sedate card parties. Clara was on her best Society behavior at all times, smiling and speaking prettily to her hostesses, playing the attentive daughter, and demurely enjoying the attentions of several gentlemen who came in her way.

But behind the mask, she was quite seriously anxious that she had lost her friend forever. Being, in reality, all the things she had claimed for herself to Lawrie, it was not in her nature to beg forgiveness, for she had never before allowed herself to be in the wrong. But where his laughter and smiling eyes had haunted her before, that moment of pain before the fire had died out of his eyes was now continually before her mind's eye, and she came to suspect she should go mad if she was not able to replace it with a memory of warmth once more.

Not being prone to self-reflection, Clara did not spend much time in conjecturing what it was, precisely, that caused her such anxiety at losing Lawrie's friendship. She allowed it to be unthinkable only, and bent her mind to discovering in what way the problem could be solved. That she must tender Lawrie an apology was certain, but in doing so she did not wish to give rise to any unmerited hopes in his breast, for this would only lead to more sorrow, and she was determined never again to pain him as she had done at the assembly.

Indeed, the suspicion that she had broken his heart was one that rested uneasily in her mind. That he had thought himself in love with her she had long understood—that it was not calf love was now less sure. However, the conviction that his was not more than an infatuation had long afforded her tranquility of mind, and thus she continued to allow herself to be persuaded. A broken friendship was easily mended, a broken heart was not.

It was why she never dallied with sincere gentlemen, and why she had never allowed Lawrie even to hope. Cold and thoughtless though she might be, she did have a conscience. She credited her brother Geoffrey for this—for he alone of the Mantells possessed natural virtue—and it was through his tutelage that she had even begun to be aware of her own small supply. But while she had granted her conscience to exist, she could not very well allow it to interfere with her plans and wishes, for then she should be even more beset by rules and restrictions than she already was.

She might well have run mad from the exertion of suppressing her anxiety of mind over Lawrie, had not she been given some relief near the end of her stay in Bristol. She and her mother had gone to a small shop that, while residing in a less fashionable part of town, was held by Mrs. Wellstone's sister to have the best bargains outside of London. They were busy about a display of men's gloves at the back, Mrs. Noyce intent upon buying Mr. Noyce a gift for their return. While her mother dawdled in her choice, Clara allowed her mind to wander, but before she could dwell too closely on her problem with Lawrie, she was distracted by the entrance of two gentlemen who were in deep discussion, the name of Lord Boltwood on their lips.

"He owes me two thousand pounds! And he dashed well better pay," said the one testily. "I've got my own debts awaiting his pleasure."

"Warned you not to play with him," said the other in lugubrious tones. "Be an age before he's out of your books. Owes old Crosby a monkey, and Pridditch twenty-two thousand. He's got some high flyer in keeping in London, and they say his estates are mortgaged to the hilt. You'll not see your money for some time."

"Not if he nabs that heiress he's dangling after in Bath. If she's half as plump as they say, he'll be at high tide even after settling his debts."

The second gentleman hummed his agreement. "Poor girl."

Moving back to her mother's side, Clara pursed her lips, first in disgust, and then in self-satisfaction. Lord Boltwood was, in fact, a gamester, and a pretty poor one at that. It was as she had suspected, of course, but if her conscience required a salve, this was as good as any.

Upon her return to Bath society, Clara was greeted by her usual round of acquaintance with delight, and in one case, relief. Lord Boltwood had assumed her flown forever—having guessed by Picton's precipitate departure on the same day as her own something of what had transpired—and had despaired ever of communicating to her his shock and ire upon the occasion. He now assured her that his devotion to her could never assume so deplorable a mien, and that he yearned to avenge her.

"I must, however, resist, ma'am," he said in his smoldering way, "until such time as I have the right. I should never presume to overstep my privilege as your very humble servant, no matter the passion which compels me."

Imagining him to be often compelled by passion, if his high flyer in keeping in London and his many gaming debts were anything to go by, Clara replied, "Your self-control does you credit, sir. Now, I must find Mr. Simpford and see how he does. One does miss one's friends so, when one is away."

"Then you have not heard—" Lord Boltwood averted his eyes, clearing his throat. "I would not pain you for the world, Miss Mantell. Nevertheless, I feel constrained to hint—perhaps Mr. Simpford has been so agreeably engaged as not to note your absence."

She cast him a quick, searching glance before saying lightly, "I feel as though I have been gone an age, and know nothing of what has been passing in Bath. Do, tell me what it is you have heard."

"Mr. Simpford has undergone an astonishing transformation, ma'am. I do not know if you should recognize him as your old friend."

"Good gracious, my lord, you terrify me! Has Lawrie become an ogre?"

He smiled, but gravely. "It is not so horrible a change as that, ma'am. However, you only can say how shocking is his transformation, for I do not scruple to tell you that he has made no secret of his defection from your circle."

"Goodness me. How unlike him." She looked away, surprised at the effort it was to preserve her air of unconcern. "And does he also make no secret of his reason for this defection?"

He had the grace to seem discomfited. "Perhaps I was uncivil to suggest he has been so ungentlemanly, ma'am. But you must comprehend my feelings in this affair, so attached to you as I am. I cannot view his sudden and complete reversal with anything but disdain. For anyone, much less a man who paints himself a gentleman, to profess to friendship for so long only to abandon it at the first provocation is despicable."

"But you must explain just how he has made his abandonment plain, Lord Boltwood."

"He avoids your family. He has forged a new circle amongst whom he moves. What's more, he seems reluctant to hear your name spoken in company, forcing the conversation into another avenue at once. If this is not defection, ma'am, I know not what is."

She was silent for a moment, contemplating this. When they had argued, Lawrie had declared his intention of renouncing her society, but it seemed he was more determined than she had imagined. If his lordship did not exaggerate, a reconciliation would, she feared, be much harder to effect than she had hoped. A brief sensation of despair assailed her, but she hastened to suppress it. Lawrie had ever been devoted to her, and she could bring him to remember it. Her absence had produced this hardening of his heart, but now that she was returned, he surely would soften toward her.

Maintaining her detachment with some difficulty, she turned a careless smile upon her companion. "It is a hard thing, to be sure, to experience such a betrayal. But I am confident it will all turn out right. While I am secure of your friendship, my lord, I cannot be cast down."

This was productive of a burst of reassurances from his lordship, that lasted until he kissed her hand and took his leave upon her doorstep. But Clara's natural sangfroid had sustained a blow, and she was hard put to maintain a civil aspect as she conversed with her parents over dinner.

"Mrs. Wellstone's sister's set in Bristol is so very superior to what is to be had here," said Mrs. Noyce, helping herself to buttered asparagus. "I must own, I never thought society in Bristol could compare favorably to that of Bath!"

"Perhaps you have simply been looking in the wrong circles, my love," said Mr. Noyce. "When first we came to Bath, the Finholdens were your guides, and I must admit them to be excessively mistaken in their notions of good society. Mrs. Wellstone, however, much like her sister, may be trusted to introduce you to more congenial company."

"I imagine you are right, my dear," she said, taking another helping of potatoes. "It does seem silly that I did not take her advice before. But Penelope Finholden was so pushing, and jealous of my company. It seemed she could not pass by without coming in to ask after our health, and then she would stay half the day. It was quite tiresome, I declare. She was particularly fond of discussing you, Clara, for she would have me believe she considers you the pinnacle of feminine perfection. But I can only conjecture she meant you for her nephew, who is, I will warn you, rumored to be very expensive."

"I am sure he is, Mother," Clara said shortly. "But you need not trouble yourself. I assure you that I am not so foolish as to contemplate marriage with a man of such questionable character."

"Well, I hope it is so, and you have not developed a secret tendre for him, for you are just the sort of young lady to do something so imprudent."

"As you have observed to me many times before," retorted Clara. "And again, I assure you I will not be so foolish as to form an attachment with such a man for, much as you imagine we are alike, I am not, and never will be, you."

Her mother gaped at her for a moment, anger and mortification coloring her features, then she stood abruptly and quitted the room.

Mr. Noyce gazed solemnly at Clara. "That was badly done, you know. She only desires your happiness."

"It is difficult to believe it while she expresses herself so poorly."

He sighed, pursing his lips. "Forgive me, Clara, but you are more like your mother than you would like to admit. She merely has learnt to acknowledge her mistakes and desires to rectify what she can. But it is new territory for her, and she is bound to struggle. You would do well to credit the virtue of her intentions."

Chastened, Clara lowered her eyes to her plate, but only pushed the food about with her fork.

"Have you seen Lawrie yet?" Mr. Noyce inquired after some minutes.

"No, sir, though I have heard he has been rather busy during my absence."

He shrugged. "I would not say that, precisely, my dear. It seems to me that he has been as active as ever in society, only he has, perhaps, widened his circle somewhat while you were away."

"Did he call upon you while we were in Bristol?"

"He did not. As I have been frequently in the baths, however, I do not see that it signifies. He did leave his card a few days ago, but I was out."

On these ominous tidings, he excused himself, and Clara was left to the discomfort of her own very lowering thoughts. The evening afforded her the opportunity of a formal apology to her mother, but she still did not know what to do about Lawrie, and continued uncertain into the following day. She had determined to allow his behavior to guide her own when they nearly collided as she came out of a shop in Union Street. Rather than cut her or bolt the other way upon seeing her, he came directly to her, bowing with all the civility of a long acquaintance.

"How do you do, Lawrie," she said, holding out her hand to him with determined affability. "I vow it has been an age since my mother carried me away to Bristol. And how have you been?"

He bowed over her hand in a negligent manner. "Extremely well, Clara. I had a notion you'd gone away. Was Bristol to your taste?"

Clara smiled mechanically, endeavoring not to note the speed with which he had dropped her hand. "Very much, I declare. You know my dislike for society, and there I was safe from all but the most sedate persons. I was with my mother's set, you must know."

"Ah," he said comprehensively. "Not many young gentlemen to flirt with?"

"None with whom I should care to engage in more than the lightest of flirtations," she answered briskly. "They were all so earnest, you see."

He gave her a knowing wink. "Say no more. I understand that you have undergone a period of purgatory, and must wish you joy in returning to the bright environs of Bath."

She was beginning to loathe his jovial manner, which grated upon her nerves. "On the contrary, I quite enjoyed the peace and quiet of Bristol. One cannot be always running about, amusing oneself with one's acquaintance, and even enlarging it, heaven forbid. It is too fatiguing."

"I am of another mind, however," he replied with complacency. "It is my belief that one can never have too many companions. Though Bath is not so large as London, it offers a diversity of acquaintance— far more broad than one could find in Southam, for example. I have for some time been eager to spread my wings, as it were, and have at last given in to the impulse."

Clara, increasingly irritated, nodded her congratulations. "And with great success, I hear. Might I venture to hint, however, that society in Bath is just as likely as that in London to provide pitfalls to the inexperienced? One must take care, or one might be brought to regret one's eagerness."

"A wise caution," he said, a wry twist to his mouth, "but there is no fear of that. I have already met some very friendly people. Mr. Hiddeston has introduced me to the Tiptons and the Ashwickes and the Drayfords—you know Miss Drayford of course—a lovely girl—and Mrs. Gravesthwaite, too. Excessively delightful people, and agreeable, too."

As most of these families were possessed of eligible and lovely daughters, Clara's smile became something of a grimace. "Delightful. Though I should rather have described Miss Ashwicke as insipid. I never begrudge one's right to a contrary opinion, however. Perhaps she is insipid only in my company."

"Indeed, it must be so, for I count Miss Ashwicke as one of the most amiable young women of my acquaintance. Would that I had met her before. I wonder that you did not think to perform the introduction."

"Goodness me, I never introduce dead bores to persons I like. It would not say much for my taste, if I did, you know, and my friends should never forgive me. No, no, acquit me of negligence at once, and believe I meant only to shield you from insupportable society."

He bowed somewhat mockingly, a hardness in his eyes. "I could have guessed as much, Clara. For such magnanimity is only of a piece with your whole character. It is just as well, I suppose, that I have been honored with Miss Ashwicke's acquaintance only recently, for earlier in my stay I might have misjudged her, having been taught to color my views to my discredit. It is always wise to keep one's eyes open, for one might discover that one has been entirely mistaken in one's friends, and that a change of scene is quite necessary."

"Indeed," said Clara, trying not to squirm under his steely gaze. She lifted her chin. "The transformation does not seem to have had a negative effect upon you, however."

"Not in the least," he said, smiling in satisfaction. "I have been quite renewed, I think."

"Certainly, in Miss Ashwicke's company one might renew one's patience, I believe."

"Perhaps, but Miss Drayford requires no patience at all, nor does Miss Tipton. Such lively minds as theirs are grateful to any gentleman's spirits, particularly those who might be jaded."

"Oh, Angelina is a darling; however, not having the pleasure of Miss Tipton's acquaintance, I cannot be a judge." She smiled brilliantly. "But I will take your word for it. A pity Miss Gravesthwaite has no conversation, or you should be quite dissipated."

"Ah, but her aunt is quite capable of perfectly rational speech, and we have sat for half an hour together discussing every sort of subject."

Clara gave a look of distaste. "Her aunt! I do not know of her, but imagine she must be a full fifteen years your senior, Lawrie. I am astonished at your having taken a fancy to so old a woman, for that is what I must conjecture you have done. It must look very odd for you to monopolize her in such a way."

He said conspiratorially, "But she is a mere seven years my senior. She came only last week to visit, while you were absent—I had forgotten. She is Mrs. Giles Gravesthwaite, the widow of Miss Gravesthwaite's uncle, poor woman, and quite eager for the comfort of good society. I have never seen her equal for amiability. She is a woman of information, too, which I find excessively attractive. There are not many ladies like her."

"I see," said Clara evenly, while wrestling down what seemed strangely like a demon of jealousy. This was a new Lawrie, who found so much to delight him in other women than herself. She mentally shook herself and said, "As your friend, I cannot but be glad you are so well-entertained. Indeed, it would shock me to find that you had not enjoyed every hour while I was away, so resourceful as you are. I must be going. My mother has looked for me this half hour, and I still must stop at the milliner's."

"I would not keep you for the world," was all he said and, bowing, took his leave, walking away down the street without another glance.

Excessively nettled, Clara turned and made her way toward the last shop on her list. It was a novel experience to take a back place in Lawrie's interest, and she found little in the situation to gratify her. She had fully expected him to offer to accompany her the few steps to the shop, and then to walk with her back to Laura Place, and perhaps even to come in to pay his respects to the Noyces. But his whole demeanor had told her he had not the slightest inclination to be long in her company, and was very well satisfied, after eight days' abstinence, with the brief chat they had just enjoyed.

That he had not forgiven her was certain. That he ever would, Clara could not as yet conjecture, and at the moment, she wished for all the world that he was seventy miles off, and not so well-pleased with his lot. Miss Ashwicke, amiable! Mrs. Giles Gravesthwaite, seven years his senior—oh! Clara almost growled aloud at the revelation that Lawrie valued women of information. If he had ever intimated such before, she had never known of it.

But it seemed there was much she did not know about her old friend, and might never know. She had only herself to blame, though she was not about to let that cast her down. She could blame—and had blamed—herself for countless mistakes in the past, and this was only one more in her sad history. Nothing had changed, precisely. She simply no longer had her old friend to await her convenience and to tease her and laugh at her. The notion was enough to make her feel a headache coming on, and she hastened through her purchase at the milliner's shop and went straight home.

Chapter 14

IF CLARA BELIEVED Lawrie to have been unmoved by their meeting, she was gravely mistaken. Though he had been preparing himself for the inevitable moment, he had almost done exactly as she had expected and turned tail to run away at sight of her in Union Street. She had hurt him more deeply than he had imagined possible, and he wished never to see her again. However, he knew that if he did not face her then, he would never do so, and would live the rest of his life in the power of his pain. Still, it was purely through a monumental act of will that he had assumed a cheerful, carefree aspect and gone to greet her.

Their dialog had gone some way toward easing his discomfort, for he was able to vent some of his spleen in revealing how he had moved past her rejection. It was with some satisfaction that he had acquainted her with his activities of the past ten days, and her visible annoyance was something of a balm to his soul. His acquaintance with the several ladies he had detailed was real, and he had enjoyed making it—as one enjoys hurtling down a rocky hill at top speed, not knowing if one will end with a broken neck or merely a skinned knee. Amiable females were everywhere—one had only to be agreeable oneself, and to wish to meet them. Whether one could forget the only female one had ever loved was another matter.

But he was determined to forget Clara—or at least to forget what he so foolishly felt for her. It could not be love, at any rate, for he believed that true love was not one-sided. True love required the meeting of hearts, the sharing of hopes and dreams, the communion of souls, and though he and Clara shared a warm and enjoyable friendship, she had never attempted to open her heart to him. He was unwilling to settle for less than true love, and if it meant quashing his hopes and dreams with Clara, so be it.

He knew he could not leave Bath, however, for to do so would only encourage those hopes and dreams to haunt him. He had resolved upon staying to retrain his heart, so that it did not leap when he saw her, and would not soften when she pleaded with him to do something outrageous for her. He would force himself to become nothing more than a friendly acquaintance, and to do so, he must meet her frequently, no matter the pain it caused.

To this end, he did not attempt to avoid Clara, but made a point of frequenting those places he might be expected to meet her. They met at card parties and concerts, on the street, at the Pump Room, and at the Assembly Rooms, and he forced himself to speak at least once to her on each occasion.

At the fancy dress ball that week, Lawrie was dancing with Miss Drayford when he perceived that Clara had come into the room. He did not allow his eyes to follow her, nor did he think long on how the celestial blue of her dress accentuated the color of her eyes, but turned his most charming smile upon his partner.

"Your steps are light tonight, Miss Drayford," he said, leading her through a figure in the cotillion.

"It is only the second dance of the night, Mr. Simpford," she said, her fine eyes sparkling invitingly. "My partner at the end of the night will regret his choice, I am persuaded."

"There is something to be said for engaging the prettiest girls early in the evening," he replied.

She blushed and looked archly. "Unless they come late. Then one must kick one's heels until they arrive."

He blinked, thinking of Clara, but then recollected that Miss Drayford had come partway through the first dance. He smiled dryly at her blithe acceptance of his compliment and watched as another couple threaded through the square. When they were finished with the figure, he again led Miss Drayford into the middle.

"It is fortunate that Bath does not suffer for company at this time of year, as London does," he said.

"Yes, though I do not believe I should ever have come to Bath but for my dear papa requiring the waters. But invalids are in constant need of society," she sighed, "and can depend upon their maladies to excite the greatest sympathy and activity among their relations." She seemed suddenly to recollect herself and simpered. "And glad I am of it, too, for it brought me here."

Lawrie obligingly smiled and led her through another figure, speaking more commonplaces as the dance wound to a close. At the end of the set, he returned her to her mama and sought out Miss Tipton, but finding that she was already promised for the next set and, perceiving Clara nearby, he determined that Miss Ashwicke would do for the country dance. She was pleasant to dance with, though a somewhat tiresome conversationalist, for she was too strictly reared to have a thought of her own, and was used to agreeing with everything her companion said. But she was really a sweet girl, and the liveliness of the country dance helped to counteract her weakness.

But Miss Ashwicke was in luck, for as they took their places in the set, Clara was led in not two couples away, and Lawrie was therefore on his mettle. He smiled and laughed at his partner's trivial conversation until she began to feel herself very clever indeed, and she ended the dance with such high spirits that she actually accepted the next gentleman who asked her to stand up with him without even seeking her mama's approval.

Lawrie was very active in demonstrating that he was quite well able to enjoy himself without Clara. He engaged Miss Tipton next, who was very pretty in a childish sort of way, and prone to stupidity, but she was cheerful and good company.

"I am glad you are come to Bath, sir," she said brightly as they awaited their turn in another country dance. "It is not every day one finds so obliging a companion. So many of the gentlemen here do not seem to enjoy dancing."

As she spoke, she looked at Lord Boltwood, who had partnered Clara in the other set. Lawrie sighed in sober agreement.

"Indeed, Miss Tipton, there are those who are sadly above their company. But do not let it disturb you. They, only, are the losers."

"To be sure!" she said, beaming upon him, and she gaily tripped along with him to go down the line.

After two more sets with younger ladies, it was with some relief that he partnered Mrs. Gravesthwaite, who was always a comfortable companion, perhaps because her experience with the male sex extended beyond mere society talk, dancing, or cardplay. During their brief acquaintance, he had enjoyed several conversations with her that delved into serious topics.

"You look fatigued, sir," she said, gazing upon him in mingled sympathy and amusement. "But you have been going the rounds, I perceive."

He shook his head and said lightly, "It is necessary that I do, ma'am, for I am bound by my duty and the scarcity of gentlemen to stand up every dance."

"And perhaps you are getting up the courage to face a particular young lady," she said.

He huffed. "You are, perhaps, too percipient for my comfort, Mrs. Gravesthwaite."

She laughed, a warm, tinkling sound. "It is the lot of a widow to comprehend much that escapes those less experienced. But come, let us dance and enjoy ourselves while we may—and perhaps you will feel equal to facing your unnamed young lady all the sooner."

Lawrie accepted this suggestion with alacrity, for the widow tended to lend him confidence. He was pleased to spend time in her company—a circumstance that was looked on askance by some for, like Clara, they wondered at his inclination for a woman seven years his senior. But others simply accepted that he, like many gentlemen of his age, was more likely to be captivated by maturity and experience.

Their mutual enjoyment of the dance was noted by many—particularly by Clara from across the room, where she danced with Mr. Frant. She had discovered that Mrs. Gravesthwaite was considered by many a bluestocking, but Lawrie—in proof of his admiration for her intellect—had been known to defend her in several instances. That the widow was grateful to him for this gallantry was evidenced by her warm smiles and shining eyes whenever they met. The present instance was no exception, and Clara felt unaccountably annoyed. The Rooms were suddenly suffocatingly full, and Mr. Frant's pat compliments insufferable. She wished she had stayed at home.

After the dance, she made her way back to where her mother was sitting, and found that Mrs. Finholden had seated herself nearby. Mrs. Noyce was stiff with indignation.

"Mother, what can have happened?" she inquired, with uncharacteristic solicitude.

Mrs. Noyce pursed her lips and said between clenched teeth, "That Woman has been discoursing all of fifteen minutes to her neighbor on the excellence of her nephew's character—as though he were not as ramshackle as herself."

"Indeed, Mother," Clara replied, "and I do not know what she can hope to accomplish by singing his praises now."

Clara had felt herself obliged to tell her mother enough of what had transpired between herself and Mr. Picton in the basement of the Rooms to make his character clear. But their removal to Bristol had been so immediate that she had not had time to say anything to anyone else. A slight hint of scandal had inevitably attached to this precipitate exit, for his removal at the same time had given rise to whispers of an altercation between them. But by the time she had returned, the rumors had quietened enough that Clara had not wished to stir them up again, and she considered the matter closed.

"Penelope is desperate to get her nephew married to an heiress, I am persuaded," her mother said, and she sniffed. "A rocky time she shall have of it, too, with his reputation. It is my belief he is a gamester and a rake, and there is no doing anything with him."

"But he is not even in Bath," said Clara, glancing about in sudden consciousness.

Her mother huffed. "He may meditate a return, which would be unfortunate. Bath is already beset by too many of his relations."

"Indeed," murmured Clara.

But reflections on the irritation of one's cast-off beaux making a reappearance were broken into by Lawrie's voice.

"You are very somber, Clara."

She looked up at him, a bit of color coming unbidden into her cheeks. "Lawrie! I did not perceive you there. You are mistaken. I am only a little fatigued."

"Then I fear my errand is vain and I will bid you good night."

"You are going?" She hesitated, still unused to his reserved manner of late. "May I ask what was your errand?"

"I came to ask you to stand up with me, but I will not make myself irksome by doing so, knowing you are tired."

He turned to go, but she stood abruptly and said, "I will dance with you, if you still wish it."

He looked back at her, a laugh in his eye that was quickly subdued.

She swallowed an ache in her throat at his readiness to quell any sort of intimacy with her. She knew a sudden urge to weep, but managed to say, "I am quite recovered."

He came to take her hand, bowing punctiliously over it. "Thank you, Miss Mantell. You are very obliging."

Her heart sank at this formality, but after having taunted and teased and then shouted at him, she must only be grateful that he did not entirely avoid her. Though, as she took her place beside him in the set and received only civilities in reply to her attempts at conversation, she wondered if it would be less painful to her to have him gone altogether.

She had begun to feel very low when he suddenly addressed her with, "You seem to have won at least one of your campaigns, Clara."

"What do you mean?" she inquired, blinking at him.

"Mr. Picton seems to have retired from the field. I admit he is not much mourned, at least by some."

"I do not mourn him," she said quickly, wondering what he was driving at. "I consider everything as settled between us, and can only be glad he has chosen to go away, for it is not for me to turn tail and run."

A tiny smile turned up one corner of Lawrie's mouth. "Indeed not. Though I imagine it must be somewhat of a relief to you to have only the one charge upon your ingenuity."

She frowned, but they were obliged to perform their figures and she could not immediately reply. When they came back together, his brief confidences seemed to be over, for he said politely, "You dance delightfully, Miss Mantell."

Clara wished to slap him. How could he be so horrid to her? She had half a mind to walk away then and there, and leave him gaping in the middle of the set. But she did not, for with every indignant thought there arose a rebuke in the memory of his injured countenance when she had said such cruel things to him weeks ago in this very building. She had earned his derision, and therefore could not justify any sort of repayment again in kind.

The remainder of the dance was passed chiefly in silence, and they parted as civilly as they had begun. Clara wanted nothing more than to go home, but her pride would not allow it. So when Lord Boltwood came to beg her hand a second time, she went with him into the set.

"I could not help but notice Mr. Simpford's manner toward you, Miss Mantell—disgraceful," he said indignantly. "I would call him out but for your attachment to him. I wonder," he added with a measuring look, "when will you see that he is not good enough even for your acknowledgment?"

"You know nothing of the matter, my lord," she retorted crossly, "and had better keep your opinions to yourself. They are ill-suited to your station, and to your sensibilities. Lawrie is my oldest friend, and I will not discuss him with you."

She accompanied this set-down with a look of reproof that silenced him immediately, and they went down the line without another word. He did not dare to speak anything but commonplaces to her for the remainder of the dance, and Clara found her mind wandering back to Lawrie and his implacable resentment. This so put her out of curl that she begged Lord Boltwood to forgo the second dance and they retired to the refreshment table.

"You are positively flushed, ma'am," said her swain, plying the fan he had taken from her.

"It is odiously stuffy," said Clara, sipping at a lemonade. "One would never conceive of its being winter outside. This room is like a hothouse!"

Lord Boltwood snapped the fan shut. "Then let us retire to the porch. If you do not fear the effects of the cold on a heated body, I will take you there instantly, so that you may be comfortable."

"I do not think I shall ever be comfortable again," murmured Clara, but she allowed him to lead her out of the ballroom and through the corridor to the porch where chairmen awaited their passengers after the ball.

The porch was much cooler, owing both to the frequent opening of its doors and the lack of persons in its vicinity. A chairman lolled at his ease by his chair and Clara, with all her discomfiting thoughts, felt safe enough.

Lord Boltwood had resumed his fanning of her heated countenance upon entering the porch, and they exchanged desultory opinions on the crush of persons always at the assemblies and the convenience of hailing a chair in the rain or cold. But after she had regained her usual countenance, and just as she was about to suggest their returning to her mother in the ballroom, the chairman slouched away from the porch. Suddenly, Lord Boltwood swept her into an embrace and attempted to kiss her.

"Oh, Miss Mantell, I cannot continue in this way—" He kissed her nose, her ear, her chin, as she struggled and strained away from him— "Your beauty, your spirit, your—your—"

She got her arm free and slapped him across the face, sending him reeling backward. "How dare you? And after assuring me you would never be so ungentlemanly as Picton!"

Adjusting her dress and patting her hair back into place, she marched to the door, but he seized her hand and pulled her back into the porch.

She wrenched free. "Provoking man! What must I do to convince you that I am in no mood for your passions? Do you mean to accost me again?"

"No, no, Miss Mantell, you mistake me utterly," said Boltwood in desperate accents. "I only must apologize to you, privately, for my despicable conduct. My passion—you are right that I too often allow it to overcome me—but it is no excuse."

"Certainly not," she said, smoothing a hand down her dress. "You are becoming tedious, Lord Boltwood, and you ought to take care. I cannot imagine it should be to your taste to lose my esteem."

He assured her in many words that it would not and believing him to be—at least for the present—in earnest, she allowed him to escort her back to her mother, who had just begun to look about for her errant daughter. As Mr. Noyce handed the ladies into the carriage, Clara considered that rakes in general were tedious creatures, and perhaps it was not so satisfactory to play their games.

As the carriage got underway, Mr. Noyce regarded Clara from the forward seat. "I am persuaded that Lawrie has not been himself of late. Can you think why, Clara?"

"I cannot say, sir," she said, shrugging a petulant white shoulder. "He has taken a pet, I imagine, because he is not first with me here in Bath."

He raised his brows. "If that is the case, I own that he has my sympathy. You are a horrid flirt, you know."

"Yes, Clara, it is a very bad habit with you," put in Mrs. Noyce, but she paused as she adjusted her shawl before continuing, "I own to having been something of a flirt myself at one time, and very enjoyable it was, to be sure, but I tell you, it did not answer. It will never get you a husband—at least of the sort that you should like. Respectable men do not want flirtatious wives."

Clara pursed her lips and retorted, "Perhaps I do not wish to get a respectable husband."

"Now, Clara," said Mr. Noyce, before his wife could reply in kind, "You do not mean that. Marriage is an excellent prospect, and will suit you very well, if you choose wisely. I may say with perfect sincerity that I am exceedingly grateful to be married, and that it has done me a world of good."

"You are the best of men, however," she said, her tone softened, "and are not given to pettishness. I stand by what I said at Wesley

Abbey, that you have ruined me for the majority of men. Until I meet with another Mr. Noyce, I shall never be satisfied."

"Nonsense," said her mother, dimpling at her husband. "There is no one like Mr. Noyce."

"Ah, my love, but there are," he said, eyes twinkling as he held up a staying finger, "They are simply different. I can think of three or four excellent young men who are very much the same as myself, but different, if Clara would only condescend to see it."

Clara forced a fleeting smile. "Perhaps I will presently, sir. However, I do not yet desire to enter the marriage state. I am afraid your excellent gentlemen must wait."

He sighed, the twinkle diminishing. "I will cease teasing you, my dear, but you must understand that even the best of men cannot be expected to hold out forever."

Clara did not answer, only turning her gaze out the window.

Chapter 15

CLARA AWOKE HEAVY-HEADED and with an unruly prepossession, for she had the most dreadful sensation that her careful plans were going awry. After her victory over Picton, she had become complacent, and then allowed Lawrie's defection to rattle her. Last night, she had very nearly brought to pass Lawrie's odious prophesy, and at Lord Boltwood's hands, of all persons.

She determined that something must be done and, after breakfast, informed her mother that she was going on errands. It was a bright day, the sun shining with only a few clouds, but December was just around the corner, and making itself felt. Walking briskly with her maid, and not stopping to look into shop windows as they passed, she made directly for the Theater Royal.

She found Miss Pratt in a small room off the stage used to receive patrons and other admirers after the shows—though Clara suspected they might be welcomed there at other times as well. But she was not inclined today to censure, nor to feel superior, and she greeted the actress with a friendly handshake.

"You seem very well, Miss Pratt," she said amiably. "I trust you have benefited from our dialog."

Miss Pratt regarded her with muted but wary interest. "I suppose so, miss, though the gentleman in question has flown the coop, as you might've heard. Don't know if that means I won, or I lost."

"Oh, decidedly you have won, for his flying was none of your doing. I'm afraid you owe that dubious honor to me."

"What happened, then?"

Clara huffed a laugh. "He attempted to force me. It was not very wise of him—I thought he knew me better than to do that. However, some men simply cannot help but try to dominate a female, I think."

"To be sure," said the actress, ruminatively. "And there's not many a girl who could stop one of them."

"Ah, but I am not many a girl. I carry a pistol with me, and am as adept with it as you are with that sword. He soon came to reason."

"*Touché,*" said Miss Pratt, with an appreciative half-smile. "I wondered what sent him off."

"I had hoped you would be pleased, but if the circumstance has cost you some anxiety, I am sorry for it."

Shrugging, Miss Pratt said, "Wouldn't go so far as to say that. I've got admirers aplenty—losing Picton wasn't the end of it for me."

"I did not imagine it would be, though the rumor has arisen that he may return."

"Oh, I wouldn't think so," said Miss Pratt, watching her blade as she slashed it through the air. "That one's pride is bigger than he can stare. Won't relish coming back to the scene of his defeat, I'd say."

Clara's eyes followed the sword's evolutions. "His aunt would beg to differ, however. She seems to be preparing the way for his return."

"If he does, won't mean much to either of us. He's had his shot and aimed low, eh?"

"I suppose you are right."

Miss Pratt met her gaze, watching her as though considering something. At last, she said, "If I'd been born a mite higher, like you, things might've been different for me."

"I imagine they might," Clara said, somewhat taken aback, and taking her turn to regard her companion in reflective silence.

Here was a woman whose circumstance had obliged her early to relinquish so much of herself without receiving anything substantial in return. Many a young wife did so, but received at least the security of a home and her husband's name. A mistress, while she could expect gifts and lodging and other material reward, would scarcely end with a lasting commitment. Clara thought of Francis's light o' love Jane, whose prospects had been bleak without his paving the way for her marriage to the butcher's son. That sort of security did not generally find a mistress at the end of her career.

She looked away in some embarrassment. She, herself, had been lucky—she had known enough to anticipate, to a degree, Picton's intentions. And she had possessed both the skill and the means to hold him off. But even had she not succeeded, he would have married her, for she had her fortune and all scandal tied to her compromised reputation would have been covered over in the respectability of marriage—wrapped in clean linen, as it were. Miss Pratt, without fortune or birth, had not even the hope of such protection, and never would.

The silence continued awkwardly, and Clara grasped for something unexceptionable to speak of. At last, her eye falling on Miss Pratt's smallsword, she said, "I have taken up fencing, you know. I went to Master Lorenzo, and he taught me."

"Is that so?" said the actress, her interest reawakening. "And how do you get on?"

"Oh, middling, I suppose," said Clara, unwilling to flaunt her natural talent to Miss Pratt. "I do enjoy it, however, just as I imagined I would."

"It's a wonder your papa allowed it. Mine, of course, pressed it on me, but I was born to the stage."

Clara eyed her keenly. "I imagined you to have wished to learn. You are well formed for it. If one is talented at something, one ought to do it, no matter the opposition."

"To be sure," said Miss Pratt, again half-smiling. "So your papa don't know?"

Clara huffed a laugh. "He knows—though I did not intend that he would. He is not my papa, precisely. My father is dead, and is probably turning over in his grave—but he would find something to disturb his equanimity even without my taking up fencing. Mr. Noyce, my mother's new husband, is the greatest dear, but even he will not wink at my fencing. It is a dead bore, I declare."

"So you were bubbled, eh?"

"Yes, and I have not practiced this age. I wonder," Clara said almost shyly, "would you practice with me? I won't be a bother, I assure you. I will only watch you at your work and attempt to mimic you."

Miss Pratt laughed, shaking her head. "That's no way to practice fencing. We'll duel, you and I. I've a notion you're better than you let on."

Clara expressed her delight in this scheme and went with Miss Pratt to the dressing room to get foils. They spent an agreeable hour exchanging hits, which Clara's maid obligingly kept a tally of, until Miss Pratt was called to the stage to rehearse. She complimented her new *protégée* on her talent and invited her to come again.

"You are very kind. I am most grateful, Miss Pratt. Thank you!" cried Clara, almost skipping away from the theater, her maid hastening to keep up.

She smiled as she made her way back toward Laura Place, feeling lighter than she had in weeks. She had allowed herself to become too caught up in trifles—Picton and Boltwood. And Lawrie—but no, Lawrie's defection was no trifle, and she would not be completely satisfied until he could be persuaded to again be her friend.

As she drew near her house, she was startled to see Lawrie descending the steps.

He slowed only a moment, then came on, tipping his hat to her. "How do you do, Clara? You have returned from your errand at last. Mrs. Noyce will be relieved. She imagined you to have run away, but with whom she could not say."

"You are quizzing, I daresay," said Clara, a trifle breathlessly. "But what are you doing here? Did you have a message?"

He shook his head, looking down. "I came for a long overdue visit. I have allowed certain ... circumstances ... to hold me back from common courtesy to Mr. and Mrs. Noyce. I have begged their pardon, and goodwill is restored between us."

"It is excessively good in you to take the trouble, Lawrie," she said, and cringed at the hopeful note in her voice. "But you are going—will not you come back in for a few minutes? I should like—"

"No, I cannot," he cut in, his gaze flitting away, as though he were reluctant to look at her. "I have been with them this half hour and should not impose longer on their time. Pardon me."

He nodded to her again and went on his way, crossing the square to walk up Henrietta Street, where he had his lodgings. Clara watched him go, her heart sinking for a moment, but the buoyancy of her visit to Miss Pratt was still high and she gave vent to only one sigh of regret as she ascended the steps of her house.

Lawrie was awfully stubborn in withholding his forgiveness, and she was inclined to think it ungentlemanly in him. She had been prepared to shake hands and forget the business days ago, but she knew she could not force the issue with him. He might do as he wished—might be so childish as to bear her a grudge, even—but she could not hold it against him. She would simply wait and hope for the moment he wished to make up their friendship, and would welcome him back with gratitude.

In this virtuous resolution she continued two more days, staying in for the mornings so that he could not avoid her when he came to call on her parents. He did not come, however, and she was inclined to be pettish, wondering what she must do to earn back his regard while stigmatizing him to herself as a self-righteous prig.

The following morning, she refused to kick her heels in her mother's drawing room, but took her maid to the theater in order to engage in a vigorous dueling session with Miss Pratt. This so relieved her spleen that she considered Lawrie with charity throughout the remainder of the day, and when they met next at a rout party, she was able to conduct herself with propriety and sweetness, and nearly to keep all irritation from her countenance when she perceived his attentions to his new favorite young ladies.

Giving in to her peevishness, Clara began flirting outrageously with Mr. Frant and even, after many assurances of his abject regret, admitted Lord Boltwood back into her court. She must reestablish her power over him, after all, if she were to emerge triumphant from this sojourn in Bath. She was cautious of where and how she met with him, however, to prevent a recurrence of an outburst of his passions. She also began carrying her pistol in her pocket or reticule at all times, and did not shrink from drawing his attention to it. He seemed to take her meaning and behaved with decorum, only increasing the broodiness of his manner and the expressions of his longing for her heart. These she chiefly found amusing—especially given her knowledge of his mistress in London. But though either of her principal beaux left something to be desired, they were the most agreeable companions available—when one could not have the companion one most wished for.

Clara often relieved the tension of her exertions through fencing, either with Miss Pratt or by herself. Miss Pratt had lent her a foil, and Clara escaped from afternoon visits as often as possible to go with her maid to a private spot she had found on Bath Common, somewhat enclosed by a hillock and some bushes, and far from the view of the few others enjoying the brisk air of the common.

One particularly fine day, she concealed the foil within her pelisse and made her way to the Common with Mary, who was obliged to chase off a small urchin who had followed them nearly all the way. Clara removed the foil from its hiding place and began to practice her forms, as always obliged to suppress the desire that Lawrie was there to practice with her.

"It really is more effective with a partner," said a male voice behind her.

Mary, the maid, squeaked, and Clara whirled to find Mr. Picton only ten paces away, regarding her with his cynical smile as the small urchin who had followed them sauntered away over the Common.

"I see you got your way, Miss Mantell," he said, doffing his hat to her. "I should not be astonished that you show such a talent for swordplay."

"I see you are as thick as you are conceited, sir," she said, lowering the foil. "I believe I made it plain that I never wished to see you again."

He sighed, taking another step or two nearer. "It desolates me to disappoint you, Miss Mantell. I would do anything in the world to please you, even hie to York—however, I simply could not keep away."

"Begging your pardon, miss," said Mary, bravely standing with Clara's reticule clutched before her, "but oughtn't we to go back?"

"Come now, Miss Mantell," said Picton, brow rising. "You are not afraid?"

Clara tossed her head. "Certainly not. It is not for me to run away. That is for improper persons who believe themselves above the rules of decorum."

He bowed. "That would be me, I collect. Well said, by the lady who flirts as recklessly as she takes up fencing. But your recklessness, it seems, extends beyond that. When I discovered that you had not made anything of our little disagreement known, I determined to come back and see for myself whether you had done it out of propriety, or out of regret." He took two steps nearer to Clara.

"Not so hasty, sir," she said. "You know what I carry in my reticule, and that I am not afraid to use it."

"Just so, ma'am. And I doubt that you would scruple to use it, even in plain sight of anybody who might come along." He smiled complacently, his eyes flicking to the maid, who stood wide-eyed and several paces away from Clara. "However, the pistol, unless I am mistaken, is in that reticule, quite ten feet from you."

Clara bit her lips, for she had not wished to fence with the pistol bouncing about in her pocket, and it was, indeed, in the reticule. She raised the foil. "You are forgetting that I have this."

"Ah, but what is that?" he said, eying the foil with derision. "Next to your pistol, that is nothing. I was far more concerned about the pistol, you know. But in the event, it is of no concern at all. I wonder if your maid could stop me from carrying you off over these hills?"

Clara opened her eyes, not having imagined he would attempt such a thing. Indeed, the idea rather thrilled her—but not in the way most maidens would feel it. She saw the danger as a challenge, for she had bested him once, and she would do so again.

She unbuttoned the foil, therefore, and set herself *en garde*, smiling rather carelessly. "Do you mean to frighten me, sir?"

"I had hoped to tantalize you, my sweet," he said, a glitter in his hooded eyes.

"Then you are a fool."

"I hope to disabuse you of that mistaken notion, Miss Mantell," he said, his lips curling unnervingly as he reached into the pocket of his coat.

"Come, Mary," Clara said, turning her head to motion the maid over, but they both stilled at the unmistakable click of a firearm being cocked in the still afternoon air. She looked quickly back at Mr. Picton to see he held a silver-mounted dueling pistol pointed negligently at the sky.

With an effort, she huffed a laugh, saying "What can you be thinking, to aim so carelessly? I suppose you wish only to frighten me—for what purpose I cannot conceive."

"It would be ungentlemanly to attempt so paltry a take-in, Miss Mantell, and whatever else I may be, I do pretend, at least, to be a gentleman. I simply wished to prove I am no fool, but I find I cannot bring myself to make an example of you. I had sooner shoot myself than mar your perfect form."

His eyes caressed her as he spoke and Clara's lip curled. "It is my belief you've no notion how to handle that pistol."

"You are ever persuasive, my sweet." He smirked. "Mark that twig where the sparrow sits, on the tree there."

Quicker than she thought possible, he pointed the gun at a tree some way away and pulled the trigger. The shot rang out, the bird burst into hasty flight, and the single twig upon which it had sat spun away into the air.

He turned again to Clara. "Believe that I know very well—better than you, even—what I am about."

The shot had been exceedingly precise, and Clara was impressed; however, she was not about to let him know it. "Ha!" she said mockingly. "You must do better than that."

"My dear Miss Mantell," he said, lowering the gun to his side and advancing as he spoke, "I am ready to do far better."

The maid made a choking sound and stumbled a few steps closer to her mistress before halting again in petrified fear at Picton's glance. He continued forward to within inches of Clara's foil, which she held pointed at his heart. The look in his eyes was hungry, and Clara was aware that her heart was pounding rather fast in her chest. The tip of her foil trembled as she reflected that perhaps persevering in this challenge was not so exciting as it had seemed.

"We could deal extremely, Clara, I am persuaded," he said softly, his eyes falling to trace the curve of her lips.

Clara blinked, swallowing convulsively. This was what she had wanted—to enthrall a rake. But she had always imagined herself to have the upper hand, to be in control. It seemed increasingly unlikely that she could maintain any kind of control with Picton if she must hold him at gunpoint or swordpoint whenever they met.

Lifting her chin, she tightened her fingers on the grip of the foil, ceasing its shaking. "We might deal extremely, sir—extremely poorly. You see, I am not quite convinced that you are what I want. I have ever so many choices, you understand."

"This is only another of your games, my sweet."

"Perhaps. However, your pistol is empty, whereas I assure you mine is not, and if I do not run you through, Mary will shoot you without compunction should you refuse to let me go my own way."

Their gazes locked, ice and steel, until he looked away at Mary. To her credit, she stood straight-shouldered as she withdrew the pistol and pointed it—though somewhat awkwardly and using two hands—at the vicinity of his head.

But Picton merely snorted and made to step around Clara's foil. With a quick swipe and lunge, she sliced his cravat through and drew a line of blood on his cheek. Retreating back a step, she set herself again, while he looked down in muted astonishment at his ruined cravat.

"You are more adept than I imagined."

"It is not the first time you have underestimated me, sir."

Touching his cheek, he regarded the blood on his fingers before giving a rueful laugh and reaching into his pocket for a handkerchief. "You have me at an impasse, Miss Mantell. But I ought to have known it would be so. Indeed, it is what I admire most in you."

He patted at his cheek, then pocketed the handkerchief, tipping his hat first to Clara and then to Mary with a roguish wink before turning to walk away over the common. When he had gone far enough that Clara felt certain he could not easily return and overpower her, she lowered the foil, closing her eyes against the rush of relief that overtook her.

Mary, who had stood frozen to the spot in her fear, now hastened to her, proffering both the pistol and tumbled excuses. But Clara heeded neither, taking Mary's hand and pressing it.

"Good gracious, Mary, you are the heroine of the hour! I did not conceive of your being so brave! I shall never forget it, and I shall think of some way to reward you, depend upon it."

Then Clara turned and, shaking herself free of the last vestiges of the encounter, walked the opposite way from Picton, taking a long route back into town, her maid following with many uneasy glances behind.

Chapter 16

I T WAS NO part of Lawrie's intention to continue to care for Clara, but his heart was recalcitrant. It gave a leap whenever they met, and continually reminded him that she had been its aspiration for too long to easily forget. He could not comprehend how it had so unaccountable a memory—to remember its admiration for Clara while forgetting so easily the pain she had caused. Either he was mad, or his heart was, and he knew he must do something to remedy the situation.

He had forced himself to invite her to stand up with him at the Assembly Rooms, which was both a necessity and a torture—he required consistent exposure to her to train himself out of love, but nowhere did Clara shine more than in the dance. She was a natural athlete with all the feminine charms, and she was a delight to partner. It made it all the more difficult to maintain his new formality with her and not to revert to their former easy ways, for it was painful to him to make her unhappy. The moment of his release from her was both ecstasy and agony, and he began to question whether dancing really was a necessity after all.

But he could not give up, for he must constantly meet her when they returned to Southam, and so, with gritted teeth, he set himself to make a proper call the following day to her house. He had not known whether to be relieved or disappointed that she was not there, but maintained a flow of inconsequential nothings with Mrs. Noyce while watching the door surreptitiously. The visit had somehow been prolonged—though he had not meant to stay so long, he really had not. It was with some embarrassment that he had realized that Mrs. Noyce was hinting for him to be off at last, and he took his leave rather abashed.

And then Clara had met him on the street, and the oddest sensation had washed over him—warm delight and cold panic, prickly apprehension and tender longing. It had been all he could do to simply greet her and say a few civil things before getting himself away without making a scene. Good heaven, the hope in her eyes had nearly driven him to take her in his arms and forgive all. When he got to his lodgings he straightway poured a measure of brandy and tossed it down, lecturing himself sternly on what is meant by renouncing love.

After another measure of brandy, he came to the conclusion that he must make a greater push to find Clara's replacement in his affections, so that there would be no more room for her in his heart. It was a simple matter to put this determination into practice, for he had already engaged himself to attend a rout that evening, and knew that Miss Ashwicke and Miss Drayford were both to be in attendance.

Through no machinations of his own, he was placed as Miss Ashwicke's partner at whist, and was soon made to reflect on her suitability as his marriage partner.

"What should I do, Mr. Simpford?" she inquired at every turn. "I do wish we could be seated side-by-side, for then you could advise me to better purpose."

"But that is not how the game is intended to be played, you know," Lawrie patiently explained, nodding his apologies for the frequent interruptions to the other players. To Miss Ashwicke, he said, "Do you have a trump?"

She responded yea or nay—as though this were a novel idea—before setting her card as he advised, and at the end of the rubber she declared, "I never can decide what is best, sir. There are ever so many cards in whist—one is continually beset by choices."

"Indeed," he said, smiling affably and reflecting that her helplessness in the matter of decision-making had never impressed him as being attractive, nor could he look forward to a lifetime of shouldering his companion's choices as well as his own. "Perhaps the round game is more suited to your taste."

She agreed to this with alacrity—having been spared the exertion of thinking of it herself—and went away, allowing him to turn his attentions to Miss Drayford. She did not play cards tonight, but held court in one of the drawing rooms where a lively party of young gentlemen were gathered around her.

"Mr. Simpford!" she cried, as he seated himself near her. "You are come just at the moment I should wish, for Mr. Hathaway has been telling the most terrific plumpers one could imagine, and you must be the voice of reason. No, no, Mr. Hathaway, I will tell him what you have been saying—there is no escape! I am persuaded you will thank me someday, for you are in obvious need of a set-down, and Mr. Simpford is the man to do it. He is telling me, sir, that he has never seen eyes the exact color of the sky, but mine."

She regarded him expectantly, but Lawrie, who could think of only one pair of blue eyes, said apologetically, "I can have nothing to do with the matter, ma'am, for he is as entitled to his opinion as the next man."

Miss Drayford seemed little pleased with his lack of gallantry, as two spots of color flew to her cheeks. "Faint heart! Do you see, gentlemen, how Mr. Simpford defies me? But I will not hear of it. There is too much nonsense in the air about here, and he has brought a whiff of rationality with him. Do you see it, sirs? Mr. Simpford positively radiates rationality. It is his greatest charm, I declare. You none of you can compare for pure reason."

This point was hotly debated, each young sprig vying for an ounce of Miss Drayford's arch approval, while Lawrie discovered he wanted no part of it. He thought he could even less spend the remainder of his life flattering his companion than he could making her choices for her. Excusing himself as soon as possible, he went to the door, but was accosted there by Lady Drayford, who had evidently been spying on her daughter and her admirers.

"Well, Mr. Simpford," she simpered, "and how are you tonight? I couldn't help but notice your seeking out my Angeline. She is, if I may say so, a bright star among the young ladies. Do not you think so? There now, I have made you blush, but it will be our secret, sir, I assure you! Angeline does enjoy herself among the beaux, but she has, more than once, declared a readiness to leave all her court behind in order that she might make a *certain* gentleman the happiest man on earth. But perhaps I am precipitate—perhaps you do not wish to be singled out just yet! Again, the blush, sir! You must not fret at your secret's being out! I am exceedingly perspicacious in matters of love. A pity we do not stay in Bath above another sennight. However, you are to go home to Southam at Christmas—you must come to us, on a visit. Oh, it is just the thing! A small, private party, with only ten or twelve guests, and you the guest of honor!"

Almost choking with dismay, Lawrie at last broke into her discourse to express his regret that he had already an engagement for Christmas, and could not at this time promise to anything past the new year. She took this graciously, but after another extended period in which she expressed her delight in his prospects and the similarity of Gosley House to her husband's estate at Black Oaks, Lawrie discovered that he had forgotten a pressing engagement and must take his leave instantly.

Opting to walk to his lodgings across town and in the dark, Lawrie breathed deeply of the cold night air. He ought to have known that it was fruitless to attempt an attachment with those particular young ladies. Having known them for weeks now, he was familiar with their manners and airs, but desperation had deluded him into believing one or the other could be a candidate for his lifelong devotion. Scarcely an hour in Miss Ashwicke's company had forcibly reminded him that she required a far more managerial disposition in a husband than his could ever be, and half that time at Miss Drayford's side had irrevocably convinced him that her arch nothings would bore him within a month.

It was a relief to him, therefore, to find himself the following day in Mrs. Gravesthwaite's company, for she perfectly understood his situation. She was also much courted, for besides being a handsome and amiable woman, she had no children and she had inherited her husband's estate. But she had often spoken to Lawrie of a Mr. Spelling, who resided in Essex, and with whom she had an understanding, but whose particular circumstance would not allow of marriage at that time.

"His mother's health is so indifferent, sir," she said as they walked together in Sydney Gardens. "If she had not taken me in such violent dislike, he should have made me an offer on the spot. However, he could not, in good conscience, vex her so completely, and I would not allow it. She cannot be blamed—her mind is so disordered that she scarcely comprehends anything properly anymore. My happiness can wait upon her comfort. The end is not far off, poor woman."

"I admire your fortitude, ma'am," said Lawrie, patting her hand on his arm. "At least you are certain of your feelings. I sometimes despair of ever understanding my own heart."

She smiled in sympathy. "My dear Mr. Simpford, your challenge is a difficult one. I own I would never have imagined a man of your steadiness to have been bewitched by a coquette! But I am unkind. Miss Mantell, I am sure, has many excellent qualities."

"To be sure, ma'am. She is quite generous to those she fancies need her assistance, and can be charmingly honest."

"Indeed!" cried his companion, with whom he had shared much of his Bath experiences. "She has not spared your feelings, certainly, when acquainting you with her wishes. But can that truly be considered a virtue?"

"I was harsh, perhaps, and have given you a wrong idea of her. She really is quite delightful to converse with, and she has high, if rather unusual, ideals. She is also a fine whip and an excellent shot, and could take to any sport, I believe, with ease."

She pursed her lips. "You surprise me. It does not seem feminine to pursue sport. And yet, you seem to find this attractive."

He chuckled, but color rose up his neck as he recalled his fencing match with Clara, and the fever of admiration that had nearly overpowered him when they had pressed so close. "Indeed, ma'am, I cannot account for it."

"I believe I know what you mean," she said, smiling ruefully. "My Henry has his own peculiarities that, in another man, I should probably find distasteful. But in him—" she sighed, her gaze fixed on a distant time and place— "I cannot but find it charming. We are a pair of fools, I think."

"I hope not," said Lawrie, kissing her hand with a warm look. "At least you are not, ma'am. You must only be patient until such time as your Henry may wed you. While I—" He shook his head. "I cannot tell if I will ever find happiness."

She nodded sadly and continued to encourage him as he saw her to her door, which was just a few steps from the gardens, before walking back to his lodgings. As this took him past Laura Place, he happened upon Mr. Noyce, who invited him up to the drawing room for a visit. Mrs. Noyce was there, and Lawrie was in momentary expectation of Clara coming into the room, and steeling himself against it. But it was several minutes before Clara at last appeared, exuding reserve.

"Goodness, Lawrie," she said, advancing with her hand held out. "I declare I thought your days of visiting us were over."

"Nonsense, Clara," said her mother in the disapproving tone she was wont to use with her daughter. "Lawrie is always welcome, and may call when he chooses."

"Certainly he is welcome, Mother. However, of late he has been so much admired that one could not expect him to remember himself to old friends."

"Clara, mind your tongue!" cried her mother, looking despairingly at her guest. "If you were not such an old family friend, Lawrie, I should beg your pardon. But you know, too well, how it is with Clara."

Lawrie did know how it was with her, and as the visit continued, there was something behind her waspishness that niggled at his sympathy and begged for his attention. In his present state of indecision as to how best to protect his heart, he endeavored to close it off from such foolishness, but was unsuccessful. It occurred to him at last that he recognized in her demeanor some of his own misery, and that, like himself, she was worn out with fighting it. He also was her oldest friend, and he was much mistaken if she was not in some sort of trouble. Perhaps they could come to an agreement—one that would leave his heart out of it—and then he could help her.

When he rose to take his leave, therefore, he requested that she see him out, and though she was at first unwilling, at Mrs. Noyce's express approval she was obliged to take his arm. At the foot of the stair, however, he took her aside into the book room.

"You look as though you are on your way to the gallows," he said instantly the door was closed.

Clara frowned, casting a glare in his direction. "How kind in you to observe it, old friend."

"Come now, Clara. I am not the only one who has behaved badly."

She turned away, a stricken look in her countenance, but replied irascibly, "If that is your opinion, I wonder that you should care that I suffer. Do not you have a lady or two to take up your sympathies? There is little room left in your heart, even for an old friend."

He sighed, rubbing his neck in a last moment of indecision before saying gently, "Clara, I have become more careful who I let into my heart of late, but I believe there is enough room yet for an old friend."

She turned quickly to him, her features uncertain, but when he offered his hand with a wry smile, she blinked several times and took it with a ragged breath. "I must own to missing my place there."

He was pained, for he momentarily wished her to mean she loved him, but he instantly repressed it. He wanted only friendship, and he said, "I have missed being your friend."

"Indeed." Her gaze was somber for some moments before she said in a rush, "It was unfeeling and rude and ungracious of me to say those things to you, Lawrie, at the assembly before—before Bristol. You have always been my closest friend, and—and I have long regretted driving you away like that. I hope you will forgive me."

Lawrie exhaled, feeling a weight lift from his shoulders. "I will. But you must forgive me, too, for I have borne you a horrid grudge."

She gave a wavering smile, visibly swallowing with emotion. "It was only my just deserts, Lawrie, so none of your apologies," she said gruffly. With a businesslike huff, she searched in her pocket for a handkerchief, which she used to dab at her eyes and blow her nose. "Now I am a fright, and it is all your doing."

"I'm much mistaken if there is not something else that has cast you into the dumps."

She glanced quickly up at him. "What makes you say that?"

"Clara, I have not known you forever without learning to discern your moods. You are in a fret over something, and as we are again friends, I wish you will allow me to help you."

She looked away again, biting her lips. "It is nothing. You are very good to offer, but I am in no need of help." When she turned to him again, it was with her characteristic sangfroid. "Our friendship is too newly reinstated to test it so soon. Allow it to suffice that you have offered, and I will promise to call on you if ever the need should arise. As old friends do."

"As old friends do," he agreed, and they shook on it.

He took his leave unsatisfied, but feeling lighter than he had in weeks. His gamble had turned out right—Clara was again his friend but no more. His heart was safe, though it still craved for something to grow out of this in time. But as he had not yet learned to enjoy torture, he ruthlessly stifled the foolish feeling.

In need of refreshment, he took himself to his club, meeting Mr. Hiddeston there and inviting him to partake of dinner with him. Their conversation was revivifying, Mr. Hiddeston choosing to relate many amusing anecdotes, and Lawrie's recent reunion with Clara had relieved him sufficiently to make him disposed to reply in kind. This pleasant exchange was supplemented by a judicious measure of wine, leading to even more fantastic stories.

The two gentlemen, fairly ripe, were still comparing various real and imagined exploits when Lawrie's attention was claimed by an unwelcome but familiar voice. He slewed about in his seat to see Mr. Picton standing in a nearby corner, speaking in a loud and boastful tone to two cronies as they sipped tumblers of brandy. Bristling in annoyance, Lawrie opened his mouth to suggest he and Hiddeston change their seats, but then Clara's name issued from Picton's lips, freezing him at attention.

"I have her in the palm of my hand, man," said Picton, in his nauseatingly assured tone.

"The last time you said that, my boy, she pulled a gun on you. Can't be too certain, I say."

"She pulled a sword on me yesterday, and dashed if it didn't resolve me to have her by the end of the week."

"Stake a pony and I'll take you."

Picton chuckled. "If I have her, I can well-afford a pony, and more. Put it in the book."

Lawrie had heard enough. This, obviously, was the source of Clara's distress, and he was not about to let the blackguard get away with it. He jumped up, pushing through a knot of men and coming right up to Picton, who stood regarding him with disdain.

Lawrie pointed a finger at his chest. "You will place no such bet in the books, sir. I will not allow you to impugn Miss Mantell's honor by making so dishonorable a claim."

"My dear Simpford, it is none of your concern," Picton said.

"As neither her brother nor her father are present, I make it my concern. I am Miss Mantell's oldest and closest friend, and you will not place a bet regarding her."

"Will I not?" inquired Picton, brows raised. "And how do you intend to stop me?"

Without hesitation, Lawrie seized Picton's tumbler and tossed the contents of it into his face. The other man swore, blinking the liquid out of his eyes and shaking droplets off his sleeves. He looked down at his ruined coat, then took his handkerchief from his pocket and began wiping his face.

In bland unconcern, he drawled, "Name your friends, sir. Brandt here will serve me."

Smiling grimly at the edge in Picton's voice, Lawrie turned to grasp his friend Hiddeston's coat sleeve, bringing him forward. "Mr. Hiddeston will be my second. He will call upon you in the morning, Mr. Brandt."

Mr. Brant, blinking at so sudden and shocking an alteration in the mood, merely nodded, taking Hiddeston's proffered card, and Lawrie whirled and strode out of the club.

Chapter 17

CLARA AROSE THE following morning in a pleasant mood, having enjoyed the first restful night in weeks. She was inclined to be vindicated, but her newfound sense of humility would not allow it. She knew she was exceedingly lucky that Lawrie had deigned to forgive her at all, and that he had done it so suddenly and easily was a matter of relief to her. She felt a veritable weight off her shoulders, and considered that she could face any of her other problems—even Picton—with complacence. She toyed with the idea of acquainting Lawrie with Picton's audacity but determined there was no point. Picton had threatened her, to be sure, but she had bested him again, and unless he was the fool he claimed not to be, he would not try a third time.

After breakfast, she took Mary to do some shopping and, hoping perhaps to meet Lawrie—or one of her flirts, of course—about town, she made for Milsom Street. An hour passed, however, with only Mr. Frant making an appearance, and as he was on his way to purchase a gun, she let him go without regret. Her desire to meet with Lawrie increased, for he was by far the most companionable of her male acquaintance, and she had been without his society too long. Luckily, she recollected a shop in Gay Street she had a great curiosity to inspect, which also happened to be near where his club was situated.

It seemed, however, that Lawrie had secluded himself for some inscrutable reason, for there was no sign of him anywhere. An inquiry of one or two acquaintances yielded no helpful information, and Clara was inclined to give up the point when she came upon Lord Boltwood outside a shop in Union Street.

"My dear Miss Mantell," he said, sweeping off his hat and bowing low over her hand. "Your beauty rivals the goddesses that once ruled these plebeian shores."

In no mood for such flowery platitudes, Clara answered lightly, "Goodness me, I must attempt to curb my beauty or it may outgrow even my conceit. What brings you out on this lovely morning, sir?"

"Nothing that will prevent me from proclaiming myself your servant, ma'am. Where do we go? Have you any burdens to place upon my willing shoulders?"

"None but the question of where my friend Mr. Simpford has got to. Have you seen him this morning?"

His lordship looked dashed. "If I am called upon only to lead you to another man, and a rapscallion at that, I must do so, for I am your slave, but it cuts me to the heart, fair cruelty."

Clara laughed merrily. "Come now, my lord, and be serious. I have made up with Mr. Simpford and his faults are all forgot—indeed, I desire to see him this morning very particularly, and I would thank you to assist me to find him. But this afternoon I promise you I shall require you to gallant me to the baths, where I am to meet my mother and Mr. Noyce."

"You delight me, ma'am," he said, brightening. "Simpford has not come in my way this morning, but it would not surprise me if he is hidden away from the world, as he must prepare for the morrow."

"The morrow?" Clara repeated, blinking. "Pray, what has he to do tomorrow?"

He bit his lips. "I ought not to have said so much. I beg you to disregard it. I am, after all, prone to dark thoughts, and his situation excited my broodings—that is, Simpford is a busy fellow. I am sure he has something important to do."

"Coming it rather too strong, Boltwood!" cried Clara, pinning him with her intent, blue-eyed gaze. "Out with it! What has Lawrie to do tomorrow? I demand you tell me!"

He sighed a trifle dramatically. "Very well, but I do so with the utmost reluctance, as it involves the honor of two gentlemen who have disappointed you, and I would rather die than be suspected of attempting to cause you to think even more ill of them."

"That is enough of your plumpers, my lord! What has he done?"

Lord Boltwood contemplated his fingernails. "He provoked Picton last night, and they are set to duel with pistols tomorrow at dawn."

Clara gasped, her intent gaze losing focus as she recalled various events leading up to yesterday. She thought of Lawrie's anger at her near-run thing with Picton at the Assembly Rooms over a month ago. She recalled Picton's threatening behavior a few days previous on Bath Common, and Lawrie's reawakened fondness yesterday for herself. But most vividly, she recalled the single twig on the tree on the common spinning to the ground, shot through at twenty-five yards.

"Good God! He will be killed!" She turned in a daze and wandered away from Lord Boltwood, reflecting on the fact that though she had learnt to shoot from Lawrie, she had bested him three of the last five times they had met to shoot at the ruin at the Abbey. He was in no way a contemptible shot, to be sure, but she knew, none better, that he was nothing to Mr. Picton.

"How could he be so foolish?" she murmured, and then said more loudly, "Oh, how dare he do this to me?"

Suddenly, she turned about again, hastening back to where Lord Boltwood stood gaping after her. "My lord, where is the duel to take place?"

"I should not say—"

"But if you do not I shall never speak to you again! Where is it to take place?"

He pursed his lips, eying her in puzzlement. "Bath Common."

"And who is Lawrie's second?"

"His second—ma'am, how come you to know of such things?"

She shook her head impatiently. "I have brothers, sir. Of course I know of these things. Who did Lawrie name as his second?"

"Why, Mr. Hiddeston, I believe."

"Thank you. I must leave you—" She paused, reaching to take his hand and pressing it. "Forgive me—our stroll this afternoon shall have to wait. However, I am most obliged to you and shall not forget what you have done for me today!" she said, leaving him with a speaking look that seemed quite to immobilize him.

Her maid skipping to keep up with her, Clara walked swiftly to Stall Street and then down Horse Street, her jaw set and her countenance fierce with determination. When she turned into Corn Street, her maid gave a little cry.

"Miss, oh miss, we cannot go there! Mr. Noyce forbade me—"

"I am not going for another fencing lesson, Mary, but to save Mr. Simpford's life."

Mary pressed her hands to her mouth. "Are you going to ask Mr. Lorenzo to fight Mr. Picton, miss? Oh, how romantic! Do you think he will?"

"He might, Mary, but that is not what I wish to ask him. I have a much better plan. Will you come with me? And will you keep it secret?"

This last was said so imperatively that the little maid blinked, then crossed her heart and held up her hand. "I will, miss. If it'll save Mr. Simpford, I'll do anything, miss. Such a fine gentleman, and so kind."

"Yes, and foolish beyond permission as well. Come along, Mary."

They entered the academy and let themselves up the back stairs, coming onto the open first floor. No one was about, but when Clara called, Lorenzo appeared from a room at the rear, wiping his neck with a towel.

"Ah, it is *la bella signorina* who wishes to fight. Do you come again for the lesson? I have missed our *piccoli duelli*. But you have not brought the Signore with you—it is *non appropriato*, but I make no complaint."

"No, Master Lorenzo, I do not wish to take another lesson, though I will apologize to you for ending our lessons without explanation. But there is no time for that now—Lorenzo, I am in need of your assistance, and desperately. Will you help me?"

"Of a surety, signorina. I will go to the ends of the earth—"

"Only to Bath Common, sir. Tomorrow morning at dawn."

His brows rose. "It is what you call an assignation?" He smiled, sidling closer to her. "I cannot say no to so beautiful a signorina. But on the Common we are *troppo visibili*—we can be too easily seen. Your Signore will perhaps find out and be angry with me and—" He made a slitting motion across his neck. "Perhaps we meet here, *in privato*, instead."

"Lord Boltwood is not my Signore, Lorenzo, and much as I am tempted, I regret that I do not wish to make an assignation with you."

"Ah! You wound me, signorina. The sword through the heart—so quick."

Clara bit back her smile. "You are incorrigible, Lorenzo! At any other time, I should fence with you, for you are a remarkably able adversary, but now, there is no time. We must plan! I must appear at a duel tomorrow morning in place of my friend, and you must be my second."

He gazed smiling at her for a moment, but the smile slipped from his face as she remained intent. "*Tu non se serio*, signorina! You wish to duel? You? Is this why you learn fencing? But you are *non competente*! You have a talent, *sì*, and you move with the grace of a goddess—*Ma no*! It is *impossibile*. You are not ready! You are as Icarus—you wish to fly, but too close to the sun. It is madness! You will be cut through—*Ucciso*!" He sliced his thumb across his throat and shook his head. "This, I will not allow!"

"You mistake me, Lorenzo," said Clara, when she could at last make herself heard. "I am neither so arrogant nor so totty-headed as to wish to duel with swords. The weapon of choice is pistols, and you do not know that I am something of an expert shot. My friend, however, is not. He has called a man out who is a far better shot than he, and I am afraid he will be killed. I cannot allow it. I will not! That is why I must take his place, and you must help me to do it."

Lorenzo regarded her, his arms crossed over his chest and his lips pressed tight. He peered behind her at the maid. "Do you help your signorina to kill herself?"

"Oh, no, sir!" cried Mary, dropping a little curtsey. "I've never seen it, sir, but I've heard tell she is a famous shot! She beat Mr. Geoffrey, sir, and Mr. Simpford."

His gaze transferred again to Clara and he chewed his lip, tapping his foot. "It is *non convenzionale*, Miss Mantell, but you, I know, are *non convenzionale*. You are a tigress in the dress of an Englishwoman." He paused, considering further. "Perhaps I help you, and then you are killed, shot, and then I am discovered and killed as well. It is not something I so desire."

"No, sir, but you will not be killed. I do not know how it is in Italy, but in England, the seconds are impartial parties—there is never a question of their safety as long as the principals are there to fight. No one will wish to harm you, even if I am killed."

"But you won't be killed, miss!" cried Mary, gripping her mistress's arm. "You can't be killed! I couldn't live with myself!"

"I will not be killed, Mary," said Clara soothingly. "Master Lorenzo and I shall come up with a plan. Shall we not, sir?"

In the early hours of the morning, Mr. Simpford's man, bidden to wake his master a half hour before dawn, brought to his bed the tidings that Mr. Hiddeston had sent round a note from Mr. Brant calling off the duel. It seemed Mr. Picton had been busy, and had got himself wounded in another duel that had taken place sometime in the night. This was most irregular, but the messenger, upon questioning, was quite adamant, and Lawrie, laying his head back down upon his pillow, evinced little desire to protest.

At about the same time, a hackney coach pulled up in front of Number 8 Laura Place, and a figure swathed in black came up the area steps and disappeared into the coach. The hackney drove away, and inside, Lorenzo critically surveyed his companion.

Clara had dressed with extreme care, choosing from Mr. Noyce's wardrobe a tall hat and long black greatcoat unadorned with showy buttons, and a dark waistcoat and coat. Mary had procured from a hawker's stall black pantaloons, and boots chosen for their antique high heels which added full four inches to Clara's height. Clara had wound a black cravat round her throat to cover any of the white linen shirt beneath and had tied her hair up in a black scarf and tucked it securely into the hat. The shoulders of the coat were padded out with buckram wadding, and the front of the coat was stiff.

Lorenzo pushed on this, saying with the flash of a roguish smile, "*Mi scusi*, signorina. I make certain the wire mesh is good. And underneath is the armor?"

"Yes, Lorenzo, and excessively uncomfortable. I feel as though I am stuffed."

"But it is better than being dead, sì?"

"I only hope I may have free movement of my arms. This greatcoat is horridly heavy. And the coat is so stiff. However do you wear these things day in and day out?"

"*È facile*. We do not wear the armor." When she only glared at him, he added placatingly, "Perhaps it is as your corsets. One accustoms oneself."

Clara simply shook her head, her lips pursed, and endeavored not to curse all well-meaning men who insisted upon treating her like a child and making her wear armor to a duel. When the carriage drew up at the common, however, she could not help but be glad of the many layers enveloping her body and chest, for the chill of the morning suddenly pressed upon her, recalling forcibly to her mind the coldness said to emanate from the grave. But she did not intend to end the morning in the grave, nor did she intend that her adversary should, so, pulling her collar up higher and pushing the hat further down on her head, she alighted.

Mr. Picton watched the arriving hackney with little interest and much loathing. Simpford had never been a favorite with him, and his insufferable gallantry night before last had set the seal on Picton's hatred of him. What right that cod's head had to defend Miss Mantell only he could tell, but Picton would soon set him straight. He wouldn't kill him, for he had a notion Miss Mantell would prove even more difficult if he did, but he would certainly make him think twice about pushing his nose in where it wasn't wanted.

He watched Simpford descend somewhat awkwardly from the coach, his stride a little odd as he approached. It must be the uneven ground of the Common, Picton thought off-handedly, and turned to speak to Brandt about the doctor. He received the news that he had just ridden up on his horse and was ready.

Simpford stopped about twenty paces away, and his second came on to meet Brandt, discussing something which seemed to take Brandt by surprise. It must not have been of moment, however, for he soon shrugged and brought out the pistols to be inspected. Picton rolled his shoulders, returning his attention to Simpford to run a critical eye over his odd preparations—the man looked like a mannequin. He must never have fought a duel before, and his second had not proved to give him very good advice. That collar turned up and the hat pulled down would avail him nothing—even did Picton wish to kill him, he would not aim at his face!

The pistols were approved and the seconds handed them to their principals, then paced off the distance, marking lines in the dirt with their boot heels. Picton assured himself his pistol was half-cocked and ready as he walked to the mark, then he turned and awaited his opponent. Simpford checked over his pistol like a man accustomed to guns and Picton knew a tiny relief to what little conscience he possessed. At least Miss Mantell could not accuse him of having called out an amateur.

Brandt stood off to the side and held up his handkerchief. He paused, looking from one to the other of the principals. Picton settled himself squarely with one foot perpendicular to the other. He was not fearful of Simpford's aim, but it was wise to set himself sideways. When he looked again at Simpford, however, he was moved to sneer. The man was imitating his stance, and Picton almost felt sorry for him.

"Ready?" called Brandt, and Picton nodded, not taking his eyes off Simpford. But in the moment before the handkerchief fell, several things happened at once—Simpford straightened himself, his chin raising in an oddly familiar manner, and in the first rays of dawn, Picton perceived a sparkle of blue eyes beneath the brim of the hat. He was certain Simpford's eyes were brown—his breath caught—it couldn't be—but there was the unmistakable nose, and those cherry lips—

The vixen!

The handkerchief dropped. Picton threw his arm straight up, his pistol aimed at the sky. Shots rang out—shouts followed as Picton jerked back and fell. His right arm was on fire, he dropped the pistol, his vision blurred, and he struggled against the many hands that all seemed to grab at him at once. There was a cacophony of voices, a rushing in his ears, but still he craned his neck to see Miss Mantell—

She stood still, her second clasping her shoulders as she stared at what she had done—he could feel her gaze though the hat was again pulled down to obscure her features. She was mad—what else could it be? What could have possessed her to take Simpford's place? Then she was bundled away into the coach and Picton resigned himself to the hands that were pushing him down, tugging at his coat, loosening his cravat.

He closed his eyes, confusion marring his thoughts. What had just happened? He had been tricked, but why? Had Miss Mantell taken them both in, he and Simpford—or had Simpford and Miss Mantell joined forces to make Picton look a fool?

A wrenching of his arm drew his anguished attention. The doctor had succeeded in removing his injured arm from his coat and shirt and was surveying the damage. He looked up at his patient with a cheerful smile.

"A clean graze, sir. Bullet only took a bit of flesh, but didn't lodge. Must only bind the wound well and it'll heal nicely." This he proceeded to do, blithely ignoring Picton's cursing, and adjured him, when he was done, to keep it clean.

"Get me up!" Picton groaned to Brandt as the doctor strode jauntily to his horse, mounted and rode away.

"Devil of a coil, Ferdy!" said Brandt as he supported him to the carriage. "Had no notion you'd delope! What maggot got into your brain? Everyone'll have it you were at fault!"

Picton, his head none too clear, was nonetheless wise enough not to spout the tenor of his thoughts before he had reached something like a conclusion. "Took pity on the poor devil," he muttered absently, and got into the coach, sitting in silent rumination through his friend's chatter. If Brandt had not been so shocked by the outcome of the duel, he might have taken more notice of the dark look on his friend's countenance, and might have felt some foreboding at what was going on inside that dangerous mind.

Chapter 18

LAWRIE AWOKE TO a clear day and a niggling suspicion that he had forgotten a most pressing appointment. A momentary panic seized him when he remembered the duel, but directly he was relieved by the recollection of the explanatory letter. A brief search produced the letter, writ in a bold and unfamiliar hand, and signed *Wm. Brandt, esq.* in flourishing letters. This thoroughly removed all doubt and Lawrie, exhaling deeply to dispel the vestiges of his panic, stood and prepared for the day.

His first call was to Mr. Hiddeston, who congratulated him on his near miss, and inquired facetiously if they ought to send a letter to Mr. Picton, condoling him on his disappointment. Lawrie expressed his appreciation of this notion, stayed to talk over the possibilities that would never occur and the felicitous chance that had caused it, and then went on his way.

He then went to his club and ordered some breakfast. While

reading the newspaper at his table, he overheard some gentlemen speaking of Picton's duel and pricked up his ears.

"Aye, man, deloped! Never thought it of a man like Picton, but so it is."

"They say he got it in the shoulder—nasty wound, bled like a stuck pig—"

"No, no, only a graze. My cousin had it from Brandt. Surgeon was mighty satisfied with it, went away humming a tune! Picton'll be tied by the heels for a few days, but nothing to signify."

"Who was the other man? Samson? St. Ford? Ah, Simpford. From somewhere north of here. Not acquainted with him myself. Well, all his cards are trumps, that's all I've got to say for it."

"I'd say! Picton's a crack shot. Put out all the candles in a hanging chandelier at Lord Dunston's hunting box once. And I saw him shoot the pips from a playing card at ten yards. If he had it in for this Simpford fellow, we'd have been reading his obsequies right now, and no bones about it."

"Wouldn't have thought Picton had an honorable bone in his body, but if he deloped, then Simpford's in the right. Wonder what it was they fought over?"

"A female, I'd lay you a monkey. Always a female. Likely that yellow-headed chit he was squiring about town before he loped off."

"It's my belief he offered her a carte blanche and she offered to send him to grass! Spitfire, that one, and well done. Believe Simpford is her cousin or some such—stands in the place of a brother. Called Picton out over it."

"Very proper, since her stepfather ain't fit for that sort of thing—though he's a bruising rider! Well, I'd say Picton has had his comeuppance. Might give him pause before he thinks to offer another young lady an insult."

Lawrie, listening from behind his newspaper, was bewildered. These men seemed to think he had dueled with Picton, when he knew, of a surety, he had not. He had dreamed of the duel, but with such a conglomeration of other actors—including Clara and Boltwood and even Lady Drayford—that he knew it without a doubt to have been pure imagination. He was tempted to stand up and inform them of the mistake, but not having the name of the other gentleman who had in fact dueled with Picton, he could not hope to answer a lot of uncomfortable questions which he felt sure would be put to him. He rather cravenly hid behind his newspaper, therefore, until the men had gone off, then stuffed down his breakfast and went back into the street, intent upon returning to Hiddeston's lodging to inquire more precisely into the matter.

Hiddeston was sanguine, assuring Lawrie it was merely a misunderstanding. "Depend upon it, old boy, they've only got it wrong because you were to duel this morning. Story's all mixed up. Poor flat who did the business last night will be out the honors this morning, but he'll be sure to set everyone straight by tonight."

Lawrie was sent on his way again, endeavoring to be satisfied, but still the situation did not sit right with him. Determined to drive away his discomfort, he called for his hack and went riding along the canal.

On his way back, he met with Mr. Noyce, who was exercising his fine bay stallion.

"Well, Lawrie, my boy! Rumor is you are to be congratulated!"

Lawrie summoned up a cheery, "Thank you, sir, though I hardly know what for."

"For a near miss! Not many men get off unhurt, and through an adversary's caprice, do they?"

Watching him closely, Lawrie said, "No, sir."

"Between us, I never made much of Picton's honor, but to agree to duel twice in one night—that smacks of overindulgence."

With a little sigh, Lawrie agreed and said, "I suppose it is all over town?"

Mr. Noyce chuckled. "Certainly! Bath is generally so quiet, I think, that a duel is something—and a duel that trumps another duel is something else!"

"Indeed, sir. But I believe there is some confusion. I have heard that I am being talked up as the victor, and I cannot but think the other man, whoever he may be, will take exception to it."

"Oho! Let him do so in his own time, but allow yourself some merit in having all the honors and none of the spoils. I'll turn back with you a while, however, for I do hope you are going to tell me what this was all about." His tone had become grave and he continued, "I am persuaded Clara had something to do with it."

In the clear light of day, without the fumes of wine to lull his reason, Lawrie was exquisitely aware of the folly of what he had done in the name of friendship to Clara. He knew that it was the height of presumption to assume Mr. Noyce's role as Clara's protector, and he was loath to own that he had gone so far as to provoke a man to duel in defense of a young lady with whom he had no understanding. His rights of friendship did not even arguably extend far enough to support what he had done, and he knew not how to excuse himself without seeming a callow youth without sense or obligation.

His hesitation, however, was enough to confirm the facts in Mr. Noyce's mind, for he said, "I see. Well, I do not hold with dueling in general, for it is a barbarous way to settle arguments, and can never be depended upon to uphold the right. However, I believe I understand what drove you to it, knowing Picton a little, and knowing Clara very well. It has long been my belief that girl will be the death of some young man or other, and it seems I was right. She very nearly was the death of Picton."

"Perhaps, sir," said Lawrie, relieved. "However, I cannot even tell you if she was the subject of Picton's argument with the other man. Indeed, I was not informed of the other man's identity. But I wish to congratulate him, whoever he may be. It seems Picton deloped, which is quite shocking in itself, even without it signifying he was in the wrong."

"Indeed! I had not heard that, but I suppose it makes perfect sense. Otherwise, I suppose murder would have been done. The man is a crack shot, they say, and we have reason to be grateful on behalf of both his opponents."

Lawrie bit his lips. "I take your meaning, sir. I own it was foolish of me to provoke him to call me out, but if you had heard what he said—however, I do not wish to vex you. I beg your pardon for acting as though I had the right to defend Clara."

Mr. Noyce regarded him quizzically. "I would think as an old friend you would have as much right, or better, to defend her than an old man who has only been her guardian these three or four months. I have very little opinion of society's notions of honor, if they would keep a man from stepping up to help someone who could not help himself. Clara was not present to defend herself, nor was I present to do so. If you had done nothing, I would have thought less of you. Now, I do not mean to say I condone the duel, but that has all ended well, so we need not revisit it."

"Thank you, sir," said Lawrie, smiling somewhat consciously. "I'm only glad Picton cannot show himself in society for a time. It will give

Clara time to prepare herself for his presence once more in Bath. Has she heard of this business?"

"It was she who told me this morning. Apparently she had it from one of her beaux she met while walking in the park. I need not say that she was thrilled at your bravery, but do not be shocked if she gives you a tremendous scold when she sees you. By the by, I am glad you two have repaired your misunderstanding—she is quite a changed creature. I imagine she suspects she was the cause of your duel, however, and will be insufferable for the next few days."

Lawrie smiled at this, but said seriously, "Would that you could carry Clara back to Southam before Picton emerges from his sickbed. I am not at all easy with his intentions. His returning at all is a great impertinence."

"As to that, we had planned to stay only a fortnight more, you know. I can hardly believe Picton will be about much before then." He cast Lawrie a sympathetic grin. "I would ask that you help me to keep Clara out of any scrapes until we can be gone, but I cannot depend upon her paying much heed to either of us."

"Unfortunately, sir, it is as you say, though I thank you for your trust. I will do my poor best, but you will pardon my saying that she is as headstrong and obstinate as she is lovely and charming."

"It is certainly a problem," agreed Mr. Noyce. "But one hopes that she will someday put her talents to better use, eh? Well, my boy, I will let you go. But you will come to dine with us today? I will tell Mrs. Noyce to expect you. Good bye!"

Clara had been busy all the morning, putting it about to select members of her acquaintance that Lawrie had been honorably relieved of his dueling commitment, while also stirring up the pot of rumors extolling his victory. She believed that if the right persons were put in possession of her version of events, the network of gossip would work in Lawrie's favor, and hopefully garble things to a point that no one could be sure of what had really happened. Her hope was that after a brief sensation in certain circles, the duel would quickly be forgotten, and Lawrie would remain none the wiser.

As the day wore on, however, she was less sanguine as to the issue. The rumors became more rampant than she had planned, and she was anxious lest Picton's circle took pains to disabuse minds as to the identity of his combatant. But she as actively hoped that Picton's pride would preclude this. He had harmed his own reputation for implacability and detachment by deloping, and the quicker the furor died down, the more satisfied he would be.

She therefore struggled between two very different sensations regarding the outcome of the duel. She was naturally possessed of extreme pride in her complete triumph in the situation. Her plan had come off without a hitch, and her shot had been precise—an injury calculated to end the duel but not to result in a threat to life. She certainly hated Mr. Picton, but only *wished* him dead without desiring precisely to bring it about.

In this, she had yet again proved herself superior to Picton. He had had murder in his eyes when he had looked at her, believing her to be Lawrie. If he had not intended to kill Lawrie, he certainly had not intended for him to win the duel. His deloping had been a complete shock and she could not conceive of why he had done so, but she was certain that he had meant no good to come of it for Lawrie. He could possibly have thought of pleasing her, in the hopes that this honorable act would soften her toward him, but she did not think he would relish the taint this would give his reputation as a dead shot and a stoneheart.

Her cogitations on the matter were relieved only by the pleasure of learning that Lawrie had been invited to dine that evening, for she had been eager to see him. Precisely why, she was not certain, for she knew all there was of the affair to know and, more to the point, could not talk to him of her part in it. She only knew that she could hardly contain her excitement as she sat quietly with her mother and Mrs. Wellstone in the drawing room, awaiting the gentlemen.

Mrs. Noyce, who had been favored with Clara's version of events, had spoken of little else all day, and now reiterated all she had gathered on the matter for the benefit of her friend.

"I never suspected little Lawrie Simpford of being so foolish as to duel, and a man of Mr. Picton's reputation! Why, even had I known Picton was a crack shot, it could not have been worse, for one never knows how these things shall end. Duels are a horrid, brutal practice, and ought to be outlawed! To think of poor Diedre Simpford's grief if it had been her son who had been shot, and we had been obliged to bring his body back to her, as I am sure Mr. Noyce would insist upon doing—you must know, Olivia, how close the families are, having been neighbors nigh on two centuries!"

"Certainly, my dear," said Mrs. Wellstone. "It would be only right for Mr. Noyce to take such a burden on himself for a friend, and I have no doubt he would do it without a thought for himself—such a kind man!"

Mrs. Noyce simpered. "There has never been a more excellent man in all the world. But as I was saying, even had Lawrie killed his man it would have been horrid for poor Diedre, for he would be obliged to flee the country! It is not so very unlikely to consider, my dear, for all Picton is so wonderful a shot, Lawrie is quite competent, and may just as well have hit him. My dear Clara, I trust things are finally at an end between you and Mr. Picton! Though his deloping hints that he is ready to turn a new leaf, you may depend upon it, it is all a take in."

"I do not think he is thought of at all highly in certain circles," added Mrs. Wellstone diffidently.

Mrs. Noyce nodded sagely. "I have long thought him grossly impertinent. How I could have considered him anything but odious, I do not know. The Finholdens, you must know, have been attempting to restore our acquaintance since Clara gave up their nephew, but I will not be taken in again. Indeed, I cannot recall what it was that attracted me to Penelope in the first place!"

"Oh, but Anamaria, she put on a show so that you would approve Mr. Picton." Mrs. Wellstone lowered her voice and added, "He is in debt to several tradesmen in town, from what I hear. He must want money."

"And his aunt only ever talked of his prospects! But she was so insinuating and plausible, I cannot be blamed for having taken her at her word. I can only be grateful that she will not dare to continue in her endeavors to re-engage me after this scandal!"

Mrs. Noyce continued to gossip with Mrs. Wellstone, who added what calming influence a rational woman does to a discussion. Clara's mind, however, was bent on what she was to say to Lawrie, and when Mr. Noyce appeared with Lawrie by his side, she stood instantly, a smile lighting her face. Allowing only for him to make his civil bow to Mrs. Wellstone and her mother, she rushed to greet him in all the pleasure of one who has done an immeasurably good deed and expects to be thanked. But as she shook hands, she recollected that she ought not to know anything of the real matter, and was obliged to act only as though she was furious with him for having put himself in danger.

Adjusting her buoyant demeanor accordingly, she said sternly, "Well, Lawrie, it is a lucky chance that brings you to dinner tonight, I hear. We might even now be mourning your loss, and that would not suit me at all."

He colored slightly, saying, "Thank you, Clara, but as Mr. Noyce has said to me, it all ended well, so we need not revisit it."

"Mr. Noyce may be satisfied with so craven an approach, but I will not forgive you so easily, Lawrie Simpford! To think that you were so careless as to insult Mr. Picton—a man ten times the shot you are—provokes me nearly to throw you off!"

"Clara, you are unjust!" cried Lawrie, goaded. "Ten times the shot? I beg to differ—"

"Yes, Lawrie, ten times," insisted Clara inexorably. "If you have not seen him shoot, I have, as I have also seen you."

"But you could not be so certain that I could not have bested him."

"Having bested you myself, sir, I think I am well able to judge between your skill."

"Clara! That was a mere game—"

But further argument was precluded by the butler's announcing dinner, and they were obliged to go into the dining room. Mrs. Noyce then took charge of the conversation, inquiring if the identity of the victor of the real duel had come to light.

"No, my dear," said Mr. Noyce. "But I have no doubt it soon will be. No man could bear to have his victory so muddled as his has been."

"And I am certain Mr. Simpford would not like to be wearing borrowed feathers much longer," said Mrs. Wellstone.

"No, ma'am," said Lawrie, with emphasis.

Clara, who had not considered Lawrie's pride when she had started the rumors, took a sip of her wine to hide her dismay. She could only hope that the business would be forgotten as quickly as she had intended, and there would be no lasting harm.

Mr. Noyce, perhaps taking Lawrie's discomfort as a hint, changed the subject. "I believe you intend to remain at Bath until Christmas, Lawrie."

"Yes, sir. I have no other obligations at home until that time."

"You must plan to travel with us on your return, then," said Mrs. Noyce graciously.

"Only if he swears on his honor not to get into another duel," Clara said, but with an arch smile that was meant to show Lawrie that he was forgiven.

Mr. Noyce said reasonably, "Oh, I am sure Lawrie does not intend to make dueling a habit, my love."

Clara raised a brow. "I am depending on it, sir."

Mr. Noyce was able, after that, to turn the conversation to other matters, and Clara encouraged it, for she never wished needlessly to mortify her good friends. She was reasonably satisfied that Lawrie had no suspicion of her involvement in the duel or the succeeding rumors, and she intended to let the matter lie. Indeed, now that all seemed to be well, she could reflect upon his actions with some pleasure, for they showed his unfailing loyalty to her, even if it did not extend beyond that of a friend.

Chapter 19

LAWRIE HAD NOT been Clara's friend for her lifetime without gaining some comprehension of her ways, and he went away from Laura Place with a deep suspicion that something was not right. While he was reasonably certain that her anger at him for calling Picton out was real, his experience of her told him she was hiding something behind it, and it could only relate to the duel. This conviction brought so serious a concern upon him that he could not sleep all night, and he awoke the next morning cross and restless.

Thinking a walk would clear his head, he set out toward High Street, intending to walk about the town before it became very busy. But as he drew near the market, he saw Clara's maid scurrying up the street with a parcel in hand, looking about in a manner he could only consider surreptitious. Puzzled and disposed by his ruminations to be curious, he followed her into the market, taking care to keep out of her sight.

His reason told him he was a fool, for the maid must merely be making purchases for her mistress or herself. But his uneasiness kept him at the watch, and she soon stopped at a hawker's stall, unwrapping the package and showing the hawker what looked like boots and a piece of black clothing. Their business was speedily finished, and Lawrie ducked behind a pie-seller's stall as the maid turned and went back the way she had come.

Lawrie watched her out of sight before going to the hawker's stall. Holding a shilling piece between two fingers, he inquired, "What did that maid just sell you?"

"Only these old things I sold her two-three days agin, sir," the man said, eying the coin as he pulled the items from beneath his counter.

Lawrie cocked his head, gazing in bemusement at the high-heeled boots and black pantaloons being displayed. "When did you say you sold them to her? What day exactly?"

"Well, sir," said the man, rubbing his stubbled chin, "This being Thursdy, and it wan't yestidy, nor the day afore that, I reckon it were Mondy, sir."

Lawrie's eyes narrowed as he did his calculations and then surveyed the items on the table once more—high-heeled men's boots and black pantaloons, sold to Clara's maid on the day before his duel. It was not right—he had only a vague suspicion, but he did not like it.

"Did she tell you why she wanted them, by any chance?"

"I can't say, sir," the man said, still eying the shilling between Lawrie's fingers. "Jes wanted the old high heels."

"I see." Lawrie continued to gaze at the boots, fingering them absently.

The hawker cleared his throat. "Would yer honor be wanting the boots, sir?"

"No—No, thank you." Lawrie handed him the shilling and walked away, pushing his hands into his pockets and thinking furiously.

The possibility that the boots and pantaloons were for Mr. Noyce Lawrie rejected out of hand. A gentleman with a spasmodic condition in his legs would never wear such high heels, even for an occasion that might merit it, such as a masquerade. There having been no masquerades in Bath during the week, Lawrie disdained even the idea of Clara's or Mrs. Noyce's having used them for such a purpose.

They might have been meant for a manservant, and been unsuitable, but Lawrie did not think so. The only menservants employed in Bath by the Noyces was the old butler—too staid and unsteady for such frankly ridiculous footwear—and a young footman who, being over six feet, had no need of an increased height.

The idea of increasing height brought him to another possibility: Clara might have desired them for her fencing, to give her better height and reach. She might have tried them, and upon finding that they did not serve, decided to return them. This was the most reasonable of all his conjectures, but it still did not satisfy him.

Returning through Laura Place, he found a decent-looking young man loafing on the street and gave him half a crown to follow the maid wherever she went that day, and to try if he could discover what it was her mistress had wanted with high-heeled boots. Promising another half crown, he instructed the young man to report to him at his lodgings in Henrietta Street at the end of the day.

After pacing about most of the day, either at home or at his club, Lawrie at last received his visitor, but with unsatisfactory results. The young man had followed the maid to Milsom Street, but she was with her mistress, and he could not get her alone. After refusing the offer to try again on the morrow, Lawrie paid the boy and sent him away, adjuring himself to cease his foolish suspicions and let the thing go.

But he could not. He dined at home without tasting the food, so disrupted were his thoughts, and would have dressed by guess for the fancy ball at the Assembly Rooms if Hiddeston had not taken him in hand. He would not have gone at all but for the growing conviction that he must find out what Clara was hiding, and the ball would be as good a place as any. He arrived at the Rooms, therefore, with only the thought of seeing Clara, and he was not disappointed. She was there, partnering Lord Boltwood in the cotillion, and he was forced to stand out, on pins and needles, until the dance was done and he could find a way to speak to her alone.

"You look the picture of consternation, sir," said a friendly voice by his side.

He turned to find Mrs. Wellstone beside him. He bowed. "Forgive me, ma'am. Something is worrying me, but I did not mean to advertise it."

"Do not mind me, for that is entirely your own affair, and I wish you well with it. However, I will give you a hint: there is nary a young lady who would dare to dance with a scowl so dark as that you are wearing."

Lawrie laughed, a bit conscious. "Dear me, is it as bad as that? I did not mean to make myself disagreeable. But I only wish to dance at the moment with Miss Mantell, who knows me well enough not to fear my scowl."

Mrs. Wellstone gazed out into the dance, where Clara seemed to be in high gig. "I can imagine what worries, you sir—but I will not be impertinent and drag it out of you with suppositions. I only hope that you may resolve the matter, and not suffer through much anxiety in the process."

"Thank you, ma'am," he said, smiling gratefully, and she went away to the matron's chairs.

The dance ended and Lawrie made his way over to intercept Clara before she had got to her mother. She saw him coming and obliged him by changing course to meet him.

"There you are, Lawrie! I thought you had decided not to come after all. It would have been very bad of you, for you are the man of the hour, you know."

"Good heavens, is everyone talking of it?" whispered Lawrie, glancing about the room. It seemed then that several eyes were upon him, and he grimaced. "You will have your wish, at least, Clara, for dashed if I'll ever call a man out again, if I am to get so much notoriety—and without even deserving it!"

Clara smiled somewhat weakly. "I am glad to hear it. I know you don't like to be spoken of—you are not like me, wishing to be foremost in everyone's thoughts."

"Heaven forbid you start calling people out!" said Lawrie in exasperation.

But Clara only looked arch and took his arm. "I am bespoken for the next set, but I might let it slip my mind, if you stand up with me."

As this was precisely what Lawrie desired, he set aside his scruples at cutting out a man of whose identity he was unaware, and agreed. He furthered his discourtesy by leading her to a corner away from her mother, so the unfortunate gentleman who wished to partner her would not find her before Lawrie could take her into the next set.

"You are in spirits tonight, Clara," he said, feeling his way. "Far better than you were last night. I thought I wouldn't come away with a whole skin."

"Nonsense," she said, with a quizzing look. "You know me too well to imagine that I would do you the least harm."

Forbearing to mention hearts and how easily they are broken, he said, "I truly am sorry to have frightened you so, but I seem to be exceedingly lucky. How fortunate that Picton would pick a fight with someone else on the very night before we were to duel."

"Intemperate persons are generally to be relied on to do precisely such stupid things." She favored him with a stern glance. "But I forbid you to allow it to go to your head, Lawrie, and assume you would be attended by the same sort of luck, should you contemplate another duel."

"I would if I am careful to provoke another intemperate person." This was received with such a wide-eyed, threatening glare that he put up his hands in surrender. "I do not mean it! You know I do not. But I wonder, truly, what sort of luck it was that attended me."

She did not meet his intent gaze, and his suspicion grew. "Clara, who told you about the duel? It is not generally the thing for a gentleman to speak to a lady of a duel."

She shrugged one dainty shoulder, still not meeting his eyes. "It was Boltwood. He is something of a rattle, to be sure. He did not mean to tell me, but once your name had escaped his tongue, I made him tell me everything. I suppose it was improper of him, but it is not as though I am missish, and would swoon or behave like a ninny at such tidings. You were not injured, so there was no need for such goings on, after all."

"No swoonings for Picton? Poor man! His injury did not merit even faintness?" said Lawrie, unable to resist a feeling of triumph.

"Certainly not. He deserved what he got."

The musicians struck up and they hurried into the set. So eager were they to evade Clara's erstwhile partner that she found herself in the lead, and they were unable to converse until they had gone down the line.

"I wonder," said Lawrie, as they caught their breath, "did Boltwood say how he had learned of the duel? It was rather quickly noised abroad."

He thought Clara looked conscious for an instant, but then she turned her provocative look on him and said, "You simply do not apprehend what a sensation you caused, Lawrie. To slip from the clutches of certain death so easily? That is something that is never too swiftly to be talked of, I assure you."

Lawrie pursed his lips. "It seems to me it was Picton who made a sensation. Two duels in one night, you know."

"Pooh! That is nothing. He might have done that a hundred times, but it would have been taken for granted he would win both. This time, he did not, and you were the beneficiary of his failure."

"And his deloping was nothing, too, I perceive?"

"Oh! Well, that was something, to be sure. However, it only made the whole of the situation more miraculous."

They went down the line and again could not speak for a time. At the end of the dance, Clara declared she was hot enough to faint, and Lawrie led her out of the ballroom and into the Octagon Room. There were several couples there, fanning themselves, and Lawrie took Clara's hand, pulling her to the corridor that led to the porch.

"I need to speak with you, privately," he said.

She looked alternately pleased and terrified, then said, "Not the porch. It is too likely to be filling up this close to eleven o'clock. Come with me."

When she led him to the narrow stair that led to the cold bath below, it was his turn to tug her back. "Clara! You are not taking me where Picton accosted you? I will not have it!"

"We will go to a different room. Do not be anxious! We shall not do anything improper, for if I know you—and I do—you are a stick in the mud."

"But that will not weigh with anyone who should discover us!"

She pulled him down the stair. "Perhaps not, but everyone knows you are as a brother to me, so it will be winked at."

Grumbling, Lawrie followed her down the steps and to a small room. Clara had taken a candle from an obliging stack in an alcove near the stair, and lighting it at the one candle in the corridor, set it in the sconce in the wall. She looked about her approvingly.

"There! This is very cozy, and it is cool and quiet. Much better than upstairs."

Lawrie was forced to agree at least partially to this, but it did not improve his mood. Clara was being slippery, and he was becoming impatient.

"Clara, I know about the boots and pantaloons."

She stilled, her eyes searching his face. "But how—What of them?" She paced away, looking carelessly about, as though there were objects of more interest in the room than a stack of towels and a stool and chair.

"You had your maid find high-heeled boots, Clara, on the day before the duel! I'm not a simpleton. It had something to do with the duel, and I'm very much afraid—Clara, how tall is that Italian fellow?"

She looked quickly at him, her eyes alight with laughter—or was it triumph? "He is of middling height, Lawrie. But I cannot conjecture why you should wish to know such a thing."

"And he is a fencing master, not a shooting master," mused Lawrie, his brain feeling thick as he puzzled it out. "You might as well have dueled Picton as he."

There was a momentary pause before Clara huffed into laughter. "I duel Picton? It is well that you do not think I could, for it is not a very flattering notion! That I could be so easily taken for a man as to duel him without a suspicion of my sex? One's opinion of Picton's intellect must be very low, indeed, to believe such a thing."

"Of his honor, perhaps, but not of his intellect," said Lawrie, more cross than ever. He followed her example, walking swiftly about the room. "You did it somehow, Clara. You orchestrated the other duel— you imposed upon someone to help you. But no one can name Picton's challenger, and the stories are so garbled—" He stopped, staring unseeing at the wall ahead of him as several hitherto conflicting pieces clicked together in his brain. "Good God. Clara, you could not. You did not!"

She shrank a little, for he had whirled on her and was looking very angry indeed. Trying for a little lightness, she said, "What horrid idea has taken possession of you now, I wonder?"

He closed the distance between them and grasped her shoulders. "Clara, did you write that note telling me there was another duel?"

"Of course I did not!"

"Do not lie to me!"

"Lawrie, I never tell untruths."

He growled low in his throat, and paused in order to command himself before going on. "Did you—good God! Clara, Did you go to the duel in my stead?"

She blinked, opening her mouth, but he shook her a little, for he knew she was about to mislead him again. "No, Clara. The truth!"

"I—I did, Lawrie," she said, as though his insistence had broken a dam within her. "But it was all for the best! Only the day before I had been a witness to Picton's skill with a pistol—I could not leave you at his mercy! He is as cold-blooded as I am—even more so. I could not let him kill you."

"Clara!" Lawrie again paused as his emotions threatened to overcome him. He let her go, his hands going to his head and his face contorting with horrified anger. "He could have killed *you*! He thought you were me! If you feared for my life, how could you think to replace me and live?"

She averted her eyes. "But I did, Lawrie. He deloped."

"You could not have guessed in a hundred years that he would do so! You must thank whatever guardian angel is watching over you that, somehow, Picton's conscience was constrained to awaken that day, and you are saved." He ran a hand over his face, grimacing with the effort of self-control. "Someone helped you, and you will tell me who it was, so that I may strangle him!"

She grasped the lapels of his coat, taking her turn to shake him. "No! Lawrie, I will not tell you, for I did impose upon him, and he was excessively unwilling. But he meant to save my life, for he insisted that I wear both an armored breastplate and a shield made of wire mesh under my shirt. Even had I been hit, it would not have killed me. But you would have taken no such measures, Lawrie, and Picton might not have deloped after all."

His eyes closed so that she could not see the relief there, for he was not done with her yet. "Clara, this is a coil you have got us into. Do you not realize what damage your reputation would receive should this become known?"

"It doesn't signify, Lawrie! I would merely be considered an eccentric—"

"Then consider my reputation!" he cried, goaded. "I would be marked out as a coward, hiding behind the skirts of a younger woman!"

She shook her head quickly. "No one will know. They all thought it was you."

"We can only pray it will not come out."

"We—we shall be gone home to Southam soon, Lawrie," she said with an uncertain half-smile, "and need not let it concern us."

"You are impossible."

He leaned away from her, closing his eyes again—it felt much better to close them, and he thought that perhaps he would be wise simply never to open them again. Life was so much simpler when he did not face it. Perhaps if he kept his eyes closed he could take up residence in the fantasy land of his mind, where Clara loved him and was reasonable and flirted only with him, and did not think to endanger her life or impugn his manliness by taking his place in duels. He gave an involuntary groan, and her hold on his coat tightened.

"Lawrie—Lawrie, I—I could not let you die." Her hand came up to his cheek, soft and gentle, and his eyes opened of their own accord. She was gazing at him with something like tenderness, and he blinked at it. "Lawrie, I would miss you terribly."

He looked at her, at her beautiful face that seemed so sweet at this moment, her red lips parted and her blue eyes intent. He would give anything to know that she meant more than what she said—that she would not only miss him, but would mourn him with a broken heart. He longed to kiss her, to assure her that he would never leave her, and that he would be hers forever, because he knew she would be his forever, too. But he could not. If he had learned anything in the past month, it was that his heart could not be trusted.

Reaching up to take her hands, he removed them from his coat. "I can only hope that this will all blow over before Picton is well enough to call me to book, for then all your schemes will have been wasted."

"Lawrie!" she cried, stunned. "You do not think he will desire a rematch?"

"If he does, I will not be the one to say nay. And I will insist upon secrecy, for I will not risk any more of your foolishness, my girl."

She grasped at his lapels again, but he intercepted her hands, bending to say in a menacing tone that masked the ache in his chest, "Now I know what you think of me, Clara, of my courage and skill, I can promise you that I will not pass over an opportunity to prove you wrong."

He strode out of the room, and didn't turn back even when she cried out after him.

Chapter 20

CLARA TRIED TO be vexed with Lawrie for again being furious with her, but she could no longer justify such a line of thinking. She had, after all, mortified him, deceived him, and put her own life in peril. These were grave offenses, and far more than their fledgling reinstated friendship could bear. It was distressing that she had managed to drive him away after only a few days, and she did not know if he would forgive her this time.

The hurt this idea caused was something of a surprise, for in general she discarded unsuccessful friendships easily. But Lawrie was a special case, for he was her oldest and best friend—and she suddenly realized that she did not know how to live without his companionship. If she had finally driven him away forever, she could only look upon the future as bleak and forbidding.

This realization was unexpected and disturbing, for it elicited several uncomfortable questions—why did she require Lawrie's friendship, when it had cost her so dearly? What did she need with his attentions when she had that of other gentlemen? And why did his rejection sting so much when she was both unwilling and unable to make a lasting attachment?

These questions exercised her mind through the following morning and into the afternoon as she sat obediently in the drawing room, netting a purse while her mother embroidered. She had just resolved that needlework was wholly infelicitous to one seeking unfathomable answers—besides being tiresome in the extreme—when an unexpected visitor burst in upon them.

"Francis!" cried Mrs. Noyce, dropping her embroidery and staring in undisguised amazement at her firstborn. "Whatever brings you here? I thought you in Leicestershire."

"I was, Mother, but—" He stopped, raking a hand through his blond locks. "Pardon me, Mother, Clara, for barging in on you like this. The truth is, I am not quite myself. Is—is Mr. Noyce at home? I should like to consult with him—on a problem—of a personal nature."

Coming to her own conclusions of what problem could be of a personal nature to Francis, Mrs. Noyce said, her lips pursed, "I trust this problem does not involve the ruin of a young lady."

Francis looked both outraged and desperate, then turned away, rubbing the back of his neck in agitation. "No, Mother, it most emphatically does not."

She regarded him disapprovingly. "If you mean by that the female in question is not a lady, I can only express my extreme disappointment, Francis."

"She is not—I have not ruined her—nor do I mean to," he said, clearly in distress. "Please, I beg, Mother—I must speak with Mr. Noyce."

"Well, I am infinitely relieved that no young woman—of any sort—has come to harm at your hands," replied Mrs. Noyce, her nose in the air. "And, I will own to some surprise at it. However, as you are clearly too agitated to string even a proper sentence together to tell me what is the matter, I shall discover for you if Mr. Noyce is at home to visitors."

She sailed from the room and Clara, her own problem effectively forgotten, pounced.

"Good heaven, Francis! What has happened? Did you finally shoot that odious toad Nathan Willoughby?"

He darted a glance at her that seemed to confirm it, saying, "I have never come so close to it in my life."

"What do you mean?" inquired Clara, all astonishment. "I was only quizzing you! Willoughby is one of your oldest friends. For all his detestable ways, you've never so much as looked askance at him before! But I can only say it is about time you took him in dislike, for I have done so these ten years and more."

"You may rest easy, for he is no longer my friend."

"Gracious me, Francis," exclaimed Clara, more and more bewildered. "What can have happened to turn you against him? For I dare not hope you have seen aught to disgust you in his morals. Did he steal one of your doxies from under your nose?"

"Hush, Clara, please!" he said almost savagely, then, going to the fireplace, leaned with a hand on the mantle, staring into the flames. "You cannot know how I suffer."

Clara sat up in her seat, gazing at her hitherto incorrigible brother, whose rakish air was entirely vanished, replaced by this broken and desperate manner. Something had shaken him, had caused him to cast away an insouciance toward debauchery she had assumed was inherited from their dissolute father, and therefore permanent to his nature. But seeing him now, she wondered if perhaps it had been merely learned, and was now, somehow, overshadowed by a higher sentiment.

In a gentler tone, she said, "Tell me, Francis. What has happened?"

He huffed, shaking his head and flashing a derisive grimace. "Would that I could, Clara, but you know I cannot trust you. You, who are as depraved as myself."

"I am quite as careless, to be sure, Francis, but I have never ruined anyone," retorted Clara, adding, "It is not the province of a woman."

"But you would have, if you were a man." He turned on her, coming to tower over her in disdain, for himself and for her. "You and I, we have learned well from our sainted father, have not we, how to manage the other sex? Control and self-gratification, that is the way—respect and esteem are not for us. There is no enjoyment, no variety, no spice in the pleasant attachment of ordinary, good people."

He fairly spat the words like venom, and Clara knew not what to think. Francis had never held himself in derision, had sought neither to justify his actions nor to excuse them. He had acted, until this moment, as though there was nothing wrong in his choice to exploit any young female who would answer his summons. Clara had always held herself to be above him and their father, for though she flirted incessantly and delighted in courting danger with a rake, she at least knew enough of right and wrong to stop short of seduction.

But she was obliged to admit that the events of the past month had changed her, and now something had happened to transform Francis from an unapologetic rogue into—she was not sure. Just what had he become? She observed him critically as he returned to his grave contemplation of the flames in the hearth. The whole of his demeanor spoke of anxiety, rage, desperation, and—yes, remorse. She was much mistaken if he had not been made to repent the habit of a lifetime.

"This is a new come-out for you, Francis. I have never seen you remorseful."

"No, Clara, you have not."

She straightened out her skirts. "It is no business of mine, but perhaps it is a good thing."

"Thus speaks the fount of virtue," was his acid response.

"I never claim to be what I am not," she said primly. "But no matter how close I have come to skirting the line of propriety, I have managed to retain my virtue."

He cast her a quelling look. "The wisdom of a coquette."

"Even the vilest of sinners may recognize the benefits of humility."

"Only if it is not too late."

The note of desperation that underlay this statement was suddenly enlightening, and she lowered her brows at him. "Francis, are you in love?"

He looked quickly at her, then averted his eyes. "I have always been as likely to fall in love as you, Clara. You are not in love. What makes you think that I could be so now?"

"Only your excessively odd behavior. What else but love could make you hate your mode of life?"

"I thought we were agreed that neither of us is capable of love."

Clara shrugged up a shoulder. "I thought you incapable of remorse, but here you are, as full of remorse as Judas Iscariot. He hanged himself, you know, but I cannot recommend it."

"Your solicitude overwhelms me."

"I never overwhelm my companions. But you are trying to fob me off. I think you have fallen in love, but unless it is with some poor housemaid of Willoughby's, or one of his light o' loves, I cannot understand it. And Mother will never countenance that sort of match, I'm afraid. You must elope."

He groaned aloud, putting both hands on the mantel. "Clara, I beg you. Be quiet!"

"Did you elope?" she cried, eyes wide. "Francis! But how romantic!"

He turned a frantic countenance to her. "Clara, I did not come here to listen to your wild conjectures, nor to submit to your strictures. I have come to speak with the only person whose counsel I trust—one who might have better advice than my devil of a father, and who will definitely guide me more surely than a chit of a sister who also happens to be the most determined flirt in all of England."

Silenced, Clara sat back, allowing him to brood as she pondered his words. Despite his protestations, she was convinced that he had fallen in love, but paid him the compliment of obeying his request to leave him in peace. When Mr. Noyce at last came into the room, Francis's patent relief further corroborated her conviction.

"Forgive me, my boy, for the delay in my coming to you," Mr. Noyce said, taking his stepson's hand in a firm grip. "I do not entirely understand it, but Mrs. Noyce was most distressed and required some careful handling. But I am now at your service."

"Thank you, sir! I am in your debt," said Francis, stopping only to nod to his sister on his way from the room. "Clara."

Clara exchanged an astonished but significant glance with Mr. Noyce before he followed his stepson from the room, and she was left to contemplate the strangeness of fate in operating so powerfully upon even the most careless of persons. As a Christian she had been taught the superiority of good over evil, and that miracles had been known to occur, but until this moment, she had not quite believed it to be true. But she could not deny that, contrary to her conviction of the impossibility, Francis was changed, and she was much mistaken if it was not due to his having fallen in love.

After further reflection, Clara saw that she ought not to have been surprised by this. She had already observed her own mother's slow but continuing transformation under Mr. Noyce's tender influence. He, she knew, would deflect praise of himself, but was not Mrs. Noyce's softening manner, her sensibility to the falseness of her friends the Finholdens, her desire to care for Mr. Noyce despite any discomfort to herself, entirely owing to Mr. Noyce's devotion? If he had not married her, she should not have desired to change. It should not be so wonderful that Francis could be worked on as well.

Whether or not it would answer was cause for speculation. Mr. Noyce was committed to loving his wife, but Francis's fate was unknowable, at least as far as Clara's lack of information could suggest. If he had fallen in love, there was no saying whether his cherished one—whoever she was—returned his affection, and if she did, it was debatable whether he could make her happy, or even come to deserve her.

Clara had not leisure to ruminate long over Francis's problem, however, for they were engaged that evening to go with Mrs. Wellstone to the concert at the Upper Assembly Rooms. Francis—though seemingly relieved somewhat after his talk with Mr. Noyce—elected to stay behind, not being, as he put it, in the mood for warbling. He was left to his brooding and his brandy, while the others went out to air their surprise over his arrival. Mr. Noyce was in a jovial but tight-lipped mood, and nothing the ladies did to try to pry any information from him on Francis's mysterious problem could succeed.

They arrived in the Octagon Room and greeted Mrs. Wellstone, and while they found seats, Clara glanced idly about in time to witness Lawrie settling Mrs. Gravesthwaite in one of the front chairs. He turned and when he met her eyes, the light dimmed from his own, his jaw tightened, and he offered her only a curt nod. She was stunned, then mortified, then resigned. Of course she had deserved that. He was still understandably angry.

She was low the rest of the evening, finding the concert tedious and disappointing. Rising during the interval to partake of refreshment in the Tea Room, she glanced toward Lawrie and instantly wished she had not. His head was bent intimately close to Mrs. Gravesthwaite, his russet coat almost pressed against her side as he exchanged quiet words with her that brought a blush to her cheek. As she watched, the shawl slipped from Mrs. Gravesthwaite's shoulders and Lawrie reached to pick it up, tenderly replacing it, and a sudden conviction overcame Clara that he meant to marry the widow. She was stricken with dread, her ears buzzing and her vision clouding. She knew an impulse to run from the Rooms and throw herself in the River Avon, and she gripped the back of her chair to keep herself from fleeing. Her heart pounding in her throat, she realized with abrupt clarity that, not only could she not live without Lawrie's companionship, but her life would be unendurable if he married anyone but herself.

This staggering conviction took from her all power, and she sank back onto her chair, passing the interval in dumb and agitated contemplation. She suspected she had been falling in love for weeks, but as she, like Francis, had been persuaded that she was incapable of tender feeling, she had thought only of Lawrie's importance to her as a friend. Even when she had replaced him in the duel, she had dismissed the truth that it was for love of him that she would risk her life, or anything else for that matter.

These admissions did little to hearten her, for she was at once painfully aware that she had crushed his love of her weeks ago, and that she could never be worthy of him. She was a horrid, heartless flirt and would sooner remain a spinster than inflict herself upon so excellent a man as he. And after her callous treatment of him, she was the last woman on earth he was likely to wish to marry. It seemed a hopeless business, and she began to wonder if a toss in the Avon was the best solution after all.

But what if she were to change? Francis's transformation again came to her mind, and with it a hope that if he could wish to renounce his debauchery, as their mother had her self-absorption, perhaps Clara, too, could cast off the depraved parts of her nature. This hope was both dazzling and disturbing. She was uncertain whether to exult in it or be terrified by it, for she had lived so long in the belief that love was a fairytale she did not want, and men were tools to be used and despised. The notion that she could actually be worthy of the love of a good-hearted, reliable man was almost too fantastic to be trusted. And yet, now that she had allowed the mere prospect of it, she could not let it go.

A vision of living in Gosley House with Lawrie sprang into her mind, of waking to his cheerful greeting, walking in the country-side with him, flirting harmlessly with him. This last she had never thought possible, for flirtation had always been her strongest weapon. But now, she thought of Geoffrey's flirting with his wife, or Mr. Noyce with her mother, the gentle hints and sweet whispers that promised of later satisfaction, of trysts kept with all the joy and fulfillment of loyalty and trust.

The idea of finally being willing and sufficiently trusting to allow the culmination of all romantic feelings, of at last giving herself wholly and completely to a man, filled Clara with a longing more powerful than she had ever experienced before. She was certain that Lawrie alone could have had the power to give her the incomprehensible freedom she required in marriage—but she had been too blind and heedless to see it.

"Good gracious, what have I done?" she murmured aloud, for it seemed she had shattered all her dreams even before they had been born.

The night brought neither solace nor counsel, and she awoke with a headache and stayed in bed. Her mother came to tut over her dissipation, tucking her in and otherwise making her comfortable, then leaving her to order a tisane. Mr. Noyce arrived soon thereafter, seating himself on a chair and regarding her with sympathy.

"Francis has gone to Southampton, and he sends you his best wishes."

Clara sighed but did not reply.

Mr. Noyce smiled kindly. "I believe there is something afflicting the Mantells of late that has them all in a muddle."

She gazed desolately at him, still not opening her lips.

"Come, you may confide in me. Francis assures me he is revived after hearing my advice. You could not do better, from such a testimonial."

Clara plucked at the coverlet. "I never understood how painful it is to break one's heart."

Mr. Noyce's eyebrows jumped up. "So you have a heart now, do you? Well, that is a beginning. A pity you did not discover it a month or six weeks ago."

"But I am sure I did, sir! I am certain that is why I tricked Lawrie into missing his duel."

Too late, she recollected that he knew nothing of the deception, and she bit her lips tight. Mr. Noyce gazed wide-eyed at her. "I think, my dear, that you should tell me the whole story."

There was nothing for it, so Clara unburdened herself to him, not in an orderly and forthright way, but haphazard and riddled with excuses. She had not yet made a full transformation, and was still commanded by habit to communicate less of her faults and more of her virtues. However, Mr. Noyce's experience with his wife had taught him much about the winding and lengthy road to redemption, and he patiently listened to her tale of woe with a candid and forgiving ear.

At the end of it, he said, "You have made a proper mull of things, my dear, and I do not trust myself to give you hope, for Lawrie is not the sort of young man to change his loyalty without just cause. But he is also big-hearted, and I should be astonished if he did not prove still to love you, and to wish as much as you do for a final reconciliation."

"I do not perceive any good in trying," she declared despairingly. "I have abused his friendship too many times, and I think he will be glad to see the last of me."

"Unless he makes Bath his permanent abode, he will find that a hard task. Recollect, you are near neighbors at Southam. He must resign himself to a glimpse of you almost every day."

Clara averted her eyes. "Perhaps he will choose to live on Mrs. Gravesthwaite's estate."

"There is where you are out." Mr. Noyce chuckled. "That lady is promised to another man—in Essex, I believe. It is a wonder what one finds out at the hot baths."

Clara gazed at him in stupefaction. "But Lawrie cannot know this! He is continually speaking sweet nothings to her and making her blush."

"I am certain you are mistaken, my dear, and they are only fast friends. He must know of her attachment in Essex, for I had it from Mr. Gravesthwaite, the lady's brother-in-law. But she is not the sort of lady to keep a secret of that kind from a gentleman making his preference known."

"Then he is not falling in love with her!"

"I believe I may safely stake my life on it."

Clara exhaled, blinked several times, and smiled rather foolishly. "Oh, Mr. Noyce, you have relieved my mind." But her countenance clouded quickly again, and she said, "But Lawrie still is determined against me. He seems not to regret me in the least, after I have treated him so abominably. I do not know what to do."

Standing, Mr. Noyce made his awkward way over to her and patted her hand. "I have every confidence in your capability, my dear. You shall find a way to his heart."

Chapter 21

DESPITE MR. NOYCE'S encouraging words, Clara's doubts continued to assail her. The vivid recollection of Lawrie's coldness the night before came again and again to her mind, and she was at last obliged to stifle it by rising from her sickbed and going out for a walk with her maid. Just at the foot of the house steps, however, an urchin ran up and presented her with a paper twisted into a screw, saying a gentleman had told him to give it to her. Heart leaping with the hope that it was from Lawrie, Clara unfolded the note.

> *Miss Mantell,*
>
> *You will pardon the liberty with which I address this letter to you, but I believe our relationship is such that you will not be shocked. I will be brief. In light of our recent engagement, I request that you meet me on Beechen Cliff as soon as may be. I trust you value your*

reputation sufficiently—and that of your friends—not
to risk displeasing me.

    Your servant,
    Ferdinand Picton

Clara's heart sank under the weight of her apprehension, and she wondered fleetingly if having a heart was rather more distress than it was worth. Crumpling the note in her hand, she looked about as though to find Picton standing there, but saw only the back of the urchin as he hurried away. She stood for several long moments in agitated indecision. Picton's note, seeming to confirm that he knew all, was anything but salutary, but the repercussions of defying his summons could encompass both herself and Lawrie, and she had already made enough trouble there.

She turned to her maid. "Mary, we will go to Beechen Cliff."

"But miss, you were only just laid upon the bed! You'll be wore out—"

"Nonsense. I was only cross, and now feel as fit as a fiddle. I have a great desire to see the view from Beechen Cliff today."

Resolutely facing the bridge, she began walking, obliging the maid to follow after. They made their way over the bridge and past the baths, down Union Street and out of town. At the bottom of the hill, Clara realized that she had not brought her pistol, which reposed in her desk in her room as she had meant only to take a short walk and not to confront villainous persons with mysterious intentions. But it was too late to retrieve it now, and Picton would not know she had not brought it. He was injured, too, and could not very well carry her off as he had threatened before. She would simply take care to stay out of his reach.

They climbed the path up the hill until they emerged at the top, overlooking the hills and streets of Bath. Mary gasped, for here, at the edge of the cliff, stood Mr. Picton, an arm in a sling.

He turned as they came across the hangar, regarding them with his lazy smile. "You are wise to come, Miss Mantell. Though, I perceive I should have stipulated that you come alone."

"I never disappoint my friends, Mr. Picton," said Clara briskly as she stopped ten feet short of him. "However, it is something of a stretch to call you my friend, thus the presence of my maid to lend me countenance. Now, what have you to say to me?"

He chuckled, looking her up and down. "You are ever enchanting, my sweet. It is one of the many things I admire in you. But I did not summon you all this way to bore you with flattery. I wish to give you an offer."

"You had better keep on with flattery, sir. I find it less of a bore than your offer."

Laughing outright, he took off his hat and bowed to her. "Bravo, Miss Mantell! I have missed that fire, and the reminder of it gives me courage to do what we neither of us will like. But first, you will get rid of your maid."

Mary inched closer to Clara's side and Clara looped arms with her, lifting her chin. "You are every bit the fool I thought you if you believe I would send away my support. We both know what a blackguard you are. I would not trust you if my life depended on it."

"It very well might," he said with a slight rise of his brows. "But no matter. She will be a witness for the both of us. You no doubt comprehend what I want of you. It is only my due, after all."

"You must pardon me, for I cannot conceive of what you can mean."

"Come now, Miss Mantell. You did not truly believe you could get away scot free after what you have done to me!"

"Pray, what have I done, sir?" inquired Clara, all innocence.

"You and Simpford combined to trick me," he said, a suspicion of a growl in his tone.

Clara eyed him sharply. "Lawrie had nothing to do with it."

"No? Then he was too much of a coward to come forward."

"He is no coward!" cried Clara, eyes flashing as she stepped toward him. "He has more honor in his little finger than you do in all your soul! He meant only to protect me, but you would know nothing of such things."

"Oh, I think I do. He is as anxious to retain his ill-gotten prestige as I am to resign mine. What would the world think if I were to explain the matter fully?"

Clara took another step, saying in a low, angry tone, "You will leave him out of this, Picton. It was all my doing—your argument is with me!"

"It certainly is, my girl! You tried to make a fool of me!"

"You made a fool of yourself! You needn't have deloped."

"Do you imagine me to be so cold-hearted as to shoot you? You wrong me, my sweet."

"I do not think I do. You were not meant to know your opponent was not Lawrie. It was not my intention to hide behind my femininity, nor to prey upon your sensibilities! I relied wholly upon my skill—but you did not trust that."

"As though I would!" he scoffed. "What a fine gentleman I should be to shoot a woman!"

"You are nothing like a gentleman, sir, but I wish you *had* tried to shoot me!" She hesitated, exhaling sharply. "Though I suppose the game would have been well and truly up if you had managed to injure me. How did you find me out?"

"Your eyes gave you away. And the tilt of your chin. And your exquisite nose." His hooded gaze caressed these members as he spoke. "How could you ever think I would risk harm to one hair of your head, my sweet?"

Clara rolled her eyes. "Enough of your meaningless words, sir. We have established, I trust, that I am at no fault for whatever stain has appended to your reputation as a gazetted scoundrel. If the world believes you now to possess a mite of honor, it was none of my doing. We can have nothing more to say to one another."

"Your trust is misplaced, Miss Mantell," he said, advancing toward her. "We have much more to say. I still require recompense, and if you refuse to pay the price, your darling Mr. Simpford must bear the weight of it. Oh, yes, my sweet. It was he who was the instigator of this affair, after all. Imagine if Society knew the truth, that he failed to defend his own challenge. His reputation would be worth that." He snapped his fingers, regarding her intently.

Her jaw worked as she stared him down. "You wouldn't dare. If anyone suspected the truth, you would be a laughingstock. It would not be worth the risk to your own reputation to attempt to expose Lawrie."

"I think you are mistaken, Miss Mantell," he said, stepping closer as though to intimidate her with his impressive height. "If rumor leaked out that you had taken Simpford's place, I would be seen as no more than the honorable man I now seem—distasteful to me, but hardly damning. But poor Simpford would be ruined. There is nothing Society despises more than a coward—except, perhaps, a fallen woman. Your reputation, you know, would be damaged as well, and your family would bear the shame with you. Think of your mother—her exquisite sensibilities. And poor Mr. Noyce's reputation as a protector—"

"He is ten times the gentleman you are, sir!" ground out Clara, scowling. She threw back her head, not giving him an inch. "What is it you want?"

"I thought I had made that clear. I want to make you an offer."

"Then do so." But suddenly his meaning came clear and Clara inhaled sharply, stepping back in her astonishment.

"Yes, I want you to marry me, my sweet." He moved toward her as he spoke, reaching to take her hand.

She pulled it out of his reach, backing farther away. "You cannot be serious."

"Oh, I am deadly serious," he said, steadily regarding her. "It is only fair, you know. You have ruined my reputation, and so you must marry me."

"You are ridiculous! You do not need marriage to redeem yourself in the eyes of Society—you are a man! Moreover, your reputation is no more ruined than mine."

"True, but I require you to marry me nonetheless. As things stand, you are eternally in my debt. My forbearance has guaranteed both your and Simpford's continued comfort, though it forfeits my own. For such a sacrifice, I will not be satisfied until you, my sweet, have submitted all you have to me—your hand, your fortune, everything."

Clara shuddered, instinctively crossing her arms over chest. She could never marry such a man—he was arrogant and selfish, immoral and false, and now he was showing himself to be cruel and implacable. Even his handsome features no longer held any attraction for her. Indignantly, she realized he was even worse than Francis had ever been, for he was a thorough-going rogue without hope of change.

But she had no leisure at present to dwell on Picton's depravity. He was impatient for an answer and, her mind in a whirl as to what could be done, she attempted to put him off.

"Then this is all about money, is it?" she said, putting on an unconcerned air while thinking furiously.

"Hardly, my sweet. I mean what I say. You are entirely pleasing to me, from your lovely head to your dainty feet, with your flashing eyes and your spitfire mouth. Your purse is only another appendage—though it is quite as necessary to me as the rest of you."

"So you would not take me without my fortune?"

He huffed a laugh. "I did not say that. Suffice it to say that you are lucky to be a wealthy woman, else my offer may not have included the protection of my name."

Clara stiffened. "And you imagine I should close with such an offer?"

"It would only be a matter of time before you had no choice, just as you have no choice now. If you care anything for your darling Simpford's reputation, you will accept my terms."

Clara, furious color flaming into her cheeks, said quietly, "You are despicable."

He took two quick strides and, before she knew what he was about, had taken her hand. Mary cried out and Clara stepped hastily back, tugging against him in vain.

"I am despicable," he said with his roguish smile. "But you knew that, my sweet. I have never deceived you—much as I tried—of that I am certain. You knew what I was when you met me. It did not seem to trouble you until recently, however."

He raised her hand to his lips before releasing it. She stumbled back, a mixture of relief and cold fear coursing through her. He did not seem intent upon forcing himself upon her at the moment, but the situation had undeniably spun out of her control. She could feel the kiss burning through her glove, and she thought with a sensation of panic how it would burn should he decide to kiss her lips. It was suddenly borne in upon her just what a fool she had been to court the attentions of such a man, and wished wildly for someone—anyone— to come to her rescue.

It seemed no one wished to climb Beechen Cliff on a dreary, cold winter day, however. Clara thought of her family, ignorant of both her whereabouts and her trouble, and unable to assist her. With an unpleasant sinking in her stomach, she reflected that other than her family or perhaps Lawrie or Boltwood, it would be better that no one come to her aid. Any other witnesses would only add fuel to the scandal Picton threatened to ignite, and speed her doom.

It was ludicrous to her, now, how woefully she had misjudged her opponent. She could see no other alternative than to give in to Picton's demands. She felt sick at the thought, yet the dreadful whirl of her mind did not yield a better option. All she knew for certain was that Lawrie must not be made to suffer still more for her recklessness, and she did not doubt that Picton was deadly serious in his intention to destroy Lawrie's reputation if she did not comply.

Picton, having watched the play of emotions on her face with some amusement, said, "I warned you not to try to shoot me, my sweet."

Her eyes snapped to his and she said, "And I warned you I never do things by halves."

"Then you ought to have shot to kill—or perhaps your aim is not so sharp as you boasted."

"I hit you precisely where I wished to. There was no cause for me to injure you badly—my only concern was for Lawrie's welfare," she said, tossing her head. "I did not—then—wish to kill you."

He regarded her with lazy interest. "I admit to some curiosity as to why you did not, if you thought it likely I would kill my opponent."

"Because I am no monster!"

He smiled wryly. "Whereas I am? It may surprise you to know that I did not, after all, intend to kill Mr. Simpford. You see, I did not at all wish to displease you."

"Then why did you call him out? If you thought I should be displeased, why did you not walk away?"

He laughed, shaking his head. "Women simply cannot comprehend the gentleman's code of honor. I could not walk away, for the same reason you cannot afford to ignore my offer. I would be quite as outcast as your dear Simpford, you understand."

"You speak of honor," she said disdainfully, "and yet you do not understand it—or you misrepresent it! You need not have called him out in the first place. Even I know that!"

"There, you are wrong," he said in an indulgent tone. "Once he had insulted me, honor required that I meet him. Though I admit to you—but to no one else—that I *had* acted badly and deserved a challenge."

"You expect me to believe you planned all along to delope? I am not so foolish!"

"Your instinct serves you well, my sweet—I would never have deloped except to save you harm. I intended to shoot Simpford, but only to wound him, just as you did me. But he was to be taught a lesson never to cross me, and to know that I meant to have you for my own."

Clara's fists clenched as she struggled against a horrible feeling of helplessness and revulsion. She closed her eyes against it but they flew open again as he instantly closed the distance between them again, taking her by the shoulders and pushing Mary away.

"Come now, Clara," he said, his heated gaze locked on her own. "We could be content together, I am persuaded. We are the same, after all, you and I. We both are ruthless and fearless and know our own minds. We dealt prodigiously well together here in Bath, despite our trifling misunderstanding. I admit, I was precipitate in that, and perhaps even a trifle crude. But notwithstanding, our acquaintance has been exceedingly satisfactory. I do not doubt our marriage would be more of the same. I think I may even love you."

Unable to move, Clara snapped, "Then do not force me to this."

He shook his head, his hands moving to cup her face as his hungry eyes roved over it. "I tell you I want you, and I must have you. I'm sorry, my sweet, but there is no other way." He dropped his hands abruptly. "Now, we must plan."

Stifling a gasp at his wildly alternating mood, Clara grasped at one, last, desperate straw. "It will not answer. Mr. Noyce will never hear your suit, and will deny you my fortune."

"He has already settled the funds on you, and you are of age." He tutted, casting her a derisive look. "You must do better than that, my sweet. My Uncle Finholden has made discreet inquiries on my behalf and has ascertained that your fortune is yours outright. I am no fool. We will elope, tonight."

Clara gaped at him. "Elope—tonight? Impossible."

"Not impossible—merely disagreeable," he said imperturbably. "However, we shall manage it. Pack wisely, my sweet, for we must travel light, and I warn you I shall throw away anything that I deem unnecessary. You will not require much—only a portmanteau and a bandbox or two to get you through a few days."

"We go to Gretna, then?"

"No, only to Gloucester. I want you safe, so will get a bishop's license to speed our union. My good Aunt Finholden is something of an acquaintance to the bishop there. We will leave early in the morning—I will come for you at three a.m. Your honorable parents ought to be asleep by then, and the rest of the household."

"How do you know that?" asked Clara, appalled at these exact calculations.

He smiled again. "I, also, never do things by halves. I have had over a week to plan, my sweet, and to gather intelligence. Amazing what one can do from the comfort of one's sickbed."

"And if I do not come?"

"That would be unwise. I need not repeat the reasons why."

She gazed at him in extreme distress, the confusion of her thoughts overwhelming. She wished she knew what to do—wished that she had not been a fool the better part of her life, and brought herself to this crisis. Struggling to organize her thoughts, she attempted to determine which was least odious of her options. She shrank from marriage to him, though he claimed to love her, for she knew that to be false. He could not know what love was, for if he did, he would never have threatened her like this. What he considered love she suspected was only fascination, and a determination to win at all costs. No happiness could result from a marriage begun on so treacherous a footing.

And yet, if she did not marry him, he would carry through his threat—of that she was certain—and then Lawrie's life would be ruined, all because of her selfish weakness. What choice did she truly have? Marriage to Picton would at least protect Lawrie from disgrace, and the wreck of her own happiness was only her own just deserts.

"What do you say, my sweet?" he inquired, breaking into her ruminations. "Will you come with me?"

"Please, I beg you, give me time—"

"I must have your promise now or I go and tell my tale to my good Aunt Finholden," he said, unbending. "There is not much to think about."

Clara, exhausted from the struggle, accepted defeat. Still, she closed her eyes against what she must say. "Yes. I will come."

Chapter 22

CLARA HASTENED HOME, having successfully refused Mr. Picton's escort, her face set and her mind a jumble of whys and what-ifs and if-onlys. Mary, skipping to keep up, inquired once or twice what she was going to do, but Clara could not spare a thought to plan—indeed, she could hardly formulate a sentence. She could only think on the horrid cruelty of fate to present her with the inconceivably precious gift of hope for love, only to crush it under the heel of justice.

For Clara could not deny that this impossible situation was only what she deserved. Mr. Noyce and Lawrie and even her mother had warned her against Picton and Boltwood, but her vanity and obstinacy had overruled them. She had insisted, resisted, and persisted, selfishly pursuing her own ends. She alone was to blame for her present situation, and she alone must pay the price.

When they gained the house, she excused Mary and went directly to her room, locking herself in. With shaking hands, she divested herself of her hat and gloves, then threw herself on the bed, indulging in a bout of unrestrained despair.

Why, oh why had she been so blind? How had she allowed cynicism to thoroughly taint her view of love and marriage, refusing to allow even the idea of happiness to belong to it? How could she have passed so easily over Lawrie—with his goodness and love—in her calculations for the future, imagining coquetry and vengeance to be more fulfilling than a life with him at her side? And how could she have used him so ill, handling his heart so carelessly that, just when she was coming to recognize its value to her, it had slipped through her fingers?

If she had been even a particle more wise, she might have won her mother's fate, to gain an excellent man who lived to love her, as she was, while patiently undoing all the evils a misbegotten view of marriage had engendered. But she had not, and now she could only look forward to a life of misery, either as Picton's wife or Lawrie's ruination.

In her despair, she saw plainly that it had been the height of conceit to imagine herself equal to Picton, with all his arrogance, cruelty, and worldly wisdom. Francis had been right to warn her away from such town beaux and their wiles. All they cared for in the world was themselves, and this selfishness was more cunning and terrible than any vice Clara possessed. They were motivated entirely by greed, self-gratification, and pride. Such animal instincts could never be treated casually, as Clara had done, without terrible consequences.

She could not imagine marriage to Picton without abhorrence. Despite his preposterous assertions to the contrary, Clara knew she would be miserable in a marriage with him, for it was born of revenge and spite and would only get worse as time wore on. Even her parents' marriage, which had begun at least with mutual complacence, had rapidly deteriorated into purgatory, with each partner despising and seeking to injure the other. There could be no hope for her with Picton. He certainly would never cherish her the way Geoffrey cherished his wife, or the way Lawrie would undoubtedly cherish his—but she could not think of that. She must think of a way out of this mess.

This resolve reawakened her spirit, and she sat up, drying her tears on the pillowcase. There must be a way to prevent the elopement without harming Lawrie's reputation, while somehow preserving her own freedom. She paced the room, racking her brain for a solution, but there did not seem to be much hope. Any way she could think to avoid an elopement with Picton left Lawrie open to ruination, and she would rather die than allow that. If she went through with the elopement in the hopes of escaping Picton at some point along the way, she must run the risk of failure and of his sure retribution—which would be swift and cruel, she was certain. Even should she succeed in escape, there was nothing to prevent him carrying through his threat to brand Lawrie a coward, which would render her exertions—along with her existence—meaningless.

She picked up a pillow and threw it across the room in her frustration. If she could consult Lawrie, he might have a cool-headed word of advice, but she could not allow him to know of Picton's threatenings. She could not bear for him to know that she had, as he had foreseen, placed him in a precarious and shameful situation, and that either her happiness or his reputation hung in the balance. She must grant him his peace and muddle through this on her own.

After an hour of feverish cogitation—the hands of the clock on her mantelpiece taunting her with their swift ticking toward the hour of her doom—only one possible option had presented itself to her. She must beg Lord Boltwood's assistance. If he were to snatch her from Picton's grasp, she could not be blamed, and Picton would perhaps transfer his desire for vengeance upon Boltwood. It was diabolical, and might not go as she planned, but it was all she could think of.

Boltwood's safety she could not consider, for it paled next to Lawrie's. He was capable, she told herself, of looking after himself. As Picton's arch-rival, Boltwood would certainly snatch at the opportunity to eliminate him from the playing field, and thus prove himself superior. His love of romance would spur his genius in concocting a plan to extricate her from Picton's clutches. He was also far less dangerous than Picton and more worshipful of herself—besides being more deeply in debt—giving her reasonably to hope that if he expected recompense for his service, a pecuniary reward may suffice. But even if it came to promising him marriage, she thought she might do so with far less loathing than with Picton.

Thus determined, she sat at her desk to write a letter, but rather than addressing Lord Boltwood, she was overcome by the necessity of leaving some sort of explanation and farewell to Lawrie, in the event that all did not go as planned. She could not tell him precisely what had forced her to this exigency, but only that she was everlastingly sorry, and she would leave the letter in a safe place, with instructions to Mary to deliver it into his hands should her plan fail.

She labored long on Lawrie's letter and had just finished it when a knock sounded on the door. She opened it to Mary, who darted glances of uncertainty mingled with concern as she entered.

"Mrs. Noyce desires you in the drawing room, miss. Mr. Simpford is here and is wishful of speaking with you."

Clara sat down hard on the stool, overcome by anxiety. What had he come to say to her? Did she dare to find out? Writing a letter to him had been hard enough, but to face him again after his coldness the day before—she was not sure she could do it. However, this may be her last opportunity of seeing or speaking to him, and she did not have time to dither, so she summoned up enough courage to go downstairs to meet him.

Lawrie stood as she entered the drawing room, bowing and asking with cool civility how she was. Her throat tight with the truth, Clara curtsied and said she was very well.

Perhaps her tone gave him pause, for he glanced narrowly at her while they took their seats, but said only, "I have just been taking leave of Mrs. Noyce. I am going back to Southam. I hoped that you would come in before I had gone."

"You are leaving—you are going home?" Clara was unable to keep the note of dismay from her voice, and he cast her another keen look as she rushed on, "But you were to accompany us—you promised to travel with us home!"

Mrs. Noyce said quickly, "Clara! Enough of this. Lawrie is his own man and owes us nothing. Certainly, it would have been much more convenient for us if he could stay but two more days and travel with us, for now we must hire an outrider or Mr. Noyce will insist on riding at least some of the way and I will not hear of it. He is an excellent rider, but he never does take sufficient care for his health, and in this cold, who knows but what he will take an inflammation of the lung. However, as I was just saying to dear Lawrie, business is business and we are not to think our preferences above his obligations."

Lawrie's countenance had closed once more and he cleared his throat stiffly before saying, "Indeed, I have business with my solicitor in London that I must attend to at once. I simply cannot spare another day or two as his schedule is quite full after this week. I greatly regret the necessity, but depend upon my long friendship with you to make my excuses. I have already asked your mother's forgiveness, Clara, and know you to be too generous not to give me yours. Now I may wish you both farewell and a good journey."

He rose as he spoke, drawing on his gloves, and Clara's heart sank at so evident an impatience to be gone from her presence. But with a sudden desperation to obtain his final forgiveness, she resolved nonetheless to detain him.

"Surely you need not go immediately," she said, trying to communicate with a look that she must speak with him.

But he would not look at her for longer than a glance, working studiously at his gloves. "Pardon me, but I must go. I have many preparations to make for my departure tomorrow."

"But Lawrie—" Clara bit her lip, for at last he looked her fully in the face, but with so grave and disapproving a countenance that she was nearly shaken from her purpose. With one last burst of determination, she said, "I will see you out."

"No need—"

"I insist!" she said and rose, sailing to the door ahead of him.

"Truly, it is unnecessary—" he muttered as they went out onto the landing.

Irritable with misery, Clara hissed, "I must speak to you. Stop fussing!"

She pushed him into the library and followed him in, shutting the door behind her. He stood, looking back with almost belligerence, while she pressed her back against the door and tried to gather her scattered wits.

"Lawrie, I—" She swallowed and tried again. "I wish to apologize—again."

"I doubt very much you know the meaning of that word."

"I might once have misunderstood it," she said, refusing to be either goaded or daunted by his tone. "But I have learnt better, and I truly am sorry for what I did to you."

He raised his brows, gazing at her from hooded eyes. "I suppose you are going the rounds of all your beaux. Did you not tender a similar apology to Picton?"

"Certainly not!" she said, lowering her brows.

"Why, then, were you seen meeting clandestinely with him today on Beechen Cliff?"

Clara gasped. "Good gracious, who told you? Who was it that saw us?" Too late, she realized the folly in phrasing it so.

Lawrie only folded his arms across his chest and set his jaw. "If you meant not to be discovered, you ought not to have chosen Beechen Cliff. You were seen by my friend Mr. Hiddeston. He did not wish to be rude, so he did not make his presence known but went back down the way he had come."

"Lawrie, I can explain—"

"Pray, spare my credulity, Clara. I have had enough of your self-exculpating periods. You may never tell untruths, but that is only because you do not live in reality. The truth is something you form to your own ends."

She gazed helplessly at him, for he was right—that is, he had been right for so long, and now he could not know that she had changed. Again, it was her just deserts for being so blindly thoughtless and obstinately selfish. But surely forgiveness was a virtue, even on behalf of someone so depraved as herself.

Quietly, she said, "I know I have been horrid, Lawrie. I toyed with your affections and broke your heart, and shamed you and mocked you. But I did not mean it. I am so very sorry—you cannot know how sorry. I do not deserve your forgiveness, or even your esteem, but I very much wish I did."

"I can only wonder at your impudence in claiming so, when you have consistently gone counter to my advice regarding the methods you employ, Clara," he said, face tight with disdain.

"Please, Lawrie, only listen! I am done with it all!"

"What of Picton?"

"Picton tricked me into meeting with him—I did not wish to, but he threatened me—" She looked up at him, regretful. "He is as despicable as you warned me, and I wish I had never met him."

His mouth was pressed in a tight line. "How disappointing for you. I wonder what will you do with no one to toy with and ill-use."

She shrunk from his coldness, so well-earned and painful. She ought not to have attempted this dialog with him—ought to have foreseen how miserable it would make her.

"Is that all you wish to say to me?" he inquired coldly.

She winced at his tone, but steeled herself to meet his icy gaze. "No, Lawrie. I wish to say that I have finally learnt my lesson. I know it is too late, but no matter what I have done in the past, I will always—" She swallowed down the lump in her throat— "I will always value you as my most constant friend."

His countenance betrayed some emotion, but it was pain rather than tenderness. He gazed at her in silence for some long moments, jaw clenched and eyes deadened by injury and distrust. "I would have gone to the ends of the earth for you once, Clara. You knew it, and you went your length to test it. I believed at one time you might change, that you had changed—but now I must believe it to be impossible. You simply cannot understand what it means to care for anyone but yourself."

He might as well have thrust a sword into her heart—which was no longer as stone but very much warm and alive, and eloquently reminding her at his every word what it meant to be well and truly broken. She gazed at him, her despair alive in her eyes, but could not bring herself to say more. Silently she opened the door, moving away and standing with her eyes averted.

"Goodbye, Clara," he said.

She could only close her eyes as he walked out of the room. After an eternity of standing so, of reliving his rejection again and again and drowning in sorrow and misery, Clara at last forced her feet to carry her back to her room. There, on the blotter, was her letter to Lawrie, which contained much the same heartfelt apologies and explanations of her guilt that she had given him in the library. Blinking her stinging eyes, she crumpled it up and threw it at the grate.

She slumped into the chair and put her head down on the desk, but she could not weep. Her head ached, her throat was impossibly tight, and her eyes stung, but the tears would only seep from the corners of her eyes. The words "just deserts" marched over and over through her mind, and she did not try to stop them. She only thought drearily that she did not care what happened anymore, as long as no one spoke to her ever again and she could be left to waste away in peace.

How long she remained in this state she did not know, but the afternoon sun slanted through the curtain when she at last rose. With an unsteady hand, she poured a glass of water and drank it, easing the ache in her throat and head. She passed a hand over her eyes, recollecting that she must importune another gentleman if she wished to save herself from Picton. She sat again at her desk and, putting Lawrie firmly from her mind, took a new piece of paper to write hastily to Lord Boltwood.

Her maid discovered her at this when she came to dress her for dinner. Glancing uneasily at her mistress, she asked, "Did you speak to Mr. Simpford, miss?"

"I did," said Clara, not looking up from her letter.

Mary hesitated, then remarked, "He's a good man. Handsome, too. He didn't say anything to distress you, did he?"

"Oh, no. He only came to take leave. He returns tomorrow to Southam."

Mary gasped. "But—if he goes away—Miss! What will you do? That Picton is the very devil—you can't run away with him! And poor Mr. Noyce—he can't fight him!"

Clara paused in her writing to blink away the sting in her eyes once more. "No, he cannot. But Lawrie does not wish to fight Mr. Picton, so I am writing to Lord Boltwood to see if he will help me."

"But he's all show, miss—he doesn't even fence," said Mary disdainfully.

Huffing a pitiful laugh, Clara answered, "Precisely. Nevertheless, he may be able to help me, without obliging me to marry him."

Mary regarded her shyly for a moment before saying, "But Mr. Simpford—don't he wish to marry you? He is so very kind and—and handsome."

"Gracious, Mary!" said Clara, absorbing herself again in her writing to hide her heartache. "I declare I am sick of Mr. Simpford."

Mary hesitated, but said in a rush, "But if you could only explain it all to him, miss, I'm sure he—"

"I made something of an attempt, Mary, and have been given to understand that I had better address a stone wall. His kindness is no longer available to me." She passed a hand over her eyes and stood, folding the missive up and searching for a sealing wafer in the desk. Affixing it quickly, she held it out to Mary. "There. Please take this directly to Lord Boltwood. Tell him it is an urgent message from me. Wait for his answer. Thank you, Mary."

The maid took it gingerly, darting a distressed look at her mistress's reddened eyes before tucking it into her apron pocket. She curtsied, pausing another moment, as though waiting to discover it was all a mistake, but Clara did not move to take back the note, and she was obliged to carry out her orders.

After she had gone, Clara went to the window, watching the maid as she hurried across the street in the direction of Lord Boltwood's lodging. Her heart sank with every one of Mary's steps. She had done it. She had sealed her fate and could only await the issue. Pressing her forehead against the cold windowpane, she closed her eyes, a vision of Lawrie's forbidding countenance rising up before her. It was all too horrible.

Chapter 23

AFTER GOING THE rounds of leave-taking, Lawrie went to his club with Mr. Hiddeston to have a celebratory dinner and last rubber of piquet. But he was restless, and when Hiddeston bade him goodbye, Lawrie remained in his chair by the fire, broodingly sipping at his port.

Clara's declaration had shocked him, both its vaunted sincerity and its cruelty. He would never forgive her for that leap of his heart when she claimed she valued his friendship above all else. It had taken all the control at his command to stride away from the room, away from the house, and out of her life. She was using him ill again, and whatever her object, he could be certain it was only for her own selfish purposes. It was more likely that she desired simply to bring him round her thumb again, and so he had responded accordingly—with firm and cool resolve.

She had either become even more adept at play-acting, or the hurt in her countenance at his rejection had been real. But in either case, he could not yield. If she was pretending, she was best served, and if she had truly been hurt at his words, it was about time she experienced the pain she so carelessly inflicted upon others. Only then might she learn.

But Lawrie did not want her to learn, for then he would subject himself to the agony of hope that she would at last be his. He had given her up, and he must be firm—he deserved better. She was too much like her father, who cared nothing for anyone but what they could give him, and had never changed—neither would she.

Despite his resolution, however, the misery in her blue eyes haunted him, and he could not forget the total dejection of her demeanor as he had seen himself out. His heart told him she was sincere, that she had learnt her lesson and would endeavor to slough off her cynical and destructive attitudes. As he watched the flames flicker on the hearth, he considered that her recklessness in taking his place at the duel had not been self-serving at all. She had risked death to save his own life, and must not that count for something?

But then he recollected her obstinate refusal to leave off Picton's society—even being so foolish as to meet him clandestinely—and he went round and round, late into the night, until he wanted to knock a hole in the nearest wall. Luckily for the venerable walls of the club—and for his own fists—a gentleman came up in the early hours of the morning and distracted him by dropping into the chair opposite with a great sigh. It was Mr. Frant.

"Guess we both lost the race, eh, Simpford?" he said, gazing forlornly at the fire.

Lawrie frowned at him. "What do you mean?"

"Miss Mantell. Gone off with Boltwood. Devil of a fellow, always looks like the Corsair or something, don't you think? Dashed ridiculous. Would rather like to strangle that Lord Byron."

"What do you mean she's gone off with him? How do you know?"

Frant sighed. "His man boasted of it to my man at the bootmaker's. Said they was to elope tonight, and must cancel some orders. Have to travel light and cheaply, I expect. Couldn't afford more than a pair of horses, with his debts."

"How can you be sure your man isn't mistaken? Do you trust him?"

Frant nodded gloomily. "Been with me for years—trust him with my life! He shaves me, don't you know! Boltwood's man is keen for gossip, and struts like a peacock, always puffing off his master's consequence. His tale is true, no doubt. Be in Gretna by the end of the week."

"Nonsense!" said Lawrie, putting down his empty glass with a click as he tried to make sense of this startling information. "She's of age—no need to go to Gretna!"

"Doesn't matter where they go, she's made her choice." He sighed again. "Devilish pretty girl—and what spirit! Would've followed her to the moon and back, if she'd had me. But it's always the same. Young ladies swoon over those Corsair types. Abominable fellows! Ought to go off and be pirates and let us have some of the pretty ones to ourselves."

Lawrie paid little heed to this diatribe. Clara had been moody of late, and had certainly been distressed this afternoon. Could she have been contemplating an elopement? But that was nonsensical, for she was dead set against marriage—especially to Boltwood.

"You're sure he didn't say Picton?" he asked, though it all must be a pack of nonsense.

Frant gazed at him, non-plussed. "Of course it ain't Picton. Said it was Boltwood, didn't I? Picton don't look like the Corsair—at least, he's got the darker coloring, but he don't wear those ridiculous clothes, and his hair looking like a wind swept through it, and he don't brood all the time. Dashed ridiculous. But Picton ain't Boltwood, and it was Boltwood's man at the bootmaker's. I tell you, he would have blubbered if it was Picton eloping with Miss Mantell."

He seemed certain, to be sure, but Lawrie was at a loss to believe it. Could this be why Clara had been so set on apologizing to him today, and not because he was quitting Bath? To be sure, he had intended to stay in London as long as it took to rid himself of his disappointment and delusion, but she did not know that. Indeed, now that he considered it, she had never before actually sought him out to beg forgiveness, but had depended on time to soften him and circumstance to bring them together.

But if she had determined on so drastic and ruinous a step—had planned to elope—she might feel the urgency to unburden herself before departing. She would have known he would deprecate such a course—indeed, she herself would deprecate it. An elopement was not only scandalous, but embodied precisely what Clara had detested and avoided her entire adult life: enforced subjection to a man.

And yet, if Frant was to be believed, she had eloped. What could she have been thinking? Had she come under the delusion that to effect a change she must make restitution to at least one of the men she had toyed with so carelessly? He would not believe that. Clara was too independent and spirited to make such a concession. He found it easier to believe that she found playing games a dead bore and meant to plague Boltwood for the rest of his life by agreeing to elope with him. Of course, if that was the case, he felt no scruple in allowing her to go her reckless way, for he had done with trying to save her from self-destruction.

But what had she said—that Picton had threatened her? Was it possible that Picton had forced her somehow to this extremity? He could not guess how Picton could make her elope with Boltwood, though he knew she had fended Picton off at gunpoint on at least one occasion. He also had a vague recollection of him saying that she had pulled a sword on him, but when that could have occurred, he could not tell, for to his knowledge, Picton had been on his sickbed—until today. Clara had said he had tricked her into this morning's meeting and that he was as despicable as Lawrie had claimed him to be. Could he have frightened her so that she believed an elopement necessary? And because Lawrie had renounced her, because he had refused even to listen to her this afternoon, she had determined to go with Boltwood.

If such was the case, Lawrie felt a veritable monster for both wronging her and abandoning her in her hour of need. But what could he do? Increasingly agitated by uncertainty, he got up to pace as Frant continued to gaze forlornly into the fire and remark on the injustices of love and the incomprehensible attractions of Corsairs. Clara had not taken kindly to his interference in the past, though she had apologized sincerely for raking him down. His considerable fear for his heart warned against taking too strong an interest in Clara's affairs, and tried to reason that if she had eloped, for whatever reason, it was only what she deserved. But then her miserable countenance swam before his mind's view and he could not believe it at all reasonable to leave anyone to such an awful penance, if it could be stopped. And if Picton had threatened her, a rescue may only bring her back into his power. He simply did not have enough information to set a course of action.

Resolving to amend this deficiency, Lawrie stood, excusing

himself from his brooding companion, who waved him distract-
edly away. Walking swiftly through the lamplit streets, he closed the
distance between Gay Street and Laura Place in a remarkably short
time, but then stopped short. Everything seemed to be peaceful and
quiet, with the only light burning in the kitchen belowstairs. He
wondered whether it would be wise to rouse the whole house before
he could find out what really had occurred and what, if anything,
could be done. At last, he determined to try the area door, and going
down the steps, he tapped gently on it. He was rewarded with an
immediate scraping of a chair and the turning of the bolt. The door
opened, and Mary, the maid, peeped out.

"Oh, Mr. Simpford!" she cried, her tone relieved. "I thought you
was that odious Lord Boltwood, and I was so frightened!"

She let him in and he asked, "Why are you up? Where is your
mistress?"

"Oh, sir! She's let him carry her off, and I was to wait up, in case
he brings her back."

Lawrie blinked at her, stupefied, and she hastened to clarify. "It is
the most tragic thing! She's gone off with that awful Mr. Picton, until
his lordship can catch them, and knock Mr. Picton on the head and
save Miss Mantell. He says as he will bring her back, but Miss told me
it may be very late and that I shouldn't worry, but I do, sir, I do! She
hadn't rather his lordship save her, though he's ever so much better
than that odious Mr. Picton, so's she reckoned she might as well go
with his lordship, as you wouldn't help her."

Lawrie's stomach clenched as though he had received a gut-punch.
It seemed Frant's tale was true, though somewhat garbled.

"Did Miss Mantell agree to go with Mr. Picton at first? Do
you know?"

"Yes, sir, though she cried and cried over it! He threatened her so's she would marry him, for she thinks him a devil, she does! After he tried to compromise her, and then he pulled his gun on her—"

"He pulled a gun?"

"But Miss only slashed him with her foil and made him go away. She's that brave, sir!"

Lawrie pursed his lips, recognizing that he had grossly misjudged Clara's interactions with Picton. "So she went with Picton to save her reputation?"

"No, sir, for that horrid Mr. Picton was a-going to tell the whole world about her shooting him in the duel, and said you'd both be ruined!"

"We both—then he did know it was her!"

"He said her eyes gave her away, sir, and she said she couldn't never live with herself if you was hurt one more time on her account."

"Good God, what have I done?" murmured Lawrie, sinking onto the bench by the kitchen table.

Mary gazed pleadingly at him, a tear dribbling down her cheek. "Oh, why did you give her up, sir? It's not my place, but I think she loved you the best of all, for she never tried to save Lord Boltwood's life."

Lawrie was stricken, for he suddenly comprehended it was true, and his own conscience had tried to tell him so. But Clara had made such a muddle of everything—if she hadn't been so provokingly foolish about Picton and Boltwood, and made him so furious about the duel, he might have been more perceptive of her trouble, and how differently this all would have turned out!

"Tell me quickly, Mary!" he said, jumping up and taking the maid by the shoulders. "Where was Boltwood to intercept them?"

"I don't rightly know, sir—only I took a letter to his lordship and he sent back a reply. It might be in her room."

"Take me up instantly!"

She did so, taking the back stairs from the kitchens. They went into Clara's bedroom and found it silent and empty, the moonlight shining through the break in the curtains to show the bed made and unused.

Lawrie took the maid's candle and went over to the writing desk, searching about the papers there, but found nothing. Then he held the candle high, shining the light about the room. By the fireplace there was a crumpled note that had got wedged beside the fender. Going to pick it up, he returned to the desk and smoothed it out. He sank onto the stool as he read.

> *Dearest Lawrie,*
>
> *Forgive me for calling you so, for I know you do not think of me anymore, and it is all my doing. I have been a greater fool than anyone alive, and now I must reap the consequences. You were right, every whit, and I can only mourn that I was too headstrong to heed you.*
>
> *My outrageous conduct has, as you prophesied, caught up with me. Picton has threatened me with something too terrible to think of, unless I elope with him. I cannot say more, but be assured that there is nothing I might do to keep him from carrying out his threat but comply with his demands—at least at first. I have reason to hope that I might be able to convince him to give me up, but even the outcome of this is not certain. Thus, I have resigned myself to my doom.*

You, my dear friend, if you will allow me to use such a term, may be forgiven a very just sense of triumph in this, for you did all you could to prevent my self-destruction. I will forever regret the arrogance and obstinacy which caused me to disregard your warnings. I know I have fatigued you with my apologies, but I beg your forbearance once more, for I have so little time before I must face my fate, and you must allow me to speak to you with what means I have.

I have known for many months now that you loved me, Lawrie. It pleased me, but I did not yet realize just how necessary your love was to my existence. I am such a selfish creature that I thought only of my own consequence, and of the delight of having another beau on my string. But you have been the best of them, always, and I knew it. That is why I never wanted to lead you on—though I even failed in that, for my liveliness makes me incautious, as you well know. But I knew you were too good for me, for I am abominable, and I did not wish to break your heart. That I managed to do just that will ever haunt me. But it was all inexcusable, and I shudder to think what I put you through.

I could place blame on my upbringing, my parentage, or my inexperience, but that would be cowardly. I nurtured my cynicism and selfishly turned everyone I could to good use— including you, my dear friend. I have willfully discarded your advice given in good faith, repaid your kindness with fickleness, and even toyed with your affections. I should not expect anything more from you but disdain. I am a horrid baggage, but I have seen changes in Francis, and my mother has changed—I hope to prove, even after this too degrading step, that it is not too late for me. I promise I will try, for there is nothing I want more in the world than to be the warm and open woman you wished and believed me to be, even if it cannot be for you.

I am sorry to have gone without a proper farewell, but I have sped my own destruction and may only say I am
Yours always,
Clara

Upon completion of this perusal, Lawrie simply sat gazing at the page, a prey to too wide a variety of sensations to do anything else. He was horrified at her predicament and ashamed that he did feel a bit of triumph over it. But what most stupefied him was the conviction that she did, at last, love him. She wished to please him, to be the woman he had known she could be. She had, at last, changed—or at least begun a transformation, just as Mrs. Noyce had begun. But it was only too late, if Picton had got away with her.

The thought awakened a sensation of activity and he stood, pacing restlessly about the room as Mary watched him in hopeful suspense. If he had only listened to Clara, had simply given her a chance to explain, she might have confided in him, and he might have saved her the horror of her present circumstances. He would have thought of some way to challenge Picton's assertions, or called him out again to prove his courage, or simply lived with the ignominy—anything would be better than Clara sacrificing herself to the rapacity of a rake.

But now she was in Picton's power, or if her plan succeeded, in that of Lord Boltwood, whose affectations of the Corsair were, Lawrie suspected, only a mask for darker motives. When they were at Oxford,

Boltwood had been quite as rapacious as Picton, though of late he had seemed far more tame. However, Lawrie did not trust that his lordship had changed enough in essentials to be trusted to care for Clara. Once either he or Picton had Clara's fortune safe, there was no telling what he would do. Her personal charms would stand her in good stead, certainly, and her fiery spirit would keep him from utterly crushing her, but once he had run through her fortune he would quickly lose interest and would have no scruple in demeaning her with low company and illicit connections.

It *was* only her just deserts, Lawrie couldn't help but think, but it did not follow that he would wish her to suffer so. If she truly did love him—and he was willing now to believe she did—he would fight to have her for his own. His only reservation, after all, had been her selfish disdain for others, but he trusted she could mend her ways, for she sincerely wished to try. He had seen the steps Mrs. Noyce had taken in the preceding months under Mr. Noyce's loving care—Lawrie could and did care for Clara that way, and she could at last let go her cynical reserve and allow herself to love and care and embrace a life of conjugal felicity like her brother Geoffrey.

He suddenly returned to the desk, rifling through the papers again and startling Mary, who waited intently while wringing her hands before her.

"Forgive me, Mary, but I must discover where they have gone. Have you any clue? Did she say anything of Lord Boltwood's answer?"

"She was that upset over everything that she never did say, sir. But that horrid Picton said as how he needed a bishop's license, and that he knew the Bishop of Gloucester."

"Good girl! Then they are on their way north. But you do not know where Lord Boltwood was to intercept them?"

"No, I'm sorry, sir."

"No matter. I have enough information to give chase." Patting her comfortingly on the shoulder, he said, "Stay up if you like, but I'd go to bed if I were you. And don't worry your master and mistress with this tonight. If I am not back with Clara by breakfast time, you may tell Mr. Noyce that I have gone after them and then abide by his instructions."

"Oh, thank you, sir!" She gazed worshipfully up at him. "I know you'll bring her back, sir!"

He looked grim. "I must, or I will never forgive myself."

Chapter 24

ICTON HAD SECURED four good horses for their elopement, despite the lateness of the hour, and their passage northward was swift. Clara had been anxious lest Picton attempt to accost her in the coach, and had brought her loaded pistol to fend him off, if need be, but he did not appear to be in an amorous mood. His jaw was tight and his fists clenched as he gazed out the window until they had cleared the outskirts of Bath, and then, with a roguish wink at her, he had tipped his hat down over his eyes and gone to sleep in his corner of the coach.

Clara could not sleep, even had she wished it. She gazed unseeing out the window of the coach, Lawrie's unforgiving countenance ever before her mind's eye, and a monstrous void in her chest. Their last interview replayed over and over in her mind, but she had become numb to it. Indeed, she had banished all her emotion down deep into a closed-off place in her soul as soon as she had sent off her plea for assistance to Lord Boltwood.

His response had been swift and loquacious, full of romantic hints and passionate proclamations, which she rapidly dismissed. At the end of the epistle he had given what she had desired—a promise to intervene and bring her to safety.

"Await my arrival during the second stage of your journey, my love, but do not faint. Blood may be spilt, but if it is mine, your liberty shall be well worth the sacrifice."

Clara was in no fear of fainting at the sight of Boltwood's blood—or of Picton's, for that matter—but she should be rather annoyed if Boltwood got himself killed while attempting to free her from Picton's grasp. She had enough on her conscience without adding his death to it.

He had not, among his protestations of violent love, stipulated a reward for his gallantry, for which she was both relieved and wary. She had made it plain that Picton's hold over her was such that she must seem entirely innocent in the breakup of his plan, and Boltwood assured her in his note that in this and in all other concerns she could rely upon him completely. She suspected this to mean he expected to figure in her concerns after today, but she did not allow herself to dwell on this point. Sufficient to the moment for the evil thereof had, of necessity, become her motto.

At all events, his romantic sensibilities had, as she had expected they would, been excessively inspired by the project, and she trusted the outcome would be spectacular. Whether it would be efficacious would remain to be seen, and she reflected that he could hardly expect the magnitude of her obligation to him to be greater than the success of his venture. Casting a furtive glance at her companion, however, she hoped that it would be a success. Picton was silent and still next to her, the lines of dissipation on his face more defined in slumber.

He seemed sinister even now, his jaw set in implacable firmness, and she shivered.

Abruptly, Clara felt the fatigue of the past twenty hours, and her impassivity began to weaken. Inevitably, her thoughts turned again to Lawrie and regret bubbled up from its hiding place in her soul. If only she had not pushed him once to often, and too far, she might not be in this predicament. He might even have come again to care for her, and wish to marry her, and though she would have required time to earn his forgiveness and esteem, she would gladly have undertaken any hardship only to be worthy of his smile.

She sighed, tears welling up and coursing down her cheeks—as they would not earlier in the day—at these visions of a future now impossible. As the towns and villages passed by outside under the full moon, she wept silently and bitterly for what would never be, all from her selfish obstinacy. She wept for what seemed an age, until the slowing of the coach outside Dunkirk made her swallow her sorrow, and she quickly wiped her cheeks before Picton could perceive her distress. She had no wish to add to his triumph.

He did not stir, however, during this first stop, and when the chaise once again started forward, Clara breathed a little sigh of relief. They were on the second stage of their journey, and her rescue was near at hand. To her mind it could not come a moment too soon.

It was nearly an hour, however, before a shot rang out, causing the horses to whinny as the post boys pulled them to a stop. Another shot was fired, along with a shout of "Stand and deliver!" There was general confusion at the front of the coach as the horses stamped and shuffled and the post boys cried out—to their assailants to hold their pops and to the occupants of the coach that it was the Collectors, and rum padders at that.

An oath erupted from Picton, who had jerked awake and was now reaching into the pocket of his greatcoat as he peered through the window into the shifting moonlit darkness. Withdrawing a pistol, he said shortly to Clara, "Stay here," and thrust open the door, leaping from the carriage. More shots were fired, among them Picton's, as Clara could see through his window, which elicited a cry from one of their shadowy assailants. Clara was certain he had hit his man and knew a pang of dismay, for the highwayman had surely been hired by Boltwood, and she wondered if he had been fully apprised of the style of his intended victim.

But then a figure loomed up behind Picton, throwing an arm about his throat and pressing the muzzle of a gun to his head. Clara moved closer to the window and saw that it was, indeed, Boltwood who held him immobile.

In sudden anxiety, she let down the glass. "Do not kill him! I demand that you do not hurt him!"

But Boltwood only smiled and winked at her before saying amiably to his captive, "It was good of you to go to all this trouble, Picton. Your preparations must have been considerable, and they are much appreciated. I shall be taking Miss Mantell from here."

Picton growled something, but Boltwood raised his pistol and struck it hard against Picton's head, letting him slump to the ground.

"Good heaven, Boltwood!" cried Clara, gazing chagrined at her erstwhile captor's still form. "That was rather crude, was it not?"

He chuckled, waving his henchmen over to him as he said negligently, all trace of the Corsair gone from his air, "It did the job, I believe, my love. Though I regret, for the sake of your sensibilities, that I was obliged to hurt him. He shall not bother you again, however."

Clara was not so sanguine. She was diverted from her troubled thoughts, however, by the henchmen throwing baggage into the road beside him.

"What are you doing?" she inquired sharply, opening the door and stepping down from the coach. "Boltwood, what is the meaning of this?"

His lordship took her hand, bringing it to his lips with a smirk. "My darling girl, I did not go to all this trouble only to have Picton follow us and perhaps take you back again. We will take the carriage to prevent that, and he will be wanting his trunks when he awakes. Horsley is not far, and he will be able to hire another conveyance from there."

She could only be satisfied, and admit to a certain degree of admiration for this plan, though it pained her. His exultant looks as he handed her back into the carriage gave her to understand that he would expect a grand recompense, which she would be hard-pressed to avoid. But she was no longer at *point non plus* with Picton, and that alone gave her courage to face the coming ordeal with fortitude.

He at last concluded his arrangements and entered the coach, disposing himself comfortably in Picton's seat. The post boys set the horses to and it was a moment before it dawned upon Clara that they continued to travel northward.

"Why are we not turned around, my lord?" she inquired somewhat shrilly.

He smiled in a lazy way that reminded Clara disquietingly of Picton. "We must continue to Horsley, for the horses are too spent to return to Dunkirk."

Clara nodded in some relief, sitting back again. Boltwood again took her hand and kissed it, and she worried for an instant that he would try to make love to her in the chaise, but he dropped her hand again, turning to gaze out the window. They arrived shortly at Horsley and the change of horses was effected, and their journey resumed. Clara's eyes drooped, and she succumbed to sleep.

She awoke to morning sunlight slanting into her eyes and sat up, looking about herself in momentary confusion. At the sight of Boltwood dozing beside her, her recollection returned and, pulling out her pocket watch, she saw with alarm that it was gone nine o'clock. She was making rapid calculations in her head as to where they ought to be when Boltwood stirred, blinking at her before looking out the window.

"Ah! Nearly there," he said cheerily. "We were forced on a detour while you slept—some sort of obstacle in the road, I believe—but only a few more stops."

Clara was assailed by distrust, but when they drove into a small town a very few minutes afterward, that she thought she recognized as one of the towns she and Picton had passed through during the night, she began to feel more at ease.

As they drew into the yard of The Crown, Boltwood said with utmost solicitude "You will like to go into the inn to refresh yourself, my love. If you are not famished, I own myself to be, so I will bespeak a private parlor and some breakfast. Then we will be on our way."

With an almost buoyant air, Boltwood handed her down from the carriage and led her into the inn, the private parlor being quickly procured and prepared for their use. As he guided her to a chair by the fire to await breakfast, he bent close to her ear to whisper, "You will understand that it behooves us to take the guise of a married couple, so that your reputation remains unquestioned."

With a startled breath, Clara realized this was too awkwardly true, and was obliged to agree, though it gave her a terrible distaste.

She had perhaps foolishly continued to cherish the hope that she could avoid marriage to him, but that hope was steadily receding. An elopement and overnight stay in the company of a gentleman must end in marriage or disgrace. She must resign herself to the inevitable.

But as the servants laid the covers and brought in the food, Clara became increasingly agitated. Boltwood's affectations of the brooding suitor had all but vanished, and she suspected he was far more expert in the game than he had led her to believe. His behavior thus far, thank heaven, had been all that was gentlemanly and proper, but she did not trust him any more than she had Picton. Even now, the secret smile about his lips spoke of his triumph, and Clara began to feel the reality of a life in his power. Only necessity motivated his solicitude now. How much of care would he spare her once he had her fortune in his grasp?

The servants finished their work and were dismissed, and closing the door after them, Lord Boltwood turned a disquieting smile on her.

"Now, my love," he said, coming across the room to her. Clara stiffened, her hand going to the pocket with her pistol—but he merely held her chair, motioning her to sit. "Eat—you must keep up your strength."

She sat, watching him warily as he assumed his own chair at the other end of the table. He smiled and reached for the wine to fill his glass, then fell to eating. Her gaze went to the food before her, and she thought at first she could not eat a morsel, her nerves were so alive. But the basket of rolls emitted so delicious a smell that she thought she could try just one, and then she thought that some kidneys and bacon would not go amiss, for really, she would faint without some sort of sustenance. She was soon eating steadily, and began to think more clearly.

There was no need of marriage to Lord Boltwood. She would offer him a substantial pecuniary reward, but if he demanded more, it was not necessary that she sacrifice herself to his whims for a lifetime. Even should he threaten to publish the events of the night, she could easily convince him that it would be the worse for him. No one of consequence had, as yet, seen them together, and Clara would make the remainder of the journey on her own. Even should word leak out, there was no one to corroborate it, and she would merely be looked on askance and ostracized by some, but after the scandal had died down, she could live her life as a spinster, retired and quiet.

Lawrie's reputation was still a problem, but she clung to the hope that Picton would not hold her accountable for the failure of the elopement. With Lawrie gone to London and her family removing back to Southam, perhaps his threat would be moot. She could not consider the alternative until her present circumstances had altered.

She looked up from her plate to find Boltwood gazing at her with smoldering eyes, and she stilled, her heart thumping distressfully. He took another sip of wine and stood, moving around the table toward her, the intent she had feared earlier plain in his eyes.

Clara jumped up. "I thank you for your trouble, my lord, but I believe we must part ways."

"I must disagree, my love." He pushed away the chair that she had placed between them. "Our ways are destined never to part again."

Clara moved backward, away from the table. "I will pay you, handsomely. You may have as much of my fortune as you wish."

He chuckled. "Oh, I intend to have it all, and all of you as well. You are so charming an heiress, you know."

"Do not be hasty, sir," she said, as he backed her into the corner. "I will not marry you—I cannot. You have done me a great service, but recollect, I never promised a thing."

He shrugged, still advancing toward her. "It does not need a promise, for now you *must* marry me."

"Nonsense. No one knows of my flight, and Picton will shoot you if you reveal his part in this. What else is there to tell?"

"Nothing but the glad tidings of our marriage," he said, placing both hands on either wall behind her, caging her in. "You will not leave here without becoming mine—whether by choice or by force, my love. I need not tell you I had rather take you by choice. I am not so crude as Picton."

He leaned in for a kiss, but found the cold barrel of her pistol pushing into his gut.

Clara's cool smile was more of a grimace. "I have had enough of your games, sir, and am convinced I will be better off without you. Now we will part."

"I wondered when you would remember that pistol, my love," he said conversationally. "I did myself the honor of inspecting it while you were sleeping, and thought to remove the ball and powder. It will not be giving either of us any trouble."

Clara's heart thudded, her eyes searching his. "You lie."

"Pull the trigger and see if I do, my love."

She hesitated then, with a growl, did as he suggested. There was a loud click as the hammer struck, but no report.

"You see? I am up to all your tricks." He bent to kiss her neck. "What is yours is now mine, and I make it my business to know my property."

Shoving him hard, she ducked beneath his arms, running for the door, but he caught her, dragging her back into his arms. "But where are you going, my love? I will have my due, now or later, you know. And we are so comfortable here—it will make the remaining journey that much more enjoyable if we are more familiar with one another."

With that, he bent swiftly to kiss her, but she swung her pistol at him and twisted away, enraged and frightened.

"I would rather walk to Bath!" she cried, reaching the door and twisting the handle. But it did not turn. The door had been locked.

He laughed and she turned to see the key held up in his fingers. "I am more experienced than you imagine, my love. There is no use in trying to escape me. The manservant is in my pay, and will see to it we are not disturbed. Now, come here—"

He reached for her again and she swung the pistol at his head, but he dodged it, catching hold of her wrist. Twisting it cruelly, he ignored her cry of pain as she dropped the gun and he drew her inexorably back toward him.

"You cannot escape me, Clara. Indeed, there is no need. Recollect, this was your idea."

"I was driven to it! I never wished to marry either of you!"

He shook his head sorrowfully, "Indeed, I know it too well. Before you begged me to help you, I had almost given up my pursuit. Between Picton and Simpford, I was simply outshone. I had considered other avenues to your fortune, but it was impossible to take you by force while you were so well-guarded. Imagine my surprise and delight at receiving your invitation to rescue you from a midnight elopement! I could hardly say no. What a honeyfall! Your beautiful person, your excellent fortune, all mine, and right under Picton's nose. I could not have wished for a better issue. You must allow me to thank you properly."

"Do not dare!" she cried as he tried again to kiss her, but she got an arm free and raked her nails across his cheek.

He let go of her with a bellow, his hand going up to cover the red welts that appeared. He felt wetness and, pulling his hand away, gazed in furious indignation at the blood there.

"You doxy!" He took an angry step toward her, and she leapt away, coming up against the table.

A knock on the door stopped him, and with a warning glance at Clara, he reached quickly into his pocket for his handkerchief. He pressed it against his cheek as the door opened and the waiter appeared to tell him the carriage was ready. In a moderate tone, Boltwood thanked him and the man went out, with a parting glance of sly curiosity between the two occupants of the room.

Boltwood turned to Clara, dabbing at his cheek with the handkerchief. "Well, my love, you have wasted an opportunity of pleasing me. But now we have another two-hour's ride to see how you will make restitution."

"Two hours—" Clara's heart nearly stopped. "Where are we? Where are you taking me?"

He smiled, a dark and sinister look. "We are halfway to Oxford, my love. There is a clergyman there who, for a price, will marry us without banns. You see, as a gentleman, I simply could not allow you to walk to Bath."

She gasped, gaping at her own stupidity. Of course he had not planned to return to Bath. He would not simply carry her back to her family like an honorable man! He was a rake and a scoundrel, and would take the opportunity he had been seeking all along to compromise her reputation and force her to marry him.

"You were never a gentleman, my lord!" she ground out, furious at her helplessness, her foolishness, and his deceit.

"Very true." He chuckled, dabbing at the scratches on his face.

"Perhaps that is why I look forward to the remainder of our journey with great anticipation. But first, I must take care of this handiwork of yours. Do not despair while you are alone, my love, for you may be secure in the knowledge that I will come back for you."

With a look that boded ill for Clara's peace, he quit the room, and she heard the unmistakable sound of a key grating in the lock.

Chapter 25

WITH A HOWL of frustration, Clara ran to the door and tried the knob, but it would not turn. She pounded on the door, but a violent knocking came back at her, along with the manservant's harsh whisper, "Quiet, you, or I'll tell 'em all you're mad, and they'll clap you up in Bedlam!"

Clara backed away from the door and stumbled over something on the floor. She bent and picked up her pistol, gazing at it in annoyance. She had been so sure of herself with that pistol, thinking to make quick work of Boltwood, but he had neatly tricked her. It was just as Lawrie had warned her, but she had not believed him. For all she had thought herself to be up to the knocker, she was still only a green country girl.

Thrusting the gun into her pocket, she ran to the window, but her captor was immediately outside, seeing to the preparations of the carriage. She rushed about the room, trying doors to see if any offered an escape. The doors out were all locked, and the cupboards were full and did not offer any effectual hiding place. She thought of pushing the table against the main door, but it was too heavy, and one of the other doors likely would be used to allow Boltwood to enter.

As she turned this way and that, rising panic threatened to consume her. She was entirely out of her element. She had been used to calling the trumps, delineating the rules, and setting the stakes, but she had chosen the wrong partners, and this game had become a much more dangerous affair than she had ever intended. She had made the mistake of judging all rakes by those in her home, but her confidence had been disastrously misplaced.

It was painfully obvious to her now that both Picton and Boltwood did not play by the rules that held Francis, and even her father, in check. While Picton and Boltwood had been constrained by Society, she had been entirely safe with her flirting and flaunting, but once they were outside those constraints, she was without control, and they could do anything to her. She wished she had realized this sooner, for a man who did not trouble himself with keeping the line in a country inn could not be relied upon to keep the line in marriage, and the girl who got herself tied to such a man might as well consign her safety to the devil.

She hurried to the window once more, to see Boltwood on the point of entering the inn. Desperately, she tried the latch and found that it opened, but the hinge was tight and she heard the key scraping in the lock before she had pushed the window half open. Her heart in her throat, she cast about for something to defend herself with, and as the door opened, she ran to the fireplace and seized the poker.

"Well, my love, all is ready," said Boltwood, closing the door and coming toward her with a patronizing smile. "Now do not raise a fuss. You know you are beaten. I promise I shall be gentle with you if you come quietly."

"Never," she said, brandishing the poker in her fencer's stance.

He narrowed his eyes, moving carefully around the table as Clara edged the opposite way. She did not wish to be herded to the door, so she backed instead toward the partially open window.

Boltwood put out his hands in a placating gesture. "Come, my love, none of this will do a bit of good. I shall only be forced to knock you on the head, and then I shall have to claim you swooned as I carry you senseless to the coach. Do not force me to such an exigency—it was no part of my program to injure one hair of your beautiful head."

"Only to injure my sensibilities? And my pride and dignity for the remainder of my days?" She punctuated her words with jabs of the poker. "I had rather fight for my freedom than give in to such a grim future."

He lunged at her suddenly, hands extended to grasp the poker, but with both hands on the handle, she parried his arms and flicked the edge of the poker at his ear. He cried out, cupping his ear, an angry glitter coming into his eyes. He lunged again and she retreated, coming against the partially open window and then lunging in tierce to make him stumble off-balance. Quick as a flash, she reversed her wrist and plunged forward again, striking him hard in the ribs.

He fell, clutching his side as his breaths wheezed from him. She did not hesitate, did not allow herself to think of what she must do next, but swung the poker against his head. It struck his temple just above the claw marks on his cheek—his eyes rolled back, his body slumped, and he went still.

Not wasting a moment, Clara swept up her hat, gloves, and reticule and rushed to the window. Pushing the glass outward, she squeezed herself through, hitching her skirts up to an unseemly height as she thrust first one leg and then her torso through. She heard a scuffle in the room and she pulled her other leg out of the window with the wrench of tearing fabric, falling to the ground as cries of alarm rang out inside.

Staggering to her feet, she took off at a run, ignoring the shouts and stares of the scattered persons in the innyard. She dashed across the main road and plunged into a side street, taking two more turns before slowing to a walk so as not to draw attention. Her chest heaved—other than her fencing lessons, she had not done more strenuous exercise than walking for the past two months. But it was well enough. She had got this far.

Ducking into an alley, she stopped to take stock of herself. Her gown had torn on the window frame, but her pelisse was in good repair, and covered the rent. She patted her hair into place and put on her hat and gloves so as not to draw undue notice. Quickly counting the coins in her reticule, she determined with relief that she should have enough to get home—if she was indeed two hours from Oxford—and must only find the means to do so.

How she was to do this was next to exercise her mind. The stages ran at odd hours, and if there was not one leaving immediately, it would have to be a horse—though she had never hired a horse before, having had a servant or an escort to do it for her. Being familiar with the charges, however, she did not think it would be difficult to make the transaction, and only worried how her request would be received. If her quality were doubted, she might be fobbed off, or might even be detained while some officious person tried to determine who ought to have the charge of her. It was entirely unjust, for a man of any station could go about hiring horses wherever he liked, and she had never heard of a man being questioned in doing so. But then again, she had never heard of a man being abducted and forced to marry.

She could not very well return to the inn where Boltwood lay senseless, so she resolved to find another posting house or inn or even a stable. Hurrying down the alley, she came out on a busy street. A couple of carts rolled past and several persons on foot walked here and there, women with shopping baskets and men swinging canes. Working class persons carried boxes with fowl inside, bags that reeked of onions, or bundles of sticks for kindling. Clara was somewhat overwhelmed being alone in such a place, and she began to imagine all sorts of evil that could be done to her.

As she wended her way down the street, the thought occurred that the simplest course would be to find a place to hide and wait for Lord Boltwood to tire of seeking for her, but she dismissed this idea out of hand. He would set up a hue and cry for her, and it would only be a matter of time, in this busy place, before she was recognized and given up to him. She could bribe as well as he, but she was not in the habit of it, and did not know how much would buy her safety, or how to discern a trustworthy person from one who would betray her for more money from her pursuer.

She came to a broad alley filled with market stalls, and wound among the housewives and servants, their baskets jostling her as she passed. A girl offered to sell her some matches, which she declined, but turning back, gave her a penny, and the girl's answering smile gave her courage.

"Pardon me," she asked the girl, "but could you tell me what this place is?"

The little girl seemed concerned at her stupidity but said, "Faring-don, miss."

Clara smiled in thanks. "And where is the next town where the stage stops?"

The little girl shrugged, looking dubious, but said, "Great Coxwell is that way." The girl pointed down the street. "Me sister lives there, but she don't take the stage."

Somewhat disappointed, Clara nevertheless thanked her, setting off in the direction of Great Coxwell. She had not got ten paces, however, when a disturbance at the far end of the market turned her blood to ice, and she ducked into a baker's shop, pressing herself against the inside wall. She stood there, heart pounding, half-hidden near the big front window for several moments, but no Lord Boltwood came into sight, and her heart gradually became comfortable once more in her breast.

"Can I help you, miss?" came a girl's voice by the counter.

Clara whirled, realizing she must present a very odd appearance, but the shop girl who confronted her looked more curious than irritated, and was young, only fifteen or sixteen. Clara glanced quickly around the shop and found that the only other customer was a bent old woman who seemed entirely absorbed by the choice of an array of breads in baskets in the corner.

Clara stepped quietly up to the counter. "Pardon me, but I must find a posting inn. Is there another besides The Crown?"

"Why, no, miss," replied the girl, her eyes wide. "There's only The Crown for hiring a carriage, though there's The Red Hen if it's a room you be wanting."

Clara shook her head. "How far is the next town where the stage stops?"

The girl looked bewildered by this strange gentlewoman who turned up her nose at a perfectly good posting inn. "It's Lechlade, seven miles down the Cirencester turnpike. Or there's Highworth, down Swindon way about six miles."

Chewing her lip, Clara considered this intelligence. Common sense told her that if Boltwood was looking for her, he would look first around Faringdon, and then in the towns along the route that went more directly to Bath, for he would assume—rightly—that she wished to return to her family there. He also would have left behind orders at The Crown that she be watched for. She must get away from Faringdon, and then try to hire a horse or board the stage as soon as may be.

"And is there a way to Lechlade across the fields?"

The girl scrunched her nose, stealing a glance at Clara's kid boots, which were more fashionable than sturdy. "It's seven miles, miss. The road's best."

"I prefer a walk through the fields," said Clara, forcing a bright smile.

"Well," said the girl, shrugging at this eccentricity, "There's a cart track what cuts down to Purvis Farm, then you can go across the fields to Lechlade from there. There's a few ponds and the river, though, and it's more'n a mite dirty."

"Very well." Clara bit her lip, considering. "I will take two buns and a cherry cake, please. And would you tell me where I might purchase some ball and powder?"

The poor girl gazed at her, utterly mystified, but perhaps judging this strange woman to be touched in the upper works, said kindly, "Harry Tipton's place, t'other end of the market."

Clara thanked her, directing her to wrap her purchases into a parcel and placing three pence on the counter. Tucking the parcel under her arm, she opened the door, casting a look up and down the street before heading in the direction of Mr. Tipton's establishment.

Here, she received much the same bewildered civility, and she left with her pistol once more loaded and primed. She was not to be caught napping a second time.

Keeping to the market street, she took her way northwest, hoping that the crowds would hide her in plain view, but they quickly dwindled into nothing as the shops gave way to cottages and then to fields. She pulled her bonnet low over her face—thinking belatedly that she ought to have purchased or traded for another that Boltwood would not recognize—and walked briskly but naturally, as though she were a young lady on an errand to a farmhouse down the way.

Coming at last upon the cart track, she glanced cautiously up and down its length before setting off along it toward Purvis Farm, and keeping an ear cocked for sounds of carriages or horses, for it had occurred to her that Boltwood may take to a horse to try if he could find her more quickly. But the track was quiet at this time of the morning, the villagers she met merely watching her in mild curiosity and nodding to her as she passed.

Purvis Farm proved to be nothing more than the usual straggling of outbuildings around a fine farm house, and before she knew it, Clara was through and confronted with miles of grazing fields beyond. She considered perhaps taking the road again, but knew that Boltwood could just as easily have enlisted aid to look for her in all directions, making the road unsafe. So she lifted her chin and set out across the fields.

It was slow going, but the ground, due to the late season, was not terribly wet. She did founder in some spongy areas near the ponds, but most were hardened by the cold, and there had been little rain or snow for several days. Despite this clemency, however, her skirts were inches deep in mud and her boots ruined after only the first two miles. A few young boys were out with the cattle that grazed in straggling groups, but she was too fatigued to give them more than a civil nod. Any romance that had lingered in her imagination at this adventure quickly faded, replaced by a dreary longing for home. The buns and cake were long devoured and she was extremely thirsty when she trudged into the town of Lechlade past one o'clock.

Avoiding the main thoroughfare, Clara found a young lady who was just finished sweeping her porch, and thinking it unlikely she would be outside long enough to be discovered and interviewed by Boltwood, inquired the direction of the posting inn. The Bull and Pidgeon was nearby, but she was obliged to wait as the ostler tended to the needs of a very smart young man and his wife, who appeared to have been just married. They certainly had eyes for no one else, and it took some time for the ostler to understand their wishes and to close with them on the hire of a fine pair of horses for the next stage of their journey.

When he turned to Clara, his obsequious attitude vanished and was replaced by suspicious disapproval. She blinked, then recollected her trudge across the fields, and the state of her dress. Putting a hand to her bonnet, she found it was slightly haphazard, and that several of her curls had become dislodged and now hung loosely about her face in frizzled disarray. She thought with dismay that she was likely also red-faced and dusty from her exertions.

Exhaling, she drew herself up and said, "I know I look a fright, sir, but I beg you will not regard it. I do not, for I have a much bigger problem. I have ... become separated from my party and must find my own way home. Do you have a horse I may hire?"

The ostler looked her up and down—an entirely unnecessary action, to Clara's mind, for he had been doing nothing else during the whole of her speech—and said, "Unless the King's highway has gone back to the likes of Devil Jack, which ain't been seen for nigh twenty years, I can't imagine what could've separated ye from yer party, ma'am."

"Well, I don't know this Devil Jack, but he sounds very like the gentleman from whom I was obliged to run away, over your fields, and into this town. However, I may remind you that the method by which I came to be here, alone and unchaperoned, and without baggage, is none of your concern, sir. You need only tell me if you have a horse I might hire to take me a stage or two toward Bath."

He crossed his arms over his broad chest and, looking down at her with hooded eyes, said, "And how might you be paying for it, ma'am? Or did this bogey man steal yer purse, too?"

Clara's jaw clenched and she held up her reticule. "I have plenty of good coin, sir, and I find your insinuations impertinent. I have told nothing but the truth, and my situation continues to be none of your concern. Will you give me a horse or no?"

"Mayhap we haven't got a woman's saddle, or do you reckon to ride astride in those skirts?" he drawled. "Yull pardon my saying, ma'am, that it wouldn't do to put yer on a horse with a good bit o' leg showing fer all to see. Unless yer what I think yer are, and then—"

"Enough!" said Clara firmly, but coloring in mortification. She had entirely forgotten that she had no habit with her, for her trunks had not followed her from Faringdon and her reticule was not so capacious. And it had not occurred to her that a posting inn would not keep a woman's saddle. She was beginning to understand why young ladies did not gallivant about the countryside—it was most inconvenient to travel on one's own, and without proper baggage.

Gathering her dignity, she said, "I comprehend your meaning sir, and your insolence is odious to me. I am nothing more than a lady in distress, but I see that you have neither compassion nor sense. I will trouble you no more for a horse, but if you will tell me where I may board the stage for Bath, I will remove myself from your vicinity forthwith."

His brows had risen higher and higher with this speech, until they threatened to leap from the top of his forehead. "Well, miss highty-tighty, I thank ye fer keeping yer legs out o' sight o' my boys, fer they can't keep their heads straight as it is. And yer welcome to git out o' my yard and go to the Angel, thataway, where the stage'll come round 'bout midnight."

"Midnight!" cried Clara, but she was answered only by a chorus of guffaws from the ostler and the interested grooms who had gathered around them during their discourse. Head held high, she pushed past the circle and, pausing only to quench her thirst at the pump, swept out of the innyard, marching down the street in the direction of the Angel.

She had never been so poorly treated in her life and was stinging from the mortification of it, which is likely the reason she did not at first give heed to some shouts of "That's her!" and "We thought she wan't right!" behind her. It was only when she heard a pounding of feet coming swiftly toward her that she jerked from her reverie and glanced quickly over her shoulder. Lord Boltwood was only yards behind her, and she burst into a run, but it was too late. He caught her by the arm, pulling her into an alley and pressing her against a wall as she struggled wildly against him.

"You have led me a dance, but no more, my girl. At least not until the knot is tied." He leered at her, enjoying her helpless anger. "Then you may run all you wish, for I shall have the chief of what I want, and I can get the rest wherever I please."

Chapter 26

CLARA GLARED AT her captor as she continued to thrash about, more angry now than ever.

"Your embarrassments must be prodigious to track me all this way, my lord," she said through gritted teeth. "I should have imagined some other young lady would be an easier victim than myself."

"But I should be required to begin all over again with another young lady," he said with a sneer, "and only think how fatiguing. I am done wooing and wish to get on with the contemplation of spoils."

"Spoils?" inquired Clara in mock innocence. "I should think you would not wish to contemplate your particular spoils, for of course you must mean your spoilt marriage to an heiress and your spoilt plans for wasting her fortune and, not least, your spoilt waistcoat."

His brow furrowed at this and he looked down, only then realizing she had pressed the barrel of her pistol up against the side of his chest. He barked a laugh, his gaze returning unafraid to her face.

"We have been through this, my love. You must think me a fool to fall for it again."

She smiled. "Oh, no. I have thought you a fool for a great many other things, however. For teaching me how to fence, which has only increased my defensive abilities. For agreeing to help me escape, which has surely earned you a lifelong enemy in Picton—you ought not to return to Bath until he is gone from it, by the by, if you value your life. But you are most foolish for underestimating me—but I am persuaded it is a universal failing of rakes, for you none of you think more of women than of the degree of their beauty and the fatness of their pocketbooks."

His hands tightened on her shoulders and he said irritably, "Hush, my love. You are nonsensical. There is no need to return to Bath, for now I have what I want, I don't care if I never see the place again."

"How glad I am to hear it, for I intend to return there posthaste. If you will release me, I should be grateful, and will wish you a speedy journey to wherever you intend to go next."

He stared at her for a moment, then laughed, shaking his head. "Your spirit is unflagging, my love. I give you credit for the attempt, but you really are too lovely to succeed in that bluff. I could not leave you without a far greater inducement than your gratitude."

"You have it, sir," she said, grinding the pistol into his ribs to remind him of its presence.

"Enough of this! My patience grows thin—"

"As does mine! Shall I pull this trigger? Or are you going to give me my due as an intelligent woman who does not repeat mistakes?"

His countenance hardened and he said after a moment, "I don't believe you. You had no time—"

"I am excessively efficient," she said, raising her bulging reticule and shaking it, to allow the ball and powder case to clank within. "It was, after all, a priority. Do not try me further. Release me at once."

Scowling darkly, he let go her shoulders and stepped back, allowing her to move sideways out from the wall, her pistol aimed at his chest. When she had backed away only a few steps, however, he lunged after her, but she was ready, coolly lowering the barrel of the gun a few inches and pulling the trigger.

The shot rang out and he fell screaming to the ground, writhing in agony, his hands clutching his left thigh. Clara regarded him coldly for a moment, then returned the pistol to her reticule and at the sound of several persons hastening toward them from the direction of the Bull and Pidgeon, took to her heels down the alley.

She dodged from side street to side street, trying to keep her bearings. She knew the Angel must be on the turnpike road, however she could not go to the posting house now. The stage did not depart until midnight, and she would not be so totty-headed as to be found kicking her heels that long. Though Boltwood was incapacitated, she was certain he would send on whatever minions he could to find her, and she was much mistaken if the impudent ostler at the Bull and Pidgeon was not one of the persons she had heard thundering down the road to find out what had happened to the nobleman. He would be first to recollect the Angel as her destination, and would no doubt be eager to assist his lordship in apprehending her.

She did not trust hiding in a shop again—Boltwood's speed in catching her must be thanks to the information of the helpful girl in the bakery. Instead, she determined very soon to make a change to her appearance, and while ruminating how this was most expeditiously to be done, spied a cloak hung with other clothing on a line behind a cottage. A moment's pause resolved her, and taking off her bonnet and pelisse, she exchanged them for the cloak, assuaging her conscience with the knowledge that her things would fetch a much higher price than the cloak was worth.

She kept to the outskirts of town, circling the Angel while keeping watch for pursuers, and endeavoring to stay parallel to the post road. Lechlade was of a size with Faringdon, and she soon found herself at the edge of town. Pausing at a stile, she regarded with loathing the stubble fields that stretched out before her, flat and open and muddy. The necessity of trudging once more over miles of fields filled her with dread but, knowing she must get away from this place, she let out a heavy sigh and climbed over the stile.

After some miles, she wished she had thought to purchase more food in Lechlade. She had perceived a farmer or two as she had passed through their domain, but they were far off, and seemed to be heading back toward town. Pushing the hood back from her head, she looked up at the weakly shining sun, which was touching the western horizon, and a glance at her watch confirmed it to be nearing four o'clock. Swallowing against the dryness in her throat, she surveyed the fields that seemed to stretch interminably before her, thinking longingly of the well-kept turnpike road just to the north. Traffic on the road would have thinned as the day drew to a close, and she decided to risk skirting the fields, using the hedgerows as cover.

She made for the level ground by the hedgerow along the road, and it was easier going, though only nominally. As she stumbled on, fatigue overtook her reason, and she began to wonder if she should wander forever, becoming lost somewhere between Lechlade and Cirencester, and never see her family again. She imagined she would become some sort of local legend, like the ghostly apparitions it was claimed could be seen wandering the fields or towns by night. As she considered, she fancied she had never been so in charity with these ghosts before now, and resolved that, should she ever meet one, she would have much to say in sympathy.

She was so taken by the piteousness of her circumstances that she did not realize she had come up along a very thin portion of the hedge. The sound of a carriage alerted her to her danger, and with a cry, she staggered forward, collapsing into a thicker set of bushes. As her cloak became hopelessly tangled in a brier, she heard the driver mutter an oath and stop the carriage, calling, "Clara?" to which she responded by abandoning her cloak, hitching her skirts, and lurching away across the field.

The sound of crunching footfalls followed her and she tripped, being so weary by this time that her legs would not carry her properly, and her blood pounded in her ears as she fell to her hands and knees. Again her pursuer called her name, and though it did not sound like Lord Boltwood, she was so terrified that she did not apprehend what that meant, and scrambled to her feet again to run.

She had taken only a few strides when she was caught by the shoulders by two strong hands, and spun around. Distraught at having been caught, she gave a sobbing push at her captor's chest before looking up with pleading, and gazed in stupefaction at the face of Lawrie Simpford. After a drawn out moment of disbelieving silence, Clara's head fell upon his chest and she burst into hysterical sobs.

Lawrie held her to him, having never been so glad in all his life to see her. Though not to compare with hers, he had had a trying day. Following Picton's trail along the main road to Gloucester, he had been obliged to ask after the fugitives at several posting houses along the turnpike road, and received only vague information. He continued on, however, and in Horsley was rewarded with the intelligence that a varlet had held up a carriage with a lady and a swell, and after knocking the swell on the head, he'd stepped into the carriage, cool as you please, and desired the post boys to drive on. Lawrie, realizing that Boltwood must have been successful in arresting the elopement, inquired as to the destination of the varlet. He was consternated but unsurprised upon being told that the gentleman in question had hired the post boys to Cirencester, and not back to Bath.

He therefore went on to Cirencester, where his inquiries were not met with luck. At least three coaches answering his description had arrived during the early hours of the morning, at different inns and traveling in different directions. One was bound for Oxford, and he had a fortuitous recollection of a fellow student and friend of Boltwood there, who had found preferment on an estate nearby, and whose predilection for a greased palm was well-known. He decided upon following the carriage paid through thither, and picked up the trail again in Fairford, where Boltwood had stopped to change horses.

Once again, the trail was easily followed, and Lawrie became confident that their destination was, indeed, Oxford, when he came upon a situation of extreme interest in Faringdon. There, at The Crown, the ostler was pleased to impart such a tale of infamy and scandal as would curl the hearer's toes.

"In they come, innocent as you please," he told Lawrie eagerly, "acting for all the world as though there weren't nothing amiss in the world. 'Might we have a private parlor,' says his lordship, and wishes for it to be away from the taproom, for his missus is mighty tired from the carriage. Then he orders a fine breakfast, just like any ordin'ry gentleman, and not one married to a madwoman, for no sooner's they done with it than she up and starts tearing about the room, and clawing her husband in the face! 'I'll be,' says Mrs. Stodson, the innkeep's wife, 'jes like a lion out of that heathen Africa! Mark me, if she ain't bound for Bedlam, she arter be!'

"But that weren't till later," he continued, relishing this telling as much as the numerous others in the hours since the events had come to pass. "For nobody knew nothing of it, my lord acting so calm, going out and locking the door quietlike behind him so's his wife couldn't get out and kill anybody afore he could take her away again. But when he goes back to collect her, she whales on him with the poker, then busts out the window and runs away, and when his lordship was found knocked cold on the floor, he was obliged to tell the whole to Stodson—soon as he was sensible. There was a to-do then, I tell you! Grooms a'running off after the mad lady and his lordship shouting orders and afraid lest she murdered everyone in her path. 'She must be found!' he says, and nobody argered, but if she were found, we ain't heard tell yet."

"Did they search the town, then?" inquired Lawrie urgently. "And they found nothing?"

The ostler shook his head, excessively pleased. "Vanished clean away, but not afore she babbled on about getting to Lechlade over the fields to little Betsy Granger, and got powder and shot from poor Harry Tipton. He's beside hisself over having assisted a mad lady to shoot anybody she likes, but he can't be blamed, never having met a murderess afore."

Lawrie blinked, taking some moments to assimilate this intelligence. She had her pistol, then. That was something, at least. Eagerly, he inquired how long ago these stirring events had transpired and was informed it had been only three hours since the fugitive had bolted from the inn.

"I'd best be gone, then. Thank you. I'm obliged to you."

Bending toward Lawrie, the ostler said meaningfully, "Best take care, sir, and be on your guard. She's a crafty one, by all accounts. All that about Lechlade was likely no more'n raving. I wouldn't trust that murderess past the end of my nose. No telling where she is now."

With a solemn wink, he let him go, and Lawrie climbed into his curricle, his countenance grim. It seemed he had been right, and Boltwood had not changed since Oxford days, though Clara had apparently bested him nonetheless—but at what cost? It was imperative to find out where she had got to now. Knowing Clara to be perfectly sane—if given to irrational starts—he rejected the ostler's wisdom and turned his pair back again toward Lechlade.

There he was at some pains to discover where Clara had gone to, for there had been no sign of her at the Angel, which was the principal posting house. It seemed she had been asked after there before, but the description of the men eluded him, until it was mentioned they were working for a lord "what been shot in the leg by a crazed woman."

Inquiries as to this incredible circumstance led him to the Bull and Pidgeon, where he was again regaled with a fantastic tale, this time of "a saucy wench what talked like a gentry mort but what looked like what the dog dragged in." Her only oddity besides this had seemed at the time to be a desire to hire a horse, though she had been wearing no habit proper for such an activity, and conclusions as to her true breeding had been various and unkind. But very soon the inmates of the inn had been apprised of the magnitude of her sins, for not five minutes after she had been sent on her way a chaise and four had come sweeping in, carrying a gentleman with his head swathed in bloodied linen who had asked after her so urgently that they knew at once she was a dangerous criminal. This had been corroborated when the gentleman had caught up to her, only to be shot, and they were all agreed that a more black-hearted female none had ever met with.

Lawrie's inquiries after the gentleman had yielded the information that his lordship had been given a room upstairs at the inn, but that he would not be seen by anyone, at the express order of the doctor. Resigning himself to not having the satisfaction of planting Boltwood a facer, and grimly pleased that Clara had quite thoroughly revenged herself, he got what other intelligence he could from the voluble inn servants and went on to the next village, where the search had apparently been carried.

But the residents there informed him with some regret that no crazed murderess had made an appearance in their town, so Lawrie turned back, thinking perhaps he had missed her along the way, or she had become mired in the fields. His eye combing the fields as he drove, he had almost passed by the bedraggled figure stumbling along the hedgerow. When she had started so violently and run away, his heart was wrenched by what horrors she had been made to endure, and it was with great relief that he had enfolded her in his arms as she wept out all her travails.

When her sobs became little more than sniffs, he said gently in her ear, "You are a horrid baggage, you know, Clara."

She began to sob anew, which was not his intent, and he hushed her, saying, "But for all that, I am glad I found you," while gently stroking her tangled hair.

She mumbled something into his neckcloth and he was obliged to lean away from her to hear, "I wonder that you came, if that is how you feel."

"You know it is not. I wish to marry a murderess, and I followed an excessively promising rumor of a crazed one running rampant through the area."

"You are either very imprudent or a philanthropist," was the muffled reply. She turned her head to peek at him. "Is that what Boltwood said of me?"

"Not only Boltwood, my love, but every innkeep and ostler and groom along the turnpike. At least between Faringdon and—where are we?"

"It is not my doing that I was obliged to trudge hundreds of miles over horridly soggy fields and ruin my dress, and shoot a man and trudge some more—oh, and steal a cloak so that I might hope to escape my persecutors."

"Well, actually," he said, lovingly wiping a smut from her cheek, "it was at least partially your doing, for you know none of this would have happened if you had not—"

She pushed him away. "Oh, do not remind me! I cannot bear to be remonstrated with, cannot you see? I have been amply punished and wish only to forget it all happened, and to go home, and never flirt again, and—and to sleep for a year or two."

With this, she collapsed again onto his chest and he chuckled, kissing the top of her frazzled head.

"You must replace the cloak, you know," he murmured.

"I left them my pelisse and hat. I am not absolutely without principle."

"And I suppose the cloak will be found sooner or later, so there is no harm done even if they do not like your pelisse and hat."

She hit a fist against his chest, but weakly, for she was scarcely able to stand, so hungry and relieved and overcome with fatigue as she was.

"Where is your pistol, by the by? Your shot was a fine one, by all accounts. Boltwood is laid up in Lechlade and cannot even receive visitors."

"I hope he dies of an infection," she replied with tired petulance. "He had the gall to empty my pistol while I slept in the carriage—he led me to believe he was taking me back to Bath! And I was so muddle-headed as to trust him. But I soon came to reason, and bought more shot and powder in Faringdon. It is in my reticule, but my pistol is in my pocket. I simply haven't had time to reload."

"Perhaps we ought to load it, so we are prepared for brigands on the road," he murmured into her hair.

She groaned. "Later. I can hardly see straight. Besides, there is no need."

He huffed a laugh, tightening his hold on her. "Very true. All's well that ends well."

"But it is not ended!" She lifted her head, gazing at him with pathetic earnestness. "I have not yet told you—Lawrie, I am everlastingly sorry! Whatever brought you after me, I am so grateful, but I know I do not deserve it. I *have* been a horrid baggage, and I likely will be for a while longer, but I will try to change, if you will help me, as Mr. Noyce helps my mother. I know it is entirely unfeeling and unjust of me to ask it, but I simply cannot live without you—"

Her declaration was cut off by his kiss, which nearly took from her what faculties she yet possessed, and would have made her close to swooning even had she not been so close to it already. But he supported her throughout, and she found after several moments that she had been in some part rejuvenated, as if by magic. Indeed, she could stand quite steadily after a time, and respond with more energy, wrapping her arms about his neck and knocking his hat to the ground in her eagerness to reciprocate.

But then a horrible thud sounded and Lawrie's ardor ceased abruptly. Clara screamed as he slumped to the ground, senseless, at her feet.

Chapter 27

PICTON LOOMED OVER his victim in the fading light, an exceedingly ugly look marring his usually handsome countenance. "I must thank you for removing his hat, my sweet. His bare head presented a far better target. Though, I thought until then he was Boltwood."

"What have you done?" she cried, crouching to gingerly touch Lawrie's still form. "You have killed him!"

"You should be glad I have not, though it is my right. I told you I would have you."

Clara rose to her feet, every limb thrilling with wrath. "I am not yours, nor will I ever be! You are despicable, and I hate you! How can you do this, and think that I should go away with you? How can you force me and threaten my family and harm my friends, and think I will forgive you?"

"I care little for your forgiveness, my sweet," he said, gazing at her in mocking satisfaction. "I want only my prize. Do you know, you look a fright, and yet you are magnificent in your fury. I think I will enjoy making you angry with me for many years to come."

"Oh, you are hateful and horrid and monstrous! I will never marry you!"

He looked amused. "Ah, but you will, my sweet. In a very few hours you will have no other option. No other man will take you. Not even poor Simpford here."

She raised a hand to slap him across the face, but he caught it easily. She tried to swing her heavy reticule at his head, but he caught that as well, ripping it from her wrist and throwing it down. Fuming, she dove her hand into her pocket and pulled out the pistol, but he instantly took hold of her wrist, twisting it until the gun fell from her grasp. He kicked it away, then, as she struggled and cursed him, he drew both her hands together so that he could kiss them with mock ceremony.

"You have not lost your fire," he said with a cruel smile. "It is what I love most about you."

"You mistake, sir! It was my defiance!"

He chuckled. "That too. You see, my sweet, there is so much to love that I will not be denied."

Clara snarled with vexation. "I would rather be ruined than live with you! Release me at once!"

Abruptly, he obeyed her, and she fell to the ground, bruised and exhausted. He merely looked away over the fields. "Where is Boltwood?"

"I shot him," said Clara, rubbing her wrists and eying him scornfully.

He laughed outright. "I ought to have guessed it. Then, you have saved me the trouble."

Clara ignored this, crawling over to caress Lawrie's face, trying to assess his condition. But Picton merely bent and seized her about the waist, heaving her up.

"Leave him. He is merely unconscious, and we must be off."

"Let me go!" cried Clara, clawing at his arms. "I tell you, I will never go anywhere with you!"

"Ah, but you will, my sweet," Picton said, dragging her toward the road. "After all, you gave me your word, and I mean to hold you to it."

"You cannot! I merely promised to go with you!" Her voice pitched higher as her panic grew. "I did as I promised, so let me go!"

"But where is your honor?" he taunted. "You implied more."

"How dare you appeal to my honor when you have none?" screamed Clara, struggling ineffectually to pry his arms free.

He suddenly clapped a hand over her mouth, pinning her against him as he pressed himself to a tree at the edge of the field. The sound of a vehicle approaching assailed her ears and she struggled harder, but her cries were too muffled to rise over the sound of the horses' hooves. The coach, drawn by four horses, swept by, and after another minute, Picton relaxed but did not let her go.

Instead, he turned her swiftly to face him, and she yelped as he hoisted her like so many potatoes onto his shoulder and carried her through the thinned portion of the hedge and into the road. She kicked and pounded his back with her fists, but he only held her legs tightly and went on as though unaffected. She began to weep, her exhaustion again overtaking her and the impossibility of her situation becoming very real. Scanning as much of the area as she could see from her position, she could perceive no farmer in the waning light, no dust of an approaching carriage, no possibility of assistance.

She could no longer see where Lawrie lay, probably still unconscious, in the field, and her heart clenched for his safety. If he were to die now, it would be even more her fault than his dying from the duel would have been, and she did not think she could survive it. Her heart, which she had considered so long to be as stone, now trembled with tender emotion, but she feared that her actions had rendered such sentiment useless. She was much mistaken if Picton possessed any sensibility, and she did not doubt that he would abuse and exploit any he perceived in her.

They passed a curricle and came to a carriage, where he halted, placing her bodily inside and shutting and locking the door against escape. She tried the other door, but it was already locked, and she kicked it in frustration. When she tried to let down the window, she found it was stuck tight, and though the other window came down, it jammed partway. She cried out in helpless anger as her captor stood outside, calmly brushing the mud and twigs from his clothes.

Looking daggers at him through the gap in the glass, she snarled, "I am glad I shot you in Bath. That satisfaction, at least, will stay with me forever."

"I imagine it will," he said, coming up to the window and smirking. "And I trust it will fuel your anger for some time to come. I like a woman with spirit." He reached up to caress her cheek, but when she jerked away, he laughed unpleasantly. "It makes no odds to me, my sweet, but you would do better to accustom yourself to this turn of events. You are to be mine, in every sense of the word, and it will go very much easier for you if you deal generously with me."

She blanched, her heart thumping in her chest at the threat. "You are heartless!"

"Indeed, I am, my sweet," he said with smug unconcern. "We are alike, you and I."

He chuckled again at her horrified expression, walking around to the front of the carriage. The carriage bobbed as he climbed up, and Clara squeezed her eyes shut against the terror that was closing in about her.

Suddenly there was a loud report, and the carriage lurched forward, tumbling Clara from her seat. A shout of agony rang out almost at the same instant, and she heard the thud of a body hitting the ground beside the carriage. Blinking against the dizziness of exhaustion and terror, she scrambled to look out the far window. Picton lay moaning on the ground, the reins tangled in his legs. Pushing to the other side, she looked out to see Lawrie, her pistol in hand, swaying in the road.

"Lawrie! Oh, my love—how did you—but do not faint away again! He has locked me in!" She pounded on the door as Lawrie put a hand to his head, trying to focus on her. "You must get me out, Lawrie! Pray, make haste and unlock the door!"

"I can't—" He panted, putting his hands on his knees and squinting across at her— "Give me a moment."

She felt as though, at any instant, Picton would rise and drive away with her, and freedom would again be snatched from her very hands. Her heart beat painfully in her chest as she endeavored to patiently await her poor rescuer, whose head, she knew, must be very bad after such a blow as he had suffered. But at last, he stood upright again and staggered toward her, and though it seemed an age, he did arrive at the door of the carriage. After some scrabbling at the handle, he managed to unlock it at last, and Clara tumbled out into his arms with a cry of relief.

Unfortunately, they were both in such a state as to be unable to support themselves, never mind each other, and they fell in a heap in the road. Free from the terrors of her prison, however, Clara was content to lie in the dirt with her head on Lawrie's chest, his arms limply around her, and allow them both to recover a little.

After some minutes, the moans on the other side of the coach penetrated their brains, and Clara rolled over to peek between the carriage wheels at Picton. It was becoming difficult to see in the dusk, but he was clutching his buttock and cursing rather fluently, and did not seem able to get up.

"A fine shot, Lawrie," she said, turning back to him. "However did you manage it?"

He chuckled weakly. "Admit that your poor opinion of my shooting was utterly unfounded, for you can see that I did very well, *and* with a bad head!"

"I would not dare to disparage you, my love, for I am thrice in your debt, and will not risk a fourth time. Only, I must mention that the leg would have been a better target."

"Nonsense! The buttock is excellent for the purpose. As you can see, he cannot do anything but thrash around and curse at us, which is precisely what I should like."

She moved her head to look up at him. "You mean that you aimed for his leg and hit his buttock."

"I admit nothing of the kind."

She sighed, stroking the front of his shirt. "Well, I shall never say a word more on the subject for, after all, you did sustain a terrible blow, and if you could see at all straight when you fired that shot, it was a wonder."

"It was, indeed," he said, rubbing her arm.

A cart came rumbling along the road then, and they scrambled to their feet, standing beside the carriage in conscious nonchalance until the vehicle had gone by.

"I wonder that Picton did not give a shout," said Clara, bending to peek at her erstwhile captor on the other side of the carriage.

Lawrie massaged the back of his head. "He wouldn't if he knew what was good for him. It would do for him at once, to call attention to himself when he has only just tried to abduct you. Though," he added, gazing at her somewhat hazily, "You are the mad lady of the area. Perhaps it would be thought more likely that you shot him as he was driving peacefully by."

"But I did not shoot him, sir, you did," said Clara, inspecting her soiled gown and patting her frazzled hair. "And so I shall tell the magistrate. I wonder if he would rather be known as the gentleman who was shot by a madwoman or the scoundrel who tried to abduct a madwoman and was shot by the man he had hit over the head."

An angry exclamation came to them from the other side of the carriage, and they went around to gaze upon Picton, who glared up at them from the verge. "It is no use gabbling on about it, for I shall deny everything you say of me!"

"An excellent notion, Picton," said Lawrie with disdain. "You are in a mortifying predicament, indeed, and should the truth get out, you would be in worse."

"I hardly know what could be worse, Simpford! You've maimed me! I may not walk again!"

"Possibly, but that would only be a just punishment," said Lawrie coldly. "It is within our rights to take you directly to a magistrate."

Picton growled but after some moments said tersely, "It seems we each have something we wish to conceal. If you do not report me, I shall keep mum about the duel."

Lawrie glanced to Clara, who sighed. "It is up to you to decide, Lawrie. I have only made a mull of things, and it is your reputation that is at risk."

"Very well." With a grimace, Lawrie turned again to Picton. "Our silence for your silence."

At that moment, Lawrie swayed and Clara, alarmed, grasped his arm, crying, "Good lord, Lawrie, you look positively sick! You must lie down, or—or sit. I do not know, but we must find you a doctor!"

"I'm the one who wants a doctor!" barked Picton.

Lawrie took a deep breath, closing his eyes for several moments before saying, "I'll be alright, Clara. It's only my head—and I am a trifle queasy. Let's just get ourselves to an inn."

Picton let out a string of curses at that and Clara sighed. "I suppose we ought to do something for him as well, Lawrie. There is a deal of blood. It would not do for him to die, you know, for then you would be a murderer and would be obliged to flee to the Continent." She turned to him, a light in her eye. "But then, I could flee with you. I am a murderess, after all."

"Cease your yammering and get me up, damn you!" snarled Picton.

They complied, binding his wound and helping him into his carriage with many groans and curses aimed at themselves. When he was situated inside, sweating and pale, Clara locked the doors and windows with grim efficiency, then turned to Lawrie.

"One of us will have to drive him, and I do not know which, for you are in no state to drive, but your curricle cannot stand here all night."

"We will tie the horses to the back of his carriage and leave the curricle," said Lawrie. "I will not let you out of my sight until he is dealt with."

Relieved, Clara nevertheless insisted that she drive. "You are not fit for it, my poor love, for you still are very pale. Does your head pain you?"

"Like the devil," said Lawrie, touching the sore spot behind his ear. "He must have used a rock—there's a dashed big lump."

Clara inspected the lump and tutted. "I am sorry for it, but that I shall get to drive us home."

"Only after you have done something with your hair," he responded. "You look dreadful."

"Good gracious, you are right! I cannot drive back to Lechlade looking like this, or they shall arrest me for accosting a peer of the realm! Here, I'll get the horses and then I shall do what I can."

"I can manage the horses," said Lawrie, waving her away.

As he unhitched the pair from his curricle and tied them to the back of the carriage, she went to the bushes where she had lost her cloak, shook it out and put it on. Recollecting her reticule out in the field, she retrieved it and Lawrie's hat and hurried back to the road, doing her best to untangle her hair by combing her fingers through it. Then she tucked her curls back up into their pins and brushed as much of the mud off her skirts as she could, scrubbing the worst off with a handful of dried grass. At last, she climbed onto the box next to Lawrie, handing him his hat.

"For appearances, you understand. Am I restored to sanity, do you think?"

He regarded her, an odd glint coming into his eyes. "Perhaps. But looks can be deceiving. Let me try another way."

And he put his arms around her, kissing her again, long and soundly. Her response apparently assured him, for he redoubled his efforts and she made no protestation, only fitting herself more securely against him and twining her arms up around his neck.

A furious banging from inside the carriage jerked them apart, and with a significant look, Lawrie passed her the reins.

"I trust in future you will be more nice in your selection of flirts."

"You may be certain I will. It has been impressed upon me in no uncertain manner that to be abducted twice in one day is bad for one's constitution."

"Not to mention one's reputation," said Lawrie, glancing at her askance. "You have lost your two most avid flirts in one day as well."

She looked archly. "Well, I must give a thought for how I shall repair my reputation, then. Perhaps, if one elopes with one flirt, is rescued by another, then is seen driving into town again the same evening with one's best friend, it would do the thing."

"Well, unless our horses have wings," said Lawrie, looking doubtful, "I doubt we shall be arriving home tonight."

Clara paused, then said with forced lightness, "Then there is nothing for it than to hie to the border."

Lawrie put out a hand and pulled the reins, slowing the horses to a stop. "Clara, there is only one way out of this mess."

"I know it," she said, blinking rapidly against the tears of shame that sprung to her eyes. "I am so sorry, Lawrie. I wish you were not forced—"

But he stopped her with another kiss, firm and insistent enough to put all apology out of her mind. When he drew back, he pressed his forehead to hers and said, "Clara, you know I love you. I have loved you for years, and though at times I questioned my reason, I now know that I was right. I wish for nothing more in the world than to marry you."

"I don't deserve you," she managed, before her throat caught.

He kissed her again, with infinite tenderness, then said, "It makes no odds, for I have too long aspired to oust Mr. Noyce as the perfect man in your estimation."

She gave a watery chuckle and they kissed again before the pounding from their passenger once more broke them apart.

Lawrie gave the coach a darkling look. "I believe we are justified in dumping him unceremoniously at the Bull and Pidgeon. He can be certain of deferential treatment there. They seem well versed in how to cater to men of his ilk."

"To be sure, there is more than one horrid baggage on this coach," remarked Clara, setting the team to, "and the sooner one of them is off our hands the better."

"I forbid you to class yourself with that scoundrel, Clara."

She pursed her lips, raising her chin. "Perhaps I was not speaking of myself."

"How am I horrid, pray, or a baggage?" he inquired in mock indignation.

"You flirted shamelessly with Mrs. Gravesthwaite, only to make me jealous—do not deny it! I know she has an understanding with a gentleman in Essex."

"I admit that was a trifle horrid," he said with a reminiscent smile.

"*And* you flirted with Miss Drayford, and Miss Ashwicke—*and* Miss Tipton!"

"Come now, Clara, you cannot in good conscience throw all my faults up in my teeth. Recollect, you flirted with every other gentleman in Bath—"

"Very well, very well," she said, adding expansively, "We shall say that we are even."

"Besides, it was not all mere flirting on my part. Miss Drayford is a lovely girl—I quite liked her, though her mother is something else. And Miss Ashwicke is so agreeable—she never disagrees with anyone, I imagine. And Miss Tipton—"

Clara pulled the team to a halt again, turning to favor him with a narrow look. "If you so much as look at any of those chits again, Lawrence Simpford, I will shoot you—either that, or I will run you through! I am become a lady of endless resource! Do not underestimate me!"

"I wouldn't dare," he said, grinning, and after another sound kiss, they were off again.

If you enjoyed this book, please consider leaving a review at the library or store site where you found it, or on your favorite review site. Reviews help others find their next favorite read and are extremely helpful to authors.

You can find review links for The Branwell Chronicles series and learn how to get a FREE book by scanning the QR code below.

Thank you!

Author's Note

ONCE AGAIN, IN researching background for this book, I discovered a wealth of information about the Regency that I didn't know before. Some of this I had heard and read a lot about, but the nitty-gritty details were a delight to find out.

Bath has a long history as a watering place, beginning in Roman times when the hot springs were discovered and their medicinal qualities first appreciated. By the time of the Regency, the town had sprung up around the baths, and a society had evolved which took advantage of the variety of people who came to either try the baths or accompany those who did. Bath society was as strict in its notions as London society, and an ever-changing group of ladies dubbed the Bath Quizzes—rather like the Almack's Patronesses—dictated who was the thing and who was not in Bath. It could be social suicide to get on their bad side, as those who disregarded their influence found to their chagrin.

Taking the waters in Bath meant to drink the mineral-rich waters that flowed from the Roman baths. Like most hot springs in England, the waters came to be known as a cure-all, with reputed healing properties for all sorts of ailments from consumption to liver disease. To meet the rising demand for the waters, and to facilitate social interaction, the Great Pump Room was erected in 1799 with a bar that dispensed the waters for a small fee and a large reception area where people could meet friends and see and be seen throughout the day. Taking the waters became a social event, and most people did it even though they hated the bitter, salty taste and did not receive any real relief from ailments.

The Upper Assembly Rooms in Bath were built in 1770 and were meant as an all-in-one amusement place for the upper class to assemble. In addition to the ballroom, card room, and tea room, there was a cold bath (re-discovered only recently) in the basement. This cold bath was meant most likely for cold plunges after a course of hot treatments or simply as a rejuvenator. In the description found in the New Bath Guide of 1778, one saw that it was "a commodious cold-bath, with convenient dressing-rooms." There must also have been storage rooms and corridors in the basement so that servants could attend those in the cold bath, and have somewhere to store the supplies. Until recently, the basement of the Upper Assembly Rooms was used to house a fashion museum, but it was moved so that excavations could move forward in the preservation of the building.

Firearms had come a long way by the Regency, and personal pistols were rising in popularity. It was not uncommon for a gentleman to carry a pistol, not perhaps to social events, but with him in his curricle or on his horse, especially if he was traveling a long distance. Because women were regarded as the "weaker sex" and expected to have fragile constitutions, it was a surprise to find one who could stand the noise of a pistol shot without fainting or going into spasms, let alone shoot a pistol. But it was not unheard of and women like Clara, who carried a pistol in their pocket or reticule, did exist. Pistols were also the weapon of choice in duels by the Regency, having almost universally replaced smallswords. Almost all pistols were flintlocks, which used a flint mechanism to create a spark that ignited a small pan of gunpowder, which in turn ignited the powder behind the ball in the barrel, causing an explosion that expelled the ball. The phrase "flash in the pan" originated with flintlocks, which sometimes didn't fire because the spark from the pan didn't travel to the barrel. Thus, after a quick, exciting spark, nothing happened. Flintlocks went out of use in the 1830's when percussion caps became standard, but the phrase "flash in the pan" has endured.

Dueling had been part of English society since before the Renaissance, and an unwritten code of honor attended all meetings. Because it was unwritten, there is no hard evidence for what rules prevailed during the Regency in England, but the Irish Code Duello of 1777 along with writings of the time and later written codes give a good idea. The basic rules seem to have been:

- There must be just cause for a meeting, which could include insult to one of the parties, or even worse, insult to a lady under the protection of one of the parties.
- Each Principal would choose up to three "Seconds" who would undertake first to effect a reconciliation, and if that failed, to set up the time and place of the meeting. The Seconds would also engage a surgeon to attend any wounded, make sure their Principals were there on time, examine the weapons to make sure they were identical, present their Principal with their

weapon, count off the distance between the two, and signal the time to fire.

- Between one and three volleys would be fired, depending on the injuries caused by each shot and on the choice of the challenger, who had the right to dictate what would give him "satisfaction."
- Once the challenger was satisfied, either by wounding the other party or accepting an apology made, the duel was over.

Just like most things involving honor in the Regency era, dueling seems a barbaric way to settle arguments, and it did cause the deaths or mutilations of countless men. But one can only suppose it was a natural consequence of living in a society where passions were routinely suppressed.

I was unable to find viable proof of ladies fencing before the 1860's, when female fencing schools became quite popular. There is an interesting painting from 1787, however, depicting one "Mademoiselle La Chevalier d'Eon de Beaumont" in a fencing match at Carlton house, with the Prince Regent and other luminaries watching. Upon further research, I discovered that this "mademoiselle" was actually born a man, and had been trained as a soldier and a spy, during which service he posed as a woman in the Russian court. At one point he was banished from France, and was reinstated as a French citizen only upon agreement that he should thereafter assume the life of a woman. He did this, living off a pension until it was ended, and then taking up residence in England where he earned money competing in fencing matches such as the one depicted in the painting. While it was disappointing to find that this was not, actually, an instance of the acceptance of female fencing in the Regency era, it was enough to convince me that it was reasonable to allow Clara to learn fencing in this story, albeit under the strictest secrecy.

Sources:

"1911 Encyclopædia Brittanica: Eon de Beaumont." Wikisource, 2022. https://en.wikisource.org/wiki/1911_Encyclopædia_Britannica/Eon_de_Beaumont

"Chevalier d'Eon." Wikipedia, 2024. https://en.wikipedia.org/wiki/Chevalier_deon#/media/File:The_Assaut_or_Fencing_Match_which_took_place_at_Carlton_House_on_the_9th_of_April_1787.jpg

"Gun Timeline." History Detectives. PBS, 2014. https://www.pbs.org/opb/historydetectives/technique/gun-timeline/

Chirashnya, Igor. "A Not So Brief History of Fencing: Part 2." Academy of Fencing Masters Blog, 1 March 2021. https://academy-offencingmasters.com/blog/a-not-so-brief-history-of-fencing-part-2-old-world-european-fencing/

Hamilton, Joseph. *The Only Approved Guide Through All the Stages of a Quarrel.* London, 1829.

Hatch, Donna. "The Flintlock, the Pistol, and the Shotgun of the Regency." The Beau Monde, 3 September 2012. https://thebeaumonde.com/main/the-flintlock-the-pistol-and-the-shotgun-of-the-regency-by-donna-hatch/

Kloester, Jennifer. *Georgette Heyer's Regency World.* Sourcebooks, Illinois, 2010.

Milligan, Mark. "18th Century Cold Bath Found in Bath Assembly Rooms." Heritage Daily, 23 October 2023. https://www.heritagedaily.com/2023/10/18th-century-cold-bath-found-in-bath-assembly-rooms/148977

Patterson, A.W. *The Code Duello: with special reference to the state of Virginia.* Virginia, 1927.

Acknowledgments

I HAVE BEEN EXCITED to tell Clara's story ever since her character sprang into life, entirely unplanned, in Book 3, *Forlorn Hope*. Her story was a challenge, as all redemption stories are, and I admit I worried at times if I could pull it off. I think I did it, but I would never have successfully done so without help!

First, to my wonderful fans and readers, I could not carry on in this sometimes monumental endeavor without your encouragement and support! I am so grateful for your wonderful reviews, your kind words, and your recommendations to friends. You are the best!

To my amazing beta readers, Alondra Uhi, Diane Paredes, Liz Prettyman, Emily Menendez, Laurie Zobell, and Karen Pierotti, you saved the day! You helped me see the forest for the trees, and all Clara's fans will be eternally grateful.

To Clare Wille and Paul Midcalf, my audiobook narrator and my producer, and to Rae Allen, my cover designer, you make my work so much more beautiful and interesting. Thank you for sharing your marvelous talents with me!

To my kids and extended family who support me in so many ways, even if you think you don't do much, it means the world to me!

And of course to the love of my life, Joe, who takes non-existent free time to alpha read, cares enough to tell me like it is, listens and helps me work things through, and always, always makes me feel like I can do this! I love you forever.

Judith Hale Everett is one of seven sisters and grew up surrounded by romance novels. Georgette Heyer and Jane Austen were staples and formed the groundwork for her lifelong love affair with the Regency. Add to that her obsession with the English language and you've got one hopelessly literate romantic.

You can find JudithHaleEverett on Facebook, Twitter, and Instagram, or at judithhaleeverett.com.

Made in the USA
Columbia, SC
11 July 2024